IT WAS BORN
IN THE DARKNESS
OF THE WOOD

J.L. HICKEY

Black Rose Writing | Texas

First printing

This is a work of fiction. Names, characters, businesses, places, events, and incidents are either the products of the author's imagination or used in a fictitious manner. Any resemblance to actual persons, living or dead, or actual events is purely coincidental.

ISBN: 978-1-68433-665-4
PUBLISHED BY BLACK ROSE WRITING
www.blackrosewriting.com

Printed in the United States of America
Suggested Retail Price (SRP) $19.95

It Was Born in the Darkness of the Wood is printed in Chaparral Pro

*As a planet-friendly publisher, Black Rose Writing does its best to eliminate unnecessary waste to reduce paper usage and energy costs, while never compromising the reading experience. As a result, the final word count vs. page count may not meet common expectations.

This book is dedicated to my family, and to the authors that kept me sane with their beautiful stories: Stephen King, Ruth Ware, Gillian Flynn, and BA Paris. Thank you.

IT WAS BORN IN THE DARKNESS OF THE WOOD

ONE

Officer Clent Moore approached the residence of Dennis and Nora Simmons with his partner, Vanessa Velasquez, in tow. The call was for a routine welfare check, the homeowner's son called in, he hadn't heard from them in a few days, and he began to worry. The house sat on the infamous Orr Rd, a beautiful two-story country home with a large white deck-like porch that wrapped around the house. The estate also came with a few acres of land surrounding it, and it sat far back from the country road atop a small knoll. Clent knew he was dealing with wealthy folk, the scarlet red 2019 BMW M6 G-Power Hurricane in the driveway was a dead giveaway. He stepped cautiously up the icy porch, gripping the handrail for good measure.

"Watch your step," He spoke to his partner. "Steps are frozen." He knocked three times on the front door. "Guess they can afford that BMW parked out front, but not any salt for their approach?"

"Guess not, I'll try not to slip," his partner Vanessa Velasquez gripped the handrail herself after almost losing her balance on a small patch of ice. Vanessa was fresh out of the academy, mid-twenties, well-toned physique. Her straight black hair was pulled neatly back in a ponytail underneath her uniformed hat. It was Vanessa's second week on the Emmett County Police Force, eager to learn and excited to be by the side of a twenty-five-year veteran. She was lucky enough to be partnered with Officer Moore, whose partner he'd spent the majority of his career with had just retired and moved out west to sunny Cali.

"Cold as hell out here. I don't think I will ever get used to these Michigan winters," Velasquez's teeth clattered from the cold.

"You haven't seen anything yet. Tonight might be your first big storm," Clent grinned. This winter's been tame so far. She had no idea what's in store for this winter.

Clent probably has forgotten more than Vanessa thought she'd ever know about being an officer of the law. Clent was decorated, he knew his way around just about anything the beat could toss at him. His presence alone was enough to make any drunken knucklehead think twice about throwing hands. Clent stood six-two with a solid toned frame, intimidating with his broad shoulders and forearms thick as dumbells. Clent was the only black officer on the force, and there were times where he got shit for it out in the predominantly white Trump-loving country folk. He was smart, collected, and experienced enough to know to defuse tense situations.

"Always this quiet out here in the country?" Vanessa's eyes shifted to the night sky. "Never get sick of these country stars." She was a city girl, born and raised in Miami, Florida. They didn't have stars like this in the city; the street lights were too bright.

"Usually peaceful," Clent responded, looking the house up and down for any signs of life. "Nearest house is almost a mile down the road both sides, and one of em' is vacant," Clent knocked again, this time harder. "Pretty isolated out here."

"Seems like it," Vanessa replied.

"Police! Anyone home?" Clent wiggled the handle to the door, locked. "Most of the calls we get out here are drunken kids getting into trouble. They like to come in from town out here in the sticks and disrupt the folk around here. Idiot teens like to hang in the woods, smoke dope, trespass where they shouldn't. Always sneaking into the old Leveille Murder house too, you know, because of the history, just city kids doing dumb city kid shit."

"Nothing attracts dumb kids like a murder house, and underaged drinking," Vanessa smirked. She'd heard the stories about the abandoned Leveille house when she took the job on the force. She was in her last year of college when the murder happened. She remembered the news coverage, the murder reached her social media timelines, due to the brutality of the crime. The story went national.

"Yep," Clent shook his head. "Wish they'd tear it down. Couple times a year, we gotta come out here and break up dumb teens trespassing on the property, spooking themselves stupid. Somebody from Detroit snatched up the place, pays for its upkeep during the summer. I hear they want to turn it into a haunted Bed and Breakfast or Air BNB."

Clent knocked again.

"No one's answering," said Vanessa.

"Hmmm," Clent grunted. "First welfare check?" he asked.

"Yep," Vanessa stepped back off the porch, she studied the two-story country home. It looks to have been renovated many times over the years resulting in a very modern aesthetic. She let her eyes drift around the outside of the house, examining for anything out of the ordinary, a jarred window perhaps, any sort of sign of a breaking and entering. Everything appeared quiet. There was one light on in the second-story window, but the shades were drawn, there was no immediate movement.

"These tend to be simple, in and out. Make sure residents are fine," Clent replied, knocking once again. This time he also rang the doorbell. "Waste of gas and time, nothing out here but farmers and rich folk. Doctors, lawyers, those types. I mean, look at this place, you think half a mill for a house this size and the land? Not on our salary," Clent huffed. "We get shot at for a living, and I can barely pay rent at for my modest three bedroom rent to own."

"Right," Vanessa replied bluntly. "You mean to tell me you signed up for the money?"

"Did you?" He walked down the porch, making his way to the front windows. "So, first welfare check, good. Tell me what you see, what we know. Time for a quiz, rookie."

"Well, someone's definitely home," Vanessa pointed to the car in the driveway. "Lights on upstairs as well."

"Yep," Clent nodded.

"The son from out of state called in the Welfare check," she went on. "It's been three days since he has spoken to his parents. They speak daily, very out of character for them to go that long without a call. Or so, he says."

"Yep," Clent replied.

"Maybe they both caught something, got ill. Just not feeling well enough to check-in?" Vanessa wasn't sure, she was musing out loud. "No signs of disturbance on the exterior of the home. Doesn't seem like any foul play."

"Maybe," Clent checked his watch, it was just after ten pm. The moon was full and hung high in the country sky, adding barely enough natural light to see their way around the yard. A soft dusting of snow had covered the frozen earth, showing no fresh footprints anywhere. Clent approached the front doublewide window, where a small opening between the shades peered into the home. He flashed his Maglite into the house.

H heard footsteps rummaging about from within the home.

"I heard something," said Vanessa.

"Yep," Clent nodded again. He saw movement too, briefly. Someone darted across the living room. "We woke someone up."

The front door opened a sliver, just large enough for a young man to stick out his disheveled face. Clent took mental notes: the man stood roughly five-eight, one hundred and sixty pounds, with shaggy brown hair, a few days of stubble on his face. He had dark brown troubling eyes, the sort of eyes that left Clent a bit uneasy. He was taking a mental picture of the man. He could see his wardrobe through the small crack of the door, a dark blue pullover hoodie, and baggy grey sweatpants. Bright blue running shoes, dirty, old, even the laces were stained brown. The young man looked fit, not in a muscular way, more like a runner. He was trim, with skinny forearms that held the door tight.

"Officers?" The man spoke, his voice low as if he had just awakened from a heavy sleep. His eyes heavy, sunken into his face like he'd come off a booze-filled weekend bender.

"Sir, are you the homeowner?" Clent stepped up onto the porch, facing the gentlemen, looking him square in the eyes. He knew he wasn't the owner. Too young to be a college student's father.

"No," he answered plainly. "Why are you here? Everything is fine; I don't need any help."

"What's your name, sir?" Vanessa asked, shining her flashlight towards the man, blinding him.

"Bob," he said plainly. Putting his hands up to block the beam. "Turn that off, please?"

"Last name?" Vanessa averted the flashlight off his face and towards his feet.

"Williams," Bob answered.

"Bob Williams, huh?" Clent added. "Short for Robert?"

"Just Bob," he added again.

"Identification?" Clent asked.

"Sorry," Bob frowned. "I misplaced my wallet. Been without my I.D. for a week now."

"Hmmm," Clent frowned. "And where did you say the homeowners were?"

"I didn't," Bob said plainly.

"Okay?" Vanessa added, growing impatient with his bluntness. "Can we speak to them? We're here on a welfare check from their son."

"Wish you could," Bob said. "They are not home. I woke up this morning to an empty house."

"I'm sorry?" Clent laughed smugly. "You telling me, you're here in their house, and have no clue where the homeowners are? What's your relation to the Simmons, Bob?"

"Friend of Dennis," Bob answered.

"Dennis Simmons?" asked Vanessa.

"Yes," Bob said.

"Mind if we look around?" asked Clent.

"I suppose not," Bob opened the front door and swayed his body from blocking the home, allowing the officers inside. He was pleasant enough. Replying with short, fast answers, but calm and collected. He did not appear nervous or under distress—all things Clent mentally noted. Yet his eyes, there was something shifty about the hollowness of them.

Before entering, Clent squared off with the man. He easily outweighed him by about forty, maybe even fifty pounds had a few inches on him as well. Clent was maybe getting up there in years, but he spent his off days in the gym. He had a regiment, ate healthily, and trained five times a week, took care of himself. He could hang if he needed to. Physically, Bob posed no threat.

"Let me hit the lights," Bob said. His hands ran up the side of the wall fingering for the switch. There was a faint *click* before the living room came to life.

"Nice place," Clent studied the living room. Wall-mounted flat-screen had to be a sixty-inches easily. There was a fancy dark-brown leather couch, two matching recliners, a small end table with a lamp on it between them. Hardwood floors, beautiful artesian rug laid out at the center, a glass coffee table pulled the room together. Very clean, extremely clean. The house smelled fresh, fresh linen with a hint of vanilla. Clent was impressed. It did not look like anyone lived in the home, almost staged for inspection. "...and clean as a whistle. You smell that, Vanessa?"

"Smells like Bleach," she replied.

"Yep," Clent nodded.

"Yes, Nora keeps a wonderful home," Bob replied. "Cleans a lot."

"How do you say you know Dennis and Nora again?" asked Vanessa. She walked herself into the kitchen, eyeing the details of the home. She found the light switch on the left-hand side of the threshold. A high chandelier hung from the center of the kitchen brought the room to life. Much like the room before, the kitchen was spotless. Not a single dirty dish in the sink, the counters freshly wiped down, not a single smear on them. The bleach smell was almost overwhelming in the kitchen. The stove looked brand new, hardly used. Too clean.

"As I said, a friend of Dennis. We share a love for old cars. He'd asked me to come up for a weekend to help him work on a project. Said he would pay me and let me stay with them for a week or two."

"Cars aye?" Vanessa frowned.

"How long have you known each other?" asked Clent

"About four months," Bob replied.

"I'm going to look around, you stay with Bob," Clent nodded towards his partner. "That okay with you, Bob?"

"If it pleases you, Officer," Bob answered. He showed no emotion.

Bob made his way into the kitchen where Vanessa was observing the contents of the kitchen fridge.

"Can I get you something, officer?" Asked Bob. "A drink? Coffee?"

"No, I'm fine," Vanessa answered. "You don't look well, feeling okay?" In the brighter light, the paleness in Bob's face was evident. She noticed the awkwardness of his eyes as well, the vacantness of them, they were dark brown, yet they had a murky like film that set in them.

"Yes, I am well," he replied.

"Any idea where the Simmons went?" Vanessa asked.

"Not really," Bob answered.

"Strange, though, no?" Vanessa frowned.

"I suppose so," Bob answered. He took a seat at the dinner table, never breaking eye contact with Vanessa.

"So, how long have you been a guest at the house?"

"About four days."

"Any idea why the Simmons aren't answering their phone?"

"No, ma'am. Did they not take them with them? Perhaps they are here? The phones I mean."

"Well, the problem, Bob, is that it's not just today that they haven't been answering? Their son, Duncan? Do you know him?"

"No."

"I see," She said. "Well, he hasn't spoken to them in a few days. Which you see is weird. Because Duncan is very close with his parents, they talk daily. Sometimes multiple times a day."

"I see," Bob replied plainly.

"No note? No nothing? You have *no* idea where the Simmons are? Just left you alone in their home?" Vanessa frowned.

"I'm sure they will be back tomorrow."

Vanessa studied the man named Bob, his facial expressions, his breathing. He gave no obvious tells. If he played poker, he'd clean house. Vanessa couldn't make him out for anything.

Clent was gone for about twenty minutes before he returned to the kitchen.

"Nothing out of the ordinary," he shrugged. "Entire house is immaculate, not a speck of dust anywhere, let alone anything suspicious. All rooms cleared."

"Nora prides herself on her home. She's the perfect host," Bob replied.

"Hmmph," Clent scratched the tip of his nose. He smelled bullshit but had nothing to go off.

"So, what's next?" Vanessa's eyes fell to Clent. Her eyes told him she thought the same. It didn't feel right; something was off.

"There is a garage, right?" Clent pointed out the side door from the kitchen. The exit opened to the side of the house where the cars were parked.

"Yes, where Dennis keeps his sixty-eight Camaro. It's a bit further back on the property, next to the woods. We shouldn't bother his stuff though; he'd be upset."

"Either way, we'd like to check that out, if you don't mind," Clent nodded.

"Sure, of course," Bob sighed. "Let me just grab the key. He keeps it next to the backdoor. Waste of time, though. Surely, they will be back tomorrow. I can have them call you?"

"We'd like just to make our rounds, and we'll be out of your hair," Clent replied.

"Yes, okay," Bob walked to the back of the kitchen near the stairs.

Clent grabbed Vanessa by her arm and pulled her into the living room.

"Stay cool," he whispered. "We don't have a warrant, all he has to do is say no, and we can't do much. It's not adding up, though, and I want to be thorough."

"Yeah, okay." Vanessa nodded. "I agree. The guy is creepy."

"All right," Bob jingled the keys in his hand. "It's this way: follow me."

The two officers followed the man named Bob outside into the wintery Michigan night. The drizzle of snow continued to fall. The driveway was slick from the thin snowy dusting, making it easy to lose balance.

"Supposed to be a big storm tonight," Bob said plainly, looking forward towards the garage.

"I hadn't heard that," Clent replied.

"Doesn't surprise me, hasn't hit the weather stations yet. They're saying a few inches tops. I follow my gut for the weather," Bob didn't look back, this was the most he's said all night. "Its gonna hit hard."

"Where you from, Bob? Asked Vanessa. "You said you were visiting Dennis?"

"Not from here," Bob said. "Little town called Ruddington. Mostly country roads."

"I've driven through Ruddington before," Vanessa added. "One stoplight, A single McDonalds, small town. Quiet."

"There's the garage," Bob pointed. "Sits right up against the woods. Mackinaw State Forest. Over seven hundred thousand acres. Beautiful."

"We're aware," Clent added. "Lived here my whole life. I hunt in those woods; most folks around here do."

"Quite a bit away from the house," Vanessa added.

"Dennis likes privacy. This is his man cave, his place to get away from the wife and work," Bob answered.

"I see," Clent smiled, admiring the exterior of the Garage. He understood that a man had to have his own space.

"Let me unlock the door, one second," Bob fiddled with the keys.

"Camaro is in here?" asked Clent.

"Yes," Bob answered.

"Nice size garage," Vanessa added. "Huge, isn't it?"

Bob opened the door cautiously, about a quarter of the way. He slipped in. "Let me get the light, so you don't bump your heads," said Bob. Before they could respond, he slammed the door and locked it shut.

"Fuck!" Clent dove for the door. He grabbed the handle, to no avail. He lunged shoulder first into the thick door. Despite his size, it barely budged. He hit a second time. It made a loud *THUD!* "Shit!" he winced. His shoulder popped.

"Damn it!" Vanessa pulled her firearm from her holster. "Wasn't expecting that!"

"Bob, open the door! Now!" Clent yelled.

This time Vanessa slammed her boot into the door, a failed attempt to kick it down.

"Son of a bitch," Clent cursed, rotating his arm in a circle, in an attempt to ease the pain. "Look around the sides; see if there's a window we can get in."

"On it," Vanessa replied. Her adrenaline was pumping, heart was racing, pounding loudly in her chest. She attempted to control her breathing.

Remember training. Stay calm.

Why had he locked them out? What was he hiding?

She holstered her weapon above her Maglite. She inspected the west side of the building. It was longer than she thought, it appeared to vanish into the thicket of the woods. The side was barren of windows and doors. No entry, no exit.

"Nothing!" Vanessa yelled.

"Not over here either," Clent inspected the opposite side. "Come here, guard the door. I'm going to look behind the garage. Maybe there's a rear door?"

They heard a rustling from the woods behind the garage.

"Shit, is that him?" Clent chased after the noise. It could have been anything, a wild animal, a god-damned bear for all Clent knew. But his gut told him it was him, escaping into the woods.

Vanessa ran back to the front of the garage. The door was still locked, firmly secured. She thought they might have been close to breaking it down; the frame looked loose. No sign of Bob exiting back out the door. Maybe she could finish the door off with a few strong kicks.

"Open up!" she yelled. She inhaled sharply, kicked again, the thud of her boots echoed into the night air.

With one final kick, the door from the front door burst open. Vanessa grunted, exasperated, she almost fell onto the floor. The snow had made her boots slick, and when they hit the smooth pavement inside the garage, she lost her balance.

"Fuck, I did it!" Vanessa blurted out to no one. She flicked her flashlight on, holstered her firearm.

"Bob? She yelled. "You in here?"

She stepped into the garage.

•　　•　　•

Clent made his way to the back of the elongated building with caution. Bob was right; the garage stood with more than a third of it enclosed within the forest. The trees and shrubbery were thick and dense. Even in the winter, where the oak tree's sprung naked branches, the pine trees stayed full, diluting most of the visibility. All of this made it very hard to traverse on foot. Visibility, even with the police high powered Maglite, was less than stellar.

Clent took a deep breath, forcing himself to breathe. Every foot was placed with attention, careful not to slip on the slick, freshly fallen snow. He worked his way through the sappy pine needles with his back against the building, his face exposed to the untamed forest. Branches scratched his face; pine needles poked him. Finally, he made it through. The building came to an end, and a small clearing opened.

Clent wiped away the sap from his face. His back against the edge of the garage. His gun raised; he rounded the corner. There *was* a back exit, a second door. This one was thick, reinforced with steel, but it remained closed. Clent approached slowly, his gun drawn and extended out in front of him, his Maglite illuminating the way.

"Where are you," Clent whispered. He reached out, checked the door handle.

Locked.

He heard rustling once again from the opposite end of the clearing. It came from deep into the forest. Tree branches snapped, bushes rustled.

"Stop!" Clent yelled. "Bob, turn around! Arms up!"

The snow fell hard now; huge white clumps invaded Clent's vision. He flashed his light towards the noise, hoping to see the man fleeing. "Bob, come back here! Why are you running?"

Clent followed pursuit into the forest. He was no tracker, and the thought of going too far into the woods made him uneasy. He understood the dangers. If got lost out here, and unprepared, it could quickly become a death sentence.

"Bob, you go too far, you get lost. You'll die out here. Bob! We got a storm brewing! You said it yourself!" Clent yelled.

Then came the sickening noise from inside the garage. It sounded inhuman, a horrid high-pitched shriek. In all his years, he'd never heard anything so disturbing. Shivers shot up his spine, the thin hairs on his neck stood up. His stomach sunk. *Vanessa...*

TWO

Haylee dropped three ice cubes in her glass. Next came the cheap vodka she purchased from the small liquor store about five minutes from her house, Seagrams. Haylee always bought the cheap kind. It did the trick, and she could buy a lot more of it. She filled her glass halfway with the alcohol. Finally came the red bull, the sweet caffeinated nectar.

Haylee hated sleeping. She hadn't had an unaided good night's sleep since the *incident*. Most nights saw her waking in terror from horrifying nightmares. There were times where screamed so loud in her sleep, her neighbor, Aaron, (they shared a duplex), would waken from her fits. The first time it happened, he'd run over to make sure she wasn't in danger of getting murdered. She knew he was joking when he said it. But he didn't know how much truth there was to it.

It wasn't funny.

Haylee took a long sip of the drink. She walked to the cupboard, above her microwave, where she kept her pills, and she dug through a half dozen pill bottles before pulling out the one she was looking for labeled Hydrocodone. Haylee took two pills into her hand, dropped them on her tongue. She took another long gulp from her cocktail. Haylee held the sweet liquid in her mouth and threw her head back, washing them down smoothly.

The guilt of her addiction to pills immediately consumed her. She thought of her dad, how disappointed he would be to see his daughter popping pills and drinking her life away.

He would never understand. He never could.

She brushed the thought aside, tightened her pink fuzzy Victoria Secret's bathrobe around her body, retying the waistband. Time for her nightly routine. She checked every window to make sure they were secured. Next, she checked the drapes making sure they were closed tightly so no one could see in. Finally, she checked the front and back door twice each, unlocking then relocking each one. She was safe. She found her puke green couch and fell into it.

She was exhausted.

Beside her laid her four-legged best friend, Trayer. He was a monster of a dog—her only real companion. Snoring lazily, he made a low grunt as she sat beside him. He hadn't even lifted his head to acknowledge her. Warm drool pooled beneath slobbery wet lips, dampening the ugly green couch with dark spots. Trayer was more than her best friend; he was her protector. He had a beautiful blue merle coat and weighted easily one-hundred-sixty pounds of thick stocky muscle. He wasn't skinny like most Great Dane's Haylee had ever known. He was tall too; when he stood next to Haylee on all fours, he could rest his head on her chest with ease.

Haylee laid down against the dog's massive frame, her head on his stomach, listening to him breathe. She was safe with him, her guardian, loyal and loving. He was a gift from her father when she moved into the duplex. He wanted her to drive home, come back to Ohio, and live with him. She wouldn't go. So, due to her stubbornness, and the fact he didn't want her living alone, Trayer became the compromise. She'd always wanted a Great Dane, and she did feel safer having him in the home. One of the few things she and her father agreed on.

Something was better than nothing.

Haylee's head was now reeling from the pills. Perhaps she should have only taken one. Or maybe one and a half. Two may have been a bad idea. These pills were new to her; she should be more careful when trying out unprescribed meds. She sighed, took a deep breath. Tried to keep focus.

She needed them, though, the pills.

She'd do anything to find the numbness, to sleep without worry. Pills were the only thing that silenced them anymore, kept them away. Especially the hideous one. The creature with the antlers, the blood-stained mouth with the jagged decayed teeth.

The mere thought of the creature sent her into a panic.

Her television was already on. She rarely turned it off, ever. The noise from random programming kept her sane. She needed the background fodder to root her in reality. If not, she was afraid she might slip away somewhere dark, somewhere rooted in her past. She opened a book, what was she even reading? She'd forgot. A self-help book, one her phycologist suggested. She hated it. The words on the page turned fuzzy, and she couldn't concentrate, all effects of the pills. It didn't matter, though, fuck the books, they never helped.

Her phone vibrated from the end table where it sat charging. She hesitated when she read the caller ID. It was her father. Her instinct was to answer. Despite their often heated differences, his voice always made her feel safe.

"Shiiit," she muttered, the word slurred from the dampness of her lips. He'd be able to tell she'd been drinking, and she knew her words weren't forming correctly.

Slurring, another effect from the pills.

She knew she took too many.

She wanted to sleep, and she needed that elation from the fuzziness in her head, the lightweight sensation of release. If she fell asleep without the pills, **the thing** would be waiting for her, behind the old wooden moss-covered door.

Her Visitor, the thing who tortured her every night before the pills, kept her safe.

She thought of the creature, its persistent haunting of her, that had followed since the incident. Her eyes were fighting her now, eyelids growing heavier by the second. The swelling of tears pooled in her eyes, and the warmth of them streamed down her cheeks.

She thought of her mother, of her sister, Camille.

Then she slipped deep into the blackness.

THREE

Aaron Hauser knocked on his neighbor's door. The roaring of a large dog resounded from inside the home. From the side window, he saw the massive head from a great Dane poking out, barking irritably. If Aaron hadn't known Trayer, he'd be intimidated by his sheer size. The dog looked menacing like it could rip one of his limbs off with ease. He averted his attention to his reflection in the glass screen of the front door. He stroked his reddish beard, nodding to himself with positive reinforcement. He leaned against his long, glossy black walking cane, waiting for Haylee to answer.

"You look, good bro," he smiled. He spoke to his reflection, fully aware of how ridiculous he would look if she opened the door at that moment. Trayer continued, the front bay window was dripping with Trayer's foamy saliva, fogging up from his hot breath. Aaron slipped the cane up under his arm and straightened his back. It cracked loudly.

Aaron was a heavier set guy, late twenty's, but he held his weight well. He prided himself on being a master of "nerd-swag." He had his own style, and he made it work, often creating outfits out of humourous tee's and sports coats, dark denim, and an array of multi-colored Nike sneakers (he was a sneakerhead) for all occasions.

It was cold—bitter cold, the kind of weather that made your bones ache. A storm hit the night prior, layered their shared duplex with about seven inches of thick snow. He braved the streets to grab breakfast. A typical fifteen-minute round trip took him forty. He looked at his watch, a quarter past ten.

He frowned.

She should be up...

Why wasn't she answering? There is no way she could sleep through Trayer's bark. Hell, if she didn't answer soon, the dog was liable to wake the whole neighborhood.

Today, Aaron wore a heather-brown sportcoat over a vintage wrestling tee-shirt. He chose the shirt specifically because it was one of his all-time favorite wrestlers, Jake the Snake Roberts. He adjusted his ball cap, a flat-brimmed Detroit Tigers hat with the old classic gothic letter "D" printed on the front.

He frowned, still no answer.

He knocked again, rang the doorbell for good measure.

"Haylee?" he yelled. He knew she was home. She hardly ever left the place, and her car was hidden under a heap of snow on her half of the driveway.

"...Hello?" He grew worried. Aaron pulled out his phone from the inside pocket of his sport coat. He rang Haylee. No answer. He redialed it...

"Hello?" A muffled voice finally picked up. She sounded woozy, half-awake, probably hungover as well (she liked to booze). "Quiet, Trayer," she snapped.

"Aye, you okay?" Aaron asked. "I'm outside; I brought breakfast."

She didn't reply.

"Hello, Haylee?" Aaron frowned.

The front door popped open, slowly.

Aaron walked into the living room, where Haylee stood sitting on the armrest of her ugly lime green couch. Her hands holding her head, she looked like death warmed over. Her skin was paler than usual, dark bags set under her sunken eyes. Her hair tousled, tied loosely in the back. Trayer immediately ran up to Aaron. He let out an inquisitive growl, his head hung lung, sniffing cautiously.

"Hey boy," Aaron put out his hand for Trayer to sniff. Immediately, Trayer lightened up; his tail began to wag haphazardly, swatting Haylee on her hip with a loud *THUD*.

"Ouch," she winced. "Big oaf," She slapped him lovingly on his hip. Trayer pranced around Aaron excitedly. Happy as ever to see his friend, the dog buried his broad snout into Aaron's crotch, huff, and snorted.

"Miss me, boy?" he laughed. "He's always so scary until he realizes it's me," said Aaron. He played with the big dog, scratching him behind the ears, rough horsing with him as he might with a little brother. "Like, oh yeah, that's not a stranger, duh—that's my buddy who brings me food," Aaron used a playful dumb voice to voice the dog. "Here yeah go bud, got you some breakfast too," he reached into a brown grease-soaked paper bag and tossed the Dane a single hash brown. Trayer wolfed it down in one gulp.

"Damn, girl," Aaron turned his attention to Haylee. "You get into a fight with the couch and lose? Lookin' rough. When's the last time you showered?"

"Thanks," Haylee frowned, rubbing her thigh where Trayer's boney tail had smacked her. "Sorry, I didn't get all dolled up for your surprise visit."

"You look sick, is all," Aaron corrected. "Hungover?"

"Too many pills last night," Haylee sank back into the couch. Her robe brushed open. Embarrassed, she covered herself up. Her head felt weighted down as if fifty-pound weights were strapped to her forehead. Her legs were also shaky; a cold sweat had come over her. She held out her two hands and tried to steady them; she failed. Trayer, now losing interest in Aaron, jumped back on the couch, burying his head in Haylee's lap.

"The pills I got you?" Aaron made his way into the living room.

"Yeah," she replied.

"The 40mg of Norco?" he asked again.

"I think," she frowned.

"I told you to take one, how many—"

"Two, with some vodka and Red Bull."

"Well, that's why you look and feel like shit," Aaron frowned. "I told you I could get you them, but you had to be careful. Can't fuck 'round with these."

"I know, I know..." Haylee shook her head, not wanting a lecture. The television was on a local news station, the volume was loud, and her head was splitting. She turned it down to a low buzz. She wasn't in the mood for company; she wanted to crawl back into her couch and sleep the day away.

"Food will help, I brought breakfast," He tossed a sausage and egg muffin on the coffee table. He placed large coffee in front of her as well. "Straight black, strong too," he said.

"You're too kind," she smiled. She hadn't realized how hungry she was.

"Listen, not to be that guy," Aaron took a seat next to her, unwrapping his breakfast sandwich. Trayer wedged himself between the two. He was always protecting her from everyone and everything, especially from men.

It didn't matter if the dog liked you or not; Trayer always wedged himself between her and anyone.

"—Then don't," she replied, her mouth full of sausage and egg.

"Look, if you want me to keep getting you these pills, you have to meet me halfway," he took a hefty bite from his sandwich, a chunk of egg fell onto his lap. Smooth, he thought to himself.

"It was an accident. I'll be careful," she added. "They're new pills. I have to figure out what works for me. Obviously, two was too many."

"I have a limited supply," he picked up the egg with a paper napkin, wrapped it up, and tossed it back into the grease-stained brown bag. "Plus, I keep a few myself, for when I get bad. They don't hand this shit out like candy. I only get a months' worth. So, take em' on bad days, and take one a day, twice a day tops. Those are strong and meant for me; I'm like three times your size little lady. That's why I told you one. You used to get the 20mg's from that dirtbag. So, just be careful. I wanna help, but I don't wanna see you blue-faced and overdosed."

"Right," she sighed. She eagerly took a second bite of the sandwich. It was greasy but tasty. She hadn't eaten much the last few days, a couple of peanut butter sandwiches, a small bag of chips. Her diet was shit.

"I'm telling you, switch over to weed," Aaron pulled out a bag from his inner pocket. "Those pills are dangerous. I wouldn't fuck with them too much. Plus, even for the physical pain, this works better for me. It's legal now too, so it's not like your dad…"

"I know," She interrupts. "It doesn't work like that for me, nothing works except for the pills," She stopped him. She didn't need a sermon on the dangers of pills, or the wonders of weed. Weed didn't knock her out like the pills; weed didn't keep *it* from visiting her dreams. She's tried everything, *every-thing*. Norco was the only thing that made her completely blackout. No dreams, no visitor. Either way, sobriety was no longer an option in her life. She had to embrace the self-medication. It was the only weapons she had to fend off *the thing*.

If he only knew. Or did he? This entire shit town knew about her past.

"Poor Haylee, what horrors she's been through.
How will she manage? How could she?
She's broken, she'll never be the same."

Haylee heard the whispers around town. She felt like a special attraction, something for the city to gossip about. When she did manage the courage to get up and leave the house (even years after the incident), the town still spread rumors about her—a freak. At least Aaron spoke to her like a person.

They'd become *semi* friends after he moved in next door about a year ago. Helped her more than she was willing to admit. He'd go with her shopping sometimes, when she was out of food, and couldn't bear going out by herself. He was her only human friend. If she wasn't such a broken, miserable, disaster of a human, she thought he might have liked her. But how could he? The mess she was—the pile of shit-bag of a human that was left after that night.

The damaged Haylee.

The Haylee three years ago? Sure, she'd never had a problem getting attention from men. Now? She was damaged goods, a lost soul with nowhere to go.

At least he brought food.

"Sandwich is good," she forced a smile. She pushed the thoughts out of her head. "I needed that."

"I'm glad," Aaron washed the last bite of his sandwich down with a large gulp of his coffee.

Haylee's phone buzzed on the coffee table, breaking the conversation.

"Shit, that's my dad," Haylee sighed. "I need to take this," she stood up, grabbed the phone, swiping the green button to accept the call.

"Morning, dad," she answered.

"Morning, I tried calling last night," His voice was soft, yet stern like a grown man talking to a frightened child. That's how he always spoke to her now. Like she was fragile, easy to break. If he said the wrong thing or his tone was too stiff, she might snap.

"Sorry, fell asleep early last night, had a bad day," she replied. She offered a smile to Aaron, putting up her finger to him, signaling for a minute.

He nodded, picked up the television remote, and turned up the volume. Haylee made her way into the kitchen for privacy.

"I'm sorry about that. Lots of bad days lately, huh?" her dad added. "Same for me, lonely here without anyone."

"Yeah," She wasn't sure how to respond. She couldn't even remember when she had a 'good' day. She was sure it was the same for him. "How's the business going?"

"Slow," her dad sighed. "Not a lot of dignified work for a Private detective who was banished from the police force. I get the regulars. Wife wants to know if the Husband is cheating and guess what?"

"What?" Haylee asked.

"They always are," He let out a half chuckle. "Picked up a few side gigs too. Gotta pay for your living, yeah know? It's not easy. I do some bouncer work on weekends now, and security here and there. Mostly bars, a night club in the city."

"I'm sorry I'm such a burden," Haylee hated feeling guilty about needing her father's support.

"I didn't mean it like," her dad fumbled his words.

"—It's okay, I get it," Haylee interjected.

"Are you eating? Staying healthy?" her dad spoke softly again, attempting to reign the conversation back under his control.

"I'm alive," Haylee half chuckled.

"I haven't been billed from Doctor Feldman lately, are you seeing him?"

"It's been a few weeks," no lies there, she didn't see the point of a shrink. She was beyond help. Her dad wouldn't listen, though. She braced herself for the same lecture he's spewed to her over the last twenty-some years.

"I wish you would see him regularly. My therapist has helped me so much."

"I will see about next week, promise," that time, it was a lie. Haylee had no intention of seeing anyone. Especially Dr. Feldman.

"Any job prospects?" He asked. He was shooting straight to the point this morning, wasting no time.

"No," she said bluntly. A swirl of anger came over Haylee's head. She didn't want to deal with this, not now, not ever.

"Look, I don't want to push you too fast. I can only pay for your rent for so long before I go broke. I'm working three jobs. Either we need to find you some income, or we need to talk about you moving back home to Ohio."

"I will start looking soon," Haylee pinched the bridge of her nose, trying to relieve the tension building. She tried getting a job last year, and it was a disaster. She had a panic attack that hospitalized her for two days. She never even made it into the first day of work. A shitty job at a Dollar General store running the cash wrap had sent her into a mental spiral into a very dark space.

"Okay, listen...I'm sorry. I am not trying to make this harder. I love and care about you. You're all I have. We're in this together."

She could hear the sadness in her Dad's voice, it stung her, like a million needles pressing against her back. Like a wave, shooting up her spine and outward. She wasn't the only victim of that night; she knew that. She relied on her dad for so much, but who did he have? Guilt replaced the anger. He had no one. He was a broken father with an adult daughter who still needed her daddy to pay her bills.

"No, I'm sorry," Haylee fell into the kitchen table. Defeated, exhausted, her head still feeling light from the pills.

"Listen, that's not even why I called. I need a favor, can you do me a favor? It's really important," his voice changed, gone was the forced politeness, the nurturing tone of a father. Replaced was the voice of Detective Dad. The voice he used when he was on duty, or when Haylee and her sister were caught being bad. When that voice came out, she knew it was serious.

"Uh, sure? Sounds important?"

"I want you to stay away from the local news and social media for the next few days. Can you do that for me?" He spoke to her again, like a child. Slow, methodic, the seriousness in his request hung in the air.

"Why, what's going on?" Haylee frowned.

"Nothing you need to worry about. But for both of us, please stay away. Just, I don't know, read some books? Watch some movies? I need you to lay low. Can you do that? Until I say otherwise?"

"Yeah, I mean, I guess," Haylee answered.

"Okay, good."

"Listen, I have a guest over," Haylee replied, "I don't want to be rude."

"—Oh," her dad was surprised, probably a little annoyed. "Yeah, um, well, I love you and just keep me posted if you need anything. I can send some money for groceries in a few days for you."

"Thanks, dad. I will call you tonight?" she asked.

"Yeah, okay. Bye." He hung up.

Click.

Silence.

Haylee put her cell down on the kitchen table, staring at the background picture of her home screen. It was her favorite photo of her and her sister. Camille had taken it at Haylee's graduation party. The two of them stood out in front of their old Ohio home, a quaint two-story bungalow. Haylee, stood with her left arm resting over her little sisters' shoulder, both with bright, broad smiles.

Haylee stood up from the table and made her way back to the living room. Aaron sat on the couch, his mouth gaped open, eyes wide. Trayer had moved, resting his head in Aaron's lap.

"Holy shit," he pointed to the television.

There, a pretty young woman in a woman's pinstripe suit jacket sat at the local WMEM TV25 news desk. An image hung in the top right corner of the screen reading, "Murder strikes Orr Road in Emmet County Once Again."

"In some wildly disturbing news," The woman spoke, her voice pleasant, the words that followed, not so much. "Police walked into what many are calling a scene from a horror movie. Two bodies have been found in a home on the now-infamous Orr road. Reports are saying the two victims were murdered in their homes and mutilated sometime in the last few days. More news to come as it develops. Stay tuned; you heard it here first."

A Video clip followed the woman with the pleasant voice, filmed late last night; they aired the residence where the crime was committed. There were multiple police cars parked outside the two-story country home, blue and red lights poured into the dark Michigan sky, reflecting off the home's window. Bright yellow police tape stretched across the hilly snow-covered front yard. There was a large group of officers and EMT's working the scene.

Haylee's knees buckled.

"Jesus!" Aaron jumped from the couch, Trayer was faster, immediately at her side. Aaron helped her to the couch. Her light frame was easy to lift, even with his bad leg. He sat her down, fetched her a glass of water from the kitchen.

She took it, guzzling down the entire glass without breathing.

"Do I need to call an ambulance? Are you okay?"

"That's my old street..." the words spilled from her mouth. "That's..."

I know," Aaron frowned. "Close to where..."

He knew. They had never spoken about the accident, but he knew.

Could you even call it an accident? She'd always spoke about that night as if it was some sort of freak turn of events. But accidents aren't premeditated. You don't unintentionally eat another human.

She should have realized he knew. Everyone in town knew. There were no secrets, especially when your name was all over local and national news.

Her fifteen minutes of fame.

"I didn't know you knew," she frowned. The news report with the pretty woman was already over. There hadn't been much to discuss, not a lot of information had been collected despite a double murder. "You don't look at me like everyone else."

"Of course, I knew," Aaron took a seat next to her. "—And what do you mean, everyone else?"

"Like a freak, everyone looks at me like I'm broken," A stream of tears rolled down Haylee's reddened cheeks.

"No one thinks you're broken. You're a victim of an awful crime," he added. He was rubbing her back in an attempt to console her.

Her breaths came heavy and deep.

"They stare at me, talk about me," she spoke through gasps of air.

This was the start of a panic attack.

"Breath," he said slowly. "We don't know much right now," he added. "What are you thinking? What's going through your head?"

"My dad," Haylee sniffled. She wiped the tears from her cheeks. She took a deep breath, tried to collect herself. "He just called, told me to stay away from the news, away from social media. He must have heard...probably from his connections."

"Too close for comfort?" Aaron questioned. "I mean, it's weird. The same road as your old home? Another, you know...murder. Violent one too."

"Yeah," Haylee went numb. "Weird..." she muttered, wiping the tears away.

FOUR

Michigan winters are brutal, with weather able to change in an instant. Haylee had packed up earlier that evening, preparing for her trip. Haylee was excited to drive down to Ohio to visit her dad. She was glad her little sister, Camille, couldn't make it. She landed a job working at the small strip mall outside of town. She wanted to stay in for the weekend to prepare for her new career.

Haylee needed to get away from everyone, even her sister. Camille and Haylee had a love/hate relationship, as most siblings do. Her little sister was a do-gooder, straight-A student, a college graduate, and of course, the apple in their daddy's eye. Haylee was the opposite; she hated college, took up smoking and drinking in middle school, and liked boys a little bit too much. Not to mention, Haylee was damaged goods, a freak, and she spent her entire childhood wishing she was more like Camille.

Camille wasn't damaged goods.

Once Haylee asked her if she too had the dreams. If she heard the voices, also?

Camille looked at her like she was a freak.

They never spoke of it again. Not even after their Mother died.

Haylee hadn't seen her dad since she moved to Northern Michigan with her fiancé Robbie about four months prior. Robbie had a job opportunity as a marketing director with THM Senior Solutions. It was about an hour commute from their cozy little home out in the countryside of Emmet County. The new position paid more than both their salaries back in Ohio.

After Robbie purposed, they packed up and moved to Michigan two months later. He'd settle in with his new position, and Haylee looked to start up a new career. She wasn't going to miss starting over. Hell, she was ready for the turn of a new leaf, excited to escape her hometown and the many demons she would hopefully leave behind.

A fresh new start. A family of her own.

Maybe she could finally get her life back on track.

After the proposal, Haylee envisioned happiness for the first time. She was due for a happy ending, after how wrong her childhood went. She dreamt of a tidy little home, a few babies, a cute dog. Something big, like a Saint Bernard, or a Mastiff to keep her safe. She didn't care for her Ohio job anyway; she'd been working as a waitress at an Applebee's. It was demeaning, half flirting with men twice her age for decent tips. She'd had a fallen out with her father years back, they spoke weekly, but there was resentment on both parties. Yet, there was still a strong family bond, unconditional love. They had gone through a lot as a family. As much damage they endured, it also strengthened as well.

So, here it is now, a few months after the move into their starter home, and Haylee was still unemployed. At least her sister Camille had better luck landing a middle management job at the nearest shopping mall. Haylee, not willing to settle with retail or the food industry, decided to keep applying for positions she lacked qualifications for.

She had her fiancé's support.

"No worries," Robbie said, reassuring her at the dinner table one beautiful summer evening. They had ordered a large pizza, double pepperoni, and cheese. The three of them, Haylee, Robbie, and Camille sitting together, eating. Robbie drank his Sam Adams Cherry Wheat. His go-to beer after a long hard day at work. Haylee limited herself to one glass of red wine, allowing her sister to partake in the rest. Haylee had learned (over the years of abusing alcohol) a bit of self-control. She was proud of that.

"I'm making enough for you to take your time—find something you love. With Camille starting her job soon, she can help with the bills. We're fine. Plus, once we get married next spring, we'll need you at home, stupid to start a career knowing we're planning our first child."

And they were going to be okay. They were better off in Michigan, too many dark secrets in Ohio, painful and hurtful secrets.

It had been four months since they moved to Michigan. They were settled into their new cozy home in the middle of a country road. Their house had a long winding dirt driveway that twisted around a small clump of a forest. Their nearest neighbors were almost a mile down the road. A beautiful quiet area out in the woods. Country livin'.

The home butted right up against the massive Michigan State Forest. A beautiful country, far away from the noisy city. Robbie had always wanted to move back to Michigan, where he grew up. He loved the outdoors, hunting fishing, and when they found the small house numbered 1228 on Orr Road, it was the perfect starter house for a family.

Camille moved in with them after a messy split with her physically and emotionally abusive husband. She welcomed her sister. Hoped she'd grow closer to her, for once she was in the position to help her little sister out, and not vice versa.

Yet, all wasn't perfect in the new home. Haylee began to notice changes in Robbie. They were subtle at first, snapping at her here and there. He'd make snide remarks. Hurtful one too, harsh and ugly words spewed from his usual charming self. Soon, he became aggressive, even violent towards her and her sister. They'd been together for years. He'd never acted that way before.

Haylee found herself slipping into the darker parts of her life even before the move. Where her depression and anxiety played, she'd come so far in silencing those inner demons to take control of her life. Now, with Robbie acting out, she felt her grip loosening.

The darkness would creep back out.

There was a strain in the relationship. They had ups and downs, and their downs were fairly dark. But no relationship was perfect, right? She needed a fresh perspective. She was losing her grip on reality in the home, with all the fighting. She decided a trip to see her father would do their relationship some good.

It was hard being in a new place; none of her friends from back home were around. She was stuck, no job. Not to mention her last breakdown, the one in the woods. The fallout left her in the psychiatric ward for a week under a suicide watch.

Found in the woods, alone, bloodied.

She *was* a freak.

Just the thought of that night made her cringe.

How could she have done that? How stupid was she?

Two wrongs...her father would always say.

Enough, she told herself. Focus on the roads.

The weather was terrible. Dreadful actually.

She drove cautiously down a two-lane highway. A substantial downpour of snow crashed into her window. The storm hit about ten minutes ago; it wasn't looking like it was slowing down. The road in front of her was already growing slick.

"Shit," Haylee cursed. She gripped the steering wheel so hard her knuckles turned white. She had heard there was a chance for snow to hit during her trip. But it looked like she was going to beat it. Unfortunately for her, she was wrong. About forty-five minutes into the drive, the severe warnings for the area hit the radio stations.

Severe winter warning.

She was nervous enough driving to Ohio by herself, let alone during a storm like this one.

Her cellphone rang, buzzing in the dash beside her. She looked at the caller ID. It was her dad. She picked it up, answered the phone. She put it on speaker, placed it on her lap. Leaving both hands on the steering wheel.

"Hi dad," she said, her words fluent with nerves.

"Hay," he said, "Hard to hear you, am I on speaker?"

"Yeah," she spoke louder. "Weathers bad, want to focus on the road."

"That's why I was calling, I was checking out the weather app for your ride here," He sounded worried. "You picked a terrible weekend for a visit," He said.

"I know," she sighed, "The radio station said we're in a warning, I'm like right in the middle of it."

"Maybe we should reschedule? How far are you?"

"Not terribly far, about an hour in..." She frowned.

"Maybe turn back, your lot closer to home than here. Drive safe, and slowly, we always have tomorrow or next week. Maybe we can do it so you and Camille can come together."

"I really need to get away..." Haylee's lip quivered. She pulled over to the side of the lone highway. She flipped on her hazards. "It's getting bad, dad. Really bad, at home."

"I know," His voice went into Detective Dad mode. "Did Robbie do something stupid?"

"No." She lied, sort of.... "But he's been so angry lately. So... mean. Ever since, you know, I had that relapse last month. It's been spiraling out of control."

"—He hit you, didn't he?" her dad's voice trembled, the anger dark, engulfing.

"No, he's not *Dave*, dad, he wouldn't do that!" Haylee found herself protecting her fiancé, and there was truth to the accusation. Little white lies, she was always good at those.

Dave was Camille's soon to be ex-husband, a drunk cop, who slapped Camille so bad he knocked her sisters filling out of her mouth. When their dad found out, he broke down their front door, grabbed his daughter from the home. He came back after getting Camille into his car, didn't say a word to the drunk Dave. Instead, his body slammed through a wall. He pulled his firearm on him. From what Haylee gathered from the little information Camille was willing to share, their father told Dave he would spray his brains all over the floor if he ever spoke to his daughter again.

Macho Dave called his bluff. Their dad discharged his weapon a few inches above his head. They hadn't heard from Dave since. Their father, a well-decorated Police detective, his career was over as fast as he'd pulled that trigger.

"Don't project, you do that when you're lying," He was a detective after all. He knew his daughter's tells. He could read them both like a book.

"Dad, Robbie is not that guy," Haylee did her best to mask the white lie.

Last week, when Camille was out of the house. Haylee had gotten upset that Robbie had been late coming home from work, something that was becoming a daily occurrence. He would come and go as he pleased. She began to think he was cheating on her.

What was the saying? Once a cheat?

She decided to confront him, tears in her eyes. He didn't reply, didn't question her accusation. Instead, his face went blank. He filled with rage. She could see the blood rushing into his cheeks; red blotches covered his face. The vein in his temple protruding throbbing Robbie clenched his fist, punched the wall as hard as he could. He hit squarely onto a mounted picture frame and shattered their engagement photo. The glass broke, the shards cut up his fist, blood dripping over his knuckles.

Haylee screamed at first. Stunned, she hadn't known what to do. She went to console him, to apologize. She reached out to him. She stood there, holding his bloody hand. That's when he pushed her away. Hard. She fell onto the floor, hit her head on the coffee table. His face-she remembered the fear in his face-like for a moment, just a small fragment of time, she thought she saw the old Robbie's eyes. Robbie, before the other woman. Robbie, before the violent streak. Robbie, before the new job in Michigan. Her fingers ran over the back of her head, a small smear of blood covered her hand.

"I'm...I'm sorry..." he muttered.

"—If he touches you, you tell me," her father said, snapping her back to reality. "You or your sister. I will do to him the same thing I did to that poor excuse for a man your sister married."

"You know he wouldn't," she lied again. "You know him, dad. He's a good guy; he wouldn't..."

"I do, but what you've been telling me lately, he isn't the man I knew back here in Ohio," he said bluntly. "Also, you know what I did for a living? I saw good people do bad things every day. It's why I taught you and your sister, how to protect yourselves. I never knew Dave was a goddamned drunk either; he knocked your sister silly. Lost my career over a loser drunk, but you two, you're all I got. I will always protect my girls. It was your mothers dying wish. We don't always get along, and I know that. I wasn't, hell...I'm not a great dad. I try, I promise I do. But I WILL protect you both."

"I know, dad." Haylee bit her smile. She didn't have much of a response.

She wasn't sure which relationship was more damaged, her and her father's, or her future husband.

"I think he's having an affair," she blurted out. "I think, maybe, he's not in love with me anymore? He doesn't want to admit it. Like he's stuck with me?" she began to weep. "We relocated, moved into this home together. Maybe he feels like now he can't go back? Does he feel stuck with me? Then, I had that incident. I'm so embarrassed over it. I think I think he thinks I'm so sort of freak. Like, who does that dad? Now he always angry."

"Haylee," her dad interjected, back to using his comforting dad's voice. "I think you need to have an honest conversation with him. Don't position him, don't insinuate he's cheating, but ask him, directly, openly. Be an adult for once."

"Yeah," she replied. She hadn't noticed the accumulation of snow that piled up on her windshield. It was coming down even harder now; visibility was worsening.

"Are you drinking again?" Her dad asked, he was sure to speak in a nonjudgmental tone, but of course, he was.

Haylee ignored it.

"Dad, I think I'm going to turn back around. We will reschedule, okay?"

"Please tell me you're still sober," Her dad pushed. "No more pills, right? No alcohol?"

"I'm trying my best. I promise," Haylee answered. This time it wasn't a white lie; it was blatant.

"I'm here for you, Hay, I love you," he added. "You guys can always come back home, always have your rooms waiting."

"Thanks, Dad," She turned off the phone. Flipped her wipers back on, clearing off the windshield. The road was still deserted, no cars on either side. She turned around. She'd drive slow and safe. She'd get back late, near midnight, but it would be safer. She would be in bed by one Am at the latest. Maybe talk with Robbie tomorrow. Over dinner, she thought. She'd make his favorite, shrimp scampi, red wine, merlot maybe. This was the plan, at least.

How was she to know her life was about to go to shit?

FIVE

"This is officer Clent Moore requesting back up at 1126 Orr road. We have a suspect that fled into the forest, repeat we need back up," Clent bellowed into his shoulder radio. He had followed the suspect about two yards into the thick forest before he'd heard the blood-curdling scream of his partner from within the garage.

"White male, about five-eight, hundred-eighty pounds. Wearing grey sweats and a blue hoody, traveling northbound on feet, suspect fled into the state forest." He'd assumed the noise came from who claimed his name was Bob Williams.

"Fucking Aye," Clent cursed. Maybe it wasn't Bob he was chasing after, could be a damn raccoon for all he knew. After all, he never saw the man flee into the forest. He backtracked towards the scream, darting through the shrubs and bushes, making his way back to the small opening. The backdoor was still secure. Clent ran as fast as his legs would take him. His right foot slipped beneath him; the snow was coming down heavy, slick. He lost his bearings, tumbled to the ground, hard.

His head hit hard on the frozen earth. It made a sickening thud in his skull. He saw bright white lights flash in front of his eyes like little fireworks were exploding in his brain. He winced in pain as he got back to his feet, holding his head. He was dazed, he gripped the side of the garage to balance himself. He shook it off, rounded the corner.

"Vanessa?" he yelled. No answer. He grabbed the back of his head; a giant goose egg had formed. Thankfully, there was no blood.

That fuckin' hurt.

The large door he failed at breaking in, now sat open, held barley on by its hinges. He could see the wet footprints of his partner leading into the garage. He raised his firearm, crossing with his flashlight in his other hand, lighting the way. The garage was spacious; it opened up directly into a workshop. Sure enough, there in the shop was the Camaro Bob had referenced earlier.

Then the smell hit him. His stomach retched immediately; the aroma hit him like a swift punch to the gut. It almost toppled him over. It was a familiar scent, something he had smelled many times over his career. No matter how many times that foul stench hit his nose, he was never ready for it. He once tried to explain it to a buddy of his, but he couldn't find words. It was simply dreadful, unholy. It stained your clothes, the sick bitter smell of decomposing flesh. Like a large waste bag of roadkill sitting out in the sun, rubbed in fecal matter, roasting.

"Vanessa?" Clent yelled again. He pushed aside the smell.

"Clent?" her voice came from the back of the shop. He turned quickly; saw the opening of a door towards the north end of the garage. It looked like a large toolbox on wheels had been resting in front of the door, possibly hiding it. It had been pushed off to the side, no doubt from Bob trying to make his escape out the rear exit, towards the forest. There, near the wall (next to the toolbox), Clent saw a small pool of blood, dried, on the floor.

"Clent, back here," Vanessa's voice wavered. She sounded foreign to him, frightened, like a lost child in a sea of people.

"Vanessa?" Clent cleared the door. A large room opened up, towards his right stood Vanessa, wiping her mouth, kneeled over, her hands resting on her knees, spitting onto the floor.

"Watch your step; I puked," she said.

"Jesus," Clent swung his Maglite around the room.

"There's a switch," Vanessa reached to her side, behind where Clent was standing. She flipped it.

Clent's flashlight had already found one of the bodies. The fluorescent lights overhead buzzed to life. Everything came into his vision. His eyes wide with horror, his mouth ajar, hands coming up fast to cover his face from the putrid smell.

"It's bad," Vanessa's legs shook. She sensed her stomach revolting, almost losing its contents again. "I'm..." her voice trembled. "I'm sorry, I froze."

Two bodies hung naked from the ceiling. A cruel makeshift pulley system (Clent could only guess, was some sort of sexual bondage device) held up the male victim about two feet from the floor. The female was hung from a blue bungee cord wrapped around her ankles. Both bodies had their hands tied behind their back. The male victim had been beheaded, no signs of the head anywhere from what Clent could see. His testicles and penis had been removed, and large bite wounds could be seen on his abdomen and thighs, to the point chunks of his flesh were missing.

Cannibalism.

The woman's body was also mutilated. Her breasts had been badly bitten, chunks of her flesh was gone as well. Her face was mutilated beyond recognition, half missing, it too, looked as it was chewed right down to the bone.

The room was about half the size of the shop where they entered. It was well lit from the hanging fluorescent tubes. Clent wagered, it must have been some sort of sex dungeon. The far wall was decorated with a myriad of sex toys, whips, chains, chokers, masks, varying size sexual toys, some boarding more on torture looking devices. All sat out on display, clean, neatly.

The opposite side held two different cameras', both mounted on tripods, and an elaborate lighting system like you'd see on a movie set. They all pointed at the center of the room where the bodies were hung.

"What the hell did we walk into?" Clent shook his head.

"So much for a quiet town," Vanessa, brushed aside her partner and made her way out of the room. If she wasn't careful, she would vomit again.

"Backups on its way, secure the area while you're out there," Clent knelt, taking in the scene. His stomach now, even more than ever, was on the verge of vomiting. He swallowed hard, fighting back the urge.

"We lost him? Bob," Vanessa asked. She stumbled her way out of the secret room of the shop.

"I think, in the woods. Watch what you touch, we need forensics," Clent replied.

"Not if he filmed it..." Vanessa whispered to herself. "Fucking psycho..."

SIX

Haylee could not understand what she was hearing; she knew the victims, recognizing the Simmons' house immediately. When she lived on Orr road, there weren't many neighbors, being a country road and all. But she drove past the home whenever they made trips into the city. She recognized it, hell, she'd eaten dinner at their table with her fiancé, Robbie.

She and Robbie had made it a point to introduce themselves to the Simmons right away when they moved in. They did their best to be neighborly, and they had no friends in town. They had a son, she remembered, he was going away to college. He had visited for we week over Christmas. She thought his name was Brandon. She may be wrong; she blocked a lot out from her memory from that winter.

They were kind, loaded with money. The husband, Dennis, he drove a BMW and was out of town on business quite a bit. He was handsome, a bit mysterious. Always had folks coming in from out of town, the house was busy. She dog-sat for them a few times before their Great Dane passed, her name was Sadie. Beautiful dog, Haylee, had asked Robbie if they could get a Dane. He laughed at her, "too big," he said. She looked at Trayer, who popped his head up excitedly. He let out an inquisitive whine. Trayer was the first purchase she made when she relocated into the duplex.

"He needs to be let out," Haylee had been so out of it, she'd forgotten about him. Poor pup, she's surprised he hadn't had an accident.

"I got it," Aaron replied. "C'mon boy," he waved to the back door. "You knew them, huh? The people in that house?"

"I did," Haylee shook her head in disbelief.

"Did you know them well?" he led the Dane through the kitchen towards the back screened sliding door.

"You could say that," she turned the television off for the first time in months. "A few times, Nora knocked on my door. I think she was lonely. We'd share some wine, talk about family. She said her husband worked crazy hours. Always had meetings out of town, always had business partners and clients over for meetings. She opened up to me. Said he loved her but wasn't *in* love with her. I believed her. Their son was older, never home much, left for college before everything..." Haylee caught herself. "You know, after what happened to me. She stayed in touch over the years, even after I moved. Got a Christmas card right before the holiday. She was kind."

"I see," Aaron opened the screen door, Trayer tore out of the house. "He okay outside for a while, in the cold?"

"Yeah, he'll bark when he's ready, he loves the snow," Haylee spoke somberly. She wanted more pills already. Even though she still felt the after-effects from the night prior. "I need a drink," she got up, made her way into the kitchen.

"It's not even noon," Aaron frowned.

"I just found out my old neighbors have been murdered," Haylee retorted, "My nerves are shot."

"Yeah, no..." Aaron fumbled, "I just meant, you sure that's a good idea? You're still recovering from last night's mishap."

"You're free to go back home, if you don't like my lifestyle," Haylee didn't need the lecture.

"Sorry, how about pouring me a shot too?" Aaron made his way into the kitchen. "I'm just trying to help, look after you."

Haylee grabbed two shot glasses from her cupboard. She pulled out the Seagrams, twisted off the top, and filled both glasses. "I'm a big girl."

"It's not that," Aaron stammered.

"—It's okay," Haylee interrupted. "Everyone means well, I appreciate it. I get it."

"Seagrams?" Aaron chortled, trying to break the uneasiness of the conversation, "the expensive shit."

"It gets the job done," She held up her shot to cheers. Aaron obliged, they clinked glasses, they downed the shot in one long gulp.

"Not good," Aaron swallowed hard. "I'm a Grey Goose guy."

Haylee poured a second, offering Aaron a shot as well. He waved it off, so she poured her fill, took the second shot with ease.

"Better?" asked Aaron.

"A little," Haylee frowned. "I didn't mean to snap at you. I get it, I do. I'm a mess."

"Let's just drop it," Aaron replied. "You think it was a robbery? They sounded rich, and you said he drove a BMW? And that house looked like it was a mansion."

"They said they were found mutilated," Haylee corrected. The words stung as they rolled off her lips so causally.

"Right..." Aaron frowned.

"I don't think robbers mutilate their victims."

"Yeah, I suppose you're right," Aaron took a seat at the table. Haylee's laptop sat folded closed, charging.

"It happened last night, the local Facebook groups are probably having a field day reporting on it already," Aaron flipped open the laptop. "You'd be surprised how much info you can find out on groups like these." He wouldn't tell her, but when news broke about what had happened in her home two years prior, he'd followed the story unfold for months through social media. Local newsgroups tended to have people close to those involved commenting. One could find shards of truths filtered through the ugly and often inhumane comments from internet trolls. Police reports leaked, transcripts of the 911 calls, screenshots of text messages, you name it, it made the rounds on the internet.

He remembered listening to her 911 call. He'd never forget the panic in her voice, the sobbing. He realized now that he was invading her privacy, and the guilt was gnawing at him. Yet, it was true. The internet had a wealth of information.

"We should see what people are saying," he spun the laptop towards her, the sign-in screen was lit up.

"I don't know if I should go digging," Haylee shook her head. "My dad wanted me to stay away. Which means he realizes something he's not telling me. Something he thinks will trigger me."

"Maybe getting some answers will help?" Aaron replied. "Your dads not here after all."

"I doubt it. I have enough issues. My stoner neighbor peddles me pain pills to keep me halfway sane."

"—Hey!" Arron took offense. "Peddling makes me sound like I'm profiting. You and I both know; you don't pay for those pills. I'm just a concerned neighbor, hoping to help out a friend."

A loud bark came from the backyard. Trayer handled his business and was ready to go in. Haylee walked to the screen door, where he waited patiently. She opened the door, Trayer ran halfway into the kitchen, and in true doglike fashion, shook his entire body from the snow he'd spent the last ten minutes rolling around in. A dog's life, Haylee wished for the simplicity. Haylee locked the backdoor and retreated to the disgusting puke colored couch.

Aaron made his way back, laptop in tow. They sat for a moment; Haylee lost in her thoughts. Aaron was not quite sure what to think. Curiosity burned inside him, what happened to the Simmons? Was it jealousy? A robbery? Revenge?

"...She was so lonely," Haylee broke the silence.

"Who?" asked Aaron. "The wife?"

"Yeah, we became..." Haylee searched for the right word. Were they friends? Chatty neighbors? Associates?

"Close enough that this has you shook up," Arron answered for her.

"Yeah," replied Haylee. "I didn't really know the husband, Dennis too well. We had dinner together once as a couple. He was more interested in Robbie than me. Took him out to show him his car he'd been restoring. Nora called it his Man's cave. She wasn't allowed anywhere near it. His space, she said."

"Yeah, I need one of those. Except mine would be a giant video game arcade some dort of giant kids wonderland. And all the weed I could smoke. Not too much into the mechanical side of manliness." Aaron joked.

"Isn't that already your apartment?" Haylee found a half-smile.

"Maybe," he shrugged.

"I don't think it's a good idea right now. I think I need to get it out of sight out of mind," said Haylee. "I promised my dad."

"I know it's eating you up inside, not knowing what happened. What's your password? You said you'd stay off the internet, not me. Let me do the dirty work. If I find anything, it's up to you if you want me to share it with you."

Haylee sighed. The curiosity was killing her. She couldn't fathom the horrors the Simmons suffered. Then again, she supposed if anyone could, it was her. She hoped it was a quick, painless death, unlike her sisters. Something in the back of her mind told her otherwise. What did her dad know? Why didn't he want her to find out about it?

"Move over," Haylee gave in. She quickly typed in her password, unlocking the laptop. "See what you can find. I'm going to put a movie on Netflix and try to relax. I'm still woozy–I need to work off these pills."

"Deal," Aaron nodded, already typing in Facebook on the web address bar and logging in under his name.

SEVEN

Detective Lewis Pike had gotten the call about a quarter to midnight. He'd laid down in bed, began the next chapter in the latest David Baldacci novel. He'd only made it to the second paragraph when his cell went off, vibrating loudly on his nightstand. The life of a Detective, it was one that he'd grown accustomed to.

No one ever calls with good news that late at night. Pike knew there would be little sleep in his foreseeable future. There never was. At least not until retirement, but he had a year to go. He wasn't exactly thrilled about it anyway.

"Pike," He'd answered the phone. He sat up, rubbing his temple. "Okay?" his eyebrows raised with curiosity.

"Orr Road, huh?" There was a long pause. "Two vics?" he stood up from his bed, made his way to his closet, dropping his flannel robe to the ground. He rummaged quickly through his closet, grabbing a pair of black slacks and a white button-up shirt. "—Yeah, I'll be there as fast as I can." He swiped the phone, ending the call.

There it was—a lot of info to digest. Pike's brain was already swimming with pieces of a larger puzzle, already formulating how some pieces fit. There was a homicide on Orr road, two vics, suspect fled on foot into a heavily wooded area. The search party was already underway. Officers were on foot searching the surrounding area. Road's been blocked off, five-mile radius. The home had been cleared, and the coroner's already on site. More backup is on the way.

It's a manhunt.

Orr road. He'd been there before, three years prior. That one still gave him nightmares.

Be ready, detective, it's a messy one. He'd been warned before he hung up.

Pike's heard that one before. Messy ones meant news coverage and nosey ass reporters.

Already disrobed, Pike slipped out of his stained grey sweats, slipped leg by leg into the pair of black slacks, they were poorly wrinkled, he didn't give a shit. He tossed off his house slippers, stepped into his work boots. Quickly buttoned up his white dress shirt (also wrinkled to shit), shoving it into his pants, he buttoned the waist, zipped his fly. He was almost ready. The most important part of the uniform was next, Pike grabbed his firearm, a Glock 22 .40 caliber, secured it within his side holster.

He glanced at his watch, 11:52 pm, near midnight.

Dress warm, he thought, he peered between the blinds. The snow was heavy, the roads already blanketed with at least three inches of snow.

Steady and slow, no need for an accident on the way. He grabbed a cup of coffee he brewed earlier in the morning, microwaved it, and poured it into a travel mug. No doubt stale, probably burnt as well. He needed the caffeine, burnt or not. The standard twenty-minute drive into the country would take him over double, if not longer.

Fucking snow.

•　　•　　•

Detective Pike pulled up to the scene a little after twelve-thirty in the morning. He found a spot beyond a few police cruisers, lights illuminating the snowy countryside around them, a swirl of blues and reds beaming out into the blackness of the sky. He exited his vehicle, where two uniformed police officers met him, hands outstretched, the stench of death on their faces.

"Detective Pike," Clent extended his hand to shake. Pike obliged. He'd recognized Clent right away, worked with him in the past, more than once. Good cop knew his shit. Strong as an Ox too, they don't make guys like Clent anymore. Pike was happy to see him onsite.

"What's that shit on your lip?" Pike pointed to the perfectly trimmed pencil-thin mustache on Clent's upper lip.

"Always on, aren't you?" Clent had half a smile, but Pike could see the seriousness behind his eyes.

"You know me," Pike took a sip of the disgustingly bitter coffee. He could barely choke it down "—always the one to break the tension."

"This makes 2017 Orr road look like a kids tea party," Clent frowned. He'd been at the site with Pike back then as well.

"Shit, that bad?" Pike frowned. "Thought this was feeling a bit of Déjà vu," Pike did not joke, it was a statement. His playful banter quickly dissolved. "So, fill me, in, and who's this?" Pike nodded to Vanessa, who stood beside her partner, her face pale white, sweat glistened off her forehead despite the bitter cold. She looked physically ill.

"Detective, this is my new partner, Vanessa Velasquez," Clent added. "First murder scene."

Pike shook her hand and nodded. "Sorry, kid, the first is always the worse."

"Especially this one," Clent added.

"Yeah," Vanessa answered. "It's embarrassing. I'm sorry."

"Don't be. Shits not easy," Pike spoke bluntly. "Unfortunately, you get used to it."

"Sort of," Clent corrected.

"What do we have?" Pike redirected the conversation.

"Backup secured the area. We got a group of about five guys looking through the woods, searching for the suspect," Clent answered. "Coroner showed up about a half-hour ago, he's in the garage now waiting for you," Clent explained.

"Who do we got on scene? Fat Man?" Pike asked.

"Isn't it always?" Clent replied.

"Okay, good. Give it to me from the beginning?" Pike asked.

"Simple Welfare check, or so we thought," said Clent.

"Okay?" Pike took a long sip of the stale, burnt coffee.

"Well, we approached the home, a young man, mid-twenties answered. No ID claimed to be a friend of the homeowners in town staying with them. Friendly enough."

"Let us into the house," Vanessa added. "He answered questions asked, did not appear to be evasive, but he was...off?"

"Claimed he woke up and Dennis and Nora had left home earlier that morning, didn't know where or why they left, no messages were left behind," Clent added.

"Home was cleared? Nothing noteworthy or foul play?" Pike led the officers towards the home, zipping his coat up to his chin.

"Home was clean, nothing to think anything suspicious went down, minus the pristine clean job and the faint odor of bleach," Clent replied.

"Okay?" Pike was waiting impatiently for the 'but...'.

"We noticed a fairly large garage outback. He led us there to have a look," Vanessa added.

"He entered the garage in front of us, slammed the door shut before we could stop him."

"He locked you out?" Pike's head tilted. "No warrant," he added.

"No warrant, it was welfare check called in from the out-of-state son."

"So, he could have just said no, or claimed he didn't have the key," Pike raised one eyebrow, thinking out loud.

"Not sure what he was thinking, he seemed a bit aloof, but not like he was hiding two bodies," Clent added.

"Panicked maybe," Vanessa responded. "We got too close, tried to keep his cool, then just bolted?"

"Good bet. So, how did you lose him? You took chase?" asked Pike.

"We think he exited the back door, fleeing into the woods. We tried to get through the front. It was sturdy, took us a minute. You'll see once we get back there, the garage extends into the woods, a good portion of it is completely covered into the forest. We didn't know there was a backdoor for him to escape through," Clent explained. "It's a bitch crawling past the side of the garage up against all the damn branches from the pin trees. I fell, knocked myself silly."

"I see," Pike shook his head, took another sip of his coffee. Still tasted like shit, but the hot liquid warmed his body from the inside out. "So, you saw him flee into the woods." This was a statement, not a question.

"More like heard, assumed," Clent replied. "I took the back, while Vanessa stayed up front attempting to break the door. By the time I made it through the damned pine trees, I heard what sounded like a man running through the forest, but I never laid my eyes on him. The backdoor was locked from the outside. I started to take after the noise when I heard Vanessa's scream."

"Scream?"

"I wasn't expecting...the site," Vanessa couldn't find the words, embarrassment overcame her face. "The garage is a bit further back, past the home. You'll see."

Pike nodded; he followed the officers around the house. They led him past the two parked cars in the driveway. They're off in the distance the garage came into sight.

"BMW," Pike noted as he walked past. "Good taste," he added. "Mr. and Mrs. Moneybags."

No one replied.

"When you enter, you'll see a restoration shop for Dennis' Camaro. The suspect claimed he came to spend a few days with Dennis to help restore the vehicle. Towards the back of the shop, left side, there was a hidden door behind a large toolbox on wheels. It had been pushed off to the side of the door when he escaped. That's where it turns bizarre," said Clent.

"You entered first," Pike's eyes turned to Vanessa.

"Yessir," she replied.

"Did you guys touch anything?"

No, we both made our way inside, her first, I followed. We were cautious," Clent explained.

"Was anything compromised? Pike took a step into the central portion of the garage. The floodlight hanging above them was bright. In the middle of the garage sat the Camaro, its hood popped open, tools neatly set to the side on a workbench. The place was clean, orderly, all tools and objects neatly set, organized. When the putrid smell of rotting bodies hit Detective Pike's nose, he almost didn't expect it.

"There it is," his nose twitched.

"The smell?" Clent asked.

"Yep..." Pike shook his head with disgust.

"I vomited," Vanessa frowned.

"Where?" Pike asked.

"When I entered the back room, the smell, and the sight of the bodies...I'm sorry."

Don't be," Pike replied. "Come back outside with me," he exited the front threshold of the garage.

"Yessir," Both officers nodded.

"You two stay out front, keep watch. We have officers in the home?" asked Pike. "We got the warrant for both, I assume?"

"Yes, and the small group searching the woods. Snow's coming down hard now though, visibility's shit." Clent frowned.

"Let me look around," Pike nodded to the officers. "I'll meet with Fat man and see what we got."

"Detective," Clent spoke up. "For real, twenty-seventeen doesn't compare to what you're about to walk into."

"Okay," Pike nodded. He appreciated the heads up. The double murder on 1228 Orr Road right down the road was terrible. That night rocked the small town, it never really recovered from it. Still very fresh in the minds of the townsfolk. Now this, one house down. Another double murder. Bizarre, he thought. Coincident?

Doubtful.

Pike didn't subscribe to the notion of coincidences.

He'd seen too much in his time as a detective. Nothing caught him off guard anymore. He wasn't sure what was waiting for him in the back of that garage, but he's sure it wasn't the last time he'd be washing the stench of death out of his dress slacks.

Pike stepped outside, gathered his bearing before going in deeper.

He took a deep breath of the cold winter air, it stung his lungs, but it made him feel alive. Grounded him in the present. This always helped him before walking into what he was sure was some form of hell on earth. He reminded himself he chose this. He knows, it hardens you, thickens your soul. He'd seen children gun down, pieces of bodies littered across streets, bodies disfigured from the vile thing's men do. These dark images stain your conscious. He'd seen everything, or so he thought. H entered the garage once again, stood before the Camaro, and began taking notes.

"Very clean," Pike walked through the main portion of the garage, taking his time before making his way back towards the secret door. He took immaculate notes, jotting down random thoughts, scribbling fast.

Organized, neat freak, old cars. Security system? Pike noticed a small security camera overlooking the vehicle. Maybe it caught something? He'd make sure to check the tapes on the security system, probably stored on the local router.

Pike approached where the toolbox was askew from the wall. He noted the bloodstain on the floor. Knelt down and took a few pictures of the blood. It was small, only a few diameters each. Possibly droplets from a murder weapon?

"Detective," A young voice came from inside the once hidden room. "Brace yourself," he said.

"Everyone keeps telling me that," Pike stepped into the room, he looked up, and his eyes immediately fell on the site.

"Fuck me," the words fell from his mouth, now agape. The site of two hanging bodies strung up from the ceiling, mutilated and on display for the world to see, caught him off guard, despite multiple warnings. "Dear lord," Pike frowned. "Poor bastards..."

More video cameras, these were not security systems like outside. These were for pleasure, set up like a porn shoot? Pike began jotting down a rush of words and half thoughts flooding from his consciousness.

Sexual Deviant? Porn Addiction? Website??? Home Made porn?

He needed to make sure he took his time surveying everything in his legal pad. His team photograph and gather evidence later. But experience told him, his first string of thoughts frequently led to clues later. So, he always wrote down his initial thoughts and reactions.

"Lew," Brenkins stood up from his kneeling position. He was observing the bodies, taking notes of his own.

"Wait," Pike held up his hand, shushing the corner. He continued his feverish scribing of thoughts. A few forced awkward silent minutes passed before Pike looked up from his legal pad.

"Fat Man," Pike shook his hand. "Sorry about that, I have a system. You were interrupting it."

"Sorry, and you know I hate that name," Brenkins said plainly. Contrary to the moniker, Paul Brenkins was not fat. In fact, the young man, in his late thirties, was quite thin, handsome with a square jaw and a picture-perfect classic cop mustache. Pike had joked with Brenkins when he first landed the Medical Examiner job, that he was the spitting image of a 'pencil-neck,' and since Paul despised that nickname as well, Lewis began calling him Fat Man. The name stuck.

"And I hate Lew," Pike countered. "This is..." Pike didn't have words. He nodded to the site before them.

"Yeah," Brenkins sighed.

"Enlighten me," Pike took in the view. The two bodies, one beheaded stung upside down, hung from the ankles. The female hung from her neck. Both with hands tied behind their backs. Adult male, adult female. Then, the camera's, two of them, pointing at the scene.

"There's a lot going on," Brenkins took a deep breath. "Judging by age, and what we can tell from the parts of the bodies that remain, we are looking at the homeowners. Dennis and Nora Simmons. My best guess from decomp is they've been dead for a few days. Both bodies, as you can see," Brenkins approached, with a blue Bic pen began to point out his thoughts, "—through the thighs here, breasts on the female, both victims' buttocks, have been bitten badly. Chewed might be a better description. To the point, the flesh was torn, possibly consumed? That's an assumption. The male's testicles and penis have been removed as well, including, well, as you see, his head. None of which has been found. Female's face also shows signs of bites. It appears the killer chewed half her face off, including her eyes, their missing as well."

"Any idea how they were killed?" Pike joined Brenkins near the body, taking in the grisly site up close. He didn't flinch, but it was apparent from the grotesque nature of the site, that he would experience many sleepless nights in the near future.

"Nora looks like she was stabbed in the back of the neck, large deep puncture wound here," Brenkins pointed to the wound with the pen. "That's a good guess due to the severity of the wound. Bite marks appear to have been made while she was still alive. At least some of them. She may have survived a while, bled out. That's my guess."

"Hmph," Pike shook his head. "The male?"

"The body is too...mutilated. I will need to get him back to the lab and run some tests."

"Yeah," Pike took a sip of his coffee.

"How can you," Brenkins face turned to revolt.

"—Oh, I'm the monster here?" Pike interrupted him.

"The smell alone..." Brenkins shook his head.

"Give me your thoughts here," Pike ignored him. "I'm pretty sure we're on the same page. Or close to it. But, maybe I'm wrong."

"Yeah okay, Brenkins added. "I mean, pretty sure we find semen in and on both vics. Obviously, some kinky shit was going on behind the scenes here. Hidden sex dungeon? BDSM? Its more common than people think, but I don't know too much about that lifestyle myself. This device that Mr. Simmons is hanging from, it's a type of BDSM torture device, free-hanging pulley, meant to hang and strap up your, umm...partner. Learned that from Google, right before you came in. So, I dunno? Things went too far with the bondage? The killer panicked? Killed them both? Maybe one was an accident, the other a necessity? You know, didn't want to get caught, innocent bystander sort of thing?"

"Maybe," Pike added, his eyes fixated on the device. "So not premeditated? Accidental, then kills the second spouse to cover his tracks? Depending who was involved with the bondage stuff? Maybe both, a threesome? Hard to tell, right?"

"Once we get the exact time of death down, that will tell us more," Brenkins added.

"Yep," Pike shook his head. "This is fucked," he had no other words.

"There's more," Brenkins went back to the woman's face. He pulled a small Maglite flashlight from his breast pocket and illuminated what was left of her. "Something has been lodged in her mouth. Looks like some sort of paper? We'll know more when we get them down and back to the morgue."

Pike stood up, made his way over to the cameras. "Digital," he said out loud. "Wonder what we'll find on these?"

"Hopefully, everything," Brenkins answered.

"So, let me ask you a question?" Pike flipped to a new page in his notebook. He clicked his black pen; he began writing scribbling his thoughts once again.

"Yeah?"

"This guy shows up, let's say it's a threesome. Simmons are swingers or something like that. They're into this, BDSM stuff we see here, sex swings, dildos plastered all over the walls, all the kinky fixings, right? Then things go wrong. Playtime turns deadly, right? Maybe the choking goes too far? Maybe someone slips knocks their head on something, either way; the sex turns deadly."

"Yep," Brenkins nods.

"So, what then? He panics, kills the wife or husband, depending on who is the first 'accidental' victim. But, after all, that is done, why does he then string the bodies up, cut off the man's head, chews on their corpses," Pike shakes his head. "That's a hard pill to swallow. Not to mention, instead of getting rid of the bodies, he lets them hang around for a while-literally-and just camps out in their home? Do I want to get caught? That's not even mentioning, where the hell is the guy's head? His dick and balls?"

"Well, when you put it that way," Brenkins stood back up. "I guess that's why you're the detective, and I just look at dead bodies." He begins to make his way out of the sex dungeon.

"Where you going?"

"I need a break from this scene."

"I'm curious, though?" Pike followed, taking another sip of the stale coffee, following behind.

"About?" Brenkins made his way past the Camaro through the broken door, and outside into the cold winter night. He took a deep breath.

"Your immediate thought is an accidental death, then manslaughter, panic to cover up his tracks. Just curious. What lead you there?"

"I dunno, man, okay?" Brenkins sounded more human than ever, gone are the medical degrees and years on the job. There in the wintery night, the dense clumps of snow falling from the skies, Paul Brenkins was shaken. He felt less than human. He understood science, formulas. When you add 'x' to 'y,' the results are 'z' because of these so-called laws he learned from a college professor that told him so. Men had laws too, but they weren't based on science. He'd never understand how anyone could do that, do what was done to the Simmons couple.

He had to get away. The Simmons hanging like animals, their bodies decimated, violated. Such evil, such vileness.

"Look that..." Pike lost his words, something that does not happen to a man of his experience "—that crime scene. That was inhuman. That's the shit nightmares are made of. You looked into the devil's playground, and you humanized the scene. That means you're one of the good ones. You tried to make sense of something that, let's face it, will never make sense to us."

"What do you mean?" Brenkins frowned. "No human I know could do that to another person. How did I humanize that?"

"Right," Pike nodded. "But humans make mistakes. Humans kill, we see it all the time. You gave this murderer, this lunatic, killing son-of-a-bitch, you gave him a reason, an excuse, an out. The sex went too far. Maybe he was choking one of the Simmons, consensual, no safe word, whoops, accidental death. Now panic sets in, sorry witness, but you gotta go. Whack, dead. That was your thought, wasn't it? It wasn't a bad thought. I just want to know what made you go there?"

"I don't know. I was just thinking, with the severity of it, the ugliness of it. Maybe there was a loss of control, an irreversible accident, then yes, panic mode sets in. The killer has to cover his tracks, right? Leave no witnesses. Then I don't know? His mind snaps? I mean, even if you accidentally kill one person, then in a state of frenzy kill a second, don't you think that might cause a break? A mental split. The guy goes crazy, loses his shit, and I dunno...cannibalism? How do you make sense of it? Any of it? How does anyone get to the point in their life they're chewing off someone's face? How does Jeffery Dahmer go from a college drop out to drilling holes in people's heads trying to make zombie sex slaves?"

"I don't know," Pike frowned. "But they do, and they will continue to because we're animals. Sick, fucking, animals."

"Yeah," The two men stood there, both staring out at the wintery night sky. Eerie silence befell them.

"—But that's our job, right?" Pike broke the silence.

"What's?" Brenkins asked.

"To make sense of it." Pike pointed to the ambulance pulling up to the scene. "Let's get you help, get the bodies down and out of that hell hole. Lots of evidence with this one. We got a lot of work ahead of us."

"A lot to collect," Brenkins added.

"We'll be here for a while," Pike shook his hand. "I look forward to your report, Fat man, wouldn't want anyone else on the job."

"I hate that fucking name, Lewis," Brenkins shook his hand back.

"Shouldn't have lost that bet," Pike smiled. "Out drink a veteran like me? Any time kid, you can have a rematch."

"Let's find this bastard, and then the drinks are on me," Brenkins replied. "I'm going to go meet with the boys."

"Sure," Pike nods. "Fuck, why did I quit smoking at a time like this?"

EIGHT

Aaron opened up multiple tabs in Google Chrome. He'd already bookmarked the town's Neighborhood Watch Facebook page, and a few local news websites. Usually, these types of groups were toxic filled dumpster fires, where entitled Facebook users troll the shit out of each other, arguing over race, religion, and politics. Through the bullshit, there were nuggets of useful information. As he expected, he'd found two posts already regarding the murders on Orr road.

The first linked to a news article, bare-boned, void of any real information other than the fact a double homicide had occurred and that a suspect had fled on foot into the surrounding woods. The other, a random post about how Orr road was cursed with two murders in less than three years, all excessively violent.

The replies started flooding in for both comments. They had only been up for a few hours, and they hit over a hundred each and counting. It was talk of the town; the comments would double within the hour. It was sure to go national soon, just due to the sheer violence and close timeline to the other murders right down the road. Aaron figured by tomorrow it would be get reposted on the NY Post and Chicago Tribune.

He clicked on both threads, opening new tabs for each. He began scrolling down, reading each reply. The comments were mostly nonsensical ramblings:

Mary Hildenbrook: This is fuckign disgusting!!!! What is wrong with Orr road? We need to find these soulless assholes and kill them

all. It's probably a cult! Find Jesus! Demons live right here! We need church and God back in this country! Make America Christian again!

Can't even proofread before spewing out their hate-filled dogma rhetoric. Aaron couldn't help but cringe.

Dip Shits. He realized the internet was flooded with entitled Karen's and gun-totin'dual-wielding-Monster-Energy-drinkin' Kyles. He understood these posts would be an array of both. Being a devote Christian himself, and coming from a father who was a respected pastor, Aaron learned early in his life to not use God's name to condemn others. This Mary woman's words were rooted in fear and hatred. She gave Christians a bad name.

Don't get triggered.

He kept scrolling:

Jarrod Henrey: I knew the Simmons. Great people, they never hurt a fly! Sick! I have ot say, I am horrified, again, at what humans are capable of doing to each other and feel terribly for the family & friends Dennis and his wife. Suspicious of the news reporters' motives reporting this case. Watch it turn into clickbait rather than a professional attempt to keep the public informed. We'll see the killer plastered all over social media, and little of the victims. Do what's right, don't publish this sick-o's name!

Does no one proofread before posting anymore? Then again, this one sounded more personal. If he did know the Simmons, and if he just found out about their friend's violent deaths over a three-paragraph Michigan Live report, Aaron supposed he wouldn't be caring about little red squiggly lines, either.

There are dozens of these types of posts—many condolences to the families involved, thoughtful yet meaningless in the long run. Plenty of "rest in peace" posts, even more, "what are the police hiding, conspiracists.

More scrolling. More wading through bullshit posts.

Then, jackpot:

Brian Bircher: I went to school with their son Brandon. We're friends on here. I saw him post that he hadn't heard from his parents in a few days and were asking friends and family to see if they could reach them. This was posted the day before yesterday. He said he was worried, and that he knew his dad had someone from out-of-town visiting them. He wasn't sure who it was but was hoping to find someone who may know. He was hoping to get ahold of that person. My guess is that guy must have killed them, I mean, there is no word of a third body, and it sounded like he had been there for a few days. Let's find this fucker!

This post alone set off a series of replies. It seemed legit. Aaron checked out Brian's profile and found Brandon Simmons as a friend. That's a good sign. Brandon's page was private, so he could not see his posts, but it was a solid lead. He took some notes on a word file doc. and continued on his search.

He heard snoring next to him. Haylee had fallen asleep almost instantly after putting on a random kid's cartoon. Rugrats, a classic feel-good, forget about your worries, cartoon. Maybe she'd turned it on to enlighten the dreadfulness of the room? Either way, it was good she'd dozed off. She needed rest. He was still upset that she didn't listen to him about the pills. Two were way too many for her first dose. What was she thinking? Recklessness like that could find her dead.

At least she was getting them from him now. No more meeting up with randoms around town. She was reasonably naïve in that respect. She would pop pills she got from strangers, friends of shady friends. Some weren't even friends; they were associates of shady associates. Who knew what she was taking? She sure as hell didn't. Shit, he didn't think she cared what she was swallowing, as long as it kept her mind at ease.

The escape.

He knew that's what she wanted.

He knew about it too well. Everyone had their demons, some larger than others.

That's when he decided to step in. When he first moved into the duplex, and he attempted to befriend her, Haylee slowly started to warm up to him.

She had asked him to go with him to make a buy, and she didn't feel safe alone. She also hated driving at night, so he obliged. They met up with some shady scrub looking guy in front of a 7-11 convenient store. They made a quick exchange. The guy was, as Aaron would say, "creepy AF."

Haylee was an attractive woman, that rare natural beauty. Dark olive skin, straight jet-black hair. She didn't even need to try, and she never did, not anymore. Aaron wouldn't admit it, but it was her physical attraction that had him knocking on her door at first. Pretty girl like her, out in the early morning hours buying pills off dirtbags, something terrible was going to happen sooner or later. In Aaron's mind, he was taking care of her. Either, he helped her, or she would go out and help herself. Lesser of two evils?

It was the cliché girl next door motif. Except that was just about the only cliché aspect of their twisted relationship.

Aaron understood it, though, more than most. He relied on pills too. He needed the Norco for the pain, and when it got bad, it was like a fire burning from the inside out. He got his prescription from his accident, a helluva nasty-ass car wreck. The one that ruined his life.

Yet, he only took the pills when the pain got bad, unbearable. He realized how toxic and addicting pain killers can be. He used them sparsely. Weed was natural, came from the Earth, weed was his choice nine times out of ten. Weed was his choice.

He went back to work.

Aaron swapped tabs on the Chrome browser. He favorite'd the Michigan Live news article, kept an eye on those comments as well. He was finding interesting theories already, copying and pasting comments he wanted to reference later. He found Dennis Simmons Facebook page after someone linked it. It was public and hadn't been taken down or blocked yet.

This was a huge find—a look into the victim's last few moments of his social idea.

Dennis, what secrets were you hiding?

Aaron smiled. Excitement rushed through his veins, like a natural high. He cracked his knuckles and began searching through Dennis's Facebook wall; it was time to dig even deeper.

NINE

Haylee found herself in a darkened room, swallowed by blackness, utterly void of light or life. She heard a familiar noise, one she'd heard many times before. There was heavy breathing, grunting, it sounded sexual, beast-like. She found a doorframe behind her, deep into the abyss. It was old, ancient, the wood warped and moldy. The handle stained with rust, the wood door itself, blood-soaked, stained with the remnants of death.

She remembered this door—this very dream.

It was a dream, right? Please, let it be a dream...

It seemed real, but Haylee knew better; she's dreamt this before. It came to her when the pills failed her. They started ever since the disaster in the woods. Sometimes despite the pills, it still managed to creep through in her dreams. It was always the same dark dream. It terrified her because she understood what secrets it hid. Behind the moldy bloodstained door, *it* was waiting. *It* was always waiting—that thing, the visitor that haunted her. Evidently, so was her sister, Camille. As always, her beautiful sister Camille. Her body, lifeless, barren, void of her love.

Haylee couldn't stop; her body was drawn to the door. Pulled by an invisible force, it grew closer and closer. She tried to break free, but no matter how hard she tried to flee, her body failed her. She didn't want to open it, but it was useless, no fighting what was about to happen. The darkness around her swallowed her, wrapped her in an icy blanket of death. Her body shook from the void, cold as an icebox.

Her breath escaped her body in bursts of steam into the abyss. Gasps of little clouds, the panic evaporating in front of her. Her chest heaved and hoed, feeling tighter with every contraction.

Please, no. Not again. Not my sister. Not that...thing.

Her voice was sullen in the void. No one to hear her scream, not even herself. She was muted, deaf. Did sound even exist in this place, could it? She could feel her lips moving, her tongue forming words, but she heard nothing. Only the frantic voice in her head, screaming to run, to flee.

Haylee's hand reached out towards the rusted handle. Her fingertips turned blue from the cold, completely numb. Her fingers wrapped around the frozen door handle. Clumps of white snow fell from the abyss. They fluttered around her, almost peacefully blanketing her from what was sure to be waiting on the other side. Her hand turned, the knob clicked, letting loose the hinge.

Not again. She choked, her words empty, meaningless in this land of grief and sorrow.

The door crept open. Within the door fell a familiar sight. The bedroom she shared with her fiancé Robbie. The same one where they were supposed to start a family in. It was the freshly decorated master bedroom that sat inside their dream home. There, on the hardwood floor, next to Haylee's pink fuzzy slippers (a Valentines' Day present from Robbie a year prior) laid the lifeless body of her sister, Camille, at the foot of their king size bed.

The scene was too familiar. Haylee sobbed. Losing control, warm tears stained her cheeks, snot poured from her nose, its warmth sticking to her lips. She begged and pleaded—worthless words lost in the nothingness that surrounded her.

Camille's corpse was pale white, a pool of thick crimson blood pooled beneath her. Her once youthful, lively body, mangled, and distorted. She laid sprawled out on her back; legs spread apart. Her silky blonde hair matted with the pool of blood, her head tilted back as if she was waiting for Haylee to enter. Except, her eyes had been removed, plucked from their sockets. Her eyelids hung loose, like wrinkled flesh-colored shades over a window.

Haylee fell to her knees, her stomach retched. She heaved, vomiting a mass of bloody maggots. They spewed from her mouth, coming out in large chunks. Their warm bodies alive, wiggling up through her throat, passing through her mouth. They squirmed, crawled about effortlessly in front of her as they collected between her legs.

Haylee gasped, barely able to breathe. There were stragglers, little demonic maggots trying to find refuge within her mouth. She spat them out one at a time, using her fingers to pull out the last remaining few. She screamed, screamed like bloody hell at the horrors before her. The larvae frantically searched for an escape. But there was none to be found. They began to shrivel up, dying in their agony beneath her. Their bodies decayed rapidly into little pools of mucus.

In-between her sister's legs, a ghastly creature kneeled, waiting for her attention. Whatever this thing was, Haylee understood it wasn't born of this earth. It was not human, not animal; it was pure revulsion. Its body was skinny, lanky, with saggy breasts dangling from its chest. It's top half feminine. Between its leg, the creature was male with an erect slim penis. It hung down between its legs, looking more animalistic than human.

A horrific sight, the creature with its head cocked awkwardly to the side. Patiently waiting to see if Haylee would advance forward. It thrust its putrid hips into Camille, penetrating her sister's corpse. Camille's mouth puckered open; a vacant moan echoed from her lips. A faint smile spread across her lifeless face. Yet, Haylee understood she was dead. There was no life there; this was indeed not her sister. The creature, grunting, snarling, having its way with her sister corpse. It's large red glowing eyes never broke Haylee's gaze. This humanoid thing, with its putrid rotting flesh dangling off its skinny frame, defiled her sister, mocking Haylee, taunting her with its grotesque guttural moans.

The smell of the creature overpowered Haylee. The odor made her dizzy. It stung her eyes, burned her nose. This thing, hunched over her Camille's body reeked of death and depravity. Long scrawny legs, even longer slimmer arms, with hoarse black hair protruding in patches all across its body. Fingers, long and slender, planted firmly on each side of Camille, supporting its weight as it continued. Its loose tits swayed from the violent thrusting motion.

Worst of all was its head, staring at her with the round glowing eyes, alien-like, inhuman. It almost put her into a trance, like it was penetrating her soul. Its head was large, disproportionate from the rest of its body, oblong. Haylee tried to focus through its mind-numbing gaze. She couldn't make out much. They were like two floodlights, glowing bright enough that it impaired her vision, blurring its facial features.

Haylee lost it.

"get out of my head!" She let out another nightmarish scream.

Then the blackness engulfed her once again. Followed by nothingness.

TEN

"Haylee!" Aaron yelled. "Wake up, Jesus fuck!"

Haylee shot awake. Her muscles burned, her back was throbbing in pain. A sudden wave of relief swept over her. Her body relaxed, went loose, limp. Did she have a seizure while she slept?

She went to speak, but her mouth hurt to open. She clenched her jaw so hard. She thought she might have cracked a molar.

Her head was in Aaron's lap. He held her up, pulling her hair back with his right hand. He protected it from the vomit. Her chest soaked from it, the puke, its acidic, sweet smell made her gag once again. Her guts heaved, expulsing more vomit, ferociously spilling from her insides while she gasped for air. Her chest burned, her head pounded.

"Get it all out," Aaron held her hair tight. "You had a nightmare, or something crazy. I think you had a seizure."

The room was spinning. Haylee's midsection was damp, her pants and underwear both soaked. She had pissed herself. She sat up from Aaron's lap entirely now. She tried to collect herself, gather her bearings. She looked down at her zip-up hoodie, chunks of the breakfast sandwich, and coffee-soaked atop her breasts.

"You got sick in your sleep, I think you puked up those pills, and your breakfast."

Haylee didn't say a thing. Her body was still shaking, her mind still trying to catch up to reality. Her head hurt, her body ached, the taste of vomit stuck at the back of her throat. The vision of her sister burned in her brain. That dream, the one that always came back. She thought she bested it. It had been weeks since she had it last. But no, somehow, it had snuck back into her life.

"You could have choked," Aaron got up from the couch, rubbing her back, "Let me get you a towel to clean up."

"No, leave, please, leave," Haylee choked out the words, almost screaming them. She was embarrassed, mortified over what happened in front of him. She smelled off piss and vile. She couldn't handle being seen like this.

"Haylee," Aaron protested, worry in his eyes. "Look, it's okay, let me run you a shower, get you cleaned up. I don't think you should be alone, do you?"

Haylee cried, sobbed, like a child who had lost her parents at a shopping mall. He'd never look at her the same way again. How could he? A dumb, fucked up girl, puked and pissed herself from a bad dream. Aaron would probably never knock on her door again. Haylee was afraid to be alone. That thing, that monster, it came back. Would it creep its way out of her dreams and into her home? She couldn't be left alone; she wouldn't be able to handle it.

"You were out for hours," Aaron added. "I thought you needed to sleep off the pills from last night."

"I'm so embarrassed," she wiped the streaming tears from her cheeks.

"C'mon, it's okay. It's been a helluva morning," he helped her to her feet. "Let's get you in the shower. I will help you get there. If you need anything, I will be out here with Trayer, cleaning up the couch for you. That's a shit ton of puke girl."

Haylee didn't have words. She muttered, "Okay, okay…" and let him lead the way. "—I,"

"—You don't have to thank me," Aaron smiled. "You need a friend in times like these. I got you, girl. It's all good in the hood."

•   •   •

The shower was scorching hot, burned her skin red. It felt amazing on her vomit-soaked body. Wash away the disgrace, she thought. Wash away the pain, let the steaming hot water take over. She scrubbed multiple times with different scented soaps. Hard, she wanted to rub away a few layers of skin, she'd peel it off if she could. No amount of soap in the world could cleanse her from that god-awful dream.

She thought of Aaron.

She let the water stream down her face, calming her. What a mess he moved next door to. A psycho who is ready to suffer a mental breakdown at any given moment. She opened her mouth, let the water fill up. She swished the hot water around her mouth, spit it out, down her chin and breasts. She sat in the tub, hung her head low, and let the heat, the steam, the pressure of the shower eases her.

Haylee had lost track of time. How long had she been in the shower? A half-hour? Maybe forty-five minutes? Longer? The refreshing steamy hot water was heavenly. She never wanted to leave.

She turned the shower knob off; the water ceased to a small drip. Haylee grabbed a towel, dried herself. She found her way into her bedroom, decided to dress like a human. She put on a pullover hoodie and a pair of dark distressed denim. The first time she wore jeans in a few weeks. She usually lounged around in leggings and baggy sweaters. She even brushed her hair, pulling it back into a ponytail before making her way back into the living room where Aaron had Trayer sprawled out over his lap. It felt good to feel semi human.

"Feeling better?"

"A little," she answered. "I'm so sorry you had to see that."

"That had to be one fucked up dream."

"It's a repetitive dream, it's...more a nightmare. I can't explain how real it feels. As you saw, it physically makes me sick. It's never been that bad, though."

"Want to talk about it?" Aaron scratched Trayer's large stomach. The dog moaned lazily. "Maybe it will help?"

"Not really," she replied bluntly. "The dream is disturbing, it has to do with my sister, and what my shrink Dr. Feldman claims is a phycological manifestation from that night, that...you know...that everything happened."

"Right, deep shit, aye?" Aaron question.

"You could say that," She sat back down. "I really want another drink."

"You should let your stomach settle first."

"Yeah," she didn't like that answer but saw it to be true.

"You believe him?" asked Aaron?

"About the manifestation thing?"

"Yeah, I mean, I know a little bit about psychology and that jazz. I got an associate's degree yea to know?" he gave her a thumbs-up as if to ask 'impressed?' He continued, "I have watched enough reality tv to know the mind can do some fucked up shit to someone's psyche. Got to love I.D. Channel."

"I don't believe it, no," Haylee said bluntly.

"Really? Not even a shred of it? I mean, the shit you've been through? I believe it."

"I can't believe it," Haylee replied.

"Why not?"

"—Because," Haylee shook her head. "I never told anyone this, but I was having dreams about *it*, the *thing* that haunts me, I saw *it* before the murder. The dream was...you know...different. Not the thing, it looks the same. But now it taunts me with my sister."

"What is *it*? The thing? Is it like a dude, a person?" asked Aaron.

"No, not human, not even close." Haylee let out a deep sigh. "I don't want to talk about it anymore."

"Okay, okay," Aaron frowned. "I've been hard at work while you took that hour shower. Found some decent stuff. Maybe a few leads. You up for that?"

"Yeah," she nodded. "What did you find out? Anything I need to know?"

"Well, it's definitely weird," Aaron pulled the laptop forward. "This is your neighbor Dennis's Facebook profile." Aaron clicked open a browser. There stood the smiling face of Dennis Simmons, his perfectly parted salt and pepper hair. More salt than pepper, but he wore it well. Just a hint of a five o'clock shadow. Fairly attractive man in his late forties.

Haylee thought he looked happy in the photo.

"Pretty normal, public, says he's married, even links to his son. Lots of photos of cars, but nothing family-wise other than the bio section linking to Brandon," Aaron explained.

"That's not too weird. I have lots of friends on Facebook that sit around all day, posting nothing but memes. Sort of like shadow profiles, at least he has real pictures. Some of my friends just use memes."

"Well, look, as we scroll down, he has lots of people commenting. They're all dudes, see..." Aaron scrolled through multiple posts on his page, pics, musings, basically the average Facebook wall from a fifty-something-year-old married man.

"I don't see what is so weird about that?" Haylee frowned.

"So, all these comments and mini conversations he's having stemming from his posts are with dudes. All of them. See?" He highlights multiple posts with the cursor. "Very few women, maybe three total, and one's his sister."

"Okay?" Haylee shook her head. "So what?"

"Well, not all of the profiles are private. So, I began trying to see if one of them may have been the guy his son posted about. You know, maybe get lucky?"

"Wait. What?" Haylee wasn't following. "What did Brandon post?"

"I forgot to mention. His son has a page too. I mean, who doesn't, right? My mom had a page for her Australian Sheppard, updates it daily," Aaron joked, Haylee did not laugh. "Right, anyway... Brandon posted the night before last about his parents not answering his calls or dm's, and that he thought someone from out of town was visiting them. He asked if any friends or family had heard from them. It's all right here, see?" He clicked another browser open to Brandon's profile and highlighted the specific post about his parents.

"I'm still confused as to why this matter?"

"Well, I noticed a theme. A lot of these guys, and I mean *a lot* of them are gay, bi, you know switch hitters. They're also open about it on their pages. Like, more than eighty percent of the people he is talking with fly the rainbow flag with pride."

"That's a good thing," Haylee suggested.

"Hey, I love gay people. I got most of my weed back in LA from my gay friend Timmy. The dude had the best smoke, way better than the stuff I get here."

"Okay, focus," Haylee tapped his laptop screen.

"I'm just saying if the shoe fits. And I think this dude had some sugar in his," Aaron smiled.

"You think he is gay?" Haylee questioned. "He's not gay."

"Well, yeah," Aaron didn't understand how Haylee wasn't making the connection. "I mean, I hang out with a diverse group of people. I have gay friends, lesbian friends. I even have a few Trump supporter friends. But I don't have an overwhelming amount of any one of those friends," Aaron explained. "Looks to me like Dennis used Facebook to meet dudes. Maybe behind his wife's back?"

"He's married and has a kid in college," Haylee protested.

"So?" Aaron shrugged his shoulders. "Why does that matter?"

"Because he's obviously not gay."

"You have a lot to learn, young one."

"Last I checked, I was *your* elder," she got up from the couch. She began pacing around the living room. "Did you find this guy who was supposed to have been spending time over there?" she asked.

"I think so," Aaron smiled. "I should have been a detective, huh?"

"If you say so," Haylee hovered beside him. "Pull up his page."

"Here it is. His name is Gary Thom. Lives in Hemlock Hills, Mi. Openly gay looks like he has a supportive group of friends. Has his family in lots of photos. Listed being single. Look at his last post…"

Gary Thom: Meeting a friend in Emmet County Up North, should be back next week! =)

"Well, he definitely came here to Emmett," Haylee sighed. "Certainly looks like it could be him. He didn't post anything after this, did he?"

"Silence, nothing. Page goes dark."

"So, I guess…what?" Haylee began to muse out loud. "Dennis had a gay friend? Why is this important? You're jumping to conclusions. Circumstantial as my Dad would say."

"Listen, Dennis had a gay friend, you said Nora was lonely. I dunno, I'm just thinking out loud. Maybe your neighbor had a secret? This is America, stranger things happen. People have secrets, you know? We all do."

Secrets.

Haylee knew about secrets.

"Nora always said it was business meetings and trips," argued Haylee. "Pretty sure gay men hold jobs, they go on trips, have straight friends."

"He didn't say he was making a business trip. Gary Thom said he was meeting a friend. Then the dude used a smiley emoji. That's not a professional post on a professional Facebook page. And, you said Nora was lonely and visited you a lot at the house. Because her husband wasn't into her anymore."

"I mean..." Haylee couldn't quite grasp the concept.

"So, you want more evidence?" Aaron smiled. "I got more."

"What?" asked Haylee.

Aaron opened up a new browser. He typed something fast, Haylee couldn't see it.

"This is Scruff, ever heard of it?"

"No," Haylee replied.

"It's a Gay hook up site, like Grindr, but not."

"Okay..." Haylee looked closer at the page Aaron had brought up, "Is that...?"

"Mr. Dennis Simmons profile on Scruff? Yes, Haylee, yes, it is," he mocked her with a telling voice.

"How did you find that?" Haylee's jaw dropped. She couldn't fathom what she was seeing.

"Reverse image search on Google. Lot's of pics Dennis posted on his Facebook page. I got a hit on the one we're looking at. Dude's gay, or Bi, whatever."

"You think? Did Nora know?" Haylee shook her head in disbelief.

The word secret popped up in her head. Sat there, haunting her. Her stomach dropped.

"No clue, but unless she had reason to think her husband was cheating on her, I doubt she was searching gay dating sites for her husband's picture. I mean, you see his name, right? Donald Sigmund, it's a pseudonym. I would have never have found it without the reverse image search."

"Okay...wait, back up," Haylee was still recovering from the nightmare. Her head still hurt. Now she had to digest this turn of events. Her brain was swimming with half-thoughts and theories, what-ifs and how-comes. "So, we found out that the Simmons had a friend over for the week. His name was probably this Gary Thom guy. Brandon, Dennis's son, who is away to college, couldn't get ahold of his parents. So, he posted on Facebook about finding out if anyone had heard or seen them in the last few days. You were able to backtrack that, somehow to Gary Thom's Facebook. Then you stalked Dennis' profile and noticed he conversates with a lot of gay men and did an image search for his pictures allowing you to find him on a gay dating ap site."

"Yep," Aaron stood up excitedly. "Nailed it!"

Haylee gave him a dirty look. "Nora was my friend," her lips pursed with anger."

"Sorry, sorry," Aaron regretted that immediately. "I mean, it makes sense, though. He invited this guy over to his house, behind his wife's back. Living this double life, and something goes wrong. Maybe this Thom guy is a serial killer, a fucking looney tune. He kills them both and makes his way back to town. Although the news is spreading on the groups as we speak, that there is a search party out there in the woods behind your old home. Cops have been scouting out the area. He may have gotten away. There's a statewide search set up and everything."

"Fucking great," Haylee dropped her face into her hands. "Murderer on the loose."

"Look, it's too early to tell, this is just a theory. We won't know what happened until tomorrow when the police release a statement if that's even tomorrow. Maybe we should take a break from this. Maybe watch a movie? I was looking at your collection while you slept. Horror buff, I see."

"I used to be. I can't watch that stuff anymore," Haylee got up from the couch. "I don't care. I'm getting a drink. I need something strong. I need vodka."

"Yeah, I suppose I could use one as well," Aaron stepped over the large Dane, who didn't flinch. The dog was passed out, snoring loudly.

"Hey, Haylee," Aaron stopped at the entrance into the kitchen as she made her way to the fridge. "I'm really sorry you're going through this."

"Thanks," she said. "It's been a rough few years. That's an understatement, to be honest. It's nice to have someone here with me. I need the company. Not a lot of people I know here in Michigan, and my own family is still down in Ohio."

"You know, I was pissed when I had to move back home," Aaron pulled two mason jars from Haylee's cupboard above the sink. "After my accident, I lost everything I had worked so hard for. I was so close to nailing my big part."

"You lived in Hollywood, right?" asked Haylee. "You've mentioned it briefly before.

"Yeah, chasing dreams, you know? A fat chubby kid from Michigan looking to make a splash in Hollywood. Silly, I suppose. But I was sort of doing it. Had some things in the works."

"Why is it silly?" Haylee untwisted the top off the vodka.

"Parents told me I was crazy. Get a real job sorta stuff. They were supportive but didn't get it either. We had a strange relationship when I moved out there. Pretty sure me moving home was their 'I told you so' moment." Aaron took a deep breath, "I don't know why I got in that damn car," followed by a deep sorrowful sigh. "I should have stayed home. I was working on a script. I planned on staying in, hard work, right? Shits supposed to pay off. Then my roommate landed a role on some shitty sitcom. It's not airing, by the way, never got picked up by any networks. It doesn't matter, we went out, partied like big shots. Alcohol, hard drugs, we lived the life, always partying. I got in the back seat. Dumb ass, he drove, his girl was with him. Boom!" Aaron clapped his hands together.

"What happened?" Haylee took the two glasses from him.

"Hit a tree, drunk ass Matt hit a fucking tree. Took a corner going eighty the cops said. We survived. I got the worse of it. He spun the damn car. The back hit a telephone pole on my side. Just fucked me up something fierce. Spent a month in the hospital, something like that? Many more in physical therapy. I had a few gigs lined up, small roles, but they were paying roles."

"You gave up?" Haylee's voice sounded defeated herself.

"Yep. I wound up giving in. Swallowed my pride. Moved back here with a coke problem. At least I was closer to my parents. Its why I get the pills, you know? I try not to use em' much, but there are days where the back pain is unbearable. It's why I have the cane, why you see my fat ass limping at times. Fucking Matt. God-damned piece of shit, Matt. Dude is a loser."

"I'm sorry," Haylee poured a large portion of vodka into the mason jar. She followed it with a handful of ice cubes. "Want pop with it? I got Pepsi."

"Naw, I'll sip it, thanks," Aaron took a long sip straight. It burned his throat. "We need to get you better vodka."

"Fuck today," Haylee nodded.

"Fuck every day," Aaron took another drink.

ELEVEN

No one was answering their phones, but maybe that was a good thing. Fewer distractions while Haylee traversed one of the biggest snowstorms Northern Michigan had seen in years. Not only was the snow thick, making her vision less than stellar on the road, but heavy winds batted her car, causing her to swerve uneasily—her knuckles, still white from gripping the steering wheel in fear of losing control.

Haylee drove an hour south down I-75 before talking to her father. It was then they decided the weather was only getting worse downstate. It would be safer to turn around and reschedule her visit. She needed to get away, though. She needed a break from the stress at home, from her sister, especially from her fiancé, Robbie. No matter the pressure, the mental health break she needed, Mother Nature was not going to allow it.

The conversation with her father was looming in her head. She needed to gather the strength and courage to confront Robbie.

Be open.

Be honest.

Come clean.

About everything.

She thought of Robbie, his sudden outbursts of violence. It was so unlike him. It has been growing; for weeks now, she could sense the friction between the two. Was he cheating, was he unhappy? Did he know? Could he have found out about her secret too? She couldn't forget about what she was hiding from him as well...She hadn't mentioned that to her father. It was too personal. She'd been up every night crying when no one was around. She'd been a basket case ever since the doctor told her the terrible news.

She held dealt with it all for months, alone.

Trying to come to terms with everything.

She also had to do this while her little sister was not in the house. She didn't want Camille to see her weak. Camille was always the strong one, the smart one, daddy's perfect angel. Finally, for the first time in their life, Camille needed her sisters help.

She was running away from an abusive husband, starting over, scared, unsure of herself. Haylee would never admit to it or say it out loud even to herself, but deep-down Haylee was happy her sister's marriage failed. Camille did everything first, and better than Haylee, even with marriage. But if things continue to go down the route, it's going with Robbie, Haylee won't have a fiancé anymore, and will be in the same boat as her little sister.

Haylee was older by four years. She was supposed to be the first Leveille girl to get married, to graduate college, to have kids. Somehow, her younger sister beat her down the aisle, both in terms of marriage and graduation. Camille was married at twenty-one to her high school sweetheart, David (he was a drunk back then too) and on a fast track to divorce all before Haylee even gotten proposed to.

That was her sister, though, always the stealer of the spotlight. The baby could never do anything wrong in daddy's eyes, unlike Haylee, who, for the most part, was a fuck up, a failure. She dropped out of college, couldn't hold a steady job, and drank way too much (for reasons nobody cared to understand). She learned to live her life in the moment. She loved the spontaneity of it. Mostly, because as a young girl, Haylee had so many of the things she loved ripped from her.

Camille was the opposite, of course, a meticulous planner. Everything came easy to her. She got A's in school, captain of the soccer team, and was valedictorian of her class. Their parents never fought about finding her the 'right' help. Perhaps she had an older sister to learn mistakes from, maybe that's why she turned out so much better than Haylee. Haylee didn't mind the sound of that. She loved her sister; she did. She wanted her to be happy, to find love, a career. She just wanted out of little sister's shadow. Not to be the screw up for once.

Where Camille had the smarts, the drive, and ambition, Haylee had natural beauty. And she knew it. Even when she was young, boys always looked at her differently. Not that Camille wasn't pretty; they both took after their long-lost mother, who was a timeless beauty. They had her eyes, soft, dark brown, her olive-colored smooth and silky skin, gorgeously curved body. Haylee had pictures of her mother all over her old bedroom back in Ohio. As a kid, she dreamt of growing up as beautiful as her, boys swooning over her. Camille was just more homely, a tom-girl who married a young Police officer, so of course Daddy Detective thought he was the perfect gentlemen.

Beauty can be just as powerful as brains; this is something Haylee learned very young, especially if the beauty had the brains to get what she wanted. She may have lacked in the academic department, but Haylee was smart. Headstrong, she understood how to get what she wanted. Her dad realized this too, detective daddy, trying to keep his two daughters safe, and away from evil men. He failed at the end when it was all said and done. His wife's one wish, to keep their daughters safe, would be his greatest failure, both as a detective and as a father.

Haylee had a long drive back home. She could only go half the speed limit due to the conditions of the road. She didn't even do that, not topping twenty miles an hour on the highway. So many thoughts swirled in her head, buzzing like a pesky flies, irritating the shit out of her. She couldn't calm herself from the noisy thoughts. Haylee wasn't a perfect sister, a perfect girlfriend, and not even close to an ideal daughter.

Haylee was a work in progress. But wasn't everyone? Then, there was the secret too. Sometimes, she had a hard time keeping the secrets straight. So many secrets, but this one was bad. It could end her relationship with Robbie once and for all, break their engagement. It could shatter everything they worked for over the last five years. When she first learned it herself, she had a breakdown. She'd been alone that day, after the doctor visit. It was roughly three weeks ago, she went alone, not expecting the conversation her doctor was to have with her. She went home; she remembers the drive was quiet. She hadn't even turned the radio on. She went numb when the Doctor spoke to her as if the words lingered in her brain, not fulling registering.

She got home, and she was alone, her sister out with friends (she'd managed to make a few, unlike Haylee). Robbie was working late, and she poured a club soda, no vodka. She sat there, repeating the doctor's words. The feeling of losing control, of being robbed of the life she tried so desperately to have. Knowing that Robbie, more than anything in the world, wanted to be a father. She thought she broke her mind, seriously. She thought something in her head snapped.

Haylee didn't care about a career or money; It had always been about motherhood for her. She was supposed to start a family with Robbie. That was the plan.

Move to Michigan.

Start a Family.

Why did her life always get so fucked up? Why wasn't she allowed to be happy? That was the only thing she wanted to accomplish in her life, become a loving mother. She'd been robbed of hers when she was thirteen. She'd always had the notion, the feeling, motherhood was her only chance of happiness.

Haylee pushed the thoughts out of her head. She played some music, a random nineties station on Spotify, and cranked it as loud as she could. Too many dark thoughts. She focused on the road and decided that once she got home safe and sound, the first thing she would do is sneak a stiff drink—no reason not to now.

She'd been doing that a lot lately. Since the secret. The secret that begot a secret, that stemmed from a bunch of other secrets. Drinking and drinking heavily. It made matters with Robbie worse. Especially after the first night when she disappeared. The night she'd blacked out for the first time in years. She wasn't ready to think of that, wasn't prepared to allow herself to face the humility of the events that transpired that night. Instead, she focused on the song blaring in the car, a terrible 90s boy band, Backstreet Boys. She tapped her fingers rhythmically against her steering wheel. She sang the simple lyrics loudly to herself in the car. Push away the darkness, focus on the now, she told herself.

The driveway was covered with four inches of snow by the time Haylee returned home. She was surprised Robbie hadn't broken out their snowblower. He was ordinarily quick to combat the Michigan weather. He liked doing things like that, mowing the lawn on the brand-new rider they bought when they first moved into the house. He'd been itching to break out their four-wheeler with the snowplow attached to its front. First heavy snow this year, and eerily, he hadn't plowed. Perhaps he was too busy. He did work from home a lot.

It was late Friday night, early Saturday morning. He probably got home late from work, finished up a few remaining things from the business day so he could enjoy a quiet weekend with her gone. He must have decided to worry about the snow until the morning. No doubt, it would still be there.

Haylee pulled in behind Robbie's big Honda truck, and her sisters little magenta-colored Subaru. Both covered with a thick blanket of some of the finest pure Michigan snow. Haylee knew about snow, Ohio had some harsh winters, but the tip of Michigan was like another world. When it snowed, it *snowed*! Hard, and a lot more often.

She stepped outside her car. The bitter winter air sent chills through her body; it ached in her bones. She locked her car from inside her door, instead of her key fob, which would make a loud honking noise. It was closer to one in the morning, and if her sister and Robbie were sleeping (probably), she didn't want the horn to wake them. Although, strangely enough, she noticed the basement light was on. Robbie had a workspace downstairs, and maybe he was up late working? Doubtful, not this late. Instead, Haylee rested on the idea that once again, Robbie forgot to turn off the lights in his study. Because you know, electricity if free.

Haylee fumbled with her keys. She found the one she was looking for and unlocked the front door, quietly making her way into the house. There was a sense of relief now as she stood inside the safety of her home. Her car currently parked securely in her driveway. The warmth was swarming over her, like the hug of an old friend. That drive was intense. It was good to be home, to be safe.

She made her way into the kitchen. Set her purse on the counter and slipped out of her jacket. She went straight to the cupboard and pulled a small glass, hit the fridge, she grabbed a handful of ice cubes, dropping them in. Above the sink was her alcohol cabinet, she pulled a bottle of Jim Beam Kentucky Straight Bourbon Whiskey. She filled her glass, let it sit for a moment. She took a seat at the kitchen table and took a long sip. Strong, she needed a stiff drink after that drive.

The secrets gnawed at the back of her head. Tomorrow she would have to find out a way to come clean to Robbie.

Her fiancé Robbie. Once, they were happy. A young couple, eager to hold one another. Falling sleep in each other's arms. She wished she could relive those days.

What would he say if he caught her immediately getting a drink? He'd scold her, no doubt. And he would be right to do so. The truth was, she was drinking too much. He was no saint, though.

Old habits, she thought, they die hard. It was easier for her to drink than to feel, to think about everything going on around her. The reality of it all was too harsh, she took a second drink, another long sip, to ease her nerves. Her mind fell to her purse. Before bed, she had to take care of her weapon, return it to the lockbox in the front closet. When she and her sister graduated from High School, her father took them both out to the gun range. Taught them to shoot himself. He wanted them always to be protected, never to fall victim without a fight. Too many crazies he would tell them, never let your guard down.

On her twenty-first birthday, he bought her a .9mm Glock 47. It was a perfect firearm for Haylee, sleek, rugged, reliable, easy to conceal, and more comfortable to shoot. She kept it in her purse whenever she left the house. She stayed up on her aim, even found a shooting range in her new town. Her and Camille had gone twice already. Her dad hammered gun safety with his children. Despite Haylee not being one to abide by many laws, a natural rule breaker, gun safety was not to fucked around with.

She wasn't tired. The drive had her adrenaline pumping. She slid her vehicle twice near her home. It got her heart rate going. The house was quiet, settling like houses tend to do. She finished her drink and thought one more should be enough. She worried about another blackout. Waking up somewhere she wasn't supposed to be...again. What a nightmare that was. It was a week after that incident when everything began to change when Robbie began the cruelties. It was her fault; she was unraveling and hadn't even told him why.

"Idiot," she muttered to herself. "Leave it to me to fuck everything up," she spoke to herself. She stood up, decided she needed another drink. This time, she wanted a mixer, pop would do just fine. Coca Cola and whiskey, a classic. One Jack and Coke on its way. She made her way to the fridge. Weird, she thought, something was smeared on the linoleum kitchen floor. She hadn't hit the kitchen light. Instead, she used the glare of her phone to find the glass and drink. She'd opened the freezer for the ice. When she opened the Fridge door for the coke, the inner light lit up the majority of the kitchen. It revealed a strange sight. There a few feet away from her near the basement door was a large smear of what? Ketchup? It looked red, dark, thick on the floor.

"What on earth?" Haylee frowned. She moved to the entrance of the kitchen, flicked on the light. The kitchen fully lit up. There it was, a smear of red liquid, except now there was more. There was splatter on the wall, near the entrance as well. She'd walked right past it when she entered the backdoor into the kitchen. There on the floor beside it was the smear. She had stepped in it, making light footprints.

It was not ketchup.

"Blood?" Haylee frowned. On the far side of the kitchen were the stairs to the basement. It was left partially open. There were large pools of blood leading to the steps. Haylee moved forward slowly, hardly breathing. She softly opened the door. More blood on the steps, a lot of it. Did someone fall? She tried to make sense of what she was seeing. She heard mumbling, heavy breathing from the basement.

Was it, Robbie?

She walked down the blood-stained stairs. She went to feel for her phone in her pocket. She had left it on the kitchen table. Shit, she thought, did she go back up to get it? She was almost at the foot of the stairs when the step let out a loud creak.

That alarmed someone, something. She heard a noise. Not so much a word as it was a deep grunt, inquisitive, almost like a *"Whose there? Or What was that?* Sort of throaty acknowledgment. Haylee quickly peered around the corner of the steps. There she saw it.

The horror, a scene from a slasher movie playing out right before her. In her very own basement. The blood, so much blood. She felt faint, her head spinning. She was going to pass out. She grabbed the railing on the steps before she lost her balance

My god, she thought. What horror!

TWELVE

The Bad Luck Lager House was Lewis Pike's favorite dive bar. It wasn't fancy, he'd didn't quite care for fancy. He liked the cheap, strong drinks, away from the glitz and glamour of the clubs the young kids visited, and far from the price a drink will cost you at one of the national chain steak restaurants. He also liked the regulars, the low-key drunks, usually older folks who did more sittin' and sippin' than talkin' and spittin'. Basically, less drama, fewer distractions, made it much easier for him to think. The last thing he wanted to deal with on a night off was some local drunk building up his liquid courage.

He also liked that a lot of the boys frequented the small hole in the wall establishment. It wasn't in the city, not quite in the country. The perfect little hideout for his brothers and sisters in blue to enjoy a few drinks and talk shop or shoot some pool. His wife left him years ago, he disowned his son, hadn't heard from him in over fifteen years. Pike didn't have any real friends outside of the force. So, it was nice seeing his coworkers out of the office. Made him remember he was more than just a Detective.

Tonight, was different though, he asked officers Clent and Vanessa out for drinks. Two nights ago, they shared an experience that would haunt them for quite some time. A lot had happened in the last forty-eight hours. He wanted to share a few drinks with them. Discuss some stuff off the record. There were a lot of pieces to the puzzle, and the more Pike dug up, the weirder the case got.

He also needed a few friendly faces so he could vent.

Keep his sanity.

Pike walked in the bar a quarter past nine in the evening. The bar was quiet, a few solo drinkers at the front of the bar, knocking back their beers. They sat around watching the Lions game on a small flat-screen television behind the bar. Sherry, the owner, waved, gave a friendly smile offering her toothless grin. She looked closer to sixty, then her real age, which was in her mid-forties. She hadn't aged well. Pike was aware she had a hard life. She shared some of her more depressing stories with him during slower nights at the bar. Abuse, lots of abuse. Mostly from the men in her life, and her favorite substances. She was clean now, proud of it as well. Still smoked a pack a day, still drank, but the hard shit was behind her.

Sherry was a natural talker, and thus she made an excellent bartender. She had the ability that allowed people to open up to her. That was the trick for tips. Same for Detective work, let them feel safe, work them, get them to spill their guts. She was sharp too, smart as a whip, born under different circumstances. Pike thought she might have been able to do bright things with her life. Yet, all those hard years left her less than stellar to look at. She brought him over a napkin, a bowl of salted peanuts, and an Old Fashion on the rocks just the way he liked it with the plastic sword skewering a maraschino cherry and an orange slice.

"Thanks, Sherry, you always know how to make a man smile," Pike smiled. He grabbed the skewer, plopped the cherry into his mouth.

"Always, Detective, first ones on me," her voice was raspy, more manly than feminine. Years of smoking, hard drugs, Pike thought. He sat alone, drumming his fingers at the table. He sat as far away from the main bar as he could, privacy for him and his companions.

He ate a few peanuts and enjoyed his drink. Vanessa and Clent entered the bar around a quarter past ten, dressed in civilian clothes. Clent, a dark pair of Levi bootcut jeans, a blue Nike zip-up hoodie that hugged his muscular frame. Vanessa, outside of her uniform, was much more attractive than Pike had noticed. She was young, vibrant. Her dark black hair was curled; he could tell she took her time doing her makeup. Her jeans clung tightly to her ass. Not bad, he thought, but immediately pushed the thought away. She would make a man much younger than he happy, at least for a while, before they inevitably grew apart.

"Evening officers," Sherry was quick to welcome.

"Howdy, Sherry," Clent waved, nodding to her. He pulled a chair out for his partner, who took a seat at the far end of the table.

"I was wondering when my tall, dark, and handsome man was going to come back in for a drink," Sherry placed her hand on Clent's shoulder, her raspy voice almost echoed inside the bar.

"Don't let my wife know," Clent winked.

"Always wanted a strong black man to keep me safe," she placed two extra bowls of peanuts down in front of them.

"How about we start with a drink?" Clent chuckled, his eyebrows raised in a bit of shock from her forwardness.

"This ones on me," Pike waved his hand, signaling for the tab.

"You sure?" Vanessa frowned. "I'm a rookie and all, but I'm a big girl."

"One-hundred percent sure, I asked you two out for my own selfish reasons, least I can do is buy you both a few drinks for your time."

"It's our pleasure, detective," Vanessa thanked him with a pleasant smile. "Clent has told me so much about you. I feel like I owe you. I would love to pick that brain of yours."

"Plenty of time for that later," Pike added. "Beers?" he asked.

"I will take a Bud Light," said Clent.

"Corona with a lime, please," Vanessa followed.

"Right away," Sherry smiled, retreating to get their drinks.

"So, what's up? Not a casual get-together, a few cops sharing drinks?" Clent asked.

"Yes and no," Pike replied flatly. "How are you holding up, Vanessa? After the crime scene on Friday?"

"Rough," Vanessa answered. "Had my doubts over the weekend, you know that I wasn't cut out for this. I knew I would see things, death, violence. We train for this stuff, but I dunno...do we train for *that*?"

"No one can train for what we saw," Clent plopped a few peanuts into his mouth. "I wasn't right either. My wife new, she pressed it. I couldn't tell her. If she knew, I mean...what the fuck was that? You can't bring that stuff up over frozen pizza with the kids at the table."

"It's been hard for everyone," Pike took a sip from his drink. "—and the damn news is leaking shit all over the place. Social media is having a field day with these keyboard detectives, spreading false info around. I miss the old days, just dealing with reporters. Now, it's every idiot with an internet connection reporting on stuff they don't know anything about."

"News spreads fast these days, hard to keep it under control," Clent replied.

"You weren't kidding," Pike looked at Clent dead in his eyes.

"About?" replied Clent.

"This making twenty-seventeen look like a play date," Pike shook his head. "Never thought I'd say that."

"That was the Leveille house, right? That was in twenty-seventeen?" asked Vanessa, feeling like this was turning into a two-way conversation.

Sherry returned with their drinks, carefully setting them down in front of each of them. "Anything else?" pleasant as always.

"Not at the moment, thanks," Pike slid her a twenty, "Keep it. If you don't mind, we'd like some privacy, keep the drinks coming through, I think we'll need them tonight."

"Thank you, detective," Sherry smiled, pocketing the twenty in her jean's back pocket. "—And no problem, I know how you officers like to talk shop. I'll keep the patrons seated near the bar, that'll give you folks all the space in the world. And don't you worry, I'll keep the refills flowin' as well, darlin'. Enjoy!" She smiled again at Clent, who tipped his beer to her.

"Yes, that's the one." Pike looked back to Vanessa, answering her question about the twenty-seventeen case.

"I'm not full-on all the details, other than it was gruesome," she added.

"Yeah," Clent frowned. "I got called there too. My old partner and I were first on the scene. We walked in with the homeowner sitting in the pool of blood. She was in shock, a catatonic state. That scene was..." Clent fiddle with the bowl of peanuts in front of him, searching for the right words.

"Horrific," Pike responded.

"So, you both were at the crime scene?" Vanessa squeezed her lime into her beer and wedged the slice down the neck of the glass corona bottle. She took a long drink.

"Yeah, we'll spare the details, for now," Pike added. "But it was–until now-my worst case. I was the head detective for that one as well. But it was open and shut. Not much work to do, everything basically lined up. Lots of paperwork."

"Same, Clent nodded. "You don't think this sort of stuff happens in a small town like ours, but twice? And worse, this time? Makes you wonder, something in the water out here?"

"Crazy times," Pike shook his head. "I blame the internet. Poisons people's minds makes everything too easy these days. You can watch just about anything on, murders, killings, it desensitized the whole damn world to the point that a double murder with cannibalism is like damn water cooler small talk."

"I can see that," Clent added. "We could be here all week discussing that topic." he chuckled.

"Right, so let's stick to why I called you out here. Back to Friday, when the shit storm hit," Pike redirected the conversation. "Obviously we're all still a little shaken up over it, some new info has come out, I'm curious about your opinions. Because, to be frank, bizarre doesn't begin to explain it. I have my thoughts, crazy as they may be, and need to talk em' out."

Clent took a long guzzle from his beer, topping almost half it off before setting it back down on the napkin. "Guys still out there, supposedly, what was his name? Gary, something?"

"Gary Thom," Pike corrected. "Probably going to find his body out in the woods once some of that storm melts off. If I read your reports right, he fled into the state forest with just a hoodie on. It's been below freezing every day. The storm hit hard, over a foot of snow. No way he could have survived out there this long."

"You don't think he could have survived? Got out of the woods that night, maybe? Hitch hiked somewhere?" asked Vanessa, downing her beer.

"I suppose anything's possible," Pike shrugged. "We had the dogs out, they lost his trail about a mile into the forest though, he got deep. He's not from these parts. He doesn't know the woods. I think he fled, and just booked it as far as he could get into the woods. He wasn't thinking. He left two mutilated bodies in the sex room for you to discover and wasn't going to stick around for you to stumble upon them."

"He definitely was not equipped to survive out there in the woods. He was on foot, no supplies, no backpack. He got lost out there. Hypothermia took him, I'm sure of it," Clent replied. "I hunt these woods, and they're no joke. People go missing out there every year; some never come back out."

"Time will tell on this one. We have a BOLO out for the guy. I'm sure you've seen the reports and news coverage. His face hit social media yesterday evening, and people are having a field day with it. So, if anyone sees him anywhere, hopefully, the words gotten out to contact us."

"One good thing about social media, huh?" Vanessa chimed in. "When this shit goes down, everyone is retweeting, reposting. His face has hit everyone's news feed in Michigan by now, multiple times."

"What do we know about him?" Clent asked, finishing off his beer. He peered over his shoulder, friendly gesturing Sherry for a second round.

"I spoke to his parents yesterday once we got confirmation who he was. Left his wallet behind in the main bedroom, he lied, by the way, go figure. We also found his duffle bag and personal belongings. We were able to get into his social media accounts with the help of his parents. Things started to come together."

"Yeah, about the crazy sex dungeon," Clent frowned. "Who would have thought a well-respected upper management big wig, married for twenty years with a kid off in college, had a double life like that?" asked Clent. Everyone would quickly learn of Dennis's second life as a member of the gay community, and his kink being active in the BDSM bondage crowd.

"So, yes, Dennis Simmons lived a double life. We've established this fairly quickly. His internet history was colorful. Nothing illegal, no kiddie porn, but he was definitely hiding his sexual lifestyle from his wife. He would often meet men from around the state, even out of state, for sexual pleasure. He used a site called Scruff, a gay hook up site, and he met men with similar tastes. That's where he met Gary Thom, and we have records of their conversations, both through the site's personal messaging app and on their cell phones. Nothing, out of the ordinary, two consensual adults discussing a meeting, and their sex life. Nothing illegal, nothing with motive."

"You're referring to the BDSM stuff in reference to similar tastes?" asked Vanessa.

"Yep," Pike nodded. "Not that uncommon I hear, really. It's bizarre walking into the hidden room like that, but I suppose if you're trying to keep it from your wife, you have to hide it. There is an extensive subculture that's into this sort of stuff. So, he found men on this Scruff site, and we assume his wife these men were business partners, or out-of-town friends. The Camaro was a cover. They were never working on a car. I guess you could say his wife and kid were covers too. You know? He didn't want anyone to know about his sexual preference. He hid it as many do. He made sure Gary understood he was married, and that everything was to be done quietly, and that she was not to know."

"Right," Clent sighed.

Sherry quietly approached, "Here you go, refills for everyone," carefully she refilled the group's drinks. "Must be something serious," Sherry frowned. "I can see it in your faces. Feel the tension."

"You could say that," Pike nodded with thanks as he plucked out the sword from his drink. This time eating both the cherry and orange slice at the same time.

"It's about that family in the country, isn't it?" Sherry frowned. "I cried when I read that on Facebook. It's everywhere I look. Those poor, poor souls."

"We're not under liberty to discuss the ongoing case, Sherry. I'm sure you understand," Vanessa thanked her for the second Coruna.

"Oh, I do, honey, and I don't think I want to know what really happened out there. You know, this place used to be so quiet, now, every year there's a killing, or a kid goin' missin in the woods, or some idiot getting drunk and shootin' someone. Hell in a handbasket I tell you, I pray for you folk, keepin' us safe from all these crazies. Lots of folks don't like cops in the cities, think you're all corrupt. I think *we're* all corrupt. It's a matter of time before the real monsters come out, and they'll be begging you guys for help then, I betchya every dollar I got."

"We appreciate your support, that's why you're our favorite place to drink," Pike smiled, slipping her another folded bill.

"No," She waved it off. "You guys get a free night; next few rounds are back on the house. It won't hurt me to give back. You do what you do, and I'll supply the beer."

"You're a doll, Sherry, really," Pike raised his glass to her. She smiled, retreating to her other patrons.

"—So, what did Gary's parents say?" asked Vanessa.

"Nice guy, Twenty-eight, works retail management east side of the state, fairly outgoing. Came out to his parents after high school, had a serious relationship in college, it ended a few years back. Pretty heartbroken over it. No signs of mental issues, clean past, hardly anything on record except for a few parking tickets. Parents looked to be supportive, didn't know about the BDSM stuff, seemed shocked, maybe appalled at the notion. Not something to talk about at Thanksgiving, right? But, I mean, squeaky clean kid, no history of mental health, a lot going for him."

"Kid just decides to kill two people, eat them, tie them up, mutilate their bodies?" Clent shook his head in disbelief. "What are we missing?"

"I mean, I'm no detective," Vanessa took another sip of her beer, "But, I agree. Where's the motive? Where's the criminal past? It doesn't seem to connect."

"Well, so we checked records. Obviously, we can't go just by what dear old Mommy and Daddy say about their precious son. Killers hide in plain sight, look at Bundy, look at Gacey. Now, Thom, he's not a serial killer at this point, but he's got the taste of blood. Maybe he's hidden the urge well, and something happened in his life his parents didn't know about. Did something tip him over the edge? We don't know. All we know is he went through his life, avoiding the system, staying out of trouble, no records. If he did torture animals as a kid, no one caught him. So, let's not rule out anything yet; he might just be really good at what he does." Pike replied. "he may have killed, and we just don't know about it until now."

"Then he shouldn't have been so sloppy? Because let's face it, he killed the Simmons and hung out in their home for a few days, right? Did we get the full report back, do we know the time of death?" asked Clent.

"Not officially, but I just got off the phone with Fat Man before I got in here. Looks like its leaning towards a few days before the welfare check. We think he stayed with the Simmons for five days judging from their text conversations. We think it happened on day two, which leaves three days before you knocked on their door."

"All right, well, that makes sense. I mean, not that he hung around, but the timeline," said Vanessa.

"Things get weirder," Pike said, spinning the ice in his Old Fashioned with the plastic sword. "There was a sheet of paper lodged in Mrs. Simmons Mouth, folded blank printer paper, half down her throat. It had the word HEL written on it in black sharpie, spelled H-E-L.

"Spelled it wrong?" Vanessa frowned.

Pike shrugged. "We still haven't found Mr. Simmons head, and we assume he ate the rest of his missing bits. Including Mrs. Simmons eyes and tongue. Some of this ring a bell, Clent?" Pike asked.

"Yes,' Clent answered bluntly.

"Am I missing something?" Vanessa frowned; the conversation had ruined her taste for beer.

"Not our first case with cannibalism, or missing eyes and tongue," Pike answered for him.

"Fuck," Clent blurted out.

"Yep," Pike half smiled, "You just figured it out, didn't you? We kept making the connection, comparing the two, but it was just a coincidence, wasn't it? Strange fact, but when is anything just a coincidence when it comes to murder?"

"It makes some sort of sense, doesn't it?" Clent was putting two and two together. His head begun to swell up with thoughts, connecting the dots.

"Wait, what?" asked Vanessa.

"Copycat killer?" Pike asked. "Sick fucker, wanting to make a name for himself? I dunno? What are your thoughts? That's why I needed to talk this one out. Not sure of what to make with the connections."

"Copy Cat?" again Vanessa was lost, she wanted answers.

"H-E-L," Clent said to her. "It wasn't Hell. It was Haylee Elyce Leveille."

"Who?" Vanessa needed more than a name.

"You probably lost your appetite, you haven't touched that second beer, but you're gonna need a few more drinks as we fill you in, trust me," Pike finished off his Old Fashion in one gulp. "Clent, I need your help on this one, because some of this is far-fetched, and I need a fresh set of eyes. You okay with that?"

"Anything to help, but first, Vanessa buckle up, we have to fill you in on a lot of history," Clent followed suit and downed his beer.

"Well then," Vanessa lifted her beer as well. "Looks like we have a long night ahead of us."

THIRTEEN

"Hello, Honey," the man's voice was muffled with a mouth full of his victim's flesh. Blood was smeared across his face, dripping from his lips. He was covered with it, at first Haylee couldn't tell whose blood it was, but judging from the mangled corpse beneath him, it became apparent, it was the female victim. The man's eyes-a familiar dark blue-gazed through the grotesque crimson mask that stained his face. They pulled her away from the site, almost in a trance. They looked tortured, like he was trapped behind them, watching in agony as the gruesome scene played out. Tears streamed down his cheeks, mixing with the victim's blood. His mouth, the sneer of his lips, the hunks of flesh dangling when he spoke, there was no questioning the man was crazed.

"Fuck!" Haylee shouted. She sprung back up the stairs, but the man was quick to react. He followed in pursuit, lurching at her. His hands gripped at her ankle, but she kicked and managed to slip away.

Was that him?

Could it have been?

It happened so fast. She hardly had a chance to take in the site.

But, those eyes...

Those blue eyes...

The same ones that used to look into her own with love and passion. The same ones that proposed to her months previously. But it was madness, the vileness of it all. It couldn't be him.

Robbie, no way it was Robbie.

The man, now snarling wickedly, reached for her again. He managed to grab ahold of her ankle, with his powerful fingers wrapping around her tightly. He yanked her down, mid-way from the stairs with such terrifying force, she tripped up. Haylee's hands reached out instinctively, catching her fall onto the steps. She spun to her side, and with all her might, she struck down with her foot, smashing her heel into straight into his nose. His cartilage crunched beneath her foot. The man grunted loudly from the blow, blood, exploding onto his face. He let up his grip, his hand covering his nose. She looked down briefly, blood freely flowing from under his hand.

Bastard!

Haylee screamed again, this time it was her who sounded guttural, crazed. She repositioned herself, back to her hands and knees. She attempted another escape this man's wrath. He was stunned from the blow and dazed long enough for her to reach the threshold atop the basement stairs.

"Come here!" he screamed. His voice demented, more like a snarl or growl than a human yell.

Haylee had one chance to make it out alive. Her purse was still sitting atop the kitchen counter, where she had left it when she got home. Inside her bag was her firearm, the Glock .47, that was her only hope. She'd fired it many times, and practice makes for a good shot, even her critical father praised the steadiness of her aim. But she'd never shot a living thing, especially a human. Her hands already shook terribly from the adrenaline, the fear. She heard the man pursuing behind her. He was close. He'd got his bearing; the pursuit was back on.

Haylee didn't hesitate. She didn't stop to look behind to gauge how far back the man was. She ran past the table, threw back a chair towards her pursuer. Her purse was there.

Thank God.

She grabbed it, pulled forth her firearm.

Not time to think.

Just act.

She spun fast; her arms extended just the way her father taught her. She steadied her weapon. There the man stood before her, now at the top of the stairs. His hand covered his face, blocking most of it from her view. He held his nose where she struck him. Blood poured freely from it, a puddle of it collecting between his feet.

She struck the bastard good.

The man went to lunge again. She did not flinch. No hesitation. She pulled the trigger, bracing for the kickback. The Glock was an easy shot. She aimed for center mass, but her aim was off. The first shot went wide, striking the wall.

The man ducked, falling to his knees to dodge the shot.

Haylee steady her breathing. She didn't flinch, pulled the trigger for a second time.

The man hadn't even got his back to his footing when the bullet struck him above the right eye. His eyebrow blew into his skull. His head shot back from the force, his brains exited the back of his skull, littering the stairs with what was left of it. His body stumbled backward two steps before he fell back. His body tumbled down the stairs. She didn't see him fall from her distance. She could only hear his body as it hit the steps, the sickening rhythmic sound of his body tumbling resonated in her head. She grabbed her phone, dialed 911. She stood in shock, waiting for an answer on the other end.

Her body trembled, her knees weak.

The operator picked up. Haylee wasn't sure what she said. She spoke briefly, not even hearing the operator questions.

"My name is Haylee Leveille," her words mumbled, broken. "1228 Orr Road, sister murdered, I shot the man, send help, please help."

She clicked the phone off, dropped it onto the floor. She had to see her sister. She had to.

Haylee, ready for the worse, approached the basement stairs. She stood, peering below at the madness beneath her. There at the foot of the stairs, the man's legs lifelessly sprawled atop the last few remaining steps. He was half-naked, blood and brain matter spread about the stairwell. His head had caved in where the bullet entered, which left his facial features unrecognizable. But those dark blue eyes from before, his voice, mad, hysterical, but familiar.

It *was* Robbie. Her sister lay dead one room over in Robbie's man-cave, his home workstation. Without thought, Haylee descended the stairs. The man was killed; her shot was fatal. Yet terror filled her body. She carefully stepped over his corpse, half-expecting his to rise from the dead, grabbing her leg. She couldn't look into his face, or what was left of it.

She found Camille...defiled, mutilated, her beautiful sister. She had been excited for the first day of her new job. Her life robbed from her, stolen, slaughtered like an animal. Haylee fell to her knees. Her gun dropped to her side. Her hand reached out. She placed it gently on her sister's shoulder. At first, she wept, she cried hard and ugly. Her mind was failing to process the events that unfolded. Then the tears suddenly stopped. A numbness rapidly spread over her body, like a fierce ocean wave crushing her beneath it. Then, blackness

Officer Clent Moore and his partner were the first to report to the scene. They approached the house with caution. There was no answer at the door, no answer to the phone that placed the distress. Clent, sensing something wrong, peered in through the back door, a perfect view into the kitchen. There he saw the blood. They acted fast.

They found Haylee, unresponsive next to her sister. Awake, but not aware. Two bodies, one mutilated, the other fatally shot in the head. Clent called dispatch, this was a homicide, and they needed Detective Pike out right away.

FOURTEEN

"So, you ready?" Aaron shifted the car into park. Once again, a drizzle of snow salted the windshield, a familiar scene throughout the last few wintery Michigan days. They parked in front of a small brick building just inside the town limits. The sign outside of the offices said Dr. Phillip P. Feldman Psychologist.

Haylee especially hated the sight before them. Doctors were not Haylee's friends. They looked at her as an enigma, a faceless puzzle waiting to be stuffed with pills and wrong diagnosis'. Time and time again, they failed her.

It was always the same.

Either she was crazy or faking it.

Or both as one specialist from the University of Michigan declared.

That one was her favorite. The doctor's name was Frank Rosenberg, an obese man who spent an hour with her one summery afternoon. He looked at her charts, her history, rallied off failed medications, without even talking to her. Then he had the audacity to claim she was making it all up. She was looking for attention. That she wouldn't be getting the attention from him, she needed therapy, perspective. She needed the truth.

"I don't want to go in," Haylee took a deep breath. Her eyes fixated at the glass door leading into the office; her anxiety was building. Her heart raced faster, her palms sweating, she nervously wiped them on her jeans.

"I can turn around. We can leave, you know? You're a grown woman, you don't have to see this guy, fuck him," Aaron cracked open a can of Monster energy drink, it fizzled loudly. He took a large gulp.

"No," Haylee shook her head. "If I miss another appointment, my dad will kill me. He may even stop paying my rent and car insurance. He's been threatening that a lot lately. So, I need to do this, for his sake, so he can have a false sense of helping me."

"You sound bitter for him wanting to help," Aaron frowned. "Isn't that a good thing?"

"No," Haylee peered out the window, away from the building. "He's as bad as the doctors. He doesn't listen to me either. Never has. It's always his way."

"Sounds like my dad too."

"Two peas in a pod," Haylee sighed.

"Well, we're a bit early," Aaron placed his Monster in the cupholder. "Wanna wait in here? Or go in?"

"I'll stay here if you don't mind, and thanks again for taking me. There's no way I would have driven myself here."

"Not an issue. I don't go into work at the café until noon, so consider it a favor," Aaron smiled, he had a natural boyish charm about him. When he wanted to turn it on, he did it well.

"So, I mean, what's up with this guy? Dr. Feldman? Is he not helping you? Like he is a shitty doctor or something?"

"No one helps me," Haylee was blunt, anger beneath her words. "I'm fucked in the head, and these doctors love stuffing me with antipsychotics. They don't work—only the Norco works. I think because it numbs me, and I can blackout with them. Alcohol used to work, but it doesn't anymore, it's not enough. I think I built up a tolerance to it now. So, I tell them they don't listen. They think I'm just an addict. But the pills they give me, the therapy, it doesn't help with the visions, the dreams."

"Like the nightmare you had?"

"Yeah, it's except its not just nightmares. Sometimes, when I get bad episodes, I see things when I'm awake too..." Haylee shook her head in disbelief. Why was she telling him this? She hadn't spoken this out loud to anyone in a long time for good reason. She gave up confiding in people. But this was different, therapeutic.

"This all stems from, you know? The incident?" asked Aaron carefully.

"Yes, and no," she shrugged. "Only my family really knows about this, a small handful of others. It's not something you talk about over dinner. Or sitting with a friend, waiting in a car, outside of a psychologist's appointment."

"I mean? I'm cool with it, no judgment here. If you wanna talk, I wanna listen," Aaron was intrigued. He'd known Haylee for a little over a year, and she'd never really opened up to him, despite plenty of him trying.

"I never even told Robbie, but I've always seen weird things, you know? They went away when I was in middle school but after the murders? Yeah, it came back tenfold. Every night was torture for me when I was a kid. Then it got better. I started feeling normal, well, sort of, I was never normal. But then after the murder, it was like the flood gates opened. Maybe even before that, it was getting bad again. I was losing control of a lot of things. Doctors like Feldman, they throw every pill at me, Abilify, Saphris, Risperdal. Nothing works. Every diagnosis they gave me, Schizophrenia, multiple personality disorder, they even thought I might have a tumor. They did so many tests. Nothing worked, no answers. Just a crazy psycho attention-seeking little girl that's making up stories of monsters and ghosts."

"Jesus," Aaron frowned.

"The only one who listened to me was my mother. My dad thought I was nuts, sick in the head. He made me see the doctors, the specialists. Even now, he's making me see Feldman. My mother, though, she was a spiritual person. She had other ideas. She listened to me."

"*Was* spiritual?" Aaron asked.

"I lost her when I was thirteen. I don't want to talk about it," Haylee glanced at her watch; they still had ten minutes to kill. She wasn't sure what was going to be more uncomfortable, the waiting room, or sitting in the car with Aaron. Now that Haylee was starting to open up, she wanted to backtrack, erase what she had already said. She was vulnerable now. She did not like it.

"So, like..." Aaron began the questions she knew would come, "How did your mom help? Like, compared to your dad?"

"You really want to hear all this?"

"Only if you want to tell me," Aaron added. "I have my own shit, and I know it makes me feel better to have someone to vent to."

"Okay..." Haylee took another deep breath. "Well, where do I begin? We tried pills when I was little too, and nothing worked then either. My mom, she listened to me about the things I was seeing. It wasn't the same nightmares back then. I was seeing these shadow-like people. Sometimes they were angry, ugly, deformed. Other times they looked just like you and me, some even talked to me. For a while, I just ignored them, but it got harder. My dad wouldn't hear it. But my mom, she pulled me aside, told me she wanted me to see someone special. Not a doctor, someone she thought could help. She reached out to a famous clairvoyant behind my dad's back, set up a few sessions."

"A clair-who-ant?" asked Aaron.

"Ever seen the show from a few years back on cable called the 'The Talking Dead'? The one about the lady who would go into people's homes suffering from hauntings? She could sense the spirits, talk to them?"

"Yeah," Aaron spent many drunk nights living in his small Hollywood apartment with his buddies watching reality shows on cable, just like that one. "She had a retired detective with her, he would do research, and she would do the ghost stuff. Good show, fun to watch high with your buddies."

"—Well, before she got sort-of-famous with that show, my mother paid her a lot of money to have some sessions with me. She was kind, listened, didn't look at me like I was crazy like the doctors do."

"Oh shit, really?" Aaron seemed excited. "I think she was cute too, for a bit of an older lady. Had tattoo's all up her arms. Cougar and whatnot."

"I suppose?" Haylee shook her head. She didn't find the humor in the statement.

"I'm sorry, go on, I wanna hear more," replied Aaron.

"Yeah, well, it caused a lot of problems with my family. My dad, he's a former detective, you know? That stuffs all bullshit in his eyes. Her name is Lydia Cayce. I only saw her maybe a half dozen times, if that. I was thirteen, so I had started experimenting with stuff, drinking, drugs. Getting into trouble as kids do. I learned that if I drank, and drank a lot to where I would blackout, it would keep the nasty stuff away. The pills the doctors gave me, the antipsychotics, had too many side effects and didn't work. Good old liquor was keeping me sane. Thirteen-year-old Haylee, the boozer."

"I mean, I drank a bit when I was a kid too, but that sounds heavy," Aaron added, taking another sip of his drink.

"Well, Lydia explained to me why alcohol worked. But it was too dangerous. I couldn't binge drink the rest of my life away. I needed to find other ways to help keep this-what she called a gift-at bay until I was ready to let it in, to conquer it."

"This all sounds so fucked up. You were just a kid dealing with this shit?"

"Yeah, well, according to my dad, it was just a means for me to get attention. To skip school, to drink. My parents constantly fought over me. My sister resented me because of it, and I resented her for being so perfect. Why did I get the fucked-up shit?" Haylee was getting emotional; her hands trembled. She hadn't spoken this stuff out loud for a long time. Not even to her psychologist, she didn't trust them. They would use it against her. They wouldn't listen. Aaron, at least he was paying attention, he seemed to care.

"So..." she continued "—this Lydia lady, she gave me all sorts of stuff. Burn this sage twice a day where I sleep. Wear this necklace, put these stones in your pockets at all times. She gave me things. Things I could do, and you know what?" Haylee looked directly into Aaron's eyes. "They worked. The crazy shit stopped for a long time. They stopped up until a few weeks before Robbie killed my sister. Things grew weird again by then, but of course, my dad didn't believe me. He wanted me to call Dr. Feldman, get seen right away. Of course, I didn't...Instead, we compromised, I was going down to see him, my dad, to get away. He thought maybe it was the stress of the engagement, not finding a job."

"I'm sorry, I thought you and your dad had a good relationship?"

"Yes and no." Haylee lips pursed together. "My mom died, and suddenly he pretended to listen a bit more. He wants me to get help, he wants me to be happy, but he wants it on his terms. He's always right, knows what's best. It's the detective in him. To him, I feel more like one of his cases he's trying to crack; that's how he treats me most of the time. I need him, you know? He's my dad, he's all I have left, but it's hard..." Haylee was feeling the anger again. "We pretend a lot."

"I think it's time for your appointment," Aaron pointed to the car radio where the bright blue numbers signaled the time.

"No," Haylee frowned. She pulled her cellphone from her inner jacket. She swiped it open, scrolled to her fathers' number, hit dial.

"What are you doing?"

"Hold on," She mumbled. "He's not answering..." she waited for the answering machine to pick up.

"Haylee?" Aaron asked again.

She angrily shoved her index finger towards his face, shushing him.

"Dad, I'm sorry you didn't pick up. I'm outside Dr. Feldman's office. My friend, Aaron, my neighbor, I had him drive me. We talked. I'm not going inside."

"What?" Aaron shook his 'no' to her, waving his hands to cut the phone off. "I don't want any part of this…"

"—I'm sorry," she explained, turning away from Aaron. "I know we've never seen eye to eye on this, on most things. You've been so great to me after Robbie and Camille, but Dr. Feldman can't help me. It does more damage than good. So, I'm sorry…I'm sorry your too stubborn to listen to me," Haylee's cheeks flushed. "I'm sorry we've pretended everything is fine between us, and that we haven't talked about what happened with Robbie, Camille, and hell, even mom. I know you're going to hate me, maybe not speak to me, cut off my rent. Whatever it's done. I'm done. I can't do it anymore. I can't handle it. It's getting worse, and it's getting out of control…" Haylee clicked the phone off, tossing it between her legs onto the floor of the car.

"Jesus," Aaron froze, unsure of how to respond.

Haylee breathed deep, almost hyperventilating. She fought the tears, wiped the few that escaped away. She counted her breaths, centered herself before speaking very softly. "Sorry about that."

"Hey," Aaron reached out, taking her hand in his. Not in a romantic notion, but as a comforting, I got your vibe. "You're damaged as fuck, girl." He smiled childishly.

Haylee couldn't help it. She blurted out in a mixture of crying and laughing. "You think?" she rubbed the tension building in her temples.

"Let's get back home," Arron shifted the car into reverse and pulled out of Dr. Phillp P. Feldman's office parking lot.

FIFTEEN

Detective Pike sat in his office alone at his desk, a hot cup of black coffee kept him company. It would be his fifth cup of the day, his bladder already an issue. His office was messy, paperwork littered everywhere, strewn about his desk. Yellow sticky notes plastered everywhere. Organized chaos is what he called it. In reality, organization was the last thing he worried about at the end of the day. His thoughts were organized, and he worked well within his means. So, why tamper with something that's gotten him this far. He tossed his sports jacket over the back of his chair and rolled up his sleeves, readied himself for another long night.

Hell, it was already a long week, day five since the double murder and the pursuit of the mad man. He hadn't much sleep and way too much coffee—dozens of questions, with little ways of answers. To make things worse, the sick fuck responsible was still missing out there somewhere. He thought the body would have turned up by now, a frozen corpse in the woods. They sent out multiple search parties, k-9's and even a copter to search the woodlands over the past few days. Zero results, nothing, the tracks went cold.

Where the hell was this kid? How would he have survived that storm?

A few of the many questions that kept Pike awake and his mind restless. His gut told him his body just hadn't turned up yet. People get lost in the woods; it happens in these parts. They may never find him. Yet, in the back of his mind, there was the probing notion, like the sting of a pesky hangnail. He could still be out there; he could strike again.

More death.

More victims.

That was unacceptable.

Pike stared at the monitor emotionless, drumming his fingers on his desk, waiting, somewhat patiently for Clent to show up for the fun. The Emmet County Police Department was quiet at this time of night. It was late, nearing midnight. Only a few souls inhabited the after-hours of the station. Pike was burning the clock; it didn't matter if he was home or in his cramped, messy office. He couldn't focus on anything outside the case.

He spent the last few nights sleeping in the office. His bed of choice on these long nights was a small little love seat that sat at the far side of his office. It was old, dusty, and hurt his back something fierce. Only a handful of cases kept Pike working into the wee hours of the night. This one, as well as the Leveille Murders a few years prior: two perfect examples of such cases.

Something wasn't adding up. Somewhere in deep crevasses of his mind, near that pesky little hangnail, there was an annoying little thought: too many coincidences between the Leveille case and the current. Maybe he was pulling at strings, wanting to connect them when there really wasn't anything there. Yet, that damn gut of his, it told him differently.

Pike already stayed two nights on that cramped love seat. Curled up in the fetal position, the only way he could fit on the damn thing. He kept a Detroit Lions fleece blanket in his office for those types of nights. His body needed a decent night's rest, somewhere he could stretch out. He wanted to call it around ten pm. He told himself he would head home, have a few choice strong drinks, hopefully, catch a few hours of sleep before hitting the office again bright and early.

That's when he saw the email sent earlier in the day from forensics. Somehow, he'd missed the incoming notification. This was big. He'd been waiting for the clearance, and the entire murder may have been filmed. If not, it had the potential of getting inside the mind of the killer. What was on those videos? Suddenly, the achy, tired body of the forty-nine-year-old Detective was refueled with adrenaline. One more night on the dusty old love seat wouldn't kill him. Waiting until tomorrow to watch the video would.

He texted Clent and Vanessa immediately, asking them both if they'd like to join him in the viewing. Vanessa was quick to pass, it was her night off, and she didn't care to see the potential gruesome scene. He didn't blame her. Clent was more curious. Texted simply "OMW." That was a half-hour ago. Pike waited eagerly, like a young kid on Christmas morning waiting for his lazy parents to wake up. He already plugged the USB drive into his computer. He wasted no time in checking it out of evidence.

Ten minutes came and went before Clent finally knocked on his office door.

"C'mon in," Pike waved, not moving from his desk chair. "I got it loaded already, did you bring the popcorn?"

"Funny," Clent let out a forced chuckle. "Midnight viewing, huh? Just the two of us?" Clent entered the Office. Again, he was dressed in his street clothes. Off duty meant on duty under the right circumstances. He didn't need to be geared up to watch alongside Detective Pike. He was honored just to get the text. This was his case too. He saw firsthand what the mad man was capable of doing.

"Vanessa passed. I think she is still adjusting to the crime scene, and if what I think is on these tapes, she probably wasn't ready for it anyway." Pike stood up, firmly shook Clent's hand.

"Fair enough, why so late?"

"I got the email earlier in the day, just didn't get a chance to check it before now. Took them long enough to clear it," Pike responded. "Pull up a chair, and brace yourself, this could get messy."

Clent nodded, pulled up a small metal folding chair from the opposite side of Pike's office that was leaned up against the side of the Love Seat. He unfolded it and took a seat. "I'm as ready as I'll ever be."

"All right," Pike took the mouse in his hand, hovered over the play button, clicked it. He then maximized the Media Player window and sat back, clearing his voice.

The video feed was high quality, shot in 4k ultra high definition from two angles. They were watching just one video. It was shot from a tripod, focused directly on the pulley machine that Dennis Simmons used as a sexual device to restrain himself or his partners. Before any sexual acts occurred, the two men sat together on two-fold out chairs in front of the pulley set up. It was easy to tell who the two men were, Dennis Simmons, who wore a one-piece latex suit that covered his torso and bottom half. Gary Thom was the second man in the scene. He was only wearing a single white linen robe.

"Dennis and Gary, first time together. Gary's first time being a sub. We've already discussed our safe word, Gary, do you mind?" Dennis asked.

"Trump," Gary gave a nervous smile. "Because, when is enough, enough?"

They both chuckled.

"So, as always, we signed a contract," Dennis lifted a clipboard from his side, attached to it was a legal document. "My personal lawyer printed this up. Standard, I always use them. It's a contract that states this is a consensual act between two adults. That the filming of said acts is for my personal enjoyment, and that under no means, will this video be distributed or ever recreated outside of its source material. If, in doing so, well, I would owe Mr. Thom here a handsome sum of money. Everything is signed and dotted. But, before we begin, and knowing that it is your first time," Dennis placed his hand on Gary's thigh gently. "You can still opt-out, and we can have the boring stuff outside of the film."

"No, I'm nervous but excited," Gary replied. He smiled wide, nervously rubbing his hands on his thighs.

The film continued. It was an awkward watch for Clent and Pike. Definitely a homemade movie, very raw, authentic. They watched, Pike taking notes per usual. The video showed two men engaged in sexually explicit bondage for roughly twenty-five minutes. Detective Pike had seen Gay porn in his life, not by choice, but it's something that everyone at some point stumbles upon. He was very much a man rooted in his conservative mindset. He didn't quite care for homosexuality; in fact, he quite despised it after it reared its ugly head into his family. He worked with only a few of "their kind" in his career. Made it a point to stay out of their personal lives. He kept it professional. But that didn't mean that when all was said and done (sitting there awkwardly with Clent watching these two men do disturbing and graphic things to one another) that he felt comfortable or okay with what was happening.

The video neared its end running time when the sexual fantasy and bondage finally stopped. Pike paused the video. He swallowed hard. The two hadn't spoken; they sat in silence as they watched the video. There were only a few minutes left of the recorded tape.

"What did we just watch," Pike stomach soured.

"Well," Clent rubbed his eyes. "No killing."

"That was difficult to watch."

"I mean, I don't watch gay porn personally, but all I saw were two men hooking up. Yeah, they had some weird kinks, pretty intense for me. But, hey, we all have our desires when the lights turn out, right? Who am I to judge as long as it was consensual?"

"Is that so?" Pike stroked his salt and peppered stubble on his chin. It had been days since he shaved, he was in the itchy phase of a beard growing in. He found himself rubbing it often in the last few days.

"Let's not fool ourselves," Clent cracked his knuckles, cleared his voice. "You don't have to be a gay man to practice BDSM, bondage, whatever it is we just saw. I have gone to strip clubs, lots of times before I was married. I saw some shit, weird shit, chicks poppin' grapes out their pussies into guys mouths, backroom specials, clown night. You name it, and there's someone out there into it. This right here? What's on this tape, it isn't that crazy. Crazy to you and me? Sure. Because it's not us, we're not into it. But this was just a sexual encounter with toys and some dude who went to long lengths to build a pulley system allowing him control over his partner. This isn't a crime, there was nothing even there, to me at least, that would leave me to believe that Gary Thom was capable of murdering those two people. He looked nervous, he looked like he was the one that wasn't in control, and obviously, he wasn't. Not in this video, it was easy to tell who was the sub and dom."

"Are you suggesting that what we just saw wasn't *abnormal*? Those men doing sadistic and abusive things to one another? You saw the same thing, right? That was violent, that looked very much to me like they both had some sort of mental illness. Normal people don't do that," Pike retorted.

"Agree to disagree, Detective. *Normal* people do that; *normal* people do a lot of weird stuff. Shit Pike, I have a thing for my wife's feet. Turns me on. Am I weird or crazy? Am I more likely to be a murderer because I find my wife's feet sexy? This is not a mental issue, not in the larger sense of the word, at least. I promise you that. If people saw this, people in this town, yeah, you're damn right, they would probably vilify them both. Because you and I both know, our county here is closed-minded. We're not progressive. You're not gay in Emmet County. You move far from here before you come out of the closet. Or you live a double life like Mr. Simmons here."

"Yeah, okay..." Pike shook his head. The video made him feel sick, dirty, it was disgusting. Clent made a good point, though. It didn't matter how it made him feel; the video they watched didn't show a murder or even a motive. It showed consensual adults engaging in sexual activities in the privacy of Mr. Simmons's home.

"This doesn't help us much, does it?" Clent stood up, folding the chair.

"Look, we know some new things. It tells us stuff either we didn't know or presumed. For starters, the wife wasn't a part of this. Not with the sexual stuff. We know, from the timestamp of the video, this was filmed the first night Gary made it to Dennis' home. We know that this was filmed in the late evening. I think it was around six pm, maybe seven. That being said, the film was what? A half-hour long, give or take? We're pretty sure both Simmons were dead for two days before we found them. That leaves the rest of the night after the filming until the following evening that the murder would have had to occur. That gives him the window of two days before you and Vanessa knock on their door."

"We have a rough timeline," Clent added. "That's good."

"Yep," Pike was jotting down more notes. "So, what happened in the next twenty-four hours that turned Gary here in a psycho killer? That's still speculation. However, we know it wasn't an accident during the sexual act."

"You stopped the video before it ended?"

"I did," Pike nodded. He clicked play.

The two men walked out of the frame for roughly 90 seconds before returning on-screen wearing terry cloth bathrobes. They brought with them folding chairs; they both set them up, taking a seat in front of the camera. Dennis spoke first.

"That was fun," he was slightly out of breath. "I very much enjoyed that; I hope you did too."

"Yes, I wasn't sure what to expect, very anxious going in, but," Gary nervously laughed, almost embarrassed to talk about it, "I would do it again. I'm glad I tried it."

"So am I," Dennis smiled, he reached his hand out, rubbing Gary's shoulder.

"I have a few more days, so I am sure we can find some more fun things to experiment with while I'm here," he spoke into the camera.

"And we have another little adventure tonight, this one won't be as physically pleasing, but it should be fun" Dennis raised his eyebrows like an evil scientist from a cheesy eighty's horror movie "Scaaaaary," he joked.

"I'm just as excited!" Gary smiled; he rubbed his hands together playfully. "We're going to the infamous Leveille Murder House to look around," he exclaimed.

"That we are," Dennis smiled, still breathing a bit heavy. He wiped some perspiration from his forehead away with the back of his forearm. He stood up and walked towards the camera. "Let's clean up, and we'll head over. Remember," he looked into the camera with a devilish grin, "Don't tell my wife."

Both men chuckled as the video feed was cut.

"Well," Pike nodded. He clicked his pen, buried his face back into his legal pad.

"That was interesting," Clent added. "The Murder House?" he mused aloud.

"Are you thinking what I'm thinking?" Pike smiled.

"I think I am," Clent added. "But I don't understand why."

SIXTEEN

Gary Thom was twenty-six years old, fresh out of college, living at his parents' home, still trying to find his place in the world. He graduated from Saginaw Valley State University with a Nursing Degree and had been applying for jobs all summer, unable to land anything worthwhile.

Frustrating.

He had the degree, yet he lacked real-world experience—a proverbial catch-22. So, there he sat, wasting away the prime years of his life in his parent's basement. Closer to thirty than twenty, working a shit job as a receptionist for a local hair salon. His life was sad, depression set in.

Loser.

It was supposed to get better outside of High School.

That's what everyone told him. It was at first, his college years turned out great. Partying, finding himself, making dumb mistakes as all college kids did. Gary never liked girls sexually growing up. He understood this at a very young age. Middle and High School proved tough. He was picked on a lot due to his feminine nature, his soft voice, his frail figure. He cared little for sports, even less about cars and hunting as his father had hoped. He found interest in fashion, technology, and a passion for music.

Gary made the drive across state to visit the man he befriended over the internet. He was nervous, excited. He'd kissed his mother and hugged his father before he left. They'd never be comfortable with him going for a week to spend time with a man he'd met online. Instead, he told them this trip was for a business opportunity and mini-vacation wrapped into one.

They were excited for him.

Gary met the man on a website called **'Scruff.'** Gary was curious, adventurous. He was still learning about his sexual nature and was willing to try new things. He had put off signing up but bookmarked the site. One very dull and equally depressing night, he stumbled across the old favorited website from years back. Bored and curious, he browsed its contents.

His interest was piqued. Gary quickly made a profile, added a few photos of himself. One was an upper-body shot. He'd try to take care of himself, watched what he ate, was proud of his body. He'd chosen selfies for the remaining two photos, showing off his personal best feature, his million-dollar smile.

It only took a few days before an interesting man had sent him a message. His name was Dennis, some fancy businessman from up north. The site allowed users to rate the person's profile based on experiences with the user on the site and IRL, a fancy internet term for In Real Life. Dennis had glowing reviews from many men, a user on the website for over five years. It was like an amazon site for gay men, with a strong subculture into bondage and BDSM, which this Dennis character played in a large part of.

This had Gary feeling, probably a bit more comfortable than he should have been, speaking with a stranger over the internet. Basically, because of the high ranking on the site for Dennis, he realized this guy was probably not a lunatic, wasn't catfishing people, and seemed like a nice guy looking to meet up with other men to experiment with. Of course, he'd heard the horror stories about the Craigslist killings, the Grindr murders, like that guy in Canada who killed that poor Asian kid, chopped up his body and mailed it all over the country. But he would be smart, careful, have a plan in place. You can never be too cautious these days–crazies lived everywhere, hiding in plain sight.

It was two months ago when Dennis first messaged Gary. They chatted almost daily through the site. After a month, they exchanged phone numbers, began texting, talking multiple times a week. They built up a relationship, a friendship, slowly getting to know each other. Dennis was forthcoming. He was a married man, who had a child in college, loved his family, but favored the attention of men. If his wife found out, he'd be ruined, and he made sure everyone he met with understood his intentions, and he was cautious of who he invited into his life.

Gary exited off the highway. He was now in Emmett County. His GPS gave him another twenty minutes before he would pull up into Dennis's driveway. There were rules. He studied them to heart.

He was to play the role of an out of town business partner.

He was staying for a week for a convention in town they would both be going to.

Dennis made sure Gary understood that although he might not be faithful to his wife, that he still loved her and his son. Very open, very truthful. Gary respected that. He'd also showed Gary photos of his playroom, was open about his taste for BDSM as a dom. This thrilled Gary. The thought of being sexually at this man's disposal was more of a turn-on than anything.

There on the right-hand side of the road. A large beautiful two-story home, very modern, expensive. He saw Dennis' BMW in the driveway. This was the place. A lump in his throat formed, his stomach knotted with anxiety.

He pulled up, and the front door opened. Dennis came out with a broad smile, followed by his wife, drink in hand, also with a smile. She was pretty, petite, in her early fifties. Her hair was done up cute with lovely blonde curls—the picture-perfect happily married couple.

"Welcome! How was the trip!" Dennis met Gary at his car, grabbing his bags for him.

"Hello," Gary exited the vehicle. He shook Dennis' hand, firm, warm. His wife offered a hug, careful not to spill her drink.

"I always get so excited when Dennis has friends come to visit," Nora sipped her drink. Gary couldn't tell what it was, but it was definitely mixed, and it was only noon. "He's been so lonely since Brandon went off to college. Nobody to play with."

"Nora, dear, please," Dennis looked somewhat embarrassed.

"I'm very grateful to you both for hosting me," Gary was slightly guilt-ridden, lying to this man's wife, but he did so anyway, and he did it convincingly well. "I'm excited to get my hands dirty with that Camaro," he smiled playfully at Dennis.

"As am I," Dennis laughed. "Plenty of time for that later, though, please come in. Let's get comfortable. A drink or two?" Dennis was cute. Older than Gary by at least twenty years, but kept in good shape, rugged, handsome look of an early two-thousands George Clooney. Gary didn't mind that at all. Salt and pepper hair, strong thick shoulders.

"No offense, I didn't know you had friends so young," Nora waived the men into the home. "You look like a baby," she said, smiling.

"That's kind," Gary smiled. "I'm not that young, but I get that a lot. It's my babyface," he joked. The lies came easy now.

"You can't be a day over twenty-five?" Nora walked carefully up the front porch.

"Add ten years," Gary replied. He shrugged his shoulders to Dennis while Nora's back was turned. Dennis smiled back.

Lies, lies, and more lies. It was part of the fun. He was enjoying this, albeit maybe too much.

"We hired Gary here to work out east for us. He spent a few months training with me at the office over the summer. We hit it off, old guys like me like to pretend we're young, you know that dear," This time it was Dennis with the little white lies, and the soft touch of playful humor.

"Well, you came at the perfect time. I've made lunch," Nora entered first. "And margaritas!"

The three of them ate, drank, and talked the early afternoon away. Gary remembers the lunch fondly, he and Dennis hit it off. His wife was even pleasant. He made sure not to focus on her too much. He was eager to spend some quality time with her husband. The less he saw her, the more he could enjoy his time with Dennis and not worry about the entire affair aspect of their sexual adventure.

The evening hit, he and Dennis excused themselves out to the garage. They left for Dennis' "Man Cave," where they could be alone to do manly things and so, that they did. Dennis showed him his garage, led him into the back room, behind the large toolbox he rolled out of the way.

"I know that seems a bit scary, hidden sex room," Dennis chuckled. "I have gone to great lengths to keep my wife from knowing. It would crush her, and I worry about how she would handle it if she was aware of my other life. So, don't be alarmed that its sort of hidden. Just extra privacy," Dennis explained to him.

Dennis was soft-spoken and very aware of Gary's needs. He went out of his way to make sure he was comfortable. Dennis assured him they could move as slow as Gary needed. But, Gary was very relaxed and had no intention to move slow. He was excited. And so, they decided not to wait until the evening and to let the fun begin.

"Of course, before we get too far with the fun stuff, did you bring the contract?" asked Dennis.

The contract, Gary got it as an email attachment, spent a full day going over it before finally deciding he was okay with it. He had it signed and ready to go. Gary was okay with the filming of the sexual act (more-so excited about it), which was what the bulk of the contract was about. He knew Dennis had too much riding on the privacy, and he thought the filming added an element of naughtiness to the act. You only live once, he thought.

•   •   •

When all was said and done, Gary was elated. The sex was euphoric. Dennis was good, and he was excited to explore the fantasy again, and hopefully soon. Escape and pleasure were needed, and it came in orgasmic shattering delight during intense sexual acts. But before round two, there was another reason why Gary was so excited to meet with Dennis.

The Leveille Murder House.

They had finished filming, cleaned up with a shared hot shower that was installed in the garage. They took a seat out in the main garage, admiring Dennis' workshop and getting to know one another. Gary couldn't help but bring it up.

"...So about the Leveille house?"

"I can see how excited you are to go see that place," Dennis teased. "You are really into that stuff, huh?"

"Oh, god, I love it. I watch all the shows, read up on all the paranormal books. It's fascinating. I even stayed at the Haunted Handley Hotel, the one the Shinning was written about."

"Really?" Dennis seemed interested.

"Yeah, it was quite an experience. This place, the Leveille home, has gotten pretty popular in the last year. I heard a new owner purchased it, going to turn it into a haunted Air BnB.

"Well. Let's not wait," Dennis stood up, took out his phone. "Let me just text the Mrs."

Dennis texted his wife not to stay up, that he and Gary headed into town to get a few drinks at a pub. Instead, the two men got into Dennis BMW and drove down the road about a mile before turning onto a snow-covered dirt driveway.

The Murder House.

SEVENTEEN

Pike woke up from a restless sleep. His back ached, his shoulder hurt from sleeping cramped on the damn love seat in his office for the third night in a row. He needed a shower and a few Advil to ease the pain. It was seven am, and he got a measly four hours of broken-up sleep. He rubbed his eyes, yawning hard. He was overdoing it, hitting it too hard. He needed to take a step back. He needed to recharge, regroup, get a solid eight hours.

He'd just awakened, and he was already pissed at the world, not a good start for the day.

Pike moved from the worn loveseat over to his disaster of a desk. He opened one of the drawers and pulled out a bottle of Listerine. He spun the top off and put it to his lips, taking in a large mouthful. He swished the liquid around in his mouth, the burning on his gums and tongue. He envisioned a million microscopic cartoon germs exploding into nothingness like on the commercials. He gargled the bright green liquid until the burning faded away. He bent over and spit into his small wastebasket.

"My hygiene has gone to shit," he fell onto his desk chair. In an hour, the department was going to be crawling with officers. Well, for a small department at least, it was going to be the busiest part of the day. He grabbed his overnight bag (a small gray fannypack) and made his way into the bathroom. He washed his face at the sink, applied deodorant, just enough to mask his foul odor. He needed a hot shower. It had been days. He started to reek, and a coat of deodorant and body spray wasn't cutting it anymore.

Pike had two goals today. Once accomplished, he'd take the rest of the day for personal and mental care. His boss was already riding him to take a step back. One thing was for sure. He needed to speak with Gary Thom's parents. Two days ago, his parents came to town, despite constant threats from the locals who wanted their son's blood. The police department warned them of the hostile threats. Yet, it was good they were willing to aid in the investigation. A lot of confusion swirled around their little boy. When people get riled up, and they set their minds to villainize someone, it often falls on the lap of the families and friends.

He had called Patricia Thom, Gary's mother late last night, before the viewing of the video. He apologized for the timing of the call; it was unprofessional of him. Yet, they told him, anytime day or night to call, so fuck it, he did. It was a quick conversation. It was essential to see the Thom's as early as possible tomorrow. He had a few questions that could be important to the case. He hadn't even woken them. How could they sleep? Their son was on the hunt by local and state police for murder, mutilation, and cannibalism. Not many nights of rest in their future, so he thought. He didn't keep them long. They agreed to meet up in the office.

The next thing on Pike's to-do-list was to pay a visit to the Leveille house. He had a hunch, and the dots were slowly connecting. He just wasn't sure what type of picture was forming.

He had a room meeting room ready for when the Thom's walked in. Fresh coffee was brewed and set out for the heartbroken parents. He spent time speaking with the two of them over the last few days. They took their coffee's black, and so he prepared them two steaming cups. There would be tears, lots of them. He readied himself for that. He went over his notes one more time to be appropriately set for the interview. They showed up at 7:30 am, right on the dot. He got them comfortable and began his questioning.

"Good morning, Patricia," Pike shook her hand, pushing her coffee closer to where she sat. "Freshly brewed, hot, black just the way you like it."

"Thank you," her voice was soft, broken. The strain of the past week weighed heavy on her face, the darkness around her eyes, sullen, lost in a sea of unyielding despair.

"Brian," Pike shook the father's hand next. The large man simply nodded in reply. "Yours, the same, straight black." Pike handed him his cup as well.

"Thanks," he took a cautious sip. He too hadn't fared well, the grief-stricken eyes, the lifeless tone in his voice.

"You folks getting any sleep?" Pike asked. He took a seat on the opposite side of the stark white table. The room was simple, small void of much of anything at all. A table with chairs, a window looking into the hallway, Bright fluorescent lights stung their eyes.

"What do you think?" Brian was blunt, almost rude, but yet not.

"I see," Pike frowned.

"It's been hard enough dealing with our son," Patricia added. "Then we get these evil stares, and people recognize us from the news when we spoke the other night. We should never have done that interview. And the hateful things online..." her voice was broken, her hands trembled. Brian's large meaty hands reached out, held them, steadied her.

"Yes, I can only imagine the pain you two are going through," Pike drummed his fingers on the table. He caught himself doing it, stopped. It was a nervous habit, one he tried to control. He craved a smoke. Instead, he popped out a small package of gum, Trident. He offered them a piece; they declined. He took a piece himself.

"What can we help you with, Detective?" Brian took over the conversation.

"I will make this quick," Pike added. "And folks, if you need to go home, be comfortable, again, we don't need you in town. We've got your statements. The rest can be done easily over the phone, or we can visit you. We must put your health first. We will remain in contact about the case. You will know everything as fast as we can inform you."

"No, we want to be here, we want to find our son," Brian cleared his throat, he squeezed his wife's hand hard.

The Thom couple, both heavier-set sat with sickly expressions, as if their life was slowly being drained from them. Brian was bald; thick dark framed-glasses sat atop his flat nose. Pike wondered if he played football when he was younger, had those broad shoulders. It looked like the man could throw a mean right if he needed too. He guessed Brian Thom was a hunter, comfortable in the woods, as well as a bar.

Patricia Thom, she seemed like the church type. The American Wife raised their son, mostly with little help from her husband. Not because he wasn't there, or abusive, but because men didn't raise kids, they disciplined them taught them how to fix shit. Underneath the extra forty pounds she no doubt added after the pregnancy, Pike thought she was probably a looker when she was younger.

"Some evidence has come into play," Pike flipped his yellow legal pad to a new page, clicked his pen and began writing.

"Okay?" Patricia asked.

"Your son and Dennis, we have them on video. They discussed going to see a home, down the road from where Dennis lived."

"Video?" Brian repeated the word.

"Yes, there was video evidence, a sexual encounter."

"Oh God, what...what was on it?" Tears rolled down her cheeks.

"I'm sorry, I'm not at liberty to discuss that. But I need to know what they may have been talking about. Had Gary discussed anything about a residence in town or doing anything with Dennis when he got here?"

"He mentioned something to me the day before he left," Brian spoke up. "He was excited because he was going to meet this guy, this Dennis guy for a job opportunity. He said he was going to stay up here for about a week, a mini vacation. I could tell he was lying. He doesn't have much of a poker face. I didn't like it one bit, but what am I supposed to say? He's a grown boy, a man. I try to be supportive, you know? He got a degree; we're trying to help him until he lands a job. I told him to go into a skill trade, and those jobs pay, he'd be set. He wanted to go into Nursing to help people." Brian shook his head, angry with himself.

"I understand," Pike nodded. "He's an adult. It's honorable to be there for him, help him get where he needs to go. You're both loving parents, it shows. No one is blaming you folks; we're still piecing everything together here."

Patricia fell into her husband's shoulders, burying her tears into his dark red flannel shirt. He put his heavy arm around her, held her tight. He comforted her.

"We appreciate that," Brian held it together. "Gary said to me, this meeting was near some famous haunted house. The one where the young lady came home to her husband, or fiancé or whatever, killing her sister. Then she killed him in self-defense. He told me he wanted to check the place out."

"Gary loved that stuff," Patricia added through sobs. She took a napkin from the table and patted the tears away. "Always watching those shows about ghost investigators, reading books about hauntings. Wouldn't surprise me that he wanted to see that house."

"What else can you tell me about Gary? Anything we may have missed, something like that, the connection to the house, his fascination with hauntings, etc.?"

"No," Patricia said.

"Still haven't heard from him? No phone calls, no texts? Mysterious numbers calling you?" Pike rallied off questions in quick succession.

"No," Brian added.

"You still think our son did this?" Patricia shook her head. "I know it may look that way. He fled from your officers. He was probably scared. He wouldn't...he *couldn't* do this; you have to believe us."

"Thank you for your statements, folks," Pike finished his sentence on his legal pad. He looked up to them with kind eyes, "...it's my job to gather evidence, hoping to find your son, safe. Bring him in for questioning and get done to the facts about what happened in that garage. Beyond that, it's up to the courts. Are you sure you folks want to stay here another night? Not that I think you need to worry, but I think it would do you both good to be around ones you love at this time. To sleep in your own bed."

"You'll see," Patricia's face turned red. "He's innocent. He's a victim here too. There's more to this thing, you're not seeing the whole picture yet."

"I hope your right, ma'am, I do. I just want to find the killer and put them to justice. Thank you again, your free to go," Pike shook both their hands, nodded with a smile. He made his way back into his office with a deep and frustrating sigh.

"Detective?" Clent lifted his own cup of coffee up high, as a gesture of good faith, a cheer to the day sort of thing. He took a slow sip. "Need this after our late night. Morning came too soon."

"Yeah, I'm sorry I missed it, Detective," Vanessa stood next to her partner. They mapped out their day, prepping their workload. "I couldn't stomach the thought of what was on those tapes."

"Just your good old fashion bondage with two consenting adults," Pike dropped his legal pad with a thud on the desk.

"So, I heard," Vanessa moved out of Pikes way, allowing him access to his desk. It was apparent the Detective was not in a good mood. He looked like shit. When Vanessa had first met the Detective on that snowy Michigan night outside the murder scene, he was a handsome, rugged Detective. He walked with confidence, had a sense of passion in his step, one of the good ones. Despite the age difference, she was struck by his handsomeness, his quick wit. But this man who fell into his desk chair, rubbing his temples, was a ball of tension.

"Anything with the parents? Thought I'd swing by before we gas up and hit the town," Clent spun the legal pad around towards him, to read it for himself. The word "Mom" was followed by "Innocent," which was underlined three times.

"Parents still having a problem coming to terms, aye?" Clent sucked air through his teeth, rubbing his thin mustache with his thumb and forefinger.

"Perfect little boy wouldn't harm a fly," Pike nodded. "Same song and dance. I needed a connection between the two homes. It looks like he did have a thing for the Haylee murders, though. He wanted to scope the house out."

"Lots of folks do, always getting calls to that house for trespassers," said Clent.

"His record is squeaky clean, though, right?" Vanessa added. "I mean, I get it. That's gotta be a hard pill to swallow for a parent. A nonviolent, normal kid, now wanted for a sadistic double murder?"

"Yet there it is, isn't it?" Pike added.

"What's that?" probed Vanessa.

"The pill, it might be a hard one to swallow, but it's not going away. You may choke on it, you may gag, but that pill is reality, and there's no escaping it. Their son murdered two people, innocent people, ate them, cut off one of their heads, cut off his testicles. This is dark shit, this is out there, fucking horror movie crazy stuff."

"And yet, he was still a human," Clent interjected. "A person, someone until supposedly the night of the murder, was just a regular guy like you and me. Innocent until proven guilty. That's how we do it."

"Innocent? That's a joke, right? Look, I don't go around fucking men, tied up in black latex, hung from ceilings for a fun Saturday night. I don't think either the victim or Gary are completely normal people. The only real victim here was Nora. Killed because these sick and twisted men." Pike argued, his words laced with anger.

"Really?" Clent was a bit taken aback at the statement.

"—Look, I get it, all right. It's the human condition. I'm a parent too. They love their kid, but the truth of the matter is, every killer we have ever put behind bars has parents. Not all of them were raised bad. Some were just born bad, twisted, sick, weird. They hid it long enough before they snapped. I'm Afraid Patricia and Brian are going to have to come to terms their little boy was a nutcase. So, whether or not the pill is big, small, hard to swallow, or whatever, it doesn't mean they don't get to not swallow it. Because we're burying two people, what's left of them at least."

"Twenty years from now," Clent spoke up, clearing his voice. "You knock on my door, tell me one of my kids murdered someone, mutilated, ate their corpse, I'd break your jaw. Tell you to fuck off; you're lying. Nothing, and I mean **nothing** you or anyone else could say that would make me believe otherwise."

"Yeah? Is that so?" asked Pike.

"Yes." Clent was blunt.

"I'm not following your point?" Pike was not backing down. "Other than you would be afraid to face truth, reality. Sometimes, officer-and you should know this-there are lots of collateral damage when sick fucks disrupt the mundane lives of the greater society. Gary Thom didn't just kill Dennis and Nora. He ruined the remaining days of his parents, his friends who cared for him, the family of the Simmons, their kid in college, all their friends. He fucked up a whole lot of people. No passes for that, none. He needs to spend the rest of his life behind bars. I don't give a fuck if he is someone's kid. He is a murdering son-of-a-bitch who deserves the death penalty."

"The world isn't black and white," Clent shook his head, almost disgraced by the conversation. "A normal person does not do that without warning signs. What happened? Did he go over twenty-five years of his life without ever having a breakdown? Without having any signs? He went to college, had a few parking tickets, nothing on his records. Nothing in all the people we've talked to, at least in his files, claims he was ever aggressive, let alone violent. You go to bed normal, wake up the next day a killer? We're missing something. It's why you can't sleep. Its why this is eating you up, because you can't make it. There's no telling, not yet at least."

"You were there. He was in the home. He fled. His fingerprints are everywhere. When the test labs come back, his bodily fluids will be on the vics. His DNA will be on them. He did this, and you know he did. So, again, tell me, what's your point here?" Pike was irritable. Anger was stemming up, almost at a boiling point. He tried to control it, to force it down, but his temper was stewing.

He was about to explode.

"My point?" Clent downed the rest of his coffee, crushed the paper cup, dropped it in the waste-paper basket. He swung his uniform jacket over his shoulder, began walking towards Pike's office door, "—Is that this shit makes zero sense. Still no motive, no reason." He looked over to Vanessa, "C'mon, we got route.".

"Yeah..." Pike looked down at his desk, his jaw tense. He'd been clenching his fists tightly.

"—And hey," Clent stuck his head back into the office. "You need some sleep, pal. You look and smell like shit. Get some rest. We can chat about this after we've cooled down."

"Hmmph," Pike huffed.

Clent closed the door. He left Pike alone with only his notes and thoughts.

Pike stood up, his hands now trembling, the anger overbearing. In a fit, he swiped everything off his desk. Papers, pencil holders, his morning coffee, they all went spilling onto the floor.

"Fuck!" he yelled.

Then he collected himself.

He counted in his head, backward from ten. He was breathing deeply between each number.

Clent was right about one thing: it didn't make sense.

But it never does.

And, yes, he did need sleep.

EIGHTEEN

Haylee pulled out a loaf of stale bread from her cabinet. Next came the peanut butter, a jar of raspberry jelly, and a butter knife. Her stomach rumbled, and although her appetite hadn't been the healthiest aspect in her life, she tried to force herself to eat something at least twice a day. Breakfast had been a half a bowl of corn flakes with skim milk; dinner was a sloppily made peanut butter and Jelly. Dessert would be a glass of wine, something dark, and one Norco to help her pass out. Keep the visitor at bay. She couldn't handle another episode like the one on the couch.

It had been an emotional day already, opening up to Aaron in the parking lot of her Psychiatrist's office. She wasn't ready for that, but it was good, a sense of calming came over her. She hadn't opened up to anyone in years. She told him about aspects of her life she hadn't even shared with Robbie. She learned to swallow her demons to bury them deep. Too many judgments, too many know-it-alls with all the answers to questions she never asked.

Aaron was different. He listened, didn't offer to change her; instead, he was just there. It lifted a bit of burden, and her shoulders felt lighter. She missed having a human connection. A shoulder to cry on. After Robbie and Camille, she withdrew. She pushed away the world. Her home was her cage, and she willingly locked herself up.

Haylee chose a Pinot Noir, cheap, just like her vodka. She'd wait an hour before bed to wash down the pill. But, as for the wine, that was to celebrate. She'd been proud of herself. She took steps today, steps into gaining some control back in her life. She should thank Aaron, but of course, she wasn't sure how to do that, she'd kept him at bay. Never really interested in listening to him, or even getting to know him past a casual neighborly relationship that started with getting her pills. They became casual friends, which led to hanging out a few times a week in her apartment watching movies. Now, they'd spent the last five days straight together.

It was nice.

Their time spent together was mostly investigating the rumors. Aaron took to combing the internet for news and information on the Simmons' death, while Haylee self-medicated. They'd sit up at night, she'd drink wine, he would smoke, and they discussed every aspect of the murder. They bonded over this terrible murder, bonded over drugs and alcohol. Not the best relationship, but hell, it was a relationship.

Haylee poured herself a deep glass of the red wine, took a bite of her peanut butter and jelly sandwich as she made her way back into her living room. Trayer was there, waiting patiently to cuddle with her on the ugly green couch. Aaron was working a late shift at the coffee shop he managed. So, tonight, for the first time since her former neighbors' murders, Haylee was alone with her thoughts.

That scared her. She liked the distractions.

She took a seat next to Trayer, he placed his large, adorable head on her lap, moaning like a grown man as he cozied up against her. She took another bite of the sandwich, the cheap white bread sticking to the roof of her mouth, forcing her to tongue it free. The television was on Nick-At-Night, airing repeats of stupid nineties sitcoms that gave her a false sense of safety. She liked that they always ended with a lesson, and happily ever after. It was hard to let the darker thoughts creep into her head when the nonsense of canned laughter and cheesy dialogue echoed throughout her living room.

Haylee hadn't heard much of anything new on the news about the case in the last few days. The last thing she and Aaron had read was the fact that the suspect, a man named Gary Thom, was still potentially on the loose. Experts thought the chance of him surviving the woods on the snowy winter night was slim, but there was not a body to confirm their thoughts. They made mention on a few news reports that Gary fled into the woods without any supplies, lacking even a coat. The temperature dropped below zero that night, and it was doubtful he would have survived a second night with the record low temps.

So, where was he?

The thought made Haylee's stomach turn.

Aaron bookmarked a few Facebook groups he found interesting so that Haylee could keep her eye on them. She pulled up the town's Neighborhood Watch group page first. Here is where they found the best information. People are quick to repost and gossip, it was like an unfiltered high school lunchroom. Lots of keyboard detectives (much like themselves) shared opinions and information, most bullshit, angry emotional responses. But there were nuggets of truths. Aaron was better at this than she was, but none the less, she found herself scrolling through the hundreds of comments.

News had broken about the sex room, the bondage, the hidden lifestyle of Dennis Simmons. It was hard for Haylee to understand. She knew them both well enough; she spent a few days over their home. More than a few if she was honest with herself. Robbie and Dennis shared a few beers. No one suspected a thing. Of course, this development brought out the trolls in full force. Lots of ugliness spread on the board; it made Haylee dizzy with anger. The same thing happened to her when Robbie killed her sister. People joked, accusations of incest with her sister sharing Robbie as a lover popped up all over the internet. The amount of cruel and disgusting filth lies, and outright slander that came from pages like these made Haylee suicidal for quite some time. A victim all over again.

She rubbed the scars on her wrist. They were subtle now, but that night in the woods. When she blacked out, she had done something to herself. She doesn't even remember it, but she has the scars to root her in the reality of it.

So, she swallowed down the large lump in her throat before she continued through the comments. She had to bite her tongue multiple times. She wrote up scathing replies to the ignorance. She had to stop herself, take another long sip of wine, and promptly delete. She would not feed the trolls. She needed some self-control in her life.

Haylee reminded herself, through the thick layer of bullshit, you could find truth in these threads. And a few minutes later, there it was, buried within the comments of the post from a few days earlier. A user had brought up her old home, that there had been recent break-ins to the residence. Somebody claimed that they saw a BMW parked in front of the old house, right around the time the murders would have happened. BMW's stand out in Emmet County, Dennis drove one. The user said it struck him weird, as he was aware of the home, a local legend, as did everyone around here.

Haylee was lost in the thread, reading all the replies when her phone loudly buzzed on the coffee table. It startled her. She jumped in her seat. She'd lost track of time; it had already been two hours since she first logged into Facebook. Trayer, who had dozed off growled at the sudden movement.

Always her knight in shining armor.

"Sorry, boy, scared myself, that's all," Haylee calmed him with a few well-placed scratches behind his ear. She grabbed her phone, answered it.

"Hello?"

It was Aaron, fresh out of work. He just pulled up into their shared driveway. "Yeah, come in," she hid a smile. It was late, nearing eleven PM. She had secretly hoped Aaron would want to hang out a bit before she passed out from the pill she was saving for bedtime. She felt safer with him there. Having a man back in her life, not even a man, just a companion—someone to share her space with, to communicate with, to feel a human connection again.

She opened the door. The cold, bitter air stung her face.

"You sure it's not too late to hang?" Aaron stepped through the threshold carrying a couple of coffee's and a brown paper sack. "I got coffee and cheesecake," he held them both up as if using them to barter his way into her living room.

"No coffee, but I'll poke at the cheesecake," she smiled, taking the bag from him. Inside the bag was a plastic container with a plain cheesecake slice drizzled with raspberry topping.

"You can reheat the coffee in the morning then, should still be better than that instant shit you gave me the last few days," he smiled. Trayer jumped from the couch, buried his head into Aaron's crotch, almost knocking him over.

"He's definitely warming up to you," Haylee sat back down, popping open the plastic container.

"You think?" Aaron dropped to one knee, allowing Trayer to roughhouse with him playfully, before joining Haylee on the couch.

"This will go nice with my wine," Haylee took a small bite of the cheesecake, it was overly sweet. She'd grown accustomed to Sugar-Free jelly and Natural Peanut Butter sandwiches. She followed the bite with a long drink from her glass.

"Research?" Aaron pointed to the screen. "Anything new that I missed while I was at work?"

"People are just saying they think they saw Dennis' car parked out in front of my old house days before the murder," Haylee shrugged. "Not sure why that's important either way. People are always breaking into my old place—stupid kids daring each other. Dennis is a grown man, though, so, why would he be doing that? Doesn't make much sense to me."

"Grown men do dumb shit all the time," Aaron took a sip of his coffee.

"These people are disgusting though," Haylee took the laptop, she highlighted a specific post about how *they* all deserved to die because 'God Hates Fags!' "—brings back painful memories. I had to leave social media for over a year when it happened to me. Probably shouldn't have ever got it back. That's why I literally only have like twenty-five friends, most family members."

"A lot of idiots say things they'd never say in real life on the internet. For real, it's the single reason why humanity is doomed. The Internet allows us to put a filter over reality. Makes it easy to spread hate, its sick." Aaron nodded. "Ever hear back from your pops?"

"Not yet," Haylee shrugged. "Thankfully. Although I wouldn't be surprised if he doesn't show up at my doorstep tomorrow and try to drag me home, he'd probably push me to go back to a psych ward again. I don't want to deal with him, not right now, not until I can get my head right. This whole murder thing has me really shook. I need to be here, slow down, get my head right."

"Well, yeah," Aaron agreed. "The two murders? It's bizarre, too many similarities."

"What about your parents?" Haylee asked.

"What about mine?" Aaron repeated the question.

"You don't talk much of them. Are they dead?" Haylee asked bluntly, forking a small piece of cheesecake into her mouth.

"Naw, I think I told you my dad is a Pastor? And my mom is a Sunday school teacher. They're Godly people."

Haylee had to stop for a second, ponder if she ever had this conversation with Aaron before. Her days muddled together, the drinking, the pills.

Maybe she had? Did she know that about his dad? There was a sense of guilt, as if she should have known, remembered.

"I remember you said you lived out in Hollywood, trying to be an actor?" She thought that sounded right.

"Yeah, I did some small gigs, standup comedy stuff. I worked on some scripts, tried to get my name out there. Then, you know the accident happened. Haven't made it back out there, hope to go again. I haven't given up that part of my life yet. Just, you know, buying time until I'm ready. Been working on a good project. I think it will be my ticket back."

Haylee did remember that. A party that went too far, his buddy smashed into a tree. He'd gotten hurt, went back home to be close with his family.

"You would have liked my mother," Haylee added.

"Why is that?" Aaron pulled a baggy of weed from his back pocket. "You mind?"

"Just smoke it outside, but roll away," Haylee replied. "She was close to God. Spiritual, you know? A Godly person, as you so called it."

"What about you?" Asked Aaron. He took out some papers, flattened one on the coffee table, and began to roll a joint.

"Not so much," Haylee sighed. She followed with another long gulp from her Wine. She barely touched the cheesecake.

"You don't believe in God at all?" Aaron asked, his voice lacking in judgment, more inquisitive.

"I have seen some things. I can't explain to you the stuff that haunts me," Haylee swished her drink in her hand. "I mean, there is stuff I don't understand, but the thought of a White-Bearded man in a long silky robe doesn't make sense to me, especially with my life. If there was a God like that, then fuck him. Seriously. Why put me through all this?"

"Harsh," Aaron licked the paper, wetting the joint closed. "But, I get it."

"Really?" Haylee seemed shocked. "Figured with how dominant the church is with your family, I assumed..."

"—What, that I was a bible thumper," Aaron laughed.

"I mean, yeah?" Haylee returned a smile.

"Well, truth be told I am. I believe I am a Christian. But, to be fair, I hold certain concepts of religion at arm's length. I had my struggles after my accident. You know, did the whole getting mad at God thing. I blamed him for it all, stopped going to church. I fought with my parents over it too. I lost my faith. I fell hard, depression, anxiety, the whole kit, and caboodle. I got on my own pill-cocktail prescribed by my family doctor. I found ways to medicate too, starting down a route that was going to bury me sooner rather than later."

"What happened?" Haylee found herself invested in someone else's story for the first time in years.

"I had driven down to Emmet Park, around 1:30 am on a Saturday night. I was meeting with this guy from the city. The normal guy I got from had told me to start buying through his friend."

"Weed?" Haylee asked.

"No," Aaron frowned. "Not proud of this, but I started using heavy. I was in a terrible mindset. One of my buddies from out West came to visit. I started using it. Bad shit, heroine."

"Oh," Haylee listened intently.

"So, this guy pulls up. Gets out of his car. I had my girlfriend with me at the time, enabler, real winner type of girl. Anyway, he walked up to my window and pulled a gun. Dude drags me out of my car, throws me onto the floor. Grabs her, does the same. He has me on my knees, both of us, my girlfriend too. Has the gun to my head," Aaron played with the joint in his fingers, looking at it, lost in thought. "Robs me, takes all my money, my wallet, my girlfriends' purse, all my cd's, both our phones. He pistols whipped me, tells my girlfriend if we say anything, he will kill us both. Knows where we live, all that good stuff."

"Jesus..."

"So, I get out of the hospital, with a concussion, staples in the back of my head. Embarrassed, broken, thinking my parents would disown me, never speak to me again. Their perfect Christians, right? Look at their fuck up, druggie son who failed at being an actor. Instead, they cried. They apologized for screwing me up. The guilt was insane. Here I fuck up, and they, what? They just forgive me, want me to get better. I'm too miserable. I'm a piece of shit, ashamed, and just a dumb kid who fucked up his life. My parents, they wouldn't stop believing in me. They wanted to send me to rehab. Trust in God, they said. Find your faith."

"They really stuck by you?" Haylee asked.

"I didn't deserve their love. Instead, I got pissed. I don't have an addiction, right? Me being a prideful jack ass, so I leave their house, stay around a few of my buddy's places for a while—couch hoppin'. One night, about a month after it all happened, I sat down, and I prayed for the first time. I told myself I could stop without rehab. But it wasn't a week before I was sneaking around looking to get it. I sat there one night, on a shittier couch than this one," Aaron looked down at the ugly green couch. "I just fucking lost it. I cried so hard. My buddy thought I was having a bad high, a breakdown, mentally. I sat there, purging myself of all these tears. I fucking prayed my heart out. Haylee, I swear to it, as I'm standing here right now-just like that, I was free. I beat the addiction, haven't shot up once. Thanks to the power of someone up there. Whether he has a white beard, or he's a damn spaghetti monster, someone or something empowered me. I stopped using. I was cured, sober."

"But, you smoke weed?" Haylee questioned.

"Heroin kills, weed doesn't," Aaron smiled "I was cured of the bad shit that was killing me. Weed is different. I got off all my anxiety pills, depression pills. I hardly need the pain pills anymore, which, if the doctors knew my history, wouldn't be a thing. So, enjoy them while I have them to give. Weed did that for me. It's my antidepressant. It's my pain reliever. It's my anxiety meds. It's not pharmaceutical poison going into my body. It's from the earth."

"If you're happy, and you got off that other stuff than smoke to your heart's content, just do it outside my house. I hate the smell of it," Haylee joked. "Listen, I'm no one to judge anyone about anything. I need those pills you get me because I wouldn't be able to live as I did in the past. I can't face those horrors again. I have been through too much. Too fucking much. It's bad enough, almost too much."

"That's also why I give you them," Aaron added. "I'm not a drug peddler. I saw firsthand what it does to someone. You're different. I get it, I do. And I don't want you getting pistol-whipped, or worse, because you're trying to buy Norco off some dumb fuck who wants to rob you. If I can't talk you out of the pills, then at least I can keep you from the weirdos."

"Look at you," Haylee teased. "Trying to protect me?"

"No," Aaron shrugged. "You are my neighbor. I just thought it was the right thing to do."

"Well, thanks," Haylee slumped onto the couch. "Honestly, I needed a friend this past week. I have no one here. And with everything going in, I may have lost my marbles more than a few times. You've grounded me, kept me sane. I owe you."

"Naw man," Aaron waved off the gesture. "We're just two fucked up people stumbling through life."

"You can crash on the couch tonight if you want." Haylee was almost afraid to ask. She wasn't sure what was happening between the two of them. She wasn't looking for love, sex, or anything from a man, or anyone. That part of her brain, her life, that was over. She was damaged goods. Yet, there was something more prominent there, something more unconditional, a bond.

"You would feel better if I did? Safer?" Aaron asked.

"I would," she replied.

"Sure," he smiled. "First, though, since I opened up to you. How about you tell me about your parents? I mean, you started too, back at the doctor's office."

"Yeah..." Haylee nodded.

"I mean, I don't wanna force you, but I'm interested, you know...if you wanna share."

"I think I need a second glass of wine for this," Haylee stood up. She refilled her glass to the brim, emptying the bottle of Pinot Noir into her cup. She drank half of it down, warmth swarmed to her cheeks, the fuzziness crashed over her thoughts. That felt better; she would sip the rest. She needed the liquid courage to help her share one of the worst moments in her life, and there had been many. It would exhaust her mentally. She'd then pop that Norco and pass out in her bedroom.

"Seriously, you don't..." Aaron protested, feeling as if he overstepped a line.

"—No, I will tell you," Haylee interjected. "I just needed to drink my courage. When I was thirteen, I had already seen a bunch of specialists, phycologists, therapists. I had been diagnosed with every psychotic disorder you could think of. Downed pill after pill to try and keep the voices and visions away. My dad's fault. He pushed them on me. No one ever listened. Anyway, my mom went more on the spiritual route. My dad forbade her to bring what he called 'voodoo shit,' his words not mine, into his home. So, my mom began sneaking me out to meet this lady, Lydia, from the cable show I was telling you about. She was sweet, very nice."

"Right, the lady with the sexy ass tattoos who talks to spirits and all that stuff?" Aaron asked.

"Yes, sexy tattoo lady," Haylee shook her head before continuing. "Things were getting better with her. She taught me a lot of spiritual stuff. I was burning the sage, wearing the crystal necklace, everything. My mom made me hide this all from my dad. They fought a lot over me. I could see, even as a dumb kid, what I was doing to their marriage. Little broken Haylee, the freak, the crazy one who heard voices. The daughter who ruined our family. It was always my fault. My dad eventually found out about Lydia, the secret visits, the voodoo lady who actually helped me." Haylee took a deep breath. Her story was wordy, flowing like a broken faucet. She was shocked at how easy it was to speak aloud. She thought she would choke on the story; her voice would tremble. No, it was as if it had been wanting to come out, waiting to be spilled. To be released deep from inside her.

Aaron held onto every word, like a six-year-old kid being read to by a loving parent before bedtime. Eyes wide, digesting everything Haylee was giving him.

"So, he flipped out, typical overprotective cop dad stuff. It was the biggest fight I'd ever seen them get into. My sister and I hid in our rooms. We held each other under my big heavy comforter, and we cried. I remember it so vividly. My mom took us both stormed out of the house. Told us we were going to our grandparents. She dropped us off there. My sister and I, confused, scared. It was terrible. It was over the summer. I remember, because my grandparents didn't have air conditioning, the house was sticky. Tears mixed with sweat. My mom didn't come home that night."

"What happened?"

"My sister and I fell asleep on the couch. Our grandparents let us stay up late watching the Cosby Show on Nick-At-Nite. I never grew out of that channel," Haylee forced a laugh, filled with remorse, laced with sadness. We got a call late; it woke my sister and I up. My grandmother picked up an old cordless phone, and they still had them back then. She just started balling. I can still hear her frantic voice. My mom had left our home after fighting with my dad all night. She returned to pack up bags, and he was waiting for her, drunk and angry. The bags were still in the car. So, I understand how one simple accident can change someone's life. Because, a drunk driver was going over ninety down a country road, the guy ran a stop sign. The son of a bitch hit my mother's car on the driver's side. They both died. Dead, just like that. I never got to see my mother ever again. Gone."

"Fuck..." Aaron muttered.

"Haylee, the poster child for a fucked-up life. Sometimes, honestly, Aaron, I wonder how the hell I am still alive. How am I still standing here? How haven't I eaten a bullet yet? Overdosed on those pills. I have fantasized about it often." Again, she rubbed the wounds on her wrists.

"That's nothing to joke about," he said.

"I'm serious," Haylee wiped away a tear that snuck its way out. She tried to fight it back, to stay strong.

"Don't say that," Aaron shook his head.

"I can tell you why," Haylee took the Norco from her pocket, popped it onto her tongue. There was one last drink of her wine, and she guzzled that down. "Because I am too damn afraid of what's waiting for me when I die. I'm too fucking scared."

NINETEEN

Aaron stepped outside of Haylee's duplex apartment, he needed a breather, to catch up with his thoughts, digest everything that was shared on the cramped puke green couch. Things got pretty intense, emotionally, and he needed to smoke. He'd been trying to make a connection with his beautiful neighbor for months, and they finally had a breakthrough.

One of the main reasons why Aaron even moved into the apartment in the first place was because he learned Haylee, the sole survivor of the Orr Road Massacre, rented out the attached apartment. He showed up to walk the premise with the landowner when he caught Haylee taking out her trash. A strikingly gorgeous woman in her early thirties, jet black hair, flawless skin. He'd describe her as drop-dead gorgeous to his parents. He'd known she was pretty just from the few photos of her that floated around the internet during the ordeal. He was not prepared for how pretty she was in person, though. He would never have known underneath her good looks; there was a broken, insecure mess of a human being. A beautiful mess, fucked up even more than he was.

And he was a pretty fucked up mess.

His front door was only a few steps from her own. He left Haylee alone with Trayer on the couch. He needed a smoke, shit; he needed it bad. It was cold as shit outside, so he hugged Haylee, and told her he would be right back. He was going to change out of his work clothes, smoke a quick joint, and then he would be back to sleep on the couch.

That made him smile. No one had ever asked him to protect them. It was a powerful feeling, manly, in a weird, sort of way. He put the joint to his lips, reached into his coat pocket, flicked his lighter, lit up the joint. He inhaled deep and strong holding it in his lungs. He reached into his pants pocket, this time grabbing his house keys. He exhaled, a cloud of dark smoke escaped his body, lost into the night sky.

Aaron entered his home. He flipped on his living room light. His home, an exact copy of Haylee's, except his had far less décor. His house was mostly barren, resembling more of a college dorm than a lived-in apartment. He had the basics, an old worn couch, a flat-screen tv mounted to his wall. He had a kitchen table, even a study where he wrote. His walls lacked anything of personality, with the exception of a myriad of professionally framed movie posters.

Aaron paid no attention to his kitchen, walked over to his desk, where he left his laptop charging. He had taken another deep inhale from his joint when he noticed his laptop was missing.

"What the hell?" Aaron coughed, the smoke spilling from his lungs.

"—You that high you didn't even see me? Sitting there in your kitchen? Seriously?" A deep voice broke the silence of the room.

"The fuck?" Aaron spun around, now facing into the kitchen. A large, well-built man sat at his kitchen table with his laptop open. He was older, late fifties, thick as an ox, his arms bulged through his tight long-sleeved under armor shirt.

"Get out of my house, man!" Aaron yelled, his voice high pitched, the joint fell from his mouth onto the stained white rug.

"Shut up," The man stood and made his move. He was as fast as he was muscular. He was on Aaron quick, his worn black boot stepping onto the joint, putting it out.

"Don't hurt me," Aaron fell backward onto his writing desk, his arms flailing above his head.

"Your name Aaron?" the man asked.

"Y-Yeah," Aaron stammered.

"Good," the man lifted his foot, bent over, he picked up the crushed joint. "Hope you weren't expecting to get your deposit back, you just burnt a hole in your shitty carpet." He handed Aaron the crushed joint.

"Have a seat," he pointed to the kitchen table. "We need to talk."

"Who are you? Get the fuck out of my house, man! Ima call the cops, you can't just break-in," Aaron was trying to stand his ground, but there was no way he wanted a physical altercation with a man this size. He looked like

Arnold and Stallone had a child. He was an old man buff like he had nothing better to do with his life than hit the gym four hours a day. In reality, there was more truth to that than Aaron would ever realize.

"My name is Gerald Leveille, former Detective, Haylee's father. I'm here on business."

"Jesus," Aaron shook his head, holding his chest with his right hand. "You almost gave me a heart attack, man."

"We need to talk," Gerald pointed to the kitchen table again.

"Dude, you can't break into my house and just make me talk to you," Aaron was pissed now, the anger was overtaking the fear.

"Oh yeah?" Gerald let out a cocky laugh, almost mocking him. "You should password protect your laptop, kid." Gerald walked over to the kitchen. He took his seat back, spun the laptop over to face Aaron. He had a word document open. It was Aaron's latest project.

"Shit..." Aaron mumbled.

"So, this is your end game?" Gerald shook his head. "Tssk, Tssk, here I thought my daughter made a friend. It's been over three years now. Yeah, know? Three years since she walked in on that fucking retard Robbie. I'm glad I taught my girls how to shoot. I just wish it was me that pulled the trigger—three years rebuilding her life. Then one afternoon she calls me, tells me she isn't going to therapy anymore, talked it over with some guy. A friend, I think, doubtful a lover, I don't think my poor daughter will ever trust like that ever again. Just another thing that man stole from her. A normal life, to love someone."

"Look, man," Aaron protested.

"He killed me fucking little girl" Gerald was almost yelling, he had to catch himself, he didn't want Haylee to hear his voice. "—He was trying to kill my other too. I trusted that man with their safety. How do you think that makes me feel? I wasn't there. I couldn't protect them." Gerald shook his head. "I got Haylee set up here. She wouldn't come home after the incident, wouldn't give me a chance to take care of her. I blew it. I know I did. I did a lot wrong raising those girls. I begged her to come home, to be with me. She wouldn't. So, here I am, trying to fix the wrongs, okay? Trying to take care of her from Ohio. Trying to get her treatment, get her help. She's all I got. I will stop at nothing to protect her. You get that, right? I pay for her medical bills, her car, insurance, I pay her damn rent. I'm going broke. I can't do it forever. I wish I could."

"Dude, seriously, why are you telling me this? I don't even know you."

"Because it was getting better, bridging the gap between us. She was letting me back in. Then you came around. Did you talk her out of treatment? She needs help. Can't you see that? She's sick. She's got issues, deep, psychological issues. You're ruining her life, and for what? This?" Gerald threw the laptop at Aaron. He caught it in his lap.

"It's not what you think," Aaron shook his head, searching for the words to explain.

"I know who you are, Aaron Hauser. I was a detective for over twenty years. I know all about your time in Hollywood. The accident with your drunk buddy. Cute, you almost died in that wreck. I know about the drug deal gone bad, too. That's twice you stole life. You think you deserve to be here? Yeah, I know things. I was good at my job. The way I see it, you're using my daughter to write this shit screenplay. Real-life sells, except you're fictionalizing it just enough. You're a fucking joke." Gerald caught his fist tightening. He wanted to break the fat fuck's nose.

"That's not true," Aaron shot back. "I'm not using anyone. I get inspired by people I know, I care about, and I write. It's therapeutic, you asshole! It's what I do. Haylee doesn't know, because there isn't anything to tell. This is my personal project. So, you have nothing, show her I don't care," Aaron retorted. Except he lied, he did care. He cared a lot. There was a great chance that if Haylee found out he had intended to move in, befriend her, gain her trust, just to learn more about her and the original murder case, so he could write a screenplay-his big break-back into Hollywood, then she very well may never speak to him again. When he thought about it now, it was a total douche move. It hadn't happened that way in real life, they became friends, with real emotions, and it just so happened he wanted to write a screenplay.

"I don't mind testing that theory," Gerald stood up, extended his hand. "Give me the laptop; we can walk over there now. Show her the evidence."

Aaron didn't say a thing. He stood there frozen, his lips pursed tightly together in anger.

"That's what I thought," Gerald shook his head. "Here's the deal. You stop talking to her, cut her out of your life. No explanation, no nothing. Just leave her alone. You're toxic to her health. She will come back around to me, and I can get her back into the right state of mind. She needs to be on meds. She needs to straighten herself back out. If I see or hear you talking to her, I will be back. Oh, and don't worry, I forwarded the word document to my email, in case you decide to get smart. It's one forward away to her."

"You think I'm a shit person," Aaron pushed back. For the first time in his life, he was standing his ground. Enough was enough. "She told me how you treated her growing up. You want to blame me for your relationship with your daughter? Try listening to her. It's her life. It's not yours. Her life is fucked up because you're overbearing, a control freak. Those are her words, not mine."

"Keep talking those words, and you won't have teeth to speak," Gerald's blood pressure boiled. It took all his self-control not to backhand the mouthy prick.

"Fuck you, man," Aaron got into Gerald's face, nose to nose, except Gerald, was about three inches taller than him. "You broke into my apartment. You're threatening me. I call the fucking cops, and it doesn't matter you're a former detective, you don't have control here. I do."

"So, call them," Gerald called his hand.

"Haylee is important to me," Aaron did not waiver, his face flushed with anger. "—yeah, she hates you, I can see it in her eyes when she talks about you. You were a shit dad, a shit husband. I know, because she opened up to me, she told me the stories of how you pushed her and your wife away. I know about your accident too, the one where your wife drove off mad, angered, because you were too stubborn to listen. I survived my accident. Haylee's mom didn't, and that's something you get to deal with. And despite that, as much as she hates you. All she wants is her damn dad to fuckin' listen to her, to help her, not control her. So, again, fuck you. Get out of my house."

Gerald's right eye quivered with tension. It had been years since the boiling rage took over him. The words stung, they hit him like a heavyweight boxer's jab, followed with an unprotected kidney shot. He could almost feel his legs get weak, wanting to double over from the blow. No one has ever spoken to him that way. Gerald was a fighter, a bully grown into a man who enforced the law, both for a career and in his home. Yet, he was a father too, and he'd become soft in the years, his sturdy exterior, the large frame, bulky muscles, all of it a front—a way of masking his own issues. Aaron not only tapped into them, but he also smashed it over his head.

Gerald took a deep breath. His hands now trembled. "I should kill you for those words."

Aaron held; still, adrenaline overcame him like a wave. He did not fear the man before him. Despite the difference in size, he pitied him, no longer afraid of an altercation. He didn't think Gerald would pull the trigger or throw a punch. He was there to intimidate him like he did his daughter and his wife. "Do it," Aaron huffed a response back.

Gerald's jaw clenched. His thick hand raised to his forehead, pulling his hair back in frustration. "You don't get it," his voice dropped, almost as if it broke in his throat. He turned, pointed to the back door. "Replace the door, flimsy lock. Popped it with a damn credit card."

"Seriously?" Aaron noticed his heart was pounding, he'd sweat through his shirt, and his forehead was soaked with beads of salty sweat.

Gerald nodded. He walked to the front door. "You're wrong, though," he grabbed the door handle, making his way out.

"I doubt that," Aaron shot back, his confidence growing. More importantly, he was lucky as fuck.

"She hasn't told you everything," Gerald stopped momentarily. "She didn't tell you about when Robbie and Camille found her naked in the woods two weeks before the murders did, she? Blood everywhere, incoherent? Complete mental break down."

"What?" Aaron frowned.

"Maybe get your facts all together before you open that fat mouth of yours next time," he turned back around, squaring off to him. "There is a shit ton about Haylee you don't know about."

Aaron wasn't sure how to respond. He stood there, staring at the man. Curiosity swirled in his brain.

"You got anything to drink around here?" Gerald released the door handle, let his guard down, loosened his shoulders. "I could use something strong."

"You're not leaving?" he muttered.

"We got off to the wrong start. But we need to talk, man to man. I want what's best for my daughter. I love her; she is the only thing keeping me here. I own my past. I live and breathe it every day. You got that part right. You stood up to me, that takes guts. You fucking prick, I think I may see what Haylee see's in you. Now, pour me a goddamned drink." Gerald reached out his hand and extension of truce.

"This night is fucking weird, man..." Aaron wiped the sweat from his bar, dried off his hand. He reached out, accepting the gesture. Gerald's overbearingly large hand practically engulfed Aarons, crushing it. "—Ouch, fuck!" Aaron winced.

"We can work on that handshake," Gerald tapped him on the back of the shoulder, they made their way together, an awkward duo, into the kitchen where Aaron grabbed a bottle of Grey Goose and two shot glasses.

"Let me text Haylee and let her know I will be late getting back over there."

'—You sleeping with my daughter?" Gerald's brow raised.

"No, No, she wants me to sleep on her couch," Aaron stammered.

"Ha," Gerald poured a shot, raised it to Aaron, and downed it quick. "I'm just messing with you."

"I can't take this man," Aaron poured his own shot, swallowed it hard. "What the hell are you talking about with the wood and blood?"

"—Yeah," Gerald frowned. "We're going to need a few more shots for this one. Sit down, kid. It's not an easy story to tell or hear..."

TWENTY

Aaron sent Haylee a text late last night, saying he would be later coming back to her apartment. She took the Norco, passed out, hoping he'd be asleep out on the couch when she woke up. He wasn't. He also hadn't texted her back.

...And that was strange.

She awoke, free from the night terrors. Thank God, the Norco did the trick. It was the only thing these days that worked. She tried the sage, the crystals in her pocket, the things that had worked when she was younger. Back when she had visions during the day, they did not, however, help her with this specific reoccurring dream. The dream with the creature. That hadn't started until right before the murders, right after they found her in the woods.

The wine, however, it muddled her head. It was too sweet; the hangover was intense.

Trayer awoke with her, excited, a one-hundred-and-sixty-pound puppy jumping eagerly around her bedroom waiting to be taken outside. Her head throbbed, and Trayer's eagerness only exuberated the pain.

Haylee slipped on her robe, along with her slippers (not the pink one Robbie bought her, she'd burned everything Robbie ever touched), and made her way to the kitchen. She let Trayer out back to do his morning business. First, she needed to text Aaron, make sure everything was okay

Had she made things weird last night? She wasn't that bad; she didn't black out the conversation they had. Perhaps she scared him away?

"Fuck," Haylee whispered to herself. Insecurity crept up her spine, sat at the base of her shoulders, clawing at her brain. She was an idiot to open up so much to one person. She scared him away.

What other option was there?

She pushed the thought away. First, she wanted to deal with the ever-growing headache. What was the best cure for a hangover? How about onset depression with a hangover? Haylee decided to skip breakfast, showering, and even brushing her teeth.

There was only one remedy that popped into her mind. Seagrams, or rather, wash the hangover away with more alcohol. Straight, on the rocks, just the way she liked it. She may even take one of her good pills, a Norco, just to help her get through the morning. She was done being a victim, being broken, embarrassed, utterly depressed. So, fuck it, she would drink.

She poured a glass of Seagram's, three ice cubes. She decided to skip the Norco, for now at least. She sat on her couch, curled up in a blanket. She pulled out a murder mystery novel she had been trying to get through. She enjoyed the mystery, the suspense, but usually, she couldn't stomach the violent parts, brought out the darkness in her. She skimmed those sections as much as possible. She let her television stay on in the background. Her good old friend, random early nineties sitcoms to keep her lonely, miserable life company. It was a quiet morning, dreary grey skies, at least it hadn't snowed in twenty-four hours. It had hit Northern Michigan hard the last few days. The schools canceled, the interstate was closed multiple times over the previous few nights.

She re-read the same paragraph three times before closing the book. She couldn't focus. Her mind kept wandering on Aaron and why he hadn't returned. At least, she realized after a strong sip of her drink, for the first time since the double murders happened, she wasn't thinking about that. One miserable thing for another, she shook her head.

Haylee decided that today was a couch day. She had a lot of those days recently. Days where facing any aspect of the world either outside her duplex or even on social media was too much for her to bear. Her anxiety was on high today. It would take a few more glasses of Vodka before her nerves let lose a bit.

She wasn't always like this. She remembers as a young girl; their family took summer trips, wonderful family vacations. They camped at Picture

Rocks, traveling across the country, museums, enjoying the world around them. She loved the adventures. But as she aged, the darkness grew, then her mother died, and everything went crazy. Then Robbie and Camille, just one shit storm after another until there was nothing left of Haley except a husk of a human, fearful of everything.

Haylee turned on a streaming service, found one of her favorite sitcoms as a kid, one she would watch on Fridays with her mother. It was the classic, corny, more canned laughter. She wished life was more like her sitcoms and less like a violent Stephen King novel.

She was halfway into the second episode and two glasses into her early morning binge drinking when a knock interrupted. Immediately, Haylee thought it was Aaron. Probably, with two cups of coffee, surprising her with breakfast like he usually did on his days off. She would act mad, even though she was more relieved than anything. But she wanted to keep him guessing, make sure he understood how much of an ass he was for what he did. She let out a sigh of relief. She stood up; the drinks hit her. Her head went weightless, fuzzy. Just enough of a buzz to keep her cool, yet not come off as a complete lush.

She collected herself, opened the door, "—Where were you..." Except there was no Aaron.

"Miss Haylee Leveille?" Detective Pike took off his hat, placing it at his chest, he nodded to her pleasantly. "It's been a while. I hope all is all right?"

Alongside him stood Officer Vanessa Velasquez, in uniform, hands held behind her back. She nodded with a smile. She was strong, stout, yet her eyes instilled with kindness. There was a softness to them, unlike the Detective, who was hardened.

Detective Lewis Pike. Haylee had met the man three years prior, with Robbie and Camille. He ran the case, and afterward, they stayed in touch briefly after the murders. Pike reached out to her a couple of times over two or three months, taking her out to dinner, just to make sure she was adjusting. He didn't have to do that. The case was open and closed. He was one of the good ones. To her, at least. He never tried anything creepy; it wasn't because he was hitting on her; he was genuinely making sure she was adjusting after the ordeal.

During the investigation, Detective Pike treated her well, respectful. He asked hard questions, but that was his job. He was one of the good ones, never judged her. But she could tell, he buried the pain inside him, just like she did. She could see it in his face. So many memories, painful, gory, visions of death, and wickedness that he had to swallow down deep into his unconscious just to get up and go to work every day.

"Detective?" Haylee was caught off guard. She was probably too drunk for this. No, she was *definitely* too drunk for this.

Haylee was wondering when the police would come knocking on her door about the murders. Now, she really wished Aaron was with her, to keep her calm, collected.

"That big dog of yours locked up?" Pike asked, noting the lack of barking.

"Hasn't wanted to come in yet, still out back," Haylee replied. "I suppose you would like to come in? My house is a mess. I wasn't expecting company." Her first white lie.

"We would," Pike smiled, offering Vanessa to enter first.

"Now's not the best time, if I'm being honest," Haylee held open the door.

Pike and Vanessa entered the premise. Pike noted immediately it smelled of alcohol. An open bottle of Seagram's Vodka, half-empty, sat beside a glass. It was freshly poured, three ice cubes filled about a quarter of the way up. Pike glanced at his wristwatch, a quarter to eleven. She started early.

"May we have a seat?" Pike asked.

"Let me just clean up," Haylee was already embarrassed. She knew why Pike glanced at his watch.

Drunk Haylee, drinking away the pain.

"Please don't," Pike insisted. "We aren't here to disrupt your life. We have a few questions about the Simmons murders. I am sure you have heard the news about your old neighbors?"

"Unfortunately," Haylee snagged the Seagram's bottle quickly, moved it to the kitchen counter. She met back with the two in the living room. She took a seat on the couch next to the two of them.

"Been all over the news, hitting the national stuff now," Vanessa added, her voice deeper than Haylee expected. "Big deal in a small town. Scary stuff. Sick stuff. Everyone is on edge."

"Yeah, people tend to do that when murder happens in their backyard," Haylee was sweating. "Somethings don't change." She was always nervous around the detective, the police in general. She had nothing to hide, but the very thought of them back in her home, questioning her, brought up a lot of painful memories. "Last I read the guy-the man you think did it-is still on the run? Gary Thom, right?"

"If he somehow managed to live through the last five days in the Michigan wilderness, with the weather we've had, then yes. But we know he ran into the woods, on foot, ill-equipped to take on that sort of weather. No jacket, no boots, just a hoodie, tennis shoes, and jeans. I think we will find his body soon enough, probably dead due to hypothermia," Pike answered. "But to answer your question, he has not been found, no."

"I know why you're here," Haylee cracked her knuckles, one at a time, a nervous habit.

"Oh?" Pike frowned. "You do?"

"The murders," Haylee frowned. "They seem, similar, right? Too close for comfort for me. I read they were stabbed, from the back right through the neck. I read he ate some of them too, just like..." Haylee struggled, choked on her words. "Robbie."

"Similarities, yes. Both in the nature of the crime scene and the location. Coincidences? Likely not," Pike added. "I am sorry that this is bringing up old memories. I am sure it can't be easy for you."

"Who is she?" Haylee pointed to Vanessa. "Where's Officer Clent? I liked him."

"They're not seeing eye to eye," Velasquez nodded, her voice stiffened with judgment. "Pike asked me to accompany him."

"Oh," Haylee frowned.

"Officer Velasquez meet Haylee, Haylee Officer Velasquez," Pike introduced the two. "She is helping me with parts of this case. As is officer Clent Moore, he's off duty at the moment, however. They both were at the crime scene. They two who got called in for the courtesy check when the perp made his escape. We are working as a team, despite what Vanessa here may have hinted at."

"Do you know Mr. Gary Thom? Have any relationship with him or his family?" asked Officer Velasquez.

"Only know of him from what I have read on the news, social media stuff like that. Personally? No, he was from the other side of the state, right?"

"He was," Pike added. "He seemed to know you, maybe though, would that make any sense to you?"

"Me?" Haylee frowned. "I don't know how. We didn't even have any mutual friends on Facebook. The only connection I found was through Dennis, just a mutual friend."

"I see," Pike began jotting down more notes.

"Are you doing okay, Miss Leveille, are you feeling well?" Velasquez asked. She had seen many victims of abuse, physical, mental, substance. It came in many forms. Haylee looked like she had been fighting a never-ending battle, losing more than winning. It was in her eyes, a sense of discomfort, complexity that Vanessa couldn't quite put her finger on.

"Not really, to be honest," Haylee sighed, she wanted another drink. She would have to wait until they left. "This double murder has stirred up a lot of...issues. I mean, not that everything was great before, but I was managing. Now, everything is pretty screwed up. It's just been hard."

"Have you been taking care of yourself, Haylee?" asked Pike, a note of concern on his face. "When we spoke last, your dad got you some help here in town. A doctor, to help, you know, sort all this out for you?"

"Yes, I am, still seeing him," Haylee lied. Another white lie. One the Detective wouldn't look up on because it didn't help his case. He was being friendly, maybe even genuine, but when he left, unless it had to do with the murders, he wasn't going to care about.

"Good," Pike smiled. "That's good to hear. Mental health is a tricky thing, and it can go south fast. Sneak up on you, you know?"

"I do," Haylee replied bluntly. "So, why do you think this Gary guy knows me?"

"Well, there was some evidence at the crime scene. They found your initials on a sheet of paper in one of the victim's mouths. H-E-L. At first, we thought the killer just misspelled Hell, which was bizarre in its own right. Then, we started noting some of the connections to your case, as you mentioned. It dawned on me...your middle name."

"Elyce," Haylee said softly. "Why would he do that, though?"

"We were hoping you could shed some light on that for us," Pike frowned.

"I swear to you. I have no connections to that guy, at least none that I know of. I mean, I was shocked as anyone to hear about Dennis' secret life. I knew them both; he and Nora well. We'd become sort of friends. I just never thought, no one did. At least I don't think."

"What about your relationship with the Simmons?" asked Velasquez.

"What do you mean? I said we were friends. I was closer to Nora than Dennis, but we all got along."

"Anyone else know about your friendship with the Simmons?" asked Pike.

"No, not really. I mean, back then, it was Robbie, myself and Camille. We didn't have many friends here. My dad knew that's really it."

"Okay," Pike nodded. "I think it's important you keep yourself on the lookout for anything suspicious. Call us for any reason, here is my card," Pike handed Haylee over his contact information. "maybe something will pop up, some sort of connection you may have overlooked. Please, let us know."

"Should I be worried?" Haylee's hand trembled as she held the card.

"Always be worried, never let your guard down," Velasquez added. "But, again, anything at all, call us. If it's an emergency, don't hesitate to dial nine-one-one. Please, always caution on safety. Here, this is my personal cell. I am available day or night. Even just to talk, okay?"

"In fact," Pike interrupted, zipping up his winter coat to his chin. "If you have somewhere to stay, out-of-town maybe? Until things blow over. That might be good. We can always talk over the phone. You're not needed here."

"Okay," Haylee nodded, placing the card on the coffee table. "Thank you, detective, officer."

"Take care, we will be in touch," Pike shook Haylee's hand and walked out into the freezing morning air alongside his partner.

•　　•　　•

"Well?" Velasquez asked. She and Pike made their way to the unmarked black SUV.

"Well?" Pike responded, pulling the car keys from his long black peacoat.

"She seemed spooked, and to put it lightly...not well, in any way," Velasquez waited for Pike to unlock her passenger side door before settling into the passenger seat.

"Yes," Pike nodded, turning the ignition. The car roared to life. "I'm sure the news of the murders put her on a downward spiral. When I saw her last, she seemed to be getting ahead of it. I can only imagine what this is doing to her. She has seen some shit, Vanessa, believe you, me."

"Struck out on a link with our perp, though," Velasquez frowned.

"I figured," Pike slowly pulled onto the street from his parked position. "We're missing something, and until we find that murdering s-o-b, we're going to be blind. Where on earth is Gary fucking Thom."

There was a moment of awkward silence. No radio, no small talk. Just the rumbling of the engine, the blinking of the turn signal, and the sound of two people breathing.

"Detective Pike?" Velasquez broke the silence. "Why did you have me come out to the residence with you?"

"What do you mean?" Pike shot back, barley giving it any thought.

"I assume it's because you and my partner got into the exchange the other day? He's been pretty hot about it. In fact, he won't stop going on about it."

"Clent?" Pike chuckled. "Fuck him, tell him to stop being a snowflake. We got a case to solve. I can't be worried about offending people. We're here to find this sick fuck. Right now, it's all I care about. If Clent wants to man up and talk, we can. I'm not apologizing, though. I'm a good cop that's seen a lot of bad shit. I don't need Clent Moore judging me about being more inclusive. I know my job, and I know how to do it. I asked you to go with me because I needed an outside perspective. I wanted fresh eyes with Haylee. Clent and I have a history with her; we were there with her three years ago. So, tell me what you saw back there, in detail. I need fresh eyes."

"Well, umm..." Vanessa stumbled. She could tell she hit a sore spot with Pike, and now he was quizzing her, deflecting perhaps? She thought for a moment before speaking. "I saw a woman, who we know has a history of abuse, survived a domestic violence attack that killed her sister. From her file, I know she has been through some psychiatric wards as a child and a young woman, recently as just a few years back. Very troubled past, not with the law, but a lot of death surrounding her. She is heavily drinking; it was a quarter to noon, and she had drunk half that bottle of vodka? She smelled of booze, words slurred, delayed responses. She was emotional, yet despite everything, she was coherent and answered seemingly truthful. Although, I doubt she is still seeing her doctor. She seemed intelligent, highly functioning alcoholic. She also seemed to be following the case quite closely."

"Good," Pike responded. "What else?"

"I dunno?" Vanessa paused for a second thinking, trying to rack her brain.

"Think," Pike replied.

"I really don't know."

"Haylee said the victims were stabbed from the back, through the neck, did you hear her?" asked Pike.

"You're right, she did," Vanessa cocked her head, thinking carefully on the statement.

"That was never leaked to the news, how would she know that?" Pike drummed his fingers on the steering wheel.

"Isn't that what happened to her sister? Attacked from behind with a kitchen knife? Stabbed in the back of the neck."

"Yes, that is correct," Pike nodded.

"Do you think she is just mixing the two events together? I mean, this has got to be a very rough position she is in, reliving this," Vanessa added.

"I'm not sure," Pike replied. "But I think we need to keep an eye on her."

TWENTY-ONE

"Well," Dennis pulled his BMW into the deserted home's driveway. He drove around back, parking it away from any late-night traffic as best he could with the snowdrifts. There wasn't much traffic down Orr Rd this late at night, but better safe than sorry. And already he was glad to play it safe, only a few minutes of parking the car behind the home a single vehicle whizzed down the street. It was illegal to be snooping around the private property of the infamous murder house, and the townsfolk are protective of intruders prying around the place. "...here we are." He set his hand gently on Gary's knee.

"Wow, this is the place, huh?" Gary clicked on his flashlight, a bright cone of light shown out in front of him. He grabbed Dennis's hand, enthusiastically. He peered around the outside of Haylee's former modest house. Her once perfect start-up family home.

"This stuff really interests you, huh?" Dennis laughed. He was a bit older than Gary, roughly twenty years older. He remembered his mid-twenties, looking to go out on adventures, driving through the supposed haunted cemetery just outside of town. Gary was thrilled to see the house. He didn't mind showing him the place, as long as they didn't draw any attention. He enjoyed Gary's time already. He was a smart young man, ambitious. A little nervous when they were intimate, but Dennis liked that.

"It does interest me," Gary added. "I love this stuff, not the murdering aspect of it, but the supposed haunting of it, if that makes sense."

"You believe in that stuff?" Dennis opened his car door and exited. It was a cold winter night, with rumors of a severe snowstorm within the next few days, as of now, they had to deal with a record low in temperature. He pulled up his hoodie from his winter jacket and tightened his scarf.

Gary joined him outside of the vehicle, his flashlight scoping out the outside of the home. "—In ghosts? Oh yeah, I run a paranormal group back on the west side of the state. My team would be very jealous knowing I got to visit the home of the Leveille murders."

"I bet," Denis chuckled. "Remember, make sure the flashlight stays on this side, we don't want to draw any attention to us. This is sort of illegal."

"Right, got yeah," Gary walked up to one of the windows looking into the kitchen. He had studied the case, how it all went down, the timeline, the whereabouts in the house. When he decided to visit Dennis, he'd ask if it was okay to sneak onto the property. Dennis was reluctant at first but gave in. Gary spent a few nights investigating the reports of the murder house.

"I was friends with them," Dennis added. "It's kind of sad for me, you know, being here."

"Oh," Gary frowned. He hadn't thought of that when he asked if it was okay to scope the place out. "I didn't realize you were close to them?"

"Close?" Dennis pondered the question. "My wife was closer to them than me. I met the fiancé a few times. We had dinner together. I never met the sister. My wife, Nora, she was pretty close to Haylee for the little amount of time they lived here. Haylee...she was a pleasant young woman."

"This isn't offending to you? That we're here?" Gary frowned. He assumed they hadn't known each other well due to the distance of the homes.

"No, it's fine, I can tell you a little bit about them if you want," Dennis added. This would be a good way for the two of them to bond. Get to know one another without Nora around, and not just in a sexual way.

"I know a bit, at least with what they think happened," Gary peered back into the window leading into the kitchen.

"What have you heard?" asked Dennis.

"Well, this is the kitchen. I read that Haylee had been dealing with some mental health issues? Robbie had been acting out in aggression with Haylee, that she had mentioned to friends and family that they had been dealing with ongoing issues with their relationship. That right here, near the basement stairs, is where Robbie took a kitchen knife when Kaylee was out of town and ambushed Camille. I read the autopsy report, they said he stabbed her in the back of the neck, and she fell down the stairs right there," Gary pointed to the closed door of the basement. "I saw drawings of the home; they filmed an episode of it on Spurned Lovers on the crime channel. They think Robbie wanted Camille, who rejected him and was going to kill Haylee when she got back home. Anger and lust drove him mad."

"That's sort of the story we got too," Dennis frowned. It was cold; his fingers and toes began to sting. "Really sad place here, I usually don't even drive past it. Hurts to know the pain in those walls."

"Why did he eat her, though?" Gary shook his head with disgust. "Like, how gross is that?"

"He snapped? I don't know. Don't like thinking about it," Dennis added.

"Then Haylee came home, right? Earlier than expected?" asked Gary.

"Yeah, they say she turned around due to a storm. She walked in, heard a strange noise from the basement, and found her sister's dead body. Robbie, on top of her, you know...doing all that sick stuff. He chased after her."

"I read she was good with a gun, her dad was a cop," Gray added.

"Self-defense. Shot him at the foot of the stairs, he fell back down. Police found her cradling her sisters' body. I guess she went mute for a while. I haven't seen or talked to her since it happened," Dennis added. "Such a tragedy...she still lives in town; heard she doesn't get out much. I tried to call her a few times. She never returned my calls."

"I thought you weren't close?" asked Gary.

"Close enough, my wife and I worried about her."

"I hear the place is haunted by spirits. They say something may have possessed Robbie, drove him mad," Gary explained. "Scary thought, though, huh? Even if you don't believe it? How can a person live a normal life, and then just turn like that, into a madman? Doesn't seem right, does it?"

"Yeah. I don't think we're supposed to know or understand how people turn like that, I don't like thinking about it," Dennis gave a nervous chuckle.

"Yeah?" Gary frowned, Dennis was right. This place was dark. There was negative energy pulsating from the home, the tension in the walls, the eeriness of the empty rooms.

"Listen, feel free to scope the place out, it's freezing, I'm going to warm up in the car. The place is locked up, so please don't break-in. I will be waiting for when you are ready, cool?"

"Okay, yeah!" Gary smiled. It was definitely cold outside, but Gary wanted to spend a little more time with the home. He dimmed the flashlight, a small Maglite he often carried on ghost hunting outings. It was small, dependable. He stared at the kitchen, his mind flooding with the horrors that stained the walls, the floor. Rumors of the sister's ghost haunting the home have been rampant. They say you can hear her screaming, falling down the stairs.

Gary took the side of the house slowly, his hand pressed up against its cold siding. To the right about ten feet down near the back of the home, was a second window. He stood on his tiptoes, looking into an empty bedroom. Vacant, lifeless, eerily quiet. He wondered who slept there. Haylee and Robbie? Maybe Camille. He wagered it was the master bedroom.

He wished he could get inside, look around. He wanted to see the basement where the murders happened. It was late, dark, freezing, the Michigan fields, the vast forest behind the home, all was quiet.

Until it wasn't.

Gary stood at the side of the home, near the back of the house, where it sat facing the forest a few yards back. He heard the most peculiar noise. Almost like a loud purring, from a large cat or perhaps what he thought a rattlesnake might sound like when aggravated. Except, it was a deep sound, almost guttural.

It was a strange sound, nothing he'd ever heard before.

"What the hell?" Gary spoke to no one, his breath forming clouds into the night sky. He hadn't expected to hear anything except save for a few random cars driving by. He decided to investigate, brightened his flashlight. He was far enough behind the property, unworried about a passerby.

He made his way around the corner. There was a double wooden cellar door that rattled as if something had just entered through its frame. It startled him, he jumped back, dropped his flashlight. "Shit," he almost shouted—his heart racing.

What the hell was that? Did something just climb into the cellar? Gary's mind raced. Should he go back and get Dennis? Should he check it out? Dennis asked him not to break into the home, but that was definitely weird.

Gary mustered up his courage, taking a deep breath himself. He walked closer to the cellar door. It was thick wood, double-wide. He centered the flashlight on the broken lock, looked as if it was ripped from the wood hinges. About three feet on the frozen grass was the broken lock, crushed to pieces.

"What is going on?" Gary kneeled to examine the thick wooden doors closer. That's when he heard it again, louder, it was almost mesmerizing. The rattling noise, the deep guttural purring, was calling out to him. The sound was—what was it? Gary couldn't think straight; the noise was muddling his thoughts. So soft, elegant, all-encompassing. He had to know what was making such beautiful noise. The hair on his skin stood upright, egging him on. He lifted the heavy door, slowly made his way down the steps into the basement. This would have been a back exit into the home. Gary assumed it would have remained locked at all times. Easy access into the house otherwise.

The purring, the rattling, it was persistent. He kept his light focused ahead of him, entered the main basement section. The noise came from the corner to his right. He slowly aimed the light towards the sound, and there, in the corner, it sat, hunched over, staring at him.

An abomination.

"My god..." Gary's mouth dropped.

TWENTY-TWO

Haylee sat on the foot of her bed. The bed she rarely slept in, still impeccably made. A small fleece blanket that normally decorated the bedspread was wrapped around her shoulders. She preferred the couch, near the television, in the center of her home where she could see the front and back doors easily. She felt trapped in her bedroom, no easy exit in case something happened, except one lone window, which wasn't easy to escape in case of an intruder. The room was mostly bare, minus a dresser that was her mothers and a vanity mirror.

The appearance of Detective Pike and Officer Velasquez shook her. She sobbed, wept hard and ugly, the empty bottle of Seagram's sat beside her on the bed. A picture of her mother framed sat on the other side. She drank the bottle down fast after they had left. She passed out on the bed, soon after polishing off the alcohol. It brought back a flood of memories of that night when Robbie went mad and the following days of mental anguish. She tried hard not to think of that time in her life, to erase Robbie from her memory, to forget about the last week of Camille's life. Then Detective Pike showed up, opened a flood gate of pain. So many raw emotions and memories washed over her.

Haylee awakened in a puddle of sweat a few hours after passing out. Her shirt drenched. It was late in the evening now, closing at six pm. She had nightmares again. She hadn't meant to drink so much she would pass out. Yet, she did. She was lucky. This time the creature didn't stalk her dreams. Instead, this was more visionary, flashes of puzzle pieces she couldn't quite put together. She hadn't dreamt it before, or had she?

There was a familiarity to it all, like a dream that escapes your memory the longer your awake. Little slivers left behind, just enough to poke you, prod you. Had she dreamt it before? A memory replaying in her head, a sense of Déjà vu?

She dreamt of the double murder. The man Gary he was in her dream. She was in his head, watched as he snuck up behind Dennis, knife in hand, stabbing him in the back of the neck and grabbing him by the hair. He pulled the knife back out, then slitting his throat, deep, across the Adam's apple. The sickening gurgling noise, blood pouring out, shooting like a fountain with every beat of his heart. So much blood. That scene replayed over and over again in her head—fractions of visions, emotions of pure anger.

It was horrifying. Too real.

She was out of liquor. Her phone was quiet, with no word from Aaron, or her dad. She thought of calling him, breaking down, crawling back to him like she always did. She hated admitting she needed him. Who was she going to turn to? Who would help her?

She gripped the photo frame of her mother in her hand.

She stood up, walked over to her dresser. She opened the top drawer, pulled out an old wooden box held closed by a string of twine. She took it back to her bed, unknotted the twine, and unraveled it. She hadn't opened the box since her mother passed; she was always afraid to relive what memories remained buried. Memories that would evoke the pain of dealing with the loss of a loved one. If Haylee was good at anything in her life, it was slipping away from reality, hiding from pain, running from sorrow, pushing back memories, both good and bad. She preferred numb.

Haylee's hand shook. She didn't know if it was from the alcohol or the fear of opening the box. Either way, she breathed hard, focused her mind. For the first time in over almost two decades, she opened its contents.

So many memories: birthday cards, photos of their family, concert tickets her mother had taken her and Camille to as kids. She relished these items. It had been so long, she took each one out slowly, allowing the memories to flood over her. She didn't rush them; each one she took time with, refamiliarizing herself with their tenderness. Treasuring the moments, she spent almost a lifetime trying to forget. She found happiness in them, not sorrow, not pain like she thought. She was surprised that through the tears streaming down her cheeks, she found a soft smile, natural and beautiful.

Then, she found what she was looking for. It had been so long ago. She was thirteen; she was thirty-five now. Would her number even work? Her email address? Her place of business still open? Haylee, after spending time with each of the box's contents, finally took out the business card of Lydia Cayce, Clairvoyant, Paranormal Detective, Psychic.

Haylee grabbed her phone. Would she remember? Would she help her?

TWENTY-THREE

Aaron paced around his kitchen all morning. Haylee's dad left before sunrise. They shared more than a few drinks. Gerald was a prick, that was for sure. However, the two of them bonded over alcohol and Haylee. Aaron wasn't sure how to move forward. He held cell in his hand, trying to figure out what to say, or to text to Haylee. He started to multiple times, only to delete the text and start over. When he poked his head out his widow, to check on her place, he saw the Police cruiser parked in her driveway. Two officers, one in uniform the other dressed in a suit, probably a detective approached her door.

Fuck, he thought. What were they doing there?

He needed to smoke. Which he did, a lot. The minute Gerald left, he grabbed his baggie and his bong. That was too intense for him, the whole ordeal. The conversation, the breaking into his house, waiting for him, the story about Haylee and the woods.

That shit was crazy, *really* crazy.

And, he was still drunk from the many shots he shared with her dad.

He needed to come clean with Haylee, about the screenplay he was writing. He didn't want Gerald to have anything over him. He wouldn't allow him to try and blackmail him ever again. He wasn't sure how she would react. Then, he wanted to hear her perspective about the woods, what happened. Because, what her dad just told him, that was not normal. That was some horror movie type shit.

He looked over at his laptop. He began to drown in his own self-loathing. Why had he started that stupid screenplay? Why, once they became closer, hadn't he stopped? But the more he learned about the story: the murders, her current state of constant fear, this was a once in a lifetime story. It truly was stranger than fiction, and he had a firsthand look into the crazy story. It was like it was made for a movie adaptation. He would fictionalize it enough, or if he got the right backing, Haylee would be paid as well. She needed help financially. Right? Maybe it wasn't such a bad thing.

He needed more weed. He needed a lot more weed.

Who was he kidding? He was misusing her trust.

"*Shit-fuck*," His brain cursed him. He always manages to screw up anything good in his life.

He pushed away the thought, first thing first. He needed to resupply.

Aaron, scoped out the front door, making sure Haylee's side wasn't stirring. He needed to get to his car without her noticing. He did not want to confront her, not yet. He didn't have a plan, no clue what to say to her. And, he stood her up after she asked him to stay the night. Sent her a single text, claiming he would be late getting back over. Except he never came back over. Another brilliant move. I

He grabbed his coat, car keys, and his favorite snapback Detroit Tigers hat and bolted to his car. First things first, he needed that weed.

TWENTY-FOUR

Gary crawled out of the cellar doors, pale, sweating, terrified. He was hyperventilating. His brain struggled to comprehend what had transpired. The cold air hit his face, stung his lungs as he breathed deep in. He crawled on all fours a few feet from the house, rolled over to his back, and stared into the night sky. His body was sore. His muscles ached, his stomach felt like razor blades were passing through him.

He started to gag. He coughed hard; his lungs burned, stomach cramped up. He rolled over to his side, vomited with intensity, his stomach spasmed. His back arched, spewing what looked like a fountain of crawling maggots. The vomit was filled with thick black mucus. It dripped from his chin into the white snow. Hundreds of larvae spilled onto the cold earth, crawling over one another. Terrified of the site, he scuttled away on his stomach. He wiped away the awfulness from his mouth. He moved back towards the Dennis' car in a panic. He looked towards the cellar; he sensed the eyes staring at him. There, the creature stood. Inside the cellar door, hunched over, peering at him with its brooding tongue hanging from its mouth. Was it following him?

"Oh god..." he muttered. The creature did not move. It stared at him, with its thin, lanky body spotted with dark coarse hairs, its skin putrid, decaying. It was a god-awful sight. It had a massive head, large eyes bright and red. Large antlers protruded from the skull, six sharp points on each side. Its skin around its face was even more decrepit compared to its body. Its flesh hung off its shredded chunks, parts of its face were utterly missing, other parts oozed with puss. And the black maggots crawled everywhere. They were moving freely through its exposed skin in and out of its muscle tissue. Even when standing upright, the creature was hunchbacked, its breasts sagged, swayed when it moved.

What happened to him? Gary's brain still weighed heavily in a fog. He remembered going into the cellar, seeing the creature in the corner, its grotesque sight, awful. The smell of·rotting flesh, formaldehyde, a strange, disgusting mixture of death and decay was overriding his senses. Then he blacked out. He awakened not long after, laying on the cold cement basement floor. He was naked; his clothes tossed aside the floor. Blood smeared between his legs, bleeding internally, no doubt. The creature was gone, nowhere to be seen. Gary gathered himself and fled. It hurt to stand, he'd been sexually assaulted by that thing. Or so he presumed. He quickly gathered his clothes, fighting through the pain.

His memory was coming back now; the creature's gaze still penetrating him. A soft whisper took his conscious.

Huuuuungry

It wasn't so much a voice, more of an urge. One that was not driven by his own needs. It was like a thought, an itch he couldn't scratch. A seed planted in his brain, ready to sprout into terror.

Gary closed his eyes, shielding his face from the creature. His body shook, both from the cold winter air and from pure horror at the creature before him. He hadn't known how long he lay paralyzed in fear. He curled up into a ball, fetal position and wept.

"Gary?" Dennis's voice broke through. "What on earth?"

Gary pulled himself back to reality. He looked up to see the cellar door closed, the creature gone. Dennis stood over him with his phone's flashlight on him.

"Dennis?" Gary's voice cracked.

"Are you okay? What happened? I stepped out of my car to smoke and heard whimpering. You've been gone for about a half-hour. Why are you laying on the ground?"

Gary stood upright. His mind was still foggy. He wasn't sure why he had been lying on the ground. His belt was loose; he readjusted it, shook off the dirt from his clothes.

"I don't know," Gary shrugged.

"Let's get you back, warm you up with some coffee. We can talk about it where its warmer."

"Yeah, okay," Gary muttered. Behind the fog, the desire was still there. The strange urge of hunger, thirst, but for something different, something he'd never experienced before. It was louder now. Stronger. What was it? Where had it come from?

"You look sick, pale as a ghost," Dennis opened the passenger car door for him.

"Yeah," Gary muttered again. Except, he only half-listened. Instead, he focused on the urge, the penetrating notion to quench the hunger.

"All right, well, get comfy, we'll get this sorted out back at the house," Dennis frowned, shutting the door once Gary got into the seat. Dennis was a bit spooked himself. The last thing he expected to find on the far side of the house was Gary curled up into a ball whimpering like a lost child.

He entered the vehicle, buckled himself in, shifted to drive and pulled out of the old murder house.

TWENTY-FIVE

Aaron pulled up into his driveway after a long night of errands and procrastination. Haylee's lights remained on next door, and he wasn't ready for a confrontation. He parked his car and turned off the engine. He waited to see if Haylee was going to stir in her apartment. Was she going to come out and confront him? It had been almost a whole day since he ghosted her. He left earlier, picked up enough weed to last him through the weekend, grabbed a bite to eat at a local restaurant. He could barely stomach the meal from all the nerves. He wasn't eager to return home; he couldn't push it off any longer; he had to speak to her at some point. Thankfully, it looked like he was being spared, for now. Her side of the duplex was quiet, one single light on in the living room. He assumed she'd passed out on the couch early.

Aaron exited his vehicle, grabbed his bags, his leftovers from the Italian restaurant in town he ate dinner at prior, a half a marinated meatball sub that he would snack on tonight if he ever got his appetite back. His body hurt today, physical reminder of the accident, so he used his cane to help him out of the car and into his duplex. He fumbled with his keys to unlock his front door, trying to move quickly, quietly as not to alarm Haylee he was home. He made it, locked the door behind him, took a deep breath. Thank God she didn't open her door.

He was in, no confrontation. Maybe his luck was changing.

He dropped his bags next to his sofa, angle his walking cane against the ledge. It was a quarter to eight pm, Friday night wrestling was about to start. He made it home in time to relax, finish his meal, smoke a bit, and enjoy wrestling. One of his favorite hobbies he'd never grown out of as a child. He needed to get Haylee out of his mind, her dad's breaking and entering as well. What a crazy week, he needed some normalcy back in his life.

Aaron took his jacket off, hung it against the back of his door. He took a seat on his sofa. It was nice to relax. He stretched out his legs, covered himself with a blanket. With the remote, he turned on the television and put it on the station for wrestling to start. He fidgeted, trying to get comfortable, it had been a long exhausting two days. He pulled out his bag of weed, his bong cleaned from its prior use sat on the table next to the sofa. He needed another smoke.

A cold breeze hit him, like a window was left open.

This struck him as weird. After the break-in last night from Haylee's dad, Aaron made sure all the windows were locked, as well as both back and front doors. He decided the weed would have to wait. There was a definite cold breeze through the home, and that was not normal. He hadn't noticed at first due to adjusting from the bitter cold outside, but his apartment was freezing.

Did the heater turn off?

Aaron stood up, placing his bag of weed next to the bong. He checked his front windows, both closed and locked, yet the breeze seemed to come from the kitchen. The backdoor? Wasn't that how Gerald broke in?

"Gerald?" Aaron called out into the kitchen. He grabbed the walking cane from the side of the sofa before inspecting. There the backdoor was locked, but he noticed underneath the side window, shards of broken glass littered the linoleum flooring.

"What the hell?" Aaron scoped out the scene. His window was covered with blinds; somehow, they had been bent. He pulled the string lifting the blinds, exposing a broken glass window. A strong, steady cold breeze hit his face. The window itself wasn't that large, not large enough for a grown person to crawl through, maybe a small child. However, it was close enough to the door handle, that someone could easily unlock the backdoor.

Aaron had kneeled to examine the broken glass. He was too taken aback from the scene to notice or hear the opening of the walk-in closet in the living room behind him. Unknowing to him, the intruder patiently lurked in the shadows of the large closet. He was stalking, waiting for his return home, anticipating an opportunity for Aaron to let his guard down.

It was Gary Thom, still in the same clothes from almost a week prior when he fled the Simmons' premise. He was skinnier, sickly looking. He'd lost nearly fifteen pounds since his escape from the Emmet County Police. His blue hoodie was worn-torn, dirty, same for his denim. His skin pale, his fingertips black from frostbite. Same as his nose and ears. The skin was decaying, gangrene setting in. His lips flakey with dead skin, cracked. The harsh elements had not been kind to Gary. Yet, he did not care. He felt nothing in the physical sense. The pain was no longer an issue.

Gary was a new man. A better man. Gone was a life wasted on monetary things; he only had one mission in his life now—the constant drive to keep *it* happy. Gary lived off survival instinct now; new, strange, yet beautiful urges had begun to course through his brain. Outside of the pure basic needs to remain alive: food, water, sleep, his only other needs were to fulfill those inner desires. The inkling necessities that popped up into his conscious, telling him, urging him, making him.

Right now, he had a particular mission, a straightforward urge he had to fill. He knew what *it* wanted. He knew what it was telling him to do. If he did so, he would receive its love, its parental guidance, let him suck from its teat, have his full, fill his belly with its love. He craved its attention, its acceptance. He lived now for its embraces, his life dedicated to its existence.

He didn't know why this man was the target. He didn't care.

Gary gripped the knife in his hand tightly, despite the numbness of the frostbit that settled in his fingertips. It was a long butcher knife he grabbed from the kitchen counter after he had broken into the back window, unlocked the backdoor. The stand-in closet was a perfect hiding spot. He could listen, hear where Aaron moved in the home. Aaron had cursed, called out to Gerald, easy to tell it came from the kitchen. He propped the closet door open, watched as Aaron kneeled to inspect the broken glass.

That was his moment to strike. He did so fast efficiently. He'd become a skilled hunter, a master of fatality by his own hands. Before the love of the creature, he'd never killed a thing. It was against his nature. Now, Gary moved forward with excitement. His brain was reliving the memories of his first two kills. Dennis and Nora, the thrilling excitement of butchering them both. The delicious taste of warm human flesh, the blood pouring freely from their dying bodies. Blood rushed between Gary's legs at the mere thought. The sweet sensation of release he'd experienced with the dead bodies, spewing his seed on them. The raw surges of animalistic aggression made him hard.

Aaron heard the footsteps of a man running towards him. He turned from the kneeling position to see Gary charging him. The knife held in his right hand, Gary lunged forward with it. Like an animal, Gary was going straight for the neck. Kill the man quickly, then have fun. He would bring back the best parts of his kill to the creature. The head, the genitals, they would feast on the flesh of a loved one.

Aaron, acting in pure instinct, swung his walking cane at the attacker. It made contact hard with Gary's right hand, across the wrist. Hard enough that it knocked the knife from his grasp. The weapon fell against the kitchen floor, making a metallic clanking noise.

Gary grunted when the strike landed—grabbing his wrist momentarily. The pain throbbed only for a second before the urge to kill Aaron overwrote any physical, sensory his brain was sending him. He went back after the knife, as did Aaron, who grabbed the handle first.

Gary foolishly grabbed the steel blade. Aaron pulled the knife from his grasp, slicing the attacker's hand deep, blood spilled from the wound. Gary yelled in pain, his eyes wild with rage. He shoved his bloody hand, palm first into Aaron's face, smearing the blood all over his mouth and nose. It blinded, choked him. Gary, struggling, saw an opening. He kneed Aaron as hard as he could in the groin.

Aaron yelped, his stomach convulsing from the blow. The throbbing pains shot through his back, causing him to double over. Aaron, trying to protect himself from the prone position, slammed his shoulder into Gary's sternum. Gary was much lighter than the heftiness of Arron. So, he lifted Gary up like a linebacker delivering a shoulder tackle. He was going to power slam him into the far wall.

Gary fought back, pulling Aaron's hair, biting his forehead. Aaron ignored the pail, lifting Gary's body high in a bear hug. He ran towards the living room, carrying Gary with ease. Gary was able to free his left arm from the hold, he wrapped it around the back of Aaron's head, around his neck into a headlock. Gary squeezed hard to try and block off the airflow. Luckily for Aaron, Gary couldn't interlock his other hand. He couldn't gather enough pressure to cut off his air completely. Instead, Aaron, with all his weight, slammed Gary into the front of the house, near the door. Gary's body hit the wall with a hard THUD! The force was strong; it knocked the air from Gary's diaphragm.

Aaron, his head being held in the headlock, had not expected the blow himself. The top of his skull hit the wall just as hard as Gary's body. It sounded like a car crash in his head, a bright white light flashed before he went black.

• • •

Gerald sat in his rental, a black Ford Escape two houses down from his daughter's Duplex. He couldn't stake out his daughter's place with his own vehicle; she would notice it immediately. So, he played it smart. Plus, the rental was a step (or two) up from the beater he drove. He'd love a new car, but paying for his daughters' vehicle, her insurance, her rent, it was too much for him. He was close to broke—no more expenses.

At least she lived in a quiet neighborhood. He'd been scoping out the area for the last two nights. He even had a straight man-to-man conversation with her friend Aaron. Despite breaking into the kids' home, scaring him half to death, he was happy with the way the conversation went. He got his point across. They shared some drinks, it was unpleasant at first, but in the end, it worked out. Aaron was terrible for his daughter's mental health. Good kid, he just met the wrong girl at the wrong time. He'd get over it. To make sure his conversation with Aaron really sank in, he decided to keep an eye out for the next few days.

Gerald had been scoping out the duplex most of the day. He'd grown hungry, though, left for a bit to drive across town to a local Pub and Grill. He grabbed a greasy burger, fries, and a strawberry milkshake to go. Gerald lived his life, usually through a strict regimen. He ate healthily, worked out daily. He missed going out on stakeouts like this. It was also the only time he allowed himself some unhealthy yet delicious food. He couldn't quite make himself a proper nutritional dinner in a rental car, after all.

Gerald unwrapped the greasy burger and bit into it. The hot juices of the burger patty filled his mouth, perfectly cooked bar food, and it was delicious. He plopped a few fries in his mouth, a bit bland, nothing fancy. He'd put his binoculars down to enjoy the meal. It had been quiet at the duplex. His daughter didn't leave, that he expected, she never left. Her lights went on and off a few times throughout the day. A little movement through the window, nothing bothersome. He was worried as to why the local Police, a detective, and a street cop knocked on her door earlier that morning and had hung around inside for almost an hour before leaving.

He thought she would call him when they left. She hadn't. He hadn't heard from her since the voicemail about not seeing her doctor. She didn't answer when he called, no texts back, nothing. This all bothered Gerald. Yes, their relationship was fragile, but she always reached out to him with trouble. He was her protector. He made things right.

Gerald wasn't just scoping out his daughters' duplex. He kept a watch on Aaron as well. He'd gotten Aaron to swear to break things off with his daughter. It took some bargaining, maybe a little blackmail, but he was able to articulate how damaged Haylee was. He was confident he got his point across and that Aaron would make the right decision. Gerald watched Aaron leave in the afternoon, come back just a few minutes after Gerald himself got back and parked a few houses down after grabbing his meal.

Gerald finished off his meal, washing it down with the sweetness of the strawberry milkshake. His stomach wasn't going to like him much later tonight, that much was a given. He crumbled up the trash from the food into a ball, tossed it in the grease-stained brown baggy the meal came with. He had just sat back to get comfy after the meal when he saw it. His daughter's door swung open. Haylee darted out frantically, knocking on Aarons door, her arms flailing wildly. Gerald was parked down the road, sitting at a bad angle. He grabbed the binoculars, tried to get a better look. He only caught a glimpse of his daughter's face. Frantic, he could hear her screaming Aarons name loudly from a few houses down.

"Shit," Gerald frowned. He wasn't sure what was going on, but he had to help. His cover would be blown, his daughter would know he'd been spying on her, but he's been in the force long enough, something terrible was happening.

Gerald turned the ignition, and his car roared to life. He shifted into drive and floored the rental down the road. He parked awkwardly, cutting off the driveway, half the vehicle on the snow-covered front lawn of the duplex. He exited the car quickly, leaving the car running.

Haylee turned at the commotion. "Dad?"

"What's going on?" Gerald was yelling now.

"Something happened in there," Haylee panicked. Her voice wavered. "I heard a loud crash, and it sounded like fighting." She didn't question her dad's sudden appearance. She was thankful at that moment. Her dad, for as shitty as he was, was always there. Even if he screwed everything up, he never abandoned her.

"Move," Gerald ordered.

"It's locked," Haylee sidestepped out her dad's way.

Gerald's fingers wrapped around the door handle.

Locked.

Shit, he thought.

His shoulder came next, hitting the middle of the door hard. It didn't budge. He'd broken in the night prior through a back window left unlocked. He was sure Aaron wouldn't have made the same mistake. Worse, he heard moaning through the door. Someone had been hurt. Gerald ran to the side of the duplex where a small slit in the living room curtains allowed him to peer inside. There he saw two men on the floor—both looking dazed. Aaron was on his back, his head bleeding. A skinner man was on his hands and knees, crawling over to him.

"Call the police!" Gerald yelled.

"My phone died!" Haylee shot back, following her dad around lost.

Gerald tossed his flip phone to her. "Call now. I'm going to try and get in from the back. Tell them there has been a break-in, we'll need an ambulance as well."

"Oh my god, what?" Haylee processed her dad's words.

"Just do it!" Gerald ran around the side of the house near the back door. He tried the door; it was locked. He noticed the window broken and found his access inside. He reached through, unlocked the backdoor entering through the kitchen. He heard the commotion from the living room. There he saw the skinny man sitting atop of Aaron. They struggled with one another. The man had both his hands wrapped around Aaron's throat, all his weight pushing down. Aaron going a shade of dark purple.

"Get off!" Gerald yelled. His hulking frame, like a human tank, pushed forward. With a mighty kick to the ribs, the madman fell over. He curled into pain, yelling from the pain.

"Are you okay?" Gerald asked. Aaron choked on the air flooding his lungs.

"Get up, you son of a bitch," Gerald lifted Gary to his feet, but Gary jabbed his thumb into his eye, clawed at his face.

"Fuck!" Gerald lost his grip.

Gary grabbed the nearby lamp from the end table. Frantically, he smashed it over Gerald's head. It made a sickening thud, shattering into sharp pieces. Gerald hit the floor, tripping over Aaron.

Gary, looking to retreat, unlocked the front door to make his escape. He'd failed the urge to kill the fat one. Now, his instincts told him to flee. If he died, then he would never get to be with mother again. Never get to suck from her sweet teats. Never get to lay within her warmth.

He wasn't ready for who stood outside the door. There on the porch between the two duplexes stood the one. She was fumbling with the cellphone, panicking. She spoke frantically to someone on the other end. Gary, for the first-time setting eyes on her, he was completely overtaken by lust, love, admiration. It was her, the true her. The one he dreams of, the one he's meant to protect.

Haylee gasped at Gary's slack-jawed stare. She couldn't talk, words choked in her throat, making it impossible for her to find her voice. The operator on the other end tried to get her attention. She could not reply; instead, she stood transfixed with Gary's soulless eyes, fear overtook her body. The man looked wild, ravenous. Instead of attacking, he stood there momentarily, smiling at her. Like a child, wide-eyed and lovingly, budding tears on his blood-soaked face.

"Stop that son of a bitch!" Gerald yelled from the living room.

His voice snapped Gary out from his trance. Gary, panicking for a moment, eyed his surroundings. He spotted his escape. The rental car parked on the lawn, still running. Gary jumped into the vehicle. He needed to return to mother, failure or not; he would go back to her, take his punishment. He would not fail in the future. He shifted the car into drive and sped off wildly into the night.

Haylee ran to her father, and to Aaron in the room. The phone in her hand. Her body shuddered.

"Did you call the police?" Gerald barked, his eye swollen from the thumb, his face scratched to hell.

"They–They're on the phone..." Haylee bent over to see if Aaron was okay.

"Give it here," Gerald took the phone, holding his head. He, too, was now bleeding from a fresh wound. "Is this dispatch?" Gerald went outside where Gary had exited, phone in hand. "Shit, he took my vehicle...Listen," he continued. "We have an issue here..."

"Aaron?" Haylee sat beside Aaron. Still bleeding from hitting his head against the wall. His throat burned, his voice hoarse from nearly being choked to death.

"I'm—I'm so sorry," Aaron's voice was hoarse, barely audible, he was still dazed, possibly concussed.

"Quiet," Haylee said, holding him in her arms. "Just, just, shut up for right now," she held his hand tight. "What the hell just happened? Was that?–Was that that Gary guy?"

TWENTY-SIX

Clent and Vanessa arrived at the scene first. Reports of breaking and entering, and an assault with a deadly weapon at 3248 Westview Apt B, the attached duplex to Haylee Leveille's residence. They patrolled nearby down Main street when the call came over. They arrived at the scene within ten minutes. The cruiser pulled up to the address.

In front of Haylee's duplex stood a bulky man holding his head, bloodied. He was still on the phone with dispatch, talking through the events. The front door to Haylee's neighbor's apartment was wide open. An ambulance was already on the scene. They had a gentleman sitting up on a stretcher, checking his vitals.

"Let's go," Clent pulled up on the side of the road, threw the cruiser into park. "Ambulance beat us. I will stand back, get details; you will clear the area."

"Copy," Vanessa swung her door open, exited the vehicle. It was her second time that day she found herself visiting the Hailey Leveille's residence. She took mental notes of the scene, her feet crunching the cold, wet snow beneath her feet. Two EMT's were dealing with the large heavier set male on a stretcher. The muscular, middle-aged man had hung up the phone, began walking towards them. Haylee was near the EMT's. A thick blanket draped across her shoulders, being checked out by the second team member.

"Officers," Gerald spoke directly. "There was a break into my daughter's neighbor residence. Assault with a deadly weapon, the perp had a kitchen knife, weapons on the kitchen floor. I entered the backdoor, fought the intruder off. The suspect stole my rental car and fled, driving north down

Pine street. I don't know the license plate number, but it was a 2019 Ford Explorer, black. That was about ten minutes ago. My rental information was on the passenger seat."

"Vanessa, Go check the residence, let's get it cleared, careful not to disturb anything until Detective Pike gets here."

"On it," Vanessa nodded, making her way to the home.

"What was your name, sir?" Clent asked.

"Gerald Leveille," He held up his hands, bloody. "Would shake your hand officer, but I need to get cleaned up. Former Detective, Ohio State Police Force, here visiting my daughter."

"Okay," Clent nodded. He spotted a visible laceration from the back of his hairline. "You need to get that checked out. Thank you for the help, let's get the EMT's to look at you. We will handle the rest. You may need to be stitched up for that."

"Officer," Gerald spoke up. "I am certain the man who broke in was Gary Thom. Fit his description, White Male, about one-hundred-sixty pounds, mid to late twenties, he had a few days' worth of stubble, dirty, looked like he was physically sick, pale, that sort of thing. I have been keeping up with the case. I knew who I was looking for when I was watching my daughter's home. It was him. He was here."

"Is that so?" Clent brow wrinkled. "Watching your daughter's home?"

"I have been watching her residence. Making sure no one has been stalking my daughter, with the odd resemblance of her case and this one. He must have broken in next door when I left for about fifteen minutes to grab a bite to eat. Through the backdoor, smashed a window, reached in unlocked. Aaron said he jumped him, must have hidden somewhere, waited for a chance."

A second vehicle pulled up along the cruiser. It was Detective Pike's car. He would be hot on this information. They needed to find the vehicle, apprehend the suspect immediately. There was a lot of work to do tonight.

TWENTY-SEVEN

Still soaked with fresh blood from the kills, Gary's clothes clung to his body. It had been a busy night. The change came fast, he fought it at first, but soon it consumed him. He allowed the urges in, let the penetrating visions into his conscious. The connection with his monstrous lover, who he knows referred to as mother, his only family. It was many things to him. It/she was everything. Gary understood immediately what it wanted; it's needs, desires.

Death, brutality, flesh.

He was hungry because she was hungry because they both needed substance. He was its caretaker now, its protector, just as much as it was to him. They became one and the same, a single entity, and their only goal was to survive. To feed. To protect *her*.

Gary had the hand saw in his grip; his mother consumed the best of the bits, the head, brains, eyes, genitals. The flesh was all his—the nose, cheeks, lips, fatty areas. The breasts and the meaty rump of the torso, he enjoyed the most, tasty delicacies. Once they were dead, he couldn't help but to gorge on their flesh. Blood still warm, he ate them raw. The wife was even still alive, barely, as he chewed through the flesh on her cheeks. Her soft low breaths, it was glorious, brutally splendid—the feast fit for only he and his new mother.

The killings were a physical rush. He'd never known the thrill of murderous delight ever before in his past existence. He'd been different since the creature came into his life. The one who was both his lover and his mother, the one who gave him new life, a reason to live. He was nothing before, just a random vessel filled with compulsory reactions to the world around him. He was a wanderer, meaningless, an existence worth nothing more than fleeting stimulated emotions that did nothing but to prevent him from becoming something more.

The head of the man, known to him before the change as Dennis, came off easier than anticipated with the aid of the saw. He would continue to feed on the wife for a few days until Mother grew hungry again. Then Nora's body would do, her head, whatever else she wanted to consume. Two kills, now that's a special thing, a rare and beautiful hunt. They could feast long on the two bodies, days, weeks if needed. The winter could keep them frozen, safe from spoiling.

He had done well.

Mother would be proud.

Gary held Dennis's head by the hair. He grabbed a sandwich baggy from the kitchen, ziplocked for freshness. Inside it was the man's genitals, removed within minutes of death.

Fresh, mother would be excited.

The hunger was crippling. The connection, the bond between him and the creature was so strong, even after having his fill of the bodily flesh of the victims, the stomach still knotted in pains of hunger. Gary had to feed both him and it to fill the emptiness.

He did not bother to change out of the bloody clothes, not yet. He enjoyed sweet aroma; the irony-metallic smell of the blood kept him hard between the legs. There was an excitement to it all, a sexual pleasure he had only begun to explore. This, too, was one of the new urges, one that was tied to the newfound connection with mother. He left the garage, the playroom, with his mother's feast in hand.

He made his way deep into the dark of the woods. The special place that was home to mother. He'd never been there, but he could sense exactly where it was. His mother's presence was his guiding light, a beacon for him to follow. Her stomach growling, her excitement spreading through his body, they shared a connection, needs, wants, desires.

The trip was long. The cold, bitter winter did nothing to stop him from his destination. His fingers burned, his toes went numb, yet physical pain was no longer a distraction. Soon, he'd be in her presence, her warmth. He walked for hours, instincts driving him. He finally came to a small clearing of woods, and old hunting lodge sat there. Desolate, neglected, lost to nature, it barley stood upright. It had become its home. Lost and forgotten, half the lodge's ceiling had caved in from a previous storm decades ago. It was big enough for her to hide, to stay hidden from the world to prey on whatever flesh she could dig her jagged teeth into.

Gary tossed the head of Dennis a few feet from what was once the front door of the small wooden lodge. From within the confines of the building, two dark red eyes peered through the blackness. It emerged, the deathly looking creature. The bright moon lit the clearing, casting just enough light to allow Gary to see it once again, full-bodied, glorious. It came out on all fours, its long lanky arms moving almost ape-like. Its large head, prolonged snout, the six-point antlers pierced into the night sky. Its half-decayed head lowered and sniffed the head of Dennis.

"For you," Gary muttered, in awe he watched.

The creature long slender fingers pulled the head closer, using them as an ice cream scoop, the creature plopped out both eyes with ease. It devoured them wildly, slurping them down, licking its decayed lips with its putrid tongue. Next, it reached into Dennis's mouth and yanked out the tongue. It too gorged itself on the meat. The creature almost put itself into a frenzy as it feasted. Finally, it held the head high and cracked it open on a nearby rock. The skull-splitting open. The creature, lifting it to its mouth, eating the brain, gulping it down.

Gary could sense the creature's fullness. He could taste the sweetness of the meal, his own mouth salivating at the site. He'd done well, made it happy. The creature had its fill. Gary would be rewarded. The thing, it's belly full, retreated into the lodge. Gary followed. The moonlight crept into the lodging. The creature sat in the corner; its legs spread open. Gary walked into its embrace, curled up on its lap. Its rancid, decayed skin gave off a wretched odor that Gary found calmness in. His stomach was rumbling now, despite his own meal of human flesh. A thirst surged through Gary's body. The creature tilted his head up, pushing its long saggy teat towards his mouth. Gary took it greedily, suckling at the things breast. He was in heaven; It had finally accepted him. He fell asleep in its warm embrace.

TWENTY-EIGHT

Haylee sat next to Aaron in the painfully dull waiting room. Despite the myriad of people currently inhabiting the large area, it seemed lifeless. Dollar store art hung framed on the stark white walls; magazines spread on tables. People trying desperately not to look uncomfortable. Since the murders, Haylee has struggled in large spaces, especially open areas filled with strangers. Add onto that her anxiety with hospitals in general, and she was ripe for a panic attack. Her nerves were shot; her right eye twitched from the stress. She was surrounded by the sick, young, old, a gathering of diseased and/or injured people. Strangers, each one, and all Haylee could think of was their staring eyes. Watching her, out of their peripherals, did they all recognize her? From the news or the dozens of newspaper articles? Were they whispering about her?

Look, mom, is that the girl from the murder house?

The crazy woman who can't leave her home, poor old Haylee, she was better off dying in that home with her sister. What a mess of a person.

She could practically read their judging minds. Her PTSD was spinning out of control. The constant noise of people chatting, the phlegmy coughs, wet and sickly. Kids ran about playfully, parents yelling at them to behave. A noisy older man in the corner who looked to have trouble breathing, hacking up a lung every five minutes into a damp handkerchief he kept shoveling back into his breast pocket. She had broken into a nervous sweat, but she had to be there because even if she detested Aaron at the moment, deep down, she needed him. She needed a friend, an anchor to the real world.

"I know this must be hell for you," Aaron finally muttered. "Thank you for staying with me. I didn't want to worry my parents. The less they know, the better, I will deal with them when it hits the news."

"Yeah," Haylee nodded. "Some of us are there for others when they need them, even when it gets uncomfortable. We don't just bail."

Aaron winced from the words. They seemed to hit him physically, like a blow to the gut. It cut him deep because Haylee was right. How many times could he mess up? Here, she was, despite everything, still by his side. He was aware of her issues with large areas, the agoraphobia, the fear of hospitals as well. He knew she was more than vulnerable.

He fucked up. He always fucked up, especially with relationships.

Aaron let her dad get into his head, with the blackmail, with the story of the woods where they found Haylee. That freaked him out, scared him, perhaps he sided with her dad after that information was shared with him, he wasn't even sure anymore. The only thing he was sure of was that he was in a lose/lose situation. Why hadn't he been upfront with her about the script? When he first met her, and they clicked. It could have been a casual thing "—Hey, by the way, I write scripts, and I'm working on something. I would love to talk to you about it, share your thoughts?" I mean, she could have told him to fuck off, but at least he wouldn't have lied to her for months.

"—Look," Aaron stumbled with his words. What could he say? Sorry didn't seem to suffice.

"No, it's okay," Haylee interjected. "The three of us are going to talk. You, me, and my dad. Until then, let's just wait. I need to get out of here bad, until then, I just want to focus on my frickin' sanity for right now."

Aaron nodded. "Okay." He avoided eye contact once again, pretending to be on his phone. He fumbled with his social media accounts, trying to focus on anything other than the throbbing pain in his head.

Haylee centered her attention on her breathing. Balancing herself, trying to take control of the situation she was losing her balance in. She was taught a trick, one of the few things she actually learned from a doctor when she was younger—the grounding technique.

Find five things she could see, count them out, focus on each.

One: Aaron, he looked broken, maybe not as broken as her, but definitely not well, physically nor emotionally. She couldn't help but feel responsible for his condition. When people let her in, she ruined them, somehow. She brought death and sadness wherever she went.

Two: Aaron's stupid wrestling shirt with Macho Man Randy Savage's big purple sunglasses on it. It had ripped down the neck during the struggle. This made her want to smile. Aaron was many things; one of those things was an ass for what he did to her that night, leaving her alone. He was also kind, caring, and very much a nerd. She had come to adore that in the last few weeks.

Three: The ugly painting of a small-town diner across the waiting room. Bland pastel colors. She needed to focus on something other than Aaron, and her eyes kept creeping up to the painting. She didn't know why, but she hated it. It seemed lifeless like the artist had no passion, just a mixture of paints and brushstrokes to make a few dollars. It reminded her of herself, she was there, present in the world, but void of real life, true meaning. Just a framed picture, pretty on the outside, frameable, but no passion or love on the inside. Hollow.

Four: The giant fish tank next to Aaron, at least a dozen or so varying fish, all lively. The only thing in the room that seemed to contain a positive life experience. The fish varied in size shapes and vibrant colors. Or was it positive? The fish safe in a small tank, never experiencing life outside in the real world.

Five: A young boy, probably five. His nose was red, as are his flush cheeks. Haylee named him Johnny, he looked sick, cuddle against his mother's lap. He played with a tablet, a raspy cough every few minutes. Haylee liked the boy; she pictured him cozied up to her as if he was her own son. Haylee stroking his feverish forehead, whispering to him that everything would be okay, and meaning it.

"Haylee," Gerald's loud voice awakened her from the daydream. "I got the car pulled up. We're ready to go, you okay?" Her father approached her, embraced her with his strong arms, like a superhero out of one of those cheesy summer blockbuster movies. His massive muscular frame absorbed her within his embrace. She loved to hate the comfort his mere presence gave her. The man who wouldn't listen to her needs yet would do everything and anything in his power to keep her safe. She didn't want to need his love, and she wanted to hate the man who forced her into the doctor's arms, more people who wouldn't listen. She tried to blame him for the loss of their mother, the returning visions, voices. Yet, she couldn't. She loved him, the bond between a daughter and a father who tried his best, yet failed time and time again—fractured yet whole. Perfectly imperfect. She wept into his shoulder. Tears of exhaustion, anger, frustration, and more than anything else, fear. It was wonderful. She knew it was going to get worse before it got better.

She would stand her ground.

They had been lucky. It was a nasty fight, but it could have been much worse.

The three of them left the hospital behind. Not much was said on the way to the car. A soft snowfall powdered the night sky, continuing the barrage of snow their small town has been battling all week—one of the worst winters in recent history, in more ways than one.

"Your head looks terrible," Haylee entered the passenger door, buckling her seat belt. She finally broke her silence.

"I have been in worse shape," Gerald responded, a reassuring smile. Gerald received his own set of injuries from the attack. Six staples to the back of his head where the lamp was smashed over him. Split his head wide open. He received stitches on his face from the scratches, sure to leave some wicked scars.

Haylee finally relaxed; the tension left her body. The waiting room was too much. The commotion put her on edge. The inner confines of the car, surrounded by people, friends, and family, she could finally breathe.

"How is he?" Gerald asked, looking over to Haylee, who took the front passenger seat.

"Ask him yourself," Haylee broke eye contact with her father. The feeling of safety aside, she realized something happened between Aaron and him. Surely, the reason Aaron had been acting funny. The hate part of her father's relationship started to override the love, the safety. Once again, he was sticking his nose in her life, ruining something that was making her happy.

"Minor concussion, head's killing me, throat hurts like a bitch," Aaron answered. "You?"

"Just a scratch," Gerald countered. "Six staples."

"Jesus," Aaron frowned. "If you didn't show up..."

"Yeah," Gerald answered back. "When I got into your apartment, he was choking you good. You went blue."

"—Why were you there? Why are you here in Michigan?" Haylee interrupted. She was thankful for her dad's involvement, but also angry he'd been spying on her.

"If I weren't there, your friend would be dead," Gerald didn't hold back. "Maybe thanking me would be a better way to start a conversation?"

"That's not what I asked," she shot back, her words thick with anger.

"I was there because I was worried about you," Gerald threw the vehicle in reverse and backed out of the parking spot. "Because you left me a message on my machine that you weren't going to see your doctor anymore. I was afraid I was going to get a call that someone found you unresponsive in the woods again, or worse, dead this time. I can't lose another daughter," Gerald spoke calmly. He tried to avoid emotional outbursts when speaking to his daughter. It was hard to do, due to the array of emotions swirling in his head. He wanted to scream at her, to try with sheer might to make her listen to him. It was the right thing to do. She needed medical help, mental help. She wasn't safe, and he was afraid she'd harm herself if left alone.

"That's not fair," Haylee replied.

"We've learned life's not fair, look at us, we're about as unfair as it gets," Gerald waited for an opening, turned carefully into oncoming traffic.

"We all need to talk, we need to straighten this out," Gerald added. "A man just broke into your apartment, Aaron, why? Why would the man Gary Thom, who murdered Haylee's old neighbors, come after you? That *was* him, right?"

"I have no idea," Aaron said. "I have never seen him before. He attacked me blindsided. I barely got a look at him."

"What about you, Haylee? Any idea why? Did you see him?"

"No idea why," she replied. "But, yes, I think so. I think it was him."

"It's all so crazy, none of it makes sense," Aaron added. "Who the hell is this guy?"

"It's about five more minutes to your duplex, Haylee. Is it okay if I come in with you guys," Gerald asked? "We can sort some of this out."

"I don't know," Haylee kept the eye contact broken.

"I think he should," Aaron added.

Haylee frowned, "Fine."

No one spoke for the rest of the ride. Haylee was lost in thought, her mind wandering, losing grip on reality. Everything was beginning to spin out of control. Of course, her dad brought up the woods. He always did; it was his way of trying to put an end to any argument about her mental health. She hated it, and he brought it up in front of Aaron, which made her fill with rage.

Yet, without her dad's protection, Aaron would surely be dead. Then, that man, Gary, stared at her, just for those fleeting moments, like they had been connected, old friends who hadn't seen each other in years. There was a weird connection to him, despite never having met him before. He didn't attack her; he didn't strike her; he was in awe of her.

TWENTY-NINE

Gary ditched the car on the side of the road. Once he hit the forest, Mother would protect him. The vehicle was not safe—a quick means of escape, but that was all. The darkness of the woods, the protection of Mother, that was his only chance of survival. He would be in her arms soon. Yet, despite this, a fear rumbled in his stomach. He had one duty to kill the best friend. The fat one, to gut him, leave his innards all over the apartment, and bring the head back to Mother. Mother was surely hungry again, and the fat man was the one to torment the girl the most.

One job, and he failed it. Mother was sure to be angry. Gary would go hungry, left unloved.

Gary's only reason for existence was to feed Mother, to keep her happy, and to keep the girl drowning in depression, despair. They both fed off that, drank from her misery, like sweet flowing nectar, it strengthened them both. They feasted on flesh and despair, like food and water to humans, their sustenance.

For Gary, failure wasn't an option. He needed another plan. He needed to eat, and so did Mother.

THIRTY

Haylee's apartment was not a part of the crime scene, and so that's where they stayed until the investigation finished. Aaron's side of the duplex was wrapped up with the yellow investigation tape. Officers have been in and out of his apartment all evening, gathering the last few bits of evidence. After sunset, it had quieted down.

When Haylee, Aaron, and Gerald entered her apartment, they brought is two large pizza's, which Gerald sat on the coffee table. The smell made Haylee's stomach growl. She hadn't realized how hungry she was. It had been almost twenty-four hours since she ate anything. Trayer, hearing them enter, loudly began barking from her bedroom.

"Glad we picked up some food. I'm sure we're all hungry after all that," Gerald went into the kitchen. He grabbed napkins and plates.

Aaron had taken a seat on the couch. Famished, he'd already eaten half a slice of pizza.

"Shit, I'm hungry," Aaron poured a two-liter of Mountain Dew into a plastic cup Gerald had bought as well.

"Let me go take care of Trayer, I will let him outside to run around," Haylee added. "He needs to run some of his pent-up energy." She let the Great Dane out into the night. He was hyper, that's for sure. She felt terrible for being gone so long, leaving her furry companion locked up. She returned to the living room, grabbed a slice of pizza. She didn't want to talk. Instead, she returned to the kitchen to watch Trayer from the window while she ate.

A perfect opportunity to sneak some Seagram's from the cupboard, taking a few long sips. Her phone vibrated in her pocket. She realized she had a few missed calls from earlier. It was her. It was Lydia.

Haylee's heart jumped into her throat.

She answered.

"Things have escalated," Gerald spoke to Aaron in the living room. "There's more going on than we know about with this Gary guy. It wasn't a random attack on you."

"Yeah?' Aaron thought the same. Except he couldn't figure out the connection. He'd been researching Gary's life online. He knew quite a bit about him.

"—Can you make it?" Haylee entered the living room, talking on her cell phone. "Thank you so much. I really need your help. I'm glad we spoke the other night too...yes...yes...You're in town already? Okay? Yes, perfect... Yep... See you soon." Haylee hung the phone up, slipped it into her pocket.

"Who was that?" Gerald asked.

"An old friend, checking up on me," Haylee sighed, rubbing the bridge of her nose. She wasn't ready for that part of tonight's discussion. It would happen soon enough. "What are you two talking about?" she deflected. She had her own questions.

"Gary, the man who murdered your neighbors and attacked Aaron," Gerald replied.

"We just can't find a connection," Aaron answered.

"We can talk about that later," Haylee took a seat next to Aaron on the couch. "But, first, we have to talk about this."

"What?" Gerald asked.

"I want to know what's going on," Haylee said, "...with you two."

"What do you mean?" asked Aaron.

"We were fine, Aaron. Then last night, you were supposed to come over, and you never showed up. You ignore my calls, my texts. That never happens. You show up at my door almost every day. Suddenly, you just ignore me? An entire day, no checkup, no courtesy check? Then my dad shows up and saves you from that madman."

"I don't always show up at your door," Aaron frowned, what did she think of him? A stalker?

"You never ignore me, though. Especially knowing everything I have been going through with those murders. And I am not saying I don't like your company. I'm telling you the opposite. It hurt me when you ignored me, knowing how messed up I am right now. I needed you."

"—Honey, it's not what you think," Gerald interjected.

"What do I think, dad? That you somehow interfered with my life? That I called you, left you a message that I was done with the psychiatric help, no more doctors, and then all of a sudden, my best friend just walks out of my life?" Haylee was angry now. Her dad is always interjecting, always knowing what was best. "You don't think that I trust you got to him? That you somehow got into Aaron's head? What? Did you threaten him? To leave me alone?"

"It's not like that," Gerald protested.

"Really? Because I think it is like that," Haylee stood up now. She was yelling, screaming at her father. "This is what you do. Is it because you want what's best for me? Or that heaven forbid, I find someone else to be there for me?"

"You need professional help!" Gerald now stood, his chiseled face red with ferocity. "This guy," he points to Aaron, his hand shaking "Knows nothing about you. Nothing! He is a damn blip in your life. I have been there since the second you were born. I know what is best for you."

"Really?" Haylee stood up, got directly into her father's face. "What's best for me? Like when mom brought Lydia into my life. The first person who listened to me?"

"—She was a hack! It was the meds that straightened you out!" Gerald yelled, interrupting her.

"Guys, guys, c'mon," Aaron dropped the half-eaten slice of pizza onto the paper plate. The yelling didn't help the headache, nor his comfort in the room.

"—She was the only person to ever listen to me. What she taught me, that's what helped—helped with the voices, with the visions, the nightmares. They all went away until you pushed mom so far. She died!"

"Fuck you!" Gerald grabbed the two-liter of soda from the coffee table. In a fury, he threw the bottle against her flat-screen television, shattering the glass.

"Jesus!" Aaron stood up, shocked at the sudden violence.

"I didn't kill her!" Gerald's broad shoulders lifted heavily with every breath.

"Right," Haylee choked back the emotion. "She was so angry over everything; she was in the wrong place at the wrong time because YOU couldn't let her try and help me. Because Mom listened, Mom got me helped that worked."

"Enough!" Aaron yelled. "Jesus fucking Christ! I just want to eat pizza!"

"Shut up!" Gerald shot back.

"No!" Aaron was done, done with everything. "You two are fucking nuts. She has a reason; she's been through hell and back." Aaron pointed to Gerald, "You? You're just as crazy. You snuck into my apartment last night, threatening me to leave your daughter alone. *That's* crazy, man!"

"—I knew it!" Haylee threw up her hands in disbelief.

"—Wait," Aaron threw up his hand to silence Haylee. "I fucked up, okay? I moved next door to you after my accident. I lived with my parents for a while. I caught wind of what happened to you. I...I just, I dunno, I was so curious about you. I was working on a new script, and I moved in to get to know you. Your dad broke into my apartment, found the script. Yes, it's about you, us, the murder, everything."

"You what?" Haylee's eyes blurred. Was it hate, anger, or the sharp pain of humiliation that caused her to kneel over?

"I was going to tell you when the time was right if there was ever a time that felt right," Aaron frowned. "I didn't think you'd ever talk to me, like, for real? Why would you? Look at me, look at you?"

"Are you serious?" Haylee muttered, her body tensed, her teeth grinding. The words hurt. Was he using her to write a movie? The thought made her sick.

"Shit head," Gerald shook his head in disbelief.

"I'm sorry," Aaron's head hung low.

"You should be," Gerald interjected.

"Right," Aaron replied. "I should be, and I am. Sorrier about that stupid script than anything in my life. It's not worth the friendship we built. But I get it. I will leave. I'll Uber to my parent's. I'm out of your life."

"Smartest thing you've said all night," said Gerald.

"No," Haylee stood up. Her eyes fell on the broken television. "Aaron stays. Dad, I want you out. Leave..."

"What?" Gerald's mouth dropped.

"I don't want you here right now," Haylee's words were soft, quiet.

"You got to be joking? I'm your father," Gerald's frowned.

"Tomorrow, Lydia will be here at noon to talk with me," Haylee walked over to the front door. She opened it. "If you want to be a part of my life going forward, then you're welcome to come. If you promise to listen to her openly."

"Is that so?" Gerald sucked in his bottom lip angrily, gritted his teeth. "I pay your bills, everything you see here? It's because of me."

"And I don't care. The only reason I am offering you this small chance is because you're my dad. I love you through everything that's happened. But we can't stay this way; it's killing us. The door will be open. Tomorrow, noon. It's up to you. Until then, I want you to go.

Gerald stood quiet for a few moments. He stared into his daughter's eyes. He nodded, walked over the broken television, and exited the door. Haylee shut it, locked it.

"Haylee," Aaron approached her. Tears in his eyes.

"Shut up," Haylee blurted out. She fell into his arms. He held her. He held her tighter than he'd ever held another human in his life.

Together, they were beautifully broken.

THIRTY-ONE

The Bad Luck Lager House was mostly empty, except for a few dedicated drunks. It was the night after Gary Thom attacked Aaron Hauser, another media frenzy had followed, taking over the local news. Social media was in an uproar as well. Everyone was spreading false information and theories like a wildfire. This alone drove Detective Pike mad. There was no controlling social media, nor the panic it seemed to create once people started throwing in their half-baked theories.

Not to mention a second terrible snowstorm hit. Further crippling the small town in less than a week. It started up last night and had steadied its course, dropping over eight inches total. This kept most patrons at home, warm indoors with their families. However, Detective Pike needed a drink, and a few inches of snow wasn't going to stop him from having a few stiff ones. He phoned a few colleagues; he needed an outlet. A lot weighted on his mind, and this newest turn of events with the attack had him enamored.

Pike took a seat at his regular table, isolated at the back of the bar. Quiet and alone, he had time to think before his comrades showed up. If they even would, the case had been stressful. Pike and Clent hadn't buried the hatchet yet, Fat Man Brenkins had just got back into town from a convention, and Vanessa Velasquez, well, he still wasn't sure how the two of them mixed. His people—the ones close to the case, and embarrassingly enough, the closest things he had to friends.

Pike pulled out his yellow legal pad. He started going over his notes and journals.

Gary Thom hadn't died from hypothermia despite his lack of survival skills and preparation for one of the coldest, brutal winters in Michigan's history. Pike was sure that he would have. He had spent multiple days in those woods. How had the weather not taken his life? Unless he had some sort of camp, something hospitable. Even if that was the case, how did multiple search parties miss it? Unlikely, they had some people very knowledgeable about the forest, and they found nothing. Hardly any tracks.

Except the weather kept the search party from hitting the forest hard. Very possible, they didn't go far enough. They wouldn't get another shot until the weather cleared up, and some of the damn snow melted.

Pike thought about the papers shoved into Nora's mouth, Hayley's initials. The solid connection and adding the close location and the similarities of the murders. Haylee was adamant that she had no relationship with Gary Thom, yet she had hinted that she was aware of more about the crime scene than what was brought out to the public. How did she know the method, right down to the stabbing in the back of the neck?

"Rough night?" Sherry's raspy voice caught his attention. It had been a quiet night for Sherry; the shit weather always took its toll on her bar and her tips.

"Rough week," Pike smiled.

"I know, I have been following the news, Whiskey?" she asked.

"On the rocks, please," Pike nodded. "Weather keeping folks at home? It's a ghost town in here."

"Oh yeah," She gave a toothy grin. "Two wicked snowstorms this week, we're still trying to get rid of the last crap the good lord dumped on us. Then, the double murder, and now the attack on that young kid. People are just hibernatin' until all this blows over. I think people are scared, yeah know?"

"I do," Pike nodded. "He is still out there, and that's a scary truth."

"You're gonna catch him, though. You always get your guy, am I right?"

"You always know what to say," Pike nodded. "Seems like this weather brings with it bad luck, every time it snows..." Pike pulled out his billfold. He handed her a ten. "Keep it."

"Be right up with the drink, darlin'," she nodded with thanks.

Pike went back to his notes. The brutality of the murders. The beheading, the cannibalism, the removal of the testicle. Haylee's sister's scene was brutal, as well. Her body had been cannibalized by the fiancé. If

Haylee wouldn't have surprised him, what would have happened to the body? Head removed? Pike wondered.

There were more similarities between the two cases. Both involved two very normal individuals. Robbie had just landed a new job, purposed to Haylee months prior. His life was going well. He wasn't into the freaky shit like Gary's hidden lifestyle. The bondage, the sexual torture. Robbie wasn't a masochist, surely with the lifestyle Dennis and Gary shared they both were. Pike had even considered the two being involved in some sort of sexual cult, but no leads proved the theory. Robbie, however, that kid was clean as a whistle.

"Just you?" Clent walked up to the table.

"So far," Pike looked up, surprised to see Clent. He flipped his notepad closed.

"On the rocks," Sherry dropped off the whiskey, "hello handsome," She put her hand on Clent's strong shoulder.

"Always a pleasure," Clent nodded. "I will take a bud light, please."

"Of course," Sherry walked away to grab his order.

"Working on the case off hours?" Clent pointed to the notebook, "Classic Lewis Pike, right there. This thing eating you alive, isn't it? Fucking with your head."

"Of course, it is, there's a mad man out there," Pike took a long sip of the whiskey. It went down smooth.

"Hey guys," Paul Brenkins swung into the bar, dusting off the snow from his jacket. "Look who I found in the parking lot?" Next to him stood a fancied-up Vanessa Velasquez. Pike always thought seeing his fellow officers out of uniform was awkward. Vanessa was stunning.

"Well damn," Clent joked. "Is that makeup? Did you get all dressed up for us?"

"Hell no," Vanessa laughed, "Take it easy, guys. I had a date with a man I met off Tinder, and it was terrible. I did get a meal out of it, though. He wouldn't stop talking about his ex-wife. So, I bailed on him. I need a drink, maybe a double."

"I got you," Brenkins laughed. "I will be back, going to hit the bar." He made his way towards Sherry.

"Tinder?" Pike asked, "aren't we running a case where a man was killed off a similar dating site?"

"Yeah," Vanessa replied. "Except, I can take care of myself. I also wouldn't be inviting any strangers back to my place off a single tinder date. I'm a lady detective. I'm also a badass cop, and I can break an arm if somebody decided to try something unwanted."

"I see," Pike smiled. "I suppose Tinder and Scruff have different clientele."

"What's that supposed to mean?" Clent asked, purposely poking the proverbial bear.

"You know what that means," Pike added, taking a second sip of his drink.

"Boys, play nice," Vanessa asserted. "I haven't even got my first shot yet."

"I'm pretty sure you are the rookie here," Clent joked. "You getting a backbone pretty quick. I seem to remember you puking at your first crime scene a week ago."

"Funny. Look, you guys obviously have a complicated relationship," Vanessa smiled as Breskin returned with her drink. "Thank god!" Vanessa held up a shot of Tequila with Breskin. They cheered the shot, liked their hand of salt, and downed it. Next came the lime.

"Damn, that's good," Brenkins smiled. "What's with all the tension? I have been gone all week on a convention. I need to relax."

"They are fighting," Vanessa added.

"Oh, well, nothing new there," Brenkins added. "Can we not with the office drama? I just got back from a convention full of wise asses."

"—No," Clent interjected. "I want to know how Tinder and Scruff are different?"

"You want me to spell it out?" Pike stirred his drink.

"Yes," Clent replied.

"Well, one's for straight folk, the other is for gays. Gays who enjoy practicing bizarre sex acts on one another. Masochists, perverts. And, in the current case, we're working, brutally kill one another." Pike countered bluntly.

"Lewis," Brenkins shook his head. "That's not fair to say."

"It's nothing but the truth," Pike slammed his drink, downing the rest of it. "Am I the only logical one here? No wonder we can't find the guy, no one is thinking clearly. Everyone is stuck on being politically correct. I could care less if the man is gay or not, but he is. He is gay, on a gay dating site, and he killed a man— a gay dating site that is known for its users being involved in bondage and sexual torture. These are the facts."

"So," Vanessa interrupted his speech. "You think the murder has to do with sexual orientation. That's the lead you are chasing?"

"It's a thought," Pike added, "a potential theory."

"Based on what? A Google search on the site?" Clent argued. "Because as far as I know, there has been zero other murders based on the thousands of users on that site. So, what's the connection? Oh, no, I get it, because you don't understand that lifestyle, its different, it's scary. Hell, Tinder has had more killings off it, as have Craigslist. All these sites have the possibility of meeting up with someone crazy. But you're stuck with the sexual orientation of the victim and the killer."

"If the shoe fits," Pike said coolly, trying not to take Clent's bait. He didn't want to lose his cool, not again. Not in front of Brenkins and Velasquez.

"I mean, you have an inside look into that world, why don't you reach out to your source? See what they say?" Clent took a swig of his beer.

"Shut the fuck up!" Pike jumped to his feet; his fist clenched tightly. He knocked his chair over from the commotion.

"Woah!" Brenkins stood up. He got wedged his body between Pike and Clent. Clent didn't flinch, nor did he stand up from his seated position.

"Step off Fat Man," Pike's face was beat red.

"Lewis, you need help. You're stuck on something that has zero to do with the case," Clent spoke calmly now. He hit the button he'd hope to. "You are lost in your own head. This murder has nothing to do with sexual preference or a sexual lifestyle. It has one-hundred percent to do with something else. You just don't want to consider it. Because it's an easy fucking connection, one that people will eat up, you can sell it, based on ignorance and hate. Easy sells, aren't they? You're better than this."

"You crossed the line," Pike wanted to lunge across the table, smack the ugly thin mustache off Clent's face.

"Okay, let's go," Velasquez took Pike by the hand, pulled him away from the table. "Let's get some fresh air."

Velasquez led the two of them out of the bar and into the nearly empty parking lot outback. It was still snowing, a fresh blanket of whiteness stretched out as far as the two could see.

The winter air blew cold against Pike's reddish cheeks. The anger still burned inside him, his fists white-knuckled with hate. He and Clent argue a lot, and they push each other's buttons, they've done that for years. Yet, they never came to blows, always worked it out. But he went too far. If Velasquez and Fat Man weren't there, he would have knocked him stupid. He didn't care how big Clent was, how often he hit the gym, if he got a nice shot to the jaw, big boy Client would crumble like a house of cards. Maybe a follow up to break the fucker's nose.

"Calm down, he was pushing your buttons," spoke Velasquez.

"He went too far, he got personal," Pike added, trying to catch his breath.

"Look, I don't know exactly what he said, but he has a point," Vanessa spoke softly, nonthreatening.

"Excuse me?" Pike wasn't sure if he wanted to curse her out, or if she just used a poor choice of words.

"Look, after the attack on Aaron, Haylee's friend, it makes more sense that she is the connection to the murder, not the sexual orientation. I'm not sure your opinions on that, and its none of my business. But, in our job, we follow facts. You said it yourself. You pointed out she knew too much. How did she know about the stabbing in the back of the neck? This has to do with her, somehow."

Pike didn't say a word. The sexual orientation, the bondage, it made sense to him, because it wasn't normal. Yet, Vanessa made sense. He had the gut feeling when he spoke with Haylee. They were missing something—the connection.

"You're thinking a copycat? Someone close to her, maybe?" Pike had thought that once too. He even had the word written in his yellow notebook, circled three times.

"I'm thinking something, maybe copycat? But, how would Gary even know all the details from the first case? I dunno, but I am with Clent on this one. I don't think that the site is a lead. I think it's right here, in this town. Something with Haylee, with the murders from two years ago. Something is happening here, under our noses."

Pike ran his fingers through his graying hair. The snow had now stuck to Vanessa's jacket, falling gently into her jet-black hair. The moonlight highlighted her soft features. Pike pushed the image out of his head. He was old enough to be her father, broken in more ways than one. The mere thought of her romantically with him made him laugh.

Never gonna happen, old man.

"You want to head back in, grab another drink?" Vanessa asked, breaking him from his thoughts.

"Not yet, the cold air feels nice. I need to calm down," answered Pike. "I saw red in there. I wanted to hurt him."

"You want to talk about it?" Vanessa brushed the hair from her face. "What happened in there? What was Clent getting at?"

"My son," Pike added. "His name is Brent. I haven't seen him in about fifteen years."

"—Oh," Vanessa frowned, she didn't want to impose. "I'm sorry."

"Don't be," Pike added. "It's my choice, my fault. I live with it, and I'm okay with it..."

"You don't seem okay with it," she replied.

"I don't condone the lifestyle he chose. Simple as that. I moved on. My job now is finding bad guys. It's what I do. It's what I'm good at."

"Then what? When you retire, when you hang up the badge?" asked Velasquez.

"I die," Pike spoke bluntly. He wanted a cigarette. He wished he'd never quit. He felt the package of Trident gum in his breast pocket.

Piece of shit gum.

"Got a smoke?" he asked.

"I do," Velasquez grabbed a pack from her purse. "Thought you quit?"

"And I thought I was the detective," Pike smiled.

•　　　•　　　•

"That got pretty heated," Brenkins came back to the table with a few more rounds for him and Clent, who downed his beer in one gulp after the spat between him and Pike. Brenkins' brought two shots and a pitcher of Bud Light to share.

"Pike is an ass, he needs to be put in his place from time to time," Clent poured himself a new glass. He nodded with an appreciation for the refill. "What's that?" he pointed at the pair of shots.

"Four Wisemen," Brenkins' handed him the shot. "This might help thicken up that so-called mustache you're trying to grow," he laughed, holding up his shot for a cheer. "This will put hair on that chest of yours as well."

"You son of a bitch," Clent laughed. He obliged, they cheered, and both downed the strong drink.

"Damn..." Clent's throat burned, he chased it with a large gulp of the freshly poured beer. "This is why I'm a beer guy, shit tastes like poison."

"That makes it good," Fat Man nodded. "We can nurse the beers, catch up."

"Where you been? I was told you were out of the office for the last week," asked Clent.

"Once I finished with the Simmons report and turned that in, I had a conference out in Boston. You know, a bunch of nerds talking about dead bodies, latest tech, decomposition rates, all sorts of good stuff. Bunch of jack asses to be honest."

"You really love that shit, don't you?" Clent shook his head in disbelief. "I still struggle with the crime scenes. That last one, man..." Clent took a swig of the beer. "That's been haunting my dreams. I can't get that site out of my brain."

"It was bad," Brenkins added. I do enjoy my job, though. I can't save people like you guys. I'm not cut out for it, just look at these weak arms," Brenkins lifted his sleeve showing off his lack of muscle. "But, if I can give the dead a voice, help out Pike and guys like you find the killers, I have done my part, right? Making the world a better place?"

"Yeah, I suppose, we would be lost without your expertise, that's for sure."

"So, anyway, I leave for a week, and I come back, and you and Pike are down each other's throats?"

"We're always like this," Clent responded. "I just get tired of his bullshit. The guy is great at his job, but he is ignorant. It limits his perspective. He's caught up on the fact Gary Thom is gay and into that bondage stuff. He won't shut up about it. He thinks it's an easy sell, just like everyone else in the ass-backward town. They don't understand it, so it must be evil."

"I mean, yeah, I get that," Brenkins nodded, taking a huge gulp of beer. "I mean, you saw that scene, though. The sex dungeon, the video recorders. You understand why he would look into that?"

"He's stuck on it," Clent corrected. "No matter what he finds, he goes back to the lifestyle of the perp. Like, it's not shocking that a gay man who likes bondage could murder two people like that. He is wrong, it's shocking, for *anyone*. I just don't think it has to do with it. Just because we live in a small-minded, racist county, doesn't mean everyone who didn't vote for Trump is a murderer. If you're different here, you're untrustworthy."

"But this guy *is* a murderer." Brenkins corrected. "I think it makes sense he would look into this. Right? I mean, what other leads are there? A man invites a stranger into his home, and he and his wife are murdered. They met on the site. Perfect example of Occam's Razor. The site makes logical sense?"

"But," Clent argued, "Nothing about the murders says logic. This is not logical. Nothing we've dealt with is logical. That's the problem. Humans, we're not logical beings, especially the people we deal with. We're emotional beings. The other problem? Pike himself. He is an old soul; he doesn't get it anymore. We're not the same place, not the same town he started out in. He's an old soul in a new generation, for better or worse. I saw the way he looked at me when I was a rookie walking into the office for the first time. I remember the way he treated me like I wasn't even there. It took him years to warm up to me. And I will tell you what," Clent chugged down the beer, pushed it off to the side. "It wasn't because I was a rookie. I had to prove myself because of my skin color."

"Really?" Brenkins shook his head. "I just, I dunno, man. I've never seen it."

"Really?" Clent laughed; it was strained, filled with annoyance. "The white guys tells the black guy, he's never noticed the racist tendencies of a co-worker. I feel like I'm talking to Pike right now."

"I just mean, I would never have thought," Brenkins corrected himself.

"Look. It was like I wasn't good enough to work with him. I was the only black guy on the force back then. Coincidence? I don't think so. We've connected, bonded maybe, over some crazy shit over the years. This small town has its past, and we got stuck in the thick of it. Mutual respect? Sure. Is he a friend? No, I wouldn't say that. I don't think that man has any friends."

"But you think Pike's a racist?"

"I think Pike is ignorant as fuck. I see the way he looks at a young black man walking down the street. I hear the way he talks about gay men, definitely homophobic. Let's not even get started on his position with the Wall and illegal immigrants. Racist, sure? Admittedly a racist? Definitely not. He would deny up and down for days and mean it. Again, its ignorance. He is ignorant. He's not out there waving the rebel flag, going to secret clan meetings. But he holds his racist thoughts."

"He always speaks so highly of you," Brenkins frowned.

"Oh yeah? What's the old bastard say about me when I'm not around?"

"That you're a good cop, one of the best," he added. "His words, not mine."

"Did he follow it with '...for a black guy,'" Clent joked.

"No, he didn't. I know Pike well enough; he definitely is stubborn. Not a lot of friends, I don't think he is an optimist when it comes to people, no matter what gender, color, or what they identify as. Political agenda's aside, he's a damn good detective."

"Well shit," Clent laughed. "You got me there; he does seem to hate just about everyone."

The two men continued with their drinks until Detective Pike and Vanessa re-entered the bar. They made their way over to them, stopping to chat with Laura for a second, gathering a few more drinks.

"You guys got a pitcher and drank the whole thing?" Vanessa pointed to the empty pitcher.

"You guys took forever," Brenkins cheeks turned blotchy with red spots. He was getting a good buzz.

"—Hey, Lewis," Clent spoke, his voice deep. "Sorry about what I said. That shit was unfair."

"No," Pike took a seat across from him. "Look, I get it. I apologize. This case is breaking me down. I can't seem to find anything to hold on to. It's just; it's eating me the fuck up."

"Still, that wasn't cool of me," Clent reached out his hand to shake Pikes.

"Keep your handshake," Pike waved it off, stood up. "I owe you a few drinks."

"I can handle that," Clent smiled.

THIRTY-TWO

"I made coffee," Aaron poured a fresh mug for Haylee, who stumbled out of her bedroom, nearing eleven in the morning. "Cream and sugar, right? Two?"

"Yeah," Haylee yawned, her head throbbing. She grabbed the back of her head. "I'm pretty hungover."

"You knocked back the drinks hard after your dad left," Aaron handed her the steaming cup of coffee. "That will help a bit. I got Trayer outside already. He slept with me on the couch."

"It was a stressful night," Haylee shot back, her eyes glaring.

"I'm not judging, I went out on the back porch and smoked a shit ton," Aaron laughed. "We've talked about this. I'm no saint."

"Sorry," Haylee added, regretting snapping at him. "I had another dream last night. I drank myself until I passed out. Never took Norco, so of course, I had the nightmares again."

"The creature?"

"Yeah, it was horrible," Haylee took a cautioned sip of the coffee, it wasn't too hot, but strong, perfectly sweetened. "It was with Gary, holding him, cradled like a child in its lap. He was breastfeeding with that thing. I saw visions again; I think it was of the murders. Visions have been popping up in my head lately, of the attack. Last night it was more fluid, in my dream."

"You are seeing visions too?" Aaron asked, he placed his coffee down on the kitchen table.

"I thought I told you?" Haylee frowned.

"No, I knew of the dreams."

"Yeah, lately, I will be sitting around doing something, and I go into like a trance. I lose time, usually only a few minutes. But it's like, I dunno how to explain it? A fractured memory? Like, I keep seeing in Gary's view of him walking up behind Dennis in a room, there is some sort of, I dunno...pulley machine near them? Dennis is messing with it, talking. I can't hear the words, but it sounds casual. Then Gary just sticks the knife into the back of his neck."

"Jesus," Aaron frowns.

"So, last night, though, it was more vivid. Like, I was there, in Gary's head. I could hear his thoughts, and there was something else in his head too. It was egging him on. I think it was the creature? It wasn't really words, like, I don't know what I'm saying, I can't explain it...Thoughts or emotions being forced into his head? It seemed so real, so fucked up." Haylee caught her hands quivering from the story.

"It was a dream. You're probably so stressed out, so tired, scared, and you're trying to understand what happened. So, you know, you created this thing, to make sense of it all?"

"Maybe," Haylee rubbed her dry eyes in her hands. "That makes sense. Doctors always threw the words 'coping mechanisms' at me, saying I always hid from my problems."

"Have you caught up on the news?" Aaron spun his laptop over to her.

"What's that?" She took a seat at the table. "Police found a stolen vehicle on the side of the road," she read aloud.

"It's your dad's rental. They found it a few miles down from the Simmons' residence, near the woods. Abandoned, the door was still open. It was a fresh snowfall that night, and tracks led into the woods. Again, he was nowhere to be found."

"Jesus," Haylee skimmed over the article. "Look at all these comments," a heavy frown took her face. "It's just so ugly. They are blaming Dennis like it was his fault."

"Yeah," Aaron replied. "People love to judge."

"Do you think he is going to show up?" Haylee asked.

"Who?"

"My dad," she replied bluntly.

"I dunno, he seemed pretty upset."

"Yeah," Haylee answered.

"What about us?" Aaron asked. "Are we cool?"

"Cool?" Haylee pondered the question. "No."

"Oh… Shit," Aaron was a bit shocked. The morning conversation seemed to note otherwise. He hoped they were back on good terms.

"I want to read the script," She added. "You wrote it about me, right? You acted like a snake, pretended to be my friend to try and write my story behind my back?"

Aaron didn't respond; he nodded.

"I want to read it."

"Okay," Aaron replied.

"Yeah?" Haylee looked surprised.

"Soon as they open my apartment back up, it's yours. I don't even want it anymore. You can delete the thing. I'm not gonna finish it. I feel terrible about it."

"Well," Haylee turned from him, making her way into the living room where the smashed television sat. It was now in the corner a heap of broken plastic and glass. Aaron must have cleaned it up. "It's a start in the right direction."

"Yeah?" Aaron smiled. "I was going to take that to the curb. Shitty, your dad wrecked your television."

"He likes to make his point being overly drastic, not the first time," Haylee explained.

"It's almost noon," Haylee looked at the clock in the room. "She should be here soon."

"The Lydia woman?" Aaron asked.

"Yeah," She answered. "I'm nervous."

"Don't be," he said, finishing off his coffee. "Maybe, she will have answers."

"That's what I'm afraid of."

THIRTY-THREE

Lydia Cayce sat in the passenger seat of the twenty-nineteen black SUV driven by her assistant, a young woman named Jeanie Dawson. Lydia was fast at work with an apple MacBook on her lap. She was lost in her digital journals, speaking out loud to herself every few minutes going over case notes. She had a travel mug she sipped from; coffee spiced up with a little Irish whiskey to keep her warm in between thoughts.

"Age, thirteen, poltergeist-like symptoms," Lydia whispered to herself, taking a sip. "Visions, night terrors, susceptible to shadow people. Potentially demonic in nature, mixture of residual and intelligent..." Lydia frowned, "...father borderline narcist, yes...I had forgotten that. Mother potentially in-tune, possible bloodline connection. Subject currently experimenting with substance abuse as a coping mechanism, emotionally off-put, scared, fragile, not ready for development."

Lydia closed the laptop. She fought back a giant yawn, the coffee proving not enough to fend off her exhaustion. She dropped the passenger seat's visor, where a small rectangle mirror exposed her smokey eyes. Lydia was tired; even the makeup couldn't hide the dark bags under her sunken eyes. She hadn't slept well since she received the frantic phone call from Haylee a few nights back. She remembered her voice, even after all the years, before she even said her name, 'Haylee,' she knew who she was speaking with. The girl she lost, the girl she wasn't able to save.

Lydia had been on edge ever since she received the phone call. She and Jeanie worked late in their office, nearing midnight. The phone call wasn't long, Lydia spoke briefly to the person on the other end. Lydia's face had gone pale, ghastly white. Jeanie figured it out before Lydia had even expressed that this was something important, not the run-of-the-mill client.

Lydia was a bit shaken up. She insisted the two of them meet with the client as soon as possible, and to start making reservations for a small little town in northern Michigan called Emmett County. They were to leave the following morning, which they did.

Lydia wasn't great company on a road trip, but Jeanie was used to that. It was her job to transport Lydia wherever she needed. A sort of twenty-four-hour assistant. She booked her hotels, flights, manage her schedule. She was compensated well, and found pleasure in her work, helping others like her. They had driven all over the United States, even traveled internationally. Lydia Cayce was world-renowned for her talents and was able to make a small fortune to fund her business.

"I'm exhausted Jeanie, ever since I spoke with her, I can't sleep, I can't eat."

"You have been high strung," Jeanie replied. "I have never seen you like this on a case? Especially one you're doing pro-bono."

"This one is special, one from my past. One that I failed; I owe it to her. I could hear her disparity over the phone. She has hanging on by a thread. I'm worried it may be too late by the time we get there. She may be too far gone."

"Worse than me?" Jeanie never liked to compare her own case with others, but when Lydia walked into her life, she saved her from the voices. Thank God, because it was almost too late for her as well. She had already tried multiple times to silence them with an overdose of pills, mangled wrists from multiple attempts of bleeding them out. She knew what it was like to be haunted, followed, preyed on by the darkness. Lydia was the only one who empowered her to reclaim her life.

"I was able to spend time with you, ease you out of it. We had time to train you to control it," Lydia smiled at her. "I was never given a chance to with her."

"I see," Jeanie drove down the long country road. She was overly cautious from the barrage of snow that had fallen over the week. Wind drifts could get nasty out in the open barren farmlands of Michigan, blowing the snow over the roads even when it wasn't coming from the sky. Large ditches on each side of the neglected Michigan road made for a bumpy ride as it was, losing control, ending up in a six-foot ditch, was not on their agenda for the day.

"About ten minutes according to the GPS," Jeanie added, both hands squeezing the wheel.

"Excellent," Lydia nodded. She was focused, tapping a pen against her thigh. "We should be there just before noon."

"Right on time," Jeanie smiled. "I'm getting good at this."

"When we get there, we will have a quick huddle session in the car. I will have a job for you to do," said Lydia, she playfully raised her eyebrows "Solo. A bit of investigating on your own."

"Yeah, Okay," Jeanie smiled with excitement. Usually, she stood by Lydia taking notes of the home, of the client's answers, facial expressions, features. She was basically a walking scribe for everything that happened. This was going to be her first time taking up a part of the investigation.

"We will be here a while, a week or two, depending on what we find. But I was doing research. I have been following Haylee since she popped back up in the news a few years back. Jeanie..." Lydia's voice turned serious, "We may be dealing with a projectile meta-identity."

"A what?" Jeanie asked

"Haven't you been keeping up with your homework?" Lydia frowned. "You're not just my travel partner. You're my protégé. You have the gift, but you need to hone the skills and ingest all the knowledge you can. We've talked about this, I will pay you as an assistant, but you also have to be my understudy. You have a gift; you can help people."

"I know, but...a Projectile Meta-Identity? I have been studying poltergeists, demonology, Babylonian mythology. I have never heard of this meta thing?"

"Then you are not studying hard enough," Lydia added. "Simple as that. We'll talk more when we get there. Until then, tell me what you know about the manifestation of demons."

"Well," Jeanie began racking her brain...

THIRTY-FOUR

Gary was failing his mother, and because of this she was going hungry. He, too, craved the taste of human flesh. The longer he went without fulfilling his pangs of hunger, the sharper the stomach pains tore at him. Like razor blades, shredding his innards. The fat one was supposed to be his feast for him and his mother. How reckless he had been, attacking him in the home, right next to *her*.

Gary was a far cry from the man he once was. He was something new, simpler. He didn't need the things his old life thought was important. His new existence was free of complexities. He had his mother, his love. She was a part of him now, they shared a conscious, needs, wants, desires. Yet, he knew he needed to stay smart, cunning. If he wanted to succeed in keeping them well fed, he had to plan, strategize.

The first thing he needed was new clothes. He looked like a feral beast; he caught the reflection in the mirror of the car before he fled into the snowy woods. A Wildman man had replaced his once youthful looks. He spent the last few days roaming the forest, noting a few different houses not too far from his mother's Den. His hunting grounds.

Tonight, after the failure of his last attack, he needed to regroup. There was a small home, and he had watched it a few times over the week. He sat in the darkness of the wood and stalked, observed. It was a few miles down the road from his first two victims. An older woman, weak, feeble, lived alone. Never any visitors.

An easy meal.

Gary had awoken the morning after his failure, the hunger overbearing. His stomach cramped, like his bowels knotting together. The pain was unbearable. Despite the physical trauma, he had made haste. The sun had just risen; he was already on foot, headed to the home. The whiteout had ceased, but traversing through the thick downfall was tiresome. When he had his full, feasting off the flesh of the Simmons, there was no pain. His muscles never burned; he never tired. But it had been almost a week since he tasted flesh and failing his mother's needs, she was not eager to let him suckle at her teats either.

Gary, or what once was Gary, made his way to the forest's edge after hours of hiking. The small home came into view once he broke the woods. It looked more like a cottage than a house, hunkered down on a small moor that looked over the forest. It was old and poor, just as Gary new the owner to be as well. It was still before noon, and the home was quiet. Gary studied its tidings, a single light shown through the kitchen window. She was awake as was her only companion.

A lone dog, medium-sized strolled about the backyard—a lab of some sort, old, matching the theme of the home and the elderly woman. The shades of white and grey had taken over its coat of black fur. The dog moved gingerly through the snow, bad hips, achy bones. Gary studied the home further, formulating his plan. It would be easy to invade; a thin backdoor faced the forest. He wagered one strong kick would fold the backdoor in half: nothing but an old mutt standing between him and his next victim.

The stomach pains were finally subsiding as his adrenaline kicked in, his mouth salivated with anticipation. He approached the home, stalking quietly. The old dog, trusting for whatever reason, barked only once and ran to him, tail wagging. It stopped a few feet in front of him, cautiously its ears lowered, as well as its head. It must have sensed something wrong. It stared at Gary, curled its lips, growled. Gary smiled at the bitch before he attacked. Gary went for the dog, but for an old mutt, it was still fast. It bit down hard onto his forearm, despite the gruesome attack, he no pain. The dog pulled and yanked at his arm, unwilling to release its grip.

Gary cursed beneath his breath. The dog growled with his forearm trapped between its jaws. Blood sprayed over the white snow, but it did not stop Gary. He was focused, numb to the pain.

Gary was able to lift the mutt with ease. Despite the dog's attack, Gary went for the kill spot. His jaws opened wide and ripped into the dog's throat. He tore into its neck. The dog yelped, releasing the bite, trying to attack Gary's face. Blood dripped down Gary's mouth as he chewed into the dog's throat. Chunks of flesh in his mouth, the sweetness of its blood, the tenderness of its flesh. Once the dog stopped fighting back, Gary slammed it hard against his knee, trying to break its back. He dropped it into the snow.

The dog lay there, rapidly bleeding out. It desperately gasped for air, the life from its eyes quickly fading. Gary kneeled, he tore at the wound with his hands, he continued his feast. He was lucky to come across the dog. A small snack, regaining some of his strength. He had grown weak without fuel. Mother would not feast from the body of a wild animal. It only feasted on the flesh of humans. Even Gary could tell the difference. Despite the easy meal, he wasn't there for the dog.

THIRTY-FIVE

"Here we are, Haylee Leveille's current residence," Jeanie came to a stop in front of modern style duplex. A cozy area, in a quiet Michigan neighborhood. It wasn't remote like her former residence on the country road, but there was enough isolation from her neighbors that gave plenty of seclusion. The nearest duplex was across the street and down away, about a quarter-mile. The duplex itself sat at the end of a cul-de-sac, which was surrounded by a tiny patch of forest. Nothing like the State Forest, but decent enough.

"What's that?" Jeanie pointed to Aaron's side, where police tape covered his side of the porch. The snow was thick, and no one had bothered to shovel the approach. The massive blitz of snow remained untouched, except for footprints and tire tracks from their vehicles going in and out the last twenty-four hours. Jeanie shifted the car into park, kept it running.

"There was a break-in, she told me all about it last night," Lydia explained.

"I see," Jeanie studied the duplex, biting her lip. "You didn't inform me of that. Is it safe here?"

"Yes, of course, it's safe. And there wasn't to inform. Her current neighbor, a friend of hers, named Aaron, was attacked by who the man who killed her former neighbors. His name is..." Lydia pulled out a manilla folder, digging through her notes. "Let's see...Gary Thom."

"That's sort of a big deal," Jeanie argued. "We're investigating a crime scene?"

"No, we're investigating Haylee and her residence. The crime scene is her friend's residence."

"OH," Jeanie didn't quite care for the explanation. Lydia was the boss, so she would go along with whatever she needed. Didn't mean she had to like it, though.

"Thoughts on energy?" Lydia quizzed.

"Already?" Jeanie tilted her head, unexpecting the question. "We haven't even entered the home."

"Right, but we are within a presence. I sensed it immediately when we pulled up. Its strong, Jeanie, lingering. Remember what we studied? Be open. What we tap into, it's not always anchored to a building, item, or even a person. It can be in the air, the earth."

"We have never investigated something like that," Jeanie frowned. She closed her eyes, steadied her breathing. She focused on the energy around her. "I don't. I don't feel anything."

"We need to strengthen your bond, because, even out here, in the vehicle, the energy is out of control. Something evil, powerful, has been here recently," Lydia took out a tape recorder from her bag. She slipped it in her coat pocket. She thumbed through the pack, checking out the contents, replacing her envelope. "I got everything I need."

"Do you want me to hang back and record?" Jeanie was curious to find out what her role would be in the investigation.

"No," Lydia unbuckled her seatbelt. "Here," she handed her a note with an address on it. "I need you to go there. Scope the place out. It's vacant. Practice what we have been working on, center yourself in each room. Find your breathing and open the gate. Meet me back here in three hours. We will compare notes. Be careful."

"What?" Jeanie looked confused. "You don't want me to be a part of the visit?"

"This is a part of the visit, there are two locations," Lydia explained. "You are going to the original home where Haylee lived before the double murder. Where Robbie killed Camille, and Haylee killed him in self-defense. I need you to do a walkthrough while I do this one. I spoke with the current owner of the home already. They gave us the go-ahead to have a look. It's been vacant since the murders; they have been trying to sell it, but nobody wants the place. He will meet you there with the keys to let you in."

"You want me to do run that part of the investigation?" Jeanie's excitement grew. She always ran as Lydia's assistant. Finally, she was given a chance to go out alone into the field.

"You are ready," Lydia nodded. "You have been my apprentice for over three years. You are more experienced in this field than almost anyone else in the world. It's time to put you to the test. Are you ready?"

"I am?"

"Good," Lydia opened her car door. She stepped out, buttoned up her winter jacket to cover her neck from the cold air. Her head popped back into view before closing the door. "—Hey?"

"Yeah?" Jeanie smiled widely.

"I know you are excited about this, but be careful. I am not sure what's going on yet, but I'm already not liking the energy out here."

"I know the drill," Jeanie replied. "I will make sure to call you if anything demonic comes up."

"No," Lydia cut her off. "I want you to leave the premises immediately if any of those signs pop up. Then call me, understood. Leave, then call."

"Yes," Jeanie nodded.

"What are the signs?"

"Violent mental images, overwhelming dread, depression, suicidal thoughts, sulfur smell, disembodied animalistic noises." Jeanie began jotting off the list.

"Good," Lydia nodded. "Be careful, the owner of the building's name is John Carey, he will show you around. He was nice enough to let us in. He was a fan of the show, so he was quite excited."

"Okay, good," Jeanie smiled.

"Good luck," Lydia shut the door.

She made her way up the approach; the snow hit past her ankles, halfway up her shin. She wadded through it, cursing herself for not wearing boots. She made it through the approach, stood before the front door. She took off the glove from her right hand. She gently touched the metal door frame; the freezing air stung her exposed skin. A sudden overwhelming emotion of fear flooded over her, like a surge of unrealistic energy came crashing through her body—fear, sadness, an uncontrollable sense of grief, and punishing anxiety. Lydia let out a small whimper, pulled her hand back quickly. She took a deep breath.

That was bad, really bad.

She knocked on Haylee's door.

THIRTY-SIX

Gary left the dog's carcass mangled in the snow. Its body in pieces, a gutted corpse. The dog was nothing, a warm-up. Once a beloved pet, now reduced to nothing but a heap of bones and blood. Its carcass soiled the snow with the brutality of death. The dog, although sweet, delicious even, did nothing to curb the constant longing for human flesh. The deprivation of it gnawed at him, drove him mad. He salivated at the mere thought of his victim, falling prey to his hands. Mother would never feast on anything short of human, and a dog would not do. He could not return to her for a second time bearing no gifts, no food. He needed the old woman.

He stalked through the kitchen window of the elderly woman's home. It was empty; the light above the sink was on. Dirty pans littered the top of the stove, a well-used skillet sill greasy from the morning bacon, a hearty breakfast, no doubt. Gary waited for a sign of life, yet the house remained silent. No movement.

It appeared empty.

Lifeless.

He studied patiently for ten more minutes before he decided to enter. Breaking in was simple. He found a window unlocked, crawled in. It led him into a small laundry room in the back of the house. He searched the space silently, barely even breathing. He found a small toolbox underneath a battered cabinet. Bingo! Just what he was hoping for, potential weapons. The contents were old, dusty, much like the house itself. He chose a hammer for his weapon of choice. He would be careful, too much damage to her head would spoil much of mother's favorite feast. The delicacy of human grey matter. The human brain.

He snuck through the small room, made his way into the kitchen. He could smell the aroma of bacon lingering from breakfast. The dirty plate still in the sink, unwashed, the iron skillet atop the stove, grease cooling. Nothing had been touched. She wasn't far. He moved swiftly into the living room; the sound of a toilet flushed. Gary took to the long curtain drape, hid behind it.

The old lady was slow-moving as she exited the bathroom. Her body hunched over from years of bad posture. She tiredly made her way towards the kitchen with the aid of a walker. Gary came out from hiding. He tried to remain calm, but he failed. His excitement got the best of him, causing him to get careless, knocking over the nearby lamp. He froze.

"Jesus!" The old lady blurted. She turned her head to see the strange man wielding a hammer. Streaks of blood discolored his clothes, his face still wet with blood.

"My God!" her voice trembled.

Gary said nothing. Instead, he snarled, exposing his blood-stained teeth. He sprang into action. Like an animal, his hammer raised high above his head. He swung it downwards with all his might. The old woman had no time to defend herself. Helpless, old, fragile. She couldn't even ger her arm raised in time to try and deflect the attack. Instead, the head of the hammer smashed into the women's right eye. The blow caved in her brow., causing her to tumble silently to the floor. Her body made a sickening thud as she hit. She was dead weight by the time she fell to the hardwood. Her legs and arms twitched; she made no noise other than a light gurgling from her throat.

Gary stood before his victim. Not an ounce of humanity left in his body; there was no humility, no remorse. The woman was not a victim. This was survival. He would feast on her flesh, take her head back to his Mother, where the brain and eyes would be a delicacy. With that, he would be treated once again by his mother with her warmth, with the milk from her breasts. He thirsted for it, as much as he craved the human flesh. Yes, there before him, all the flesh he could eat.

Gary kneeled beside the woman. He opened his mouth full. He began, he started with her neck, tearing her throat open just to be sure she would not regain any sort of consciousness. He would move to her thighs, her breasts. He would take his time with the woman. Enjoy his full.

Mother would be proud.

THIRTY-SEVEN

A young woman opened the door. Her face was tired, beaten, bags lined her eyes. Her hair, jet black, fell to her shoulders. Lydia could tell the woman tried to hide the pain, the suffering. But it was still present. Her makeup was done, her hair styled, eyeliner, lip gloss. She looked like she had dressed and readied herself for a job interview. But behind the cosmetics was a layer of pain, nothing could soften.

Lydia recognized her immediately.

"Haylee?" Lydia's heart gave way. Before her, with a faint smile, stood Haylee. The young woman she had known as an early teen. Naturally beautiful even back then, with or without the cosmetics. Her dark brown eyes remained the same, resilient. Her face hardened from the many emotional wars she no doubt endured. There, on the other side of the door, stood a warrior. Brave, stronger than she would ever give herself credit for.

"Lydia?" Haylee asked back.

Haylee flung her arms open with an embrace, hugging Lydia tightly. She wept into her shoulder like a couple of long-lost friends reunited. The tears wet Lydia's jacket, probably mixed with snot as well. Haylee sobbed; it was ugly, hard. She cried a lot recently, and she hated it. It made Haylee weak, needy, out of control of her emotions.

"Lydia," she caught her voice. "Thank you for coming. Thank you so-so-so much." She failed to control the tears.

"Darling, I'm happy to have come," Lydia pulled away softly. She looked into her eyes, studied them. "Dry those eyes. It's a pleasure to reconnect with you after so many years."

"I'm so sorry," embarrassed, Haylee wiped away the tears.

"Don't be," Lydia replied. "We had a powerful connection when you were younger. I'm sorry we couldn't continue with our visits. I got your letters, and I have them all. I brought them here with me. I saved them until they stopped coming," she patted her large messenger bag.

"You got them?" Haylee frowned. "You never replied? I thought you never received them or hated me because we stopped our visits."

"Oh, I did reply. I promise you I did. I figured you weren't getting them when you grew desperate for me to reply. When I realized you were not receiving them, I tried calling even. I promise you I did."

"I threw them out," Gerald had snuck up behind them. He spoke bluntly, to the point. "Sorry, parked down the road. You said noon. I'm a few minutes late."

"You threw them away?" Haylee's face burned red. It was intense anger, pure. Her jaw clenched tightly, holding back a flurry of emotion.

"Yes," Gerald replied. "Am I still invited to this gathering?" he looked at Lydia, his eyes unwavering. "I would like to be here."

"Mr. Leveille," Lydia offered a sincere smile. "We never met before. But I know much about you."

"I'm sure you do," Gerald did not offer his hand.

"I can't believe you," Haylee lost it. Anger overrode her entire body. Her mind warped with hatred. She slapped her father as hard as she could. The noise echoed through the house.

"Shit!" Aaron jumped. He hadn't wanted to intrude on the reunion, stood back for his turn to meet Lydia.

Gerald didn't raise his hand to block the slap; he stood there and took it. He let her have that, that moment of aggression, taking out years of frustration on him. He stared into his daughter's eyes. His face now swelled with the shape of a handprint across his right cheek. He turned his head, spit out a small amount of blood into the snow.

"Nice hit," he wasn't joking. His daughter packed some power. A bit of him was proud of that.

Gerald was not angry; he showed no aggression. His eyes watered, not from the blunt force of her slap. It did hurt, but he had been in his share of brawls. Fights that broke jaws, cracked clavicles. No, this was a worse pain, the pain of a failing parent. Or was it even worse than that? Was it failure mixed with jealousy? Haylee was so happy to see this woman, this crook. This woman barely spent any time with her as a child. How could she be so excited to see her? He was there every day, through the death, the blood, the pain, the murders.

Gerald was crushed.

Betrayed.

Failure and jealousy, a potent mixture.

"Haylee," Lydia grabbed her by the arm. She pulled her away from her dad. "Honey, it's okay."

"I deserved that," Gerald nodded. "I'm sorry I did that."

"What?" Haylee's jaw dropped. Her father apologized? Never?

"Its cold out here, can we go in? Warm-up?" asked Lydia, trying to break the tension.

"Uh, yeah...of course," Haylee stepped back into her home.

Lydia made her way passed into the living room as well.

"Hi!" Aaron waved with a broad smile, his hand extending for a handshake. "I'm Aaron, can I get your coat? Maybe an autograph? Both? I'm kidding, not really, though. That shit was intense, no? Sorry, I talk a lot when I get nervous."

"—Aaron! Not now," Haylee shot a stern look. She stepped in front of her father, blocking him from entering. "We're not done with this conversation," She whispered to him, calming herself. The slap helped. It felt empowering. It felt damn good. "If you walk through that door, you are to listen and not argue. Understood?"

"I do," Gerald nodded.

"Okay..." Haylee nodded. She let him pass. She closed the door, locked it behind him. Haylee looked over to Aaron, disappointed. "Sorry, Lydia, Aaron has a crush on you. Big fan of your old show. I asked him to behave. He obviously can't."

"Sorry," Aaron's cheeks flushed. "She's right, though," he stammered. "I mean, about the behaving part."

"Oh darling, that's cute. I could be your mother," Lydia chuckled.

"My mom doesn't have badass tattoo's like you," Aaron helped Lydia slip out of her winter coat, admiring the artwork on her arms.

Lydia was nearing fifty, and she embraced age gracefully. Her hair was naturally black with slivers of silver styled through it. It was natural but enhanced. Whether it was her age or the talents of her hairstylist, she wore it well. Sophisticated, confident, Lydia had an aurora about her. When she walked into a room, people took notice.

She let Aaron take her jacket. Her body was trim, thanks to her daily routine. Morning workouts, afternoon yoga, and a strict carb-free diet. She wore a black blouse that highlighted her tattoos. She had a canvas of them, full sleeves on both arms. A monument of ghostly images, various spirits on one arm wrapped within a colorful and vivid floral background.

Her other arm was tattooed with a sleeve of a blackened shaded forest. Thick woods stretched up through her forearms to her elbow, where the trees bloomed in full explosive shades of green—above that, nearing her shoulder, a beautiful colored night sky lined with stars and a bright yellow moon. The two pieces on her arms connected across her chest and through shoulders, creating one intricate body mural, spilling into one another. Forest meeting coral, spirits meeting stars.

It was evident the attention Aaron was showing Lydia. Perhaps a small part of Haylee felt a tinge of jealousy, which she quickly waved off. Ridiculous, jealousy was something she was not ready to handle.

"I love your ink," Aaron admired the work. "I want to get a sleeve myself, thinking maybe of my favorite horror movies. Jason, Freddy, the creature from the black lagoon."

"Oh," Lydia sniggered. "I like that idea. Yes, my artist is amazing. I dated a tattooist for quite a while. She did all the work for free over a few years. She is amazing with a tattoo gun. If your ever in New York, I can give you her number."

"Oh," Aaron was caught off guard with the subtleness of her reply. "Yeah, that's awesome. She's good. Very good." He corrected himself.

Gerald snickered. "Smooth, kid. That's one way of telling him to keep it in his pants."

"—So," Lydia continued, turning towards Haylee. "Haylee, I just wanted to tell you how thrilled I was that you reached out to me after so many years. After we lost touch, I felt terrible. We never reconnected. My life got busy, the television show, the book deal I signed. Excuses, I know. I am sorry for that."

"No, it's not your fault," Haylee waved off the apology. "If I would have received your letters," she shot her dad a terrible look. "We would have never lost touch."

"That is true," she said. "It would have been nice."

"I'm just glad I kept your card," Haylee added. "I was afraid to call you because I thought when you never replied to my letters...I dunno, I just, I was afraid maybe you hated me."

"I'm glad you still had it after all those years. I'm here now. We can catch back up. A lot has happened."

"Yes, so how do we do this?" asked Haylee.

"Well, normally, I have my assistant run through the home. Take notes, get an understanding for the place. Just like we would do on the television show, then you and I, we would talk. Fill me in with everything that's been going on. I know you said briefly on the phone things have escalated, you are at your wits end?'

"Yes," Haylee replied.

"It's been horrible lately," Aaron added. "We've been sort of dealing with it together. Ever since the double murder in town shits been whacky as fuck."

"I'm glad you had a friend," Lydia replied. "This will be a bit different than how we ran the show, so bear with me. My assistant is working a secondary case so that I will do the walk through myself after our meeting."

"Okay," Haylee replied.

"As a former client, I know a little bit about your history. I will need to be brought up to speed over the last twenty-some years. When did things escalate? When did it go from bad to worse? Be sure to fill me in with any certain aspects of your life that may have triggered these issues. I know we have your father and your friend, Aaron, was it? But these questions could get very intimate, and I need one-hundred percent honesty if we are to do this right. Remember, no secrets, I can't help with false information."

"Yes, I know," Haylee nodded. "They can stay. I want to be open with them about everything too. They need to hear this. All of it."

"So, where *do* we start?" Lydia posed the question back at her. "Our last meeting, you were thirteen. There was an improvement in your life. I remember the visions were dimming; the voices were muting. The crystal I gave you to wear around your neck, the sage burnings when things got thick. They seemed to be helping you control it."

Haylee took in a deep sigh. "Yes, then my dad found out and forbid our meetings. He and my mother got into a huge fight about it, which inadvertently caused her death. It was a car wreck. After all, that, the crystal and the sage burning at night before bed; it all stopped working. Things escalated quickly. Everything got worse, darker, violent."

Lydia peered over to her Gerald, studying him. He sat, his head down towards the floor, staring between his legs, his mouth pursed into a frown. He said nothing; he was tense, labored breathing. She could sense the raw anger emitting from his core.

"I had to hide that stuff from my dad for as long as I could. It became hard to, and when the sage ran out, I had no real way of getting any more. Not till I was older, but by then, I had given up. It stopped working anyway. I was a wreck when my mom died. I think, with all the pain, emotional stress, it was like amplifying it somehow."

"Yes," Lydia nodded. She pulled out a recorder and hit play. "Do you mind? For my notes?"

"Of course not."

"Okay, great. Yes, the stress of any kind can weaken the wall we were trying to build. Something so prolific in your life at such a young age? It probably shattered any defense you had from the veil. You remember, of course, when we spoke back then when you were a child. The gift, the ability to see through the veil, your connection with the spirits, the unnatural beings that call the darkness home. When it goes unchecked, it can warp your mind, bleed into your life, causing a lot of bad things. It can very much weaken you mentally and physically. Break you down."

"I remember, yes," Haylee replied.

Gerald sighed heavily. His mind wandered memories of his wife, the argument, the destruction of his family. He'd hated his wife for bringing Lydia into their home. A hack, a fake, someone who took a financial gain over other people's misery. He sat there, listening to them talk, wanting to interrupt so bad. To throw her out of the home, drag her by her hair and toss her down the porch steps.

It was hard. Very hard. But he kept himself in check, bit his tongue.

"Despite people who may not believe you, Haylee, or in us, what I do. We know the truth, and how very evil it can be. Go on, how did you cope? How did you manage it?"

"I didn't," said Haylee.

"I got her to some specialists," Gerald broke into the conversation. "They gave her medicine, anti-psychotics. Things got better in her high school years. Yeah, they got worse at first, obviously after the accident. She was depressed, who wouldn't be?" Gerald interjected. "But she got better. Thanks to me, to the doctors."

"Let them talk," Aaron stopped him.

"She got better, until the shit with Camille," Gerald swallowed the lump in his throat, ignoring Aaron. His voice broke, cracked. He choked on the name of his daughter.

"Dad," Haylee shook her head. "The pills never helped. I just lied, hid it. I faked it to them, so they would leave me alone. To keep the doctors away. I told them what I thought they wanted to hear. I got sick of people not listening."

"That's not true, I remember. After a while, you began to smile again. The fear was fading in your eyes. You had good years in high school."

"Sort of," Haylee explained. "Truth is, it did get better for a while when I started drinking a lot. You never saw that I hid it. Every night, *every* single night through high school. I drank heavy. Blacking out would keep the dreams away. When the dreams went away, the visions, the sightings during the day, faded as well. When drinking got hard to keep up, I started doing harder drugs. Mostly opioids, pills that would knock me out with no hangover. Drugs offered me the escape."

"You did what?" Gerald's mouth fell agape. He dropped his head into his hands. "You were a pill popper? My daughter, a junkie? Right under my nose?"

"I escaped, the only way I knew how because you stopped me from going to the one person who was helping me!" Haylee stormed off into the kitchen. She returned with a large plastic bag of pill bottles. She dropped them onto the coffee table. "See? This is my life. I take pills. Norco works best, but anything that alters my mind numbs me, lets me blackout. Every day dad, I take these. If I somehow miss, I don't find a way to numb myself, that thing returns. In my dreams, visions of horrid shit will pop into my brain at any time. This is how I cope. Pills. Pills and liquor."

"You're an addict," Gerald rummaged through the pills, he tossed numerous empty pill bottles to the floor in a childish fit.

"Gerald," Lydia spoke up. "I will ask you to leave if you can't keep your acquisitions to yourself.

"Accusations?" Gerald was the one now in a rage. He tried to remain calm, but he lost it. In a fit, he flipped over the coffee table, holding the pills. They spilled, scattered across the carpet. "You are a criminal. You poisoned her mind with all this witchcraft bullshit. You made money off her pain, her misery. Now she's an addict. She needs therapy. She needs to get clean. She needs help from professionals! You are a god-damned piece of shit! You ruined my life. You killed my wife! It's your fault!"

"Dad!" Haylee began screaming. "Get out! Get the fuck out of my life! Go! I don't want you here!"

"Fine!" Gerald yelled back. "I'm done with this. I have given you my whole life! I have tried to help you, fix you! You're just an addict! Pill popping junkie! My daughters, one dead, one wants to be!" He opened the front door, making a dramatic exit. He slammed it as hard as he could; the walls shuddered from the force.

"Fuck!" Haylee screamed. She collapsed to the couch. Drained, she had no more tears to shed. She went numb. She wasn't even angry anymore. She'd simply given up. It was too much.

"He doesn't understand," Lydia took the seat next to her. Haylee laid her head on her shoulder. "Most people don't darling. They don't walk in our shoes. They don't know the horrors we see. They think they have an answer for everything. What they fail to realize, is that there are things in this world, we just can't explain."

"I'm so sorry," Aaron sat on the other side of Haylee. He slipped his hand into hers. She squeezed him tightly.

"What about you?" Haylee looked at him. "You think I'm just an addict? Just a junkie? Making all this up?"

"No," he said plainly. "I have seen the fear in your eyes—the terror. I was attacked by a man who tried to kill me. Who has some sort of connection to you and that house? I don't know what to believe, to be honest. But I don't think you are lying. And I am no one to judge how you cope with everything."

Haylee didn't say anything.

"—But," he continued. "Your dad is sort of right on one thing. You can't keep abusing those pills. They will kill you."

"They are the only thing that works," Haylee's voice was a soft murmur.

"He is right," Lydia nodded. "The cold truth. Many of us who share this gift, or curse, whatever you define it as. We battle through the same demons. Numbing your mind is easy. Drugs, alcohol, the stuff that can alter your reality, these are the simplest means of escape, but the damage is the same. They steal your life. We get you clean; we get you sober, and with my help, we take your life back."

"I'm too far gone," Haylee shook her head. "I feel it, like a candle burning inside my head. The flames almost out, it's been too long. I can't be helped."

"That's not true. Not at all," Lydia protested. "First, we need to figure out what attached to you. What this dream signifies, who was this person who attacked Aaron? What does it have to do with the other home? I need every little detail of what happened."

"Where do I begin?" Haylee straightened herself upright, doing her best to compose herself.

"Let's start with anything leading up to the night of your sister's murder. Anything that was life-altering I need to know about. Then, I need to know in detail the events of the murder. I am sorry, I know it's hard to talk about but, I need to know every single little detail. We will slowly work our way up to today."

"Oh god," Haylee frowned. "Okay...I think I should start with the woods..."

"The woods?" Lydia questioned.

"No," Haylee corrected herself. "I should start with Dennis Simmons."

"Dennis?" Aaron squinted his brow in confusion.

"I have not been totally honest with everyone," Haylee's hand was shaking, her legs trembling. "I didn't know, though. I never saw the dungeon or would have thought he was bisexual. He was handsome, smart, and Robbie and I were already having issues..."

"It's okay, dear," Lydia rubbed her back in a circular motion, soothing her. "You are in a safe place. We are here to help."

"Okay..." and Haylee started with the truth.

THIRTY-EIGHT

Jeanie pulled her vehicle up to the abandoned home. There, a white Subaru was parked, it remained running. A man sitting in the driver seat, window rolled down, smoking. It was a quarter past noon when she arrived at the home. The man saw her pull up, exited his vehicle, dropped the cigarette onto the unshoveled driveway. It fizzled out. He was a short, stocky man. A black winter hat pulled over his head, and a thick matching winter coat zipped to his chin.

The residence was lovely, comfortable looking, a shame of its history. Beautiful location, nestled cozily against the national forest. Large front and back yard, quiet, no neighbors nearby. A lovely home for a family. In Jeanie's past life as a realtor, prior to her mentorship with Lydia, she could have sold this home effortlessly, except for the grisly murders. Even noting that she thought she could make a pretty easy sale.

It was modern, well taken care of, even now with its new owner. They didn't live on-site, but they kept it up. Windows were newer, roof too, good shape. She wasn't sure what she expected pulling up, a wreck of a home? Some derelict cabin with blood-stained walls right out of a horror film? Old rickety and dilapidated? A lot of the homes she and Lydia visited had storied pasts, usually multiple generations of lives sharing their lives within the walls.

This home was much newer, maybe five years tops. And yet, there it stood, vacant, lifeless. Despite its short time on this earth, the stories it could tell, the violence it had seen. Jeanie couldn't wait to explore the inside.

Jeanie enjoyed the research part of the investigations. With her experience as a realtor, she was good at digging up information on the locations. Part of her job was to research the homes for Lydia. Find out the past, the secrets, the rumors. Lydia would go in blind, get a feel for the house, the rooms, and the two would compare notes.

Lydia rolled down her car window before exiting. Always one to play it safe, she did not know this man and wasn't about to put herself in danger out in the middle of nowhere. "Are you the owner of the property?" she smiled.

"Yes, ma'am." He returned the kindness with a friendly wave. "Name's Brian."

"Hello, I'm Jeanie. I work with Lydia. She wanted me to meet up with you," Jeanie, confident enough, exited the vehicle. She shook the man's hand and shook it, locking her car with the key fob.

"I recognize you from your old show, The Talking Dead" he smiled brightly. "My wife and I are big fans. One of the reasons we bought the home was due to the hauntings. We're big-time followers. It would have been perfect for your show. Any chance of bringing it back? All sorts of weird stuff going on in there."

"The show? Afraid not," Jeanie replied. "We enjoyed filming, but Lydia did not like how the network was forcing storylines. What we did was real, the way they portrayed it wasn't. So, we made some decent money, and used it to keep our little business afloat."

"Damn network greed," Brian shook his head, "—loved the show, just loved it."

"We appreciate that. What can you tell me about the house, the murders?" Jeanie asked.

"Not much, really. A rich guy built the home as a rental. The young couple was the first to rent. They got it quick. Houses out here go fast. Nice and quiet, away from the city, nice yard. People love the isolation. It was a newer model, real nice inside. Of course, then the murders happened. That can affect value. Locals dubbed it the murder house. The original owner who built the place, wanted nothing to do with it after a while. Wife and I own a few different places, and we rent as well. We picked it up, been renovating a bit of the inside."

"Right," Jeanie nodded.

"Anyway, as for the murders? The woman's name was Haylee, she and her fiancé at the time. I think his name was Robbie? They rented the place from the original owner. She didn't stick around long, for obvious reasons. The owner tried to rent it back out, but no takers. Whispers of hauntings, you know, that sort of stuff. He was a motivated seller, so my wife and I stepped up, bought it. We're thinking about setting it up as an Air BnB. We're currently saving up for some modifications to the home, mostly in the basement. That's where the murders happened. You'd be surprised how popular the home is, though. Always having people breaking in, young kids walking around the outside, stirring up trouble. We have let a few paranormal groups stay overnight, working investigations. One group bailed before midnight. So, stuff seems to go on in there."

"Local tourist trap, huh?" Jeanie approached the front porch. She scoped out the front of the house, peered into the windows.

"Definitely," the man said, following. "Normally, we don't let people onto the site. Only done it a few times for a few local paranormal groups. Super excited to get a call from you and Lydia, though. Like I said, big fans. I have the key here," Brian fiddled in his pocket until he found the keys. He unlocked the front door. "The house is yours as long as you want to be in it. Just lock it on your way out."

"You're not staying with?" Jeanie asked. "I was hoping you could give a tour?"

"Sorry," Brian frowned. "I own a few homes around here. I have some work to do on a rental, the other side of town, and a showing for another. Gotta catch up on shoveling some of the driveways and approaches, damn blasted winter snow. I trust you will be respectful. Nothing in there to steal, so, no harm in letting you have as much time as needed."

"I promise to lock up," Jeanie shook the man's hand once again. "Thank you."

"Pleasure's mine, let me know what you guys find out. I would love to hear about the findings. The basement's through the kitchen, that's where everything went down. It's also where the few groups who came in before you said was the most haunted parts of the home."

"Thank you," Jeanie waved to the man as he made his way back down the porch and into his vehicle.

Jeanie entered the home. She closed the front door, settling herself in. The windows, completely exposed, no curtains keeping out the sun from spilling onto the hardwood floor. The interior was barren. She took a seat in the middle of the living room. She sat where the sun hit, as the home had no power, no running water, it was freezing inside. She welcomed the warmth of the rays.

The first thing she was to do was meditate. Sit, connect, breathe, feel the home. Center her mind, open herself up to her surroundings. She would do this in every room, for roughly ten minutes each place. Soak the energy from the surrounding space, the air, the walls, the floor beneath her.

Jeanie knew the story well enough. Lydia told her in great detail about Haylee's life, about the basement and the kitchen, both probable hotspots. Although experience taught her every room needed meditation. She was never to let her guard down. Sometimes when a home was active, it could very well be in the least expected area—a closet upstairs, an attic, maybe a crawlspace in the basement. Somethings enjoy the small nooks and crannies.

Jeanie took a seat in the sun, sitting Indian style. She pulled out a small recorder from her bag. She hit the red record button, placing it in front of her.

"Living Room: 12:26 pm ten-minute meditation. Recording now. Jeanie solo."

Jeanie sat, breathing in slowly, deep into her diaphragm. Counting to twenty, she released each breath as slow as possible. She envisioned her surroundings in her head. She visualized herself, sitting cross-legged in the middle of the room with the warmth of the sun beating down her back. She imagined her spirit, her core, leaving her body, floating above her physical form. Looking down at herself, she tried to piece together the room from her memory. She absorbed the energy in the walls, the floor.

Ten minutes passed, and nothing. Clean. Jeanie stood up, stretched her legs.

She would hit every room on the main level. Once finished, she would hit the two bedrooms upstairs and the half bath. She would then move downstairs into the basement. She had a long time ahead of her. Ten minutes was a minimum, but if she was to start experiencing anything unnatural, she was to remain there. Tap into the energy. She would provoke it, push it out, attempt communication. If it was demonic, she was to leave immediately. Her first time alone, she thought she would be afraid. She was not.

She was excited.

Jeanie took out her recorder: "Living room, 12:37 pm, ten-minute meditation. Clean. Nothing of note. She clicked the recording off.

Lydia had built up her confidence.

Where would she be if Lydia hadn't found her? There was no way she would still have her job at the Realtor company. She was rapidly breaking down at that point in her life. For her, the gift came late. Lydia had explained to her that when she was young, she was probably able to cut it off. Subconsciously ignoring it to the point, the veil weakened. Jeanie was lucky. Her childhood was boring in a good way, with two loving parents, decent grades. Lydia explained that it fed on weakness, fear, anger, the black emotions that poison the human condition. Because she was loved, cared for, and able to stay away from tragedy, the creatures from the veil were never able to gain control. They gave up. The veil was too weak.

That all changed in college. One stupid night, a frat party. The ingredients that ruined her life: Four men, camera phones, and a pill to knock her out.

It was rape.

Violent.

Revolting.

Her entire life physically and mentally was invaded by these monsters. Not a month after, still dealing with the emotional wreckage. The embarrassment, the pain that would never leave her. That wall she had built up to keep the veil out, it came crashing down.

Voices snuck into her head.

Shades of creatures stalked her day and night.

She managed to graduate, despite it all she was able to land a job with the realtor. For five years, she felt her mind crumbling, slowly decaying. She was barely hanging on, drinking heavily to keep them at bay. She remembers when she finally snapped. A bottle of pills washed down with a box of wine. She had moved back into her parents' home by then, afraid to live by herself. They found her. Her stomach was pumped, lucky to have survived.

That's when Lydia heard about her. She knocked on her parent's door one evening, offering her help.

No one before Lydia ever understood her about the voices, the visions. It was her coping mechanism, a reality broken from the violent men. They said the mind was a fragile thing, and her mind was raped by those men just as her body was.

Lydia thought otherwise. Lydia paid for the best counseling, her own doctor she worked with for people like her. She healed that part of her life, coming to terms with the rape. Lydia helped her with the other part of her life. The voices, the shadows, the dreams.

Without Lydia, Jeanie wouldn't be alive today.

Lydia stood up from her seat in the living room, made her way into the master bedroom on the western side of the home. Jeanie readied herself for a long isolating afternoon. She repeated the same steps for the bedroom. She sat cross-legged, eyes closed, meditating. There was an energy to the house, something unnatural; she continues breathing, connecting.

Then something happened that shook her.

A gush of cold struck her back. A loud rush of footsteps clamored across the floor of the living room. She jumped, a natural reaction from the startlement. Jeanie, heart thumping in her chest, hurried to her feet. She swung around, looking out into the living room—a lump formed in her throat, causing her to swallow hard.

"What the hell?" Jeanie's eyes fell on the front door. It hung open; the cold winter air wafted into the home.

But she closed it, hadn't she? When she entered? Yes, she remembered feeling the door mechanism latch. There was no way she would leave the door open in the middle of winter.

Now it sat open.

And the footsteps? They sounded like they went towards the kitchen. Jeanie was unsure what to think. Her eyes fell to the wooden floor. Wet footprints...leading into the kitchen.

"Brian?" she whispered. She grabbed her phone from within her inside jacket pocket. Just in case, she pre-dialed out 9-1-1, her thumb resting on the green phone, ready to call for help. "Hello?"

She made her way slowly into the kitchen.

THIRTY-NINE

Haylee wasn't sure where to begin or how to start. Everything in the last few years has spun out of control. One mistake spiraled into a tsunami of blood and death. There was so much to tell Lydia, about Robbie, about her sister, about the Simmons, about the woods, and what happened underneath the blanket of fern trees. Lydia asked to start at the beginning. But Haylee didn't even know where it all began. When did she stop living her life? When did she become the victim of happenstance time and time again?

"It's okay, just breath, there's a lot to unpack here," Lydia encouraged her. "We have all afternoon if need be."

"Dude, for real, I can leave if it's an issue," Aaron saw the unease on her face. "I don't want to complicate things. I want to help."

"No, stay. It's just…" Haylee paused. "I don't even know how to put everything in words."

"Be blunt; be honest," Lydia replied. "Be unapologetic."

"Okay…back in Ohio, after high school, I was failing at college. I met Robbie. I fell for him hard. I had boyfriends in high school, a few in college. But I never fell in love, not like this. That was Robbie, charming, handsome, a bit shy. He allowed me to put my guard down. I never told him about my issues with the voices. But he was aware of everything else. He was my rock, because my family, my father, our relationship has always been love and hate. Anyway, Robbie and I were together through college. We moved into an apartment during our last year. He cheated on me that first year we moved out, some girl he worked with. He said it was an accident and that he needed to come clean, that lying to me every day was killing him. I would have never known because I trusted him, so much, I would have never guessed he'd cheat on me. It hurt so bad fucking bad... I had never felt so low, not since I lost my mother. We decided to, you know, make it work? I guess...Before he cheated, I was so happy with my life. The bad things started to clear up. I wasn't getting the visions, the voices, the dreams seemed to be less active. Then, when all that pain came from him fucking that girl behind my back...it all flooded back. Even stronger. Day and night, the voices, the visions, weird memories, violent, nasty things would pop into my head. That's when I went back to what I had done in High School. The drinking, the pills. I did this for a year behind his back. He worked a lot anyway. We tried to repair the damage."

"Okay," Lydia nodded.

"He purposed after he landed the new job here in Michigan. Around the same time, my sister's fiancé, who was an abusive asshole, put his hands on her. My dad attacked him, lost his job, Camille was scared and asked to move in with us out to Michigan. I said, yes. I was scared to move away from my family with Robbie, anyway. I told him I trusted him again, but it was a lie. I was afraid to live without him but hated living with him. To this day, I have no idea why he cheated. He claimed he still loved me and that it was a stupid mistake. But I could never trust him again. I was always jealous, checking his phone behind his back. I even thought, maybe...he and my sister..."

"Here," Lydia pulled a Kleenex from her purse.

"No," Haylee shook her head. "I won't cry again. I'm stronger than that. I know my sister would never have done that. It was just me losing control of my reality." Haylee rubbed her eyes, rolled her neck. It cracked multiple times. "We moved to Michigan. I was confused, still angry. My sister was doing well, and she landed a job right before she passed away. Robbie was thriving at work, working late ours again. We began fighting a lot at home since we moved. He started staying out late. He cheated once already. So, you know? My mind started wandering even more. We met our neighbors the Simmons within the first week. We had befriended them, sort of, it was more for me than Robbie. He didn't care for them. But he saw I was struggling with the move. Until the murders...I had no idea about the sex dungeon? I knew Dennis and Nora well. More than I admitted to anyone. I was close with Nora, sure. We met weekly, talked almost daily. I know she had no idea about Dennis' second life."

"I read that he had a hidden sex dungeon in his garage? Hid it from his family? He had sex with men behind his wife's back?" Lydia questioned.

"I had no clue, but, yes, it looks like he did. He had been for a long time. I didn't know, and she didn't know, either. It's all his fault. He was a monster. An addict"

"Gary?" Arron questioned?

"No, Dennis," Haylee corrected. "I didn't know, I swear it. I felt bad enough as it was. I liked Nora, but Dennis? He was there, this older handsome man that had everything, and yet he still wanted me? I don't know why, but I let him. Maybe to get back at Robbie? Maybe because I was confused and wanted to be wanted again? Maybe because I was losing control all around me with voices and shadows everywhere. Because being wanted like that, made me forget about the pain."

"Wait. What?" Aaron's mouth fell open.

"I thought I was the only other one. He never asked me into that place, and it was always when Nora was out. Or he would get a hotel room in the city, and we would meet for lunch. But then he left his laptop open afterward. He went to shower, and a message popped up on his messenger. It was a naked woman, younger, not illegal, but probably just in college. She was bent over, spreading herself for him. It was disgusting. I read the messages. She was one of his many girls in his messages. No men, only women. He must have hidden the men from his social media profile that he left open. He was sick."

"Jesus," Aaron was at a loss for words.

"He had issues," Lydia spoke calmly, without judgment. "Sex is a human act, but when it controls our lives? When it becomes a necessity that hurts the ones we love? Then it defines us, and we lose control of it. He was losing that inner war. That's evident. We can't forget, he was human, just like you and I. We make mistakes, but they don't define us. Not if we can learn and adapt from them."

"There's more. Part of the problem between Robbie and me was that I was told that pregnancy would take a miracle. Before I made the mistake, multiple times with Dennis, I had visited my doctor. I learned about Endometriosis, and what it was doing to my body, and why Robbie and I would never have our family."

"Endo what?" Aaron asked.

"All I wanted was to be a mother. To pick up where my mom left off," Haylee frowned. "Endometriosis, it's when the egg becomes blocked. Basically, I can't have kids. It hurt me so bad. I was spinning out of control. Another part of my life ruined, stolen from me. That's when Dennis found me at my weakest. There was a comfort to be in a man's arms who wanted me. I was broken in so many ways. At least he wanted me for something. Robbie did everything he could to not spend time with me. Not that that makes it right...I never even told him about it. He died before I could muster the strength."

"I'm so sorry," Lydia held her hand tight. "What about the woods?"

"Jesus," Haylee's knees trembled. "I was late. A miracle, I was pregnant."

"What?" asked Aaron.

"I took a pregnancy test at home. It was positive. It was Dennis', I know because Robbie and I hadn't made love in months. I told my sister, I was panicking. I was in shock. I wanted a baby so badly. I wanted to be a mother, to hold my own child in my arms, to feel that love. What was Dennis going to say? What was Robbie going to do? I just...I broke down. Every day I felt myself losing it, slipping away from reality. Camille told me to getaway. Go see dad, get my head straight. I called him, set up a time to visit. But I never made it. I stayed in my room for two days. I was supposed to leave that weekend. On the second night, my stomach hurt so bad. Like a razor was shredding my insides. It was so painful; I was vomiting blood. Robbie was at work; Camille was out with friends. Everything went black that night. I had no clue how far along I was. I was afraid to go to the doctors. I had told myself I would when I got back home from Ohio after I visited my dad. After I figured out what I was going to do. But I never got to go, blackness. It's all I remember. When I woke up, I was in the hospital. I was told my sister and Robbie came home, that the door was open. The followed the droplets of blood into the woods. They found me a few yards in. I had dug a hole, naked from the waist down. Blood everywhere, my hands, my crotch."

"Jesus," Aaron stood up. He began pacing throughout the room. Haylee avoided his eyes. Was he judging her? Did he hate her for the infidelity? About keeping it a secret?

"I lost the baby, a miscarriage. I crawled into the woods, my mind broke. I spent a week at a psych-ward, being evaluated. They thought I tried to kill myself, that I had slashed my wrists with something. I was able to go home with my sister and Robbie after a while. But it wasn't like before. Robbie thought the baby was his, even though it couldn't have been. I think he wasn't able to come to terms with it. He decided I had been pregnant for longer, forcing it to make sense, I guess. We never spoke of it. I withdrew even more. I was only home a few weeks before I tried to leave for my father's again. That's the night when the snowstorm hit. When I returned home...and the madness."

"Haylee," Lydia's voice was soft. Gentle. "Have you told anyone?"

"No, who could I tell?" Haylee managed to keep strong throughout the story. But her stomach was sick with nerves, her eyes thick with tears, and then she let it all go. All of the pain, the suffering, the tears poured down her cheeks. She sobbed. She sobbed harder than she had ever in her life. All the pain she had tried to hide away, tried to swallow down, the confrontation of the events, they spilled it out of her, like a gunshot wound, a gaping hole in her soul.

"I'm a mess," her words wet with spit. Tears hit her hard, her nose and cheeks red, gasping large gulps of air in-between heart-breaking moans.

"Let it out, purge the toxins from within you," Lydia pulled Haylee's head back into her shoulder. She rubbed her back like her mother used to do when she got hurt as a young child. "There, there, darling. Release it all, cry it out." Her hand rhythmically circled around her shoulders, soothing her.

Haylee breathed hard, tried to collect herself. "After the woods. The dreams started with the creature. The voices went away, the shadows too. All that was left was the visions of that thing—the dreams with my sister, with Robbie. I see things now too, it's like, it's attached to me. I had visions of that Gary man killing the Simmons."

"I see," Lydia looked to Aaron. He stood in the corner, pale as a ghost.

"You said you were attacked by a man? The man who supposedly killed Dennis and his wife?

"Yes," Aaron replied.

"How long ago was this?"

"Yesterday," He replied.

"Did the man come into this room? Here in Haylee's apartment?" she asked.

"No, he attacked me in my home. Next door."

I need to get there. If it was just yesterday, I might be able to pick up on it," Lydia stood up. "Take me there."

"We can't," Haylee explained, wiping away her tears. "It's a police crime scene."

"I don't care. I need to be as close to the person as possible. This is a must," Lydia explained.

"Okay, I have my key. Follow me," Aaron led the way-out apartment and towards his home.

"Let's find out what we are dealing with Haylee. Follow me." Lydia held her hand out, helping Haylee to her feet. "Time to conquer our fears. Time to take control of your life."

"Okay..."

FORTY

Robbie needed to get out of the home. He and Haylee hadn't stopped arguing since the move, and it had gotten worse since the incident in the woods. He had hoped with the new job, the new home, the proposal, that they would be able to put his infidelity behind them. Start fresh, start new. How stupid was he?

Why had he slept with that girl? He wanted to wish it away. Yet, things would never be the same.

He left the house, a beautiful winter evening, warmer than it should be. Robbie loved the woods. When his mind weighed heavy, he often hiked behind his new home. The forest behind them was a big selling point for Robbie. He'd grown up in the country and missed the isolation. He'd spent a lot of time hiking when he needed to get away from the stress.

He'd found an abandoned shed a ways behind their property, far back deep into the woods. He explored it a few times, wondered about the building, and he assumed it was an old hunting lodge. He was on his way back to the lodge when he came across the area where he and Camille found Haylee a week prior.

The site of her body was mortifying. They found her pantless, blood everywhere, she slumped over within deep hole, it looked to him like a grave. The ground was partially frozen, they think she dug it out with a rock and her fingers. Then she sat in the hole, tore at her wrists, passed out from the loss of blood.

Haylee remembered nothing.

Then, the miscarriage. But how? He was afraid to ask her in her fragile state. Who had she slept with? He played along, acted dumb, let her believe he thought it was his. But he realized the truth, that it couldn't have been. He stood there, looking down at the shallow looking grave. Tears rolled down his cheeks. Warm, even in the winter air. Where had it all gone wrong?

Of course, the answer was right in front of him. He just didn't want to admit it.

It went wrong when he met Amanda. A few nights of loveless sex. Pointless, not worth losing Haylee over. But yet it would not go undone. He had excuses, plenty of them—all bullshit.

This was his fault. How could he be angry with her own infidelity? Yet, he was. Bitter, angry, wasn't even the right word. It was darker than anger. Worse than hate. He despised her. He couldn't look at her any longer.

He left the hole. Wiped the tears away. Made his way back towards where he'd found the hunter's lodge.

He heard a rustling from behind him. It startled him. Something following him? He snapped his head back to a thicket of fern trees. There, in the darkness of the wood, about six feet over the ground, hovered two red glowing eyes.

"Jesus…" Robbie whispered to himself.

The eyes, they fascinated him. They called for him, reached out to him. He wasn't sure how much time passed as he gazed within them. Without his realization, he began making his way towards the eyes. Fear started to creep up. His brain was fighting with itself. Part of him wanted to flee, to turn and run. But his control over his body was limited, and something stronger was egging him forth. He couldn't overcome the sensation. Why was he walking towards this thing? Jesus, he could smell it, the rank stench of death. It made his stomach retch. The thing's body came into view. It was skinny, decrepit. Its head large, awkward, bobbing up in down as he approached. Its flesh was dangling from the bone, short antlers protruding from its head.

Robbie would become the first host. His humanity would be ripped from him. Buried, blurred, he would try and fight it at first. He would last longer than the future victims. He would keep it at bay, slowly going mad from the creature's ethereal connection. It had poisoned him. Soon he would be completely overtaken.

FORTY-ONE

Gary was proud of himself, basking in the joy of the kill. His stomach was full of its fleshy splendor. The old woman was easy prey. He feasted for as long as he could. Once he had his fill, he searched the home.

Tools, he needed tools.

First, he needed to remove her head, keeping the eyes and brains for mother. He found a hand saw in the old woman's garage. Old tools from a long dead partner. Dust was thick on them. Luckily the saw was still sharp. It proved to get the job done with ease. Next, he found a burlap sack and placed her head into it. Easier to carry, easier to hide.

Mother would be happy.

The sudden rush of blood between his legs made his knees weak. Even better than human flesh was the sweet milk from mother's teats. He found his mouth salivating at the thought, his cock hardening.

It was both nurturing and sexual. He wanted it more than anything.

Finally, he needed a shower. Not because he cared for hygiene. Gary had to hide in plain sight, and foul odor would draw attention to his presence. His primary instinct was to hunt, kill, feed himself, and mother. He needed to stay undetected. He washed himself of the blood. He found scissors in the bathroom, and with them, he cut his hair as close to the scalp as possible. Next, he found an old razor, shaved himself bald. He searched for her bedroom. Photos of the woman and a man on her dresser. Probably a deceased husband. His clothes still hung in the closet. For how long? It didn't matter; Gary's clothes laid soaked in blood on the bathroom floor. He needed a change, and these would suffice. A bit large on his skinny frame, but he found a belt.

Gary left home with his prized possession, her head in the sack. He also found an old hiking bag in the back of the women's closet. He filled it with tools, hammers, the saw, and other instruments he could hunt with. He would walk along the woods, hidden within its thicket, staying hidden enough from the edge to keep an eye out for people. He would pass a few homes, looking, watching, taking notes on future hunting opportunities.

Gary was eager to make it back to mother. Her hunger resonated deep within him, torturing him like some distant itch. It grew more intense the closer he got to Haylee's old residence, where he and mother first met. The site of the home meant he was close to their new lair. He knew to turn deeper into the woods, travel north until he came across the isolated hunting lodge.

Haylee's old home came into view, and to Gary's surprise, a lone car was parked in the driveway. He stopped mid-track, curious as to the scene unfolding. He bent down, concealing himself further within the woods. He watched eagerly from afar. Someone was inside; someone was lurking around. Gary smiled, his mouth pulled wide, his blood-stained teeth showing. Today was proving to be primed for hunting.

He placed the burlap sack containing the old woman's head inside a large bush to conceal it. He also grabbed the hammer and hand saw. He would bring mother two heads to feast from. How lucky he was.

Good boy, he told himself.

He left the thicket of the woods and made his way to the home.

FORTY-TWO

"She is not answering," Lydia frowned, this was her second phone call in five minutes to her partner, Jeanie. "I don't understand why she isn't answering. This isn't like her at all. She knows to keep in contact during investigations."

"Maybe she has bad cell service?" Aaron responded. He swiped away the police yellow tape from his doorstep.

"That house was terrible for cell service," Haylee nodded. "Can we get in trouble for this? It's still a crime scene, right? Like, is this okay?" she followed Aaron's lead.

"Perhaps you're right," Lydia pushed aside the negative thoughts. "Cell service makes sense," Jeanie would show up on time after she was done investigating the home.

"We're okay entering," Aaron unlocked the front door. "I got a voice mail during that intense convo you two had. Detective Pike said I was allowed back into my place. So, we're fine now. Said I could remove the tape."

"Oh, good," Haylee answered.

Lydia calmed herself. She readied her mental state before entering Aaron's home. This was not like Lydia. She was usually cool, calm, level headed. She noted when she and Jeanie drove up to the duplex that she sensed something dreadful nearby. The residue of something unique outside Haylee's home. During the interview, as Haylee went through her deepest secrets, Lydia could sense the energy growing stronger. A lingering aroma, a stench of death. Not strong enough for her to tap into, but it was there, evident that something was afoul. She needed to be closer to it, narrow the hot spot down. She had a good idea where that was. Aaron's apartment could be the epicenter of the lingering energy she was feeling.

"Shit, there goes my deposit," Aaron entered first. He led them into the living room, where the majority of the scuffle ensued. The room was as they left it, lamps toppled over, a massive dent in the plaster of the wall, like a small crater. Even the blood spots remained on the carpet.

"Can we enter?" Lydia asked, following behind Aaron and Haylee.

"Yeah, come in. Man, that asshole did a number on my place," Aaron frowned, he held the door open for the women.

Lydia followed in behind Haylee warily. She always took investigations cautiously. But in all her years of experience (over two decades worth) couldn't prepare for what was about to happen. She hadn't walked three feet into Aaron's living room before she was hit with a wave of malevolent energy. She was knocked back like a rag doll, flung off her feet and tossed outside of the house.

Lydia fell hard on her back. Her stomach immediately retched. She crawled out onto the snowy lawn, trying to escape from the home, vomiting violently along the way, leaving a trail of stomach bile behind her. Her body temperature spiked, she broke into a sweat that drenched through her clothes. Her skin turned clammy; her face went white as a ghost. She heaved in between the spasms of her stomach. Her head flooded with a whirlwind of emotions. Anger, rage, and the most intense hunger and thirst she'd ever known. She was being overrun with dreadful emotions. Abhorrent, revolting sensations of bloodlust pounded her brain like a four-year-old on a drum set.

"Fuck!" Aaron jumped back. He'd never seen a human tossed so violently from thin air. It looked like an unseen vehicle struck her. One minute she was behind him, the next she was gone. He ran outside to her aid. Lydia was quivering, seizing in the snow. A horrible noise came from her. It was awful, demonic.

"Lydia!" Aaron panicked. "Help me with her!"

"Jesus, okay..." Haylee snapped out of it. The site of Lydia's body being tossed and the violent aftermath froze her in fear.

The two of them tried to embrace Lydia. She fought them, screamed, clawed at them both. She was still suffering some sort of seizure. Still projecting stomach bile as she fought them both. They struggle to contain her. It seemed to last forever before the fight went out of Lydia. The seizure stopped; her body loosened.

Lydia curled into a ball, holding her stomach. She rocked herself in the winter snow. She stopped fighting them off, her eyes vacant. She whispered unintelligible words.

"What the hell just happened?" Aaron was horrorstruck. He was out of breath from the struggle.

"Jesus, how should I know?" Haylee knelt down beside her. "Lydia, Lydia?"

"Let me go grab some water," Aaron ran into Haylee's home.

"I need to call an ambulance," Haylee grabbed her cell.

"No," Lydia whispered. "No ambulance..."

"What happened?" Haylee placed her hand on Lydia's forehead. It was burning.

"My god..." Lydia's eyes burned like hot coals had been pressed into them. Her throat was on fire as if she swallowed red hot razor blades. Her body constricted; every muscle cramped up on her.

"Shit, okay, shit," Haylee stood up pacing. "No ambulance?"

"Here, try this," Aaron came running back with some water. He held her head up in his lap. Lydia slowly sipped.

"Okay," Haylee pulled out her phone and scrolled down to Vanessa's number. She had given her, her card the other day. She had programmed her name into her phone almost immediately. Call for anything she said.

Shit, she needed someone here, a professional of something. Haylee dialed. It rang a few times.

"Hello?" Vanessa picked up.

"Vanessa? This is Haylee. I'm in trouble..."

"Haylee?" Vanessa repeated. "What going on?"

"Please come help me. Something has happened. I need some help."

"Did you call 9-1-1?" she asked. "I'm off duty."

"No, I can't call 9-1-1," Haylee explained. "Please, you said to call for anything," she continued. "Please, I need you. Now."

"Okay, okay, are you at your duplex?" Vanessa asked.

"Yes," Haylee replied.

"Be there in ten. Stay safe." Vanessa hung up.

"Who was that?" Asked Aaron. He held up Lydia's head in his lap, aiding her with the water.

"A woman officer left me her card. Said to call for anything. She's off duty right now."

"No ambulance," Lydia choked on her words, coughing up some of the water she'd just swallowed.

"No, she said she would come by herself."

"What's going on?" Aaron offered Lydia some more water. "What the fuck just happened to you?"

"Give a minute…" Lydia was still gasping to catch her breath. Barely able to sit upright. She was weak, exhausted from the struggle.

"Let's ger her inside to warm up?" Aaron asked, looking at Haylee.

"No," Lydia moaned. "I'm burning up…"

They sat there, nearing ten minutes before officer Vanessa Velasquez pulled up in her civilian vehicle. Lydia said nothing; she concentrated on her breathing, drinking down the water. Velasquez exited the car, quickly made her way over to the three of them, sitting out on the front lawn in the snow.

"What's going?" asked Velasquez.

"Lydia got violently sick," Haylee explained. "Something attacked her."

"Okay? Attacked her?" Vanessa frowned; her eyes darted around the yard. "Why are you out here in the cold? Why did you call me and not an ambulance?"

"—No," Aaron interjected. "You don't understand. She didn't just come down with something. She walked into my apartment, and she like, got attacked by something. It fuckin' threw her out of my place. We were both standing there, and she got hammered by something."

"Attacked? Hammered?" Vanessa shook her head; they had gone crazy. Nothing made sense. "She needs to see a doctor, call her an ambulance. I don't know what sort of help I can be."

"No," Lydia blurted out. Her voice seemed to come back, the color returning to her face. "I'm not sick," she added. "I told you not to call," she took Aaron's hand to help her get to her feet. Her legs still weakened. "They won't listen to us. Police never do."

"What? Listen to what?" asked Aaron.

"Whoever attacked you in your home, he's not human. Not any longer," Lydia explained. "Gary is a part of the creature now."

"What did she just say?" Vanessa asked? "Not human? Who is this woman? What does she know about Gary Thom?"

"My name is Lydia," it was still hard for her to speak. "And my guess is, you won't believe any of the information I am about to share... You are not needed here. I am sorry, Haylee called you. We won't need your assistance, after all."

"Is that so?" Vanessa looked at Haylee with disbelief. "I came out here to honor my word. I'm off duty. So, why don't we head inside, we'll brew some coffee, and you try me?"

"Yea, it's freezing out here," Aaron blew his hot breath into his freezing hands. "It's been a fucked-up day. I could use some caffeine and a fuckin' fifth."

They regrouped back inside Haylee's living room. Lydia made Aaron close the door into his duplex before she walked past. Her stomach retched again as she made her way passed it. She sat on the far side of Haylee's home. Staying as far away from Aaron's side of the duplex as possible. Aaron brew the coffee strong; he brought it out with four mugs.

"Thanks," Lydia forced a smile. The coffee was strong, and despite the incident, the hot beverage soothed her throbbing throat.

"Okay, where do we begin?" Vanessa asked.

"I'm sorry," Lydia explained, drinking down the rest of the water Aaron had fetched for her previously, before taking a second sip of the coffee. "I have been doing this for over two decades. I have never gotten that physically ill from a walkthrough. Hell, I didn't even get a chance to start the walkthrough. It hit me so fast. I didn't have time to prepare myself."

"Prepare for what?" Vanessa interrupted.

"I am a paranormal investigator," she explained slowly. "I'm not sure if you are a believer in the paranormal or not, but regardless, I am what most people label as a clairvoyant. I can tap into...different worlds, realms, however you wish to comprehend it, or how you label it. The things you can't see, but sometimes feel? The energies in the world and the things that live in those different realms. All of it, I am sensitive to them. So is Haylee. It is why she is so troubled. She was never given the right help, the opportunity to understand and control it. So, in her case, it warped into something sinister. Using her as a sort of vessel, overtaking her."

"Wait, we're talking ghost stuff?" Velasquez asked. "House on haunted hill, Amityville horror? That stuff?"

"Yes, ghost stuff, I suppose that works too," Lydia held her head. A throbbing pain still lingered between her eyes. "Anyway, I felt something was off when we pulled up. That's how strong it was here. I should have known..." Lydia frowned. It was a cautious mistake. "I sent my partner to your old house Haylee, to do her own walkthrough. When we came here, we discussed your history. I could feel the presence or the energy that was coming from the other side of the duplex, Aaron's apartment. It's here too, but the presence is weaker. It's hard to explain, but the connection isn't as strong, weakened. I believe that is because the man was never actually in your apartment. I think in here, I can sense the dreams, the visions, your part of the connection. Which isn't as pure as the man who was in Aaron's apartment just yesterday."

"That's why my place affected you so much? Aaron asked.

"Yes, a closer connection to the source. You were attacked by the man who killed Haylee's neighbors. He was in your home. It's the energy he left behind that hit me so hard. When I entered your place, it was like a kick in the stomach. Worse than that, you saw me, it knocked me off my feet. Threw me with force. These things, these creatures, ghosts, spirits, we don't understand much about them. But someone like me, like Haylee? We feel them, and that man, Gary? He isn't human anymore. I can tell you that for certain. His energy hit me like a wrecking ball of sickness. That's how it can transmute through different realities, through energies. Whatever this thing is, it's powerful, very powerful. Gary is a puppet now; something is controlling him. Something that has been terrorizing Haylee ever since her fiancé killed her sister, and she killed him in self-defense. Although Robbie wasn't going to kill you, the creature and the host need you alive. He may have been trying to chase you out. Or hold you captive? I don't know..."

"You mean Gary Thom is brainwashed?" Velasquez asked.

"More like mind-controlled, it works like a hive mind, from my limited understanding. This thing, creature, spirit, whatever it is. It shares a collective consciousness with its puppets. I only know that because I could feel both Gary and the creature's presence. The remnants of both their beings. The sickness, it was a manifestation of the creature. But Gary was definitely in there too. Like a whisper, trapped in his mind. He has no control."

"This is fucking nuts man, is this real?" Aaron looked towards Haylee for answers. She sat there, emotionless. Taking everything in. "

"Oh, God, Jeanie?" Lydia took out her phone. She attempted to call again. "She didn't answer. She is in trouble."

"Who?" asked Vanessa?

"My partner, she went to Haylee's old home to investigate. She is in trouble, I know it." Lydia tried to stand, but her knees buckled out.

"Hold on, I have you," Aaron grabbed her.

"We need to go there. Get her out. If that place is its nest, she will never make it out."

"Okay, listen," Velasquez helped Aaron move Lydia to the couch. "Keep her here. Watch her. Haylee, can you go with me to your old home? We can check on Jeanie, and get everyone safely back here."

"Uh, god, back to that house?" Haylee swallowed hard. She hadn't set foot near her old home since the murders.

"That might now be a good idea," said Lydia. "Aaron, can you go with Vanessa? Haylee, stay with me. We still need to talk."

"I just need directions, give me the address," Vanessa replied.

"No, I'll go with you," Aaron grabbed his jacket. "I know the way, been there lots of times."

"To the home?" Vanessa asked?

"Yes, I'm sort of doing some research on the house.

"OK, we are in and out of the house. We'll check on her friend and double back here. It's illegal to be snooping around the property," Velasquez said.

"We got permission from the homeowner," Lydia replied. "She was let in."

"Okay, well, that will make it easier. C'mon, let's go," Vanessa opened the front door. "Car is running, let's move."

FORTY-THREE

Jeanie's heart was pounding; she found it hard to swallow, adrenaline pumping. The front door was open, wet footprints from the snow, freshly made led into the kitchen of the empty home. Her first instinct was to call 9-1-1. She had it pre dialed, her finger on the green phone button to dial. Perhaps it was Brian. Maybe he forgot to tell her something, looking for her, assuming she started in the basement? She didn't think to look for his vehicle. She didn't think of leaving the house. No, her instinct was to investigate.

"Brian?" the word came out of Jeanie's mouth, feeble, weak. Almost a whisper.

"Brian?" she tried again; this time louder. The house quiet, silent.

"Hello?' Anyone?" she asked.

No one replied.

The wet prints went to the basement. She grabbed the closed door, slowly opening it towards her. It flung open, violently. The thick door smashed into the bridge of her nose. She heard a loud crack as it struck her. Her vision blurred; bright lights popped in her eyes. She fell backward, keeping her footing, but hunched over from the blow. She had just enough time to look up when she saw the man lunging at her, his arm high above his head with a metal object in his hand. It came down fast, lethally. She felt something hit the top of her head, followed by the sickening sound of her skull cracking. She was surprised; there was no pain—only numbness which shot through her extremities. A bright light flashed in her head; more stars exploded around her.

Then came her final visions of her life.

The four men at the party on campus. Visions of young drunk faces, pink lips, reddish cheeks. Still, boys, boy's doing sick grotesque manly things. The visions came over her in waves of shattered recollections. Each a sharp shard of pain, misery being stabbed into her fading conscious, forced to relive the worst of her life during her last living moments.

Not of her loving parents, not of her best friend in middle school enjoying the summer pool at her parents' home downstate, not of Lydia, who took her under her tutelage, teaching her how to help with the demons that came before the four boys. Or her loving guidance helping her conquer the scarier demons that came after the boys. No, her last moments were shared with the entitled football kids, with futures more important than her body.

They Mocked her.

Slut.

Whore.

Cum faced bitch.

They each took turns, sticking things inside of her, not just their disgusting dicks, anything they could find, playing would it fit. They paraded her around the party unconscious. When they were done, the last one took out his flaccid skinny pecker and pissed on her, then shoved her back into her car, where she awoke the next morning.

They filmed the atrocity on their phones.

Showed their friends.

The flashback lasted for a few minutes, as Jeanie's brain released the euphoric chemical DMT (N-Dimethyltryptamine) that flooded her head with her most profound memories in a dreamlike state. These few minutes felt more like a trapped eternity of her most painful life experiences. She laid helpless on the floor, stuck somewhere between near-death and total annihilation. Those sick fucks, the pain, the damage they caused her both in life and now even in death. This is what came to Jeanie during her last few precious moments among the living, before the final and fatal blow to her head.

Next came blackness, then came nothingness.

Death.

FORTY-FOUR

"It's down this road. We got a few miles to go still." Aaron said. "Can I go in?"

"In?" Velasquez questioned?

"The house, to check on Jeanie? I have never set foot in it."

"No," Velasquez replied. She grabbed her phone from the dash, dialed.

"Who are you calling?" asked Aaron.

"A colleague," Velasquez answered.

"Hello? Pike?" Velasquez spoke. "Listen, it's probably nothing. I know Clent's on duty tonight, but I got a call. I'm headed to Haylee's old home on Orr Rd. Weird shit is going down. Thought I would see if you wanted to meet up ask some questions to the group?"

"The detective?" Aaron asked. "Tell him I said hi?"

"Are you serious?" Velasquez shot him a dirty look.

"Sorry," Aaron muttered. "Shit, I'm trying not to go insane, *excuse* me."

"—Sorry, yeah, I'm with the kid who was attacked by the suspect Gary Thom. I'm just picking up this woman named Jeanie. We're going back to Haylee's to figure this crazy shit out. If you give me twenty minutes, we should be back to Haylee's. Trust me. You will want to meet us there."

"Any word on the Gary dude who broke into my place? They catch that idiot?"

"—Yes, okay. See you soon." Vanessa hung up. "No, he is still out there. We found the car he stole from Gerald Leveille, left on the side of the road near the state forest."

"So...?" Aaron posed as a question.

"So what?" Velasquez asked, annoyed with Aaron already.

"What the fuck is going on? You heard that shit back there from Lydia. You didn't hear the crazy shit I heard before that. I think I'm starting to go crazy."

"Nonsense," Velasquez answered. "We're dealing with a guy who lost his grip on reality. That's all. Something made him snap. He's killed two people who took him in. For some reason, he tried to kill you. It seems like he has some sort of fascination with your friend if you ask me. She is the link between you and the other murders. This guy, he's been lucky so far. His luck will run out."

"You didn't see what happened to Lydia. That was not normal. I'm telling you that shit was like something from a horror movie."

"Could have been lots of things. Vomiting? Maybe food poison."

"She was like, talking in tongues, saying weird stuff, mumbling, she didn't even sound human," Arron took off his flat-brimmed ball cap, and ran his hands through his sweaty hair.

"Look," Velasquez spoke bluntly. "I don't know what you want me to say. We aren't fighting a demon, or someone possessed. We're dealing with a potential serial copycat killer. If it is, and we don't catch him, there are going to be more murders. I don't want that. Do you?"

"No, of course not."

"You're only with me right now, to make sure I get to the right place, and because they insisted. You're going to wait for me in my car; I will check on the woman. Hopefully, she is willing to come back to Haylee's for a group discussion. We'll have a conversation, all of us, including the Detective working on the case, you remember Pike, obviously."

"Yeah, okay." Aaron nodded. "Slow, down, though. Next house on the right. Where the vehicle is parked out in the driveway. Must be Jeanie's."

"Okay," Velasquez pulls up alongside Jeanie's vehicle. "Stay Put. I will be back in just a few minutes." She exited the car, feeling for her side-hip belt holster and her firearm.

"So, just like? What? Wait here?" Aaron asked.

"That's what I said," she repeated, scoping out the home.

"What if you don't come back?"

"That won't happen, but if it does, call 9-1-1."

"Yeah, okay," Aaron nodded.

Velasquez made her way to the home, nearing three pm. The sun hung high in the sky—a warm day for a Michigan winter. The bountiful snow was finally melting a bit beneath the warmth of the rays. The home appeared empty. Velasquez scoped out the main window on the porch, looking into the living room.

All clear.

She checked the front door; the handle moved freely. It was unlocked. She knocked first. "Jeanie?" she yelled. "Jeanie, are you in there? My name is officer Vanessa Velasquez, your friend Lydia asked me to check up on you. Jeanie?" she yelled again.

Aaron sat anxiously in the running vehicle. He was sweating, tapping his thumb on his pant leg. He looked down at the dash; there in the cup holder was Vanessa's phone. She forgot her phone.

Shit! Aaron wasn't sure what to do. She hadn't entered yet. He could hear her voice from the car, knocking loudly at the door. He stepped out, waving her phone. "Hey! Vanessa!"

"Get back into the car!" She yelled back.

"But!" Aaron waved the phone. That's when he saw a skinny man darting from the back of the house. He ran towards the woods from the backside of the house. "Dude!" he yelled, pointing to the back.

"What?" Vanessa shook her head in anger. "Get back into the fucking car, Aaron!"

"A guy!" He yelled again, pointing like a mad man to the backyard.

"What?" Vanessa ran down the porch, swinging around the house towards the side where she parked her car. "You saw someone?"

"Dude was running into the woods!"

"Stay! Call 9-1-1 now!" Vanessa took off towards the woods. She saw briefly the image of a man scurrying through the woods, his head bobbing against the snowy backdrop. She went to grab her phone. She stopped briefly. "Shit!" she realized now what Aaron was waving, was her phone. She was so worried about her firearm; she forgot it on her dash. She didn't have a choice; she knew this was the guy—this was Gary. No time to grab it. She had to get this fucker.

"Gary Thom, stop, or I will shoot!"

"Shit-fuck-shit-fuck," Aaron's hands quivered. He called 9-1-1, doing his best to explain what happened. "I need help. I'm with Officer Vanessa Velasquez, and she just chased a dude into the woods. We're at 1981 Orr Road. Send help!"

FORTY-FIVE

"Are you feeling better?" Haylee came back to the sofa with a second bottle of water. Lydia had finished off the coffee. Haylee poured herself a drink as well, a stiff one. Seagram's Vodka and Red Bull, mostly vodka.

"You're drinking," Lydia didn't ask, nor was her words judging.

"I need it right now. My nerves are shot," Haylee took a sip. "I really want to pop a pill and numb myself. It's taking everything I got not to. If you weren't here, I won't lie, it's probably the first thing I did."

"I see, and yes, I am getting my strength back," Lydia was now sitting up. "I hear your dog whining in your room? Is he okay in there?"

"Yes, he's been locked up most of the day, with all the visitors," said Haylee. "I'm sure he is getting restless, though."

"Let him out. He shouldn't be tied up. I like dogs. It won't bother me."

Haylee let Trayer out of her room. Hyper from being holed up, he ran straight for Lydia. His tail wagged wildly. He buried his snout into her lap, snorting and drooling all over her.

"Good boy," Lydia smiled for the first time since she got sick. "Animals are just like humans, you know? You can read their essence, their energy. Trayer here is a very kind, compassionate, dare I say, a bit of a trouble maker?"

"Yes, that about sums him up," Haylee let out a nervous laugh. She followed it with another drink, this time bigger, longer. "I don't have that, though," said Haylee.

"Have what?" she asked.

"That gift, to see or feel, whatever, energies from people and animals. If I did, I would have probably seen how evil Robbie was. You know, I struggled with it for so long. I have researched about people like him. People who live double lives, sort of like Dennis, I suppose. You know?' Haylee asked. "People who live behind the mask, people who think they're perfect, or close to it. Like, how could this sweet man do this? I read about lots of people like him: Ted Bundy, that kid from the UK, Brian Blackwell who killed his family, that bastard Chris Watts. I read up on narcissism too, and personality disorders. Then there's me, like a magnet to these people. How do I allow two of them into my life?"

"You don't have that ability, because we were never able to finish what we started all those years ago," Lydia explained. "You, Jeanie, myself, we are rare people. So rare that of all the so-called 'specialists' in the fringe science or paranormal field, of all the cases I have dealt with over the last two decades, we are the only three I know of here in the states that are pure. Some have weaker connections. But they usually grow out of it during puberty. They don't become stronger, like you and I. So, at this point, you have been defending yourself from it, instead of learning how to control it. This has allowed it to distort itself, to use you instead of you harnessing it. We can still fix it, but it will be a long journey."

"I see," Haylee took the explanation in slowly.

"It's not your fault. You were never given the opportunity to protect yourself."

"So, what do you see in me?"

"In you?" she asked.

"You said you could see Trayer's essence. You sensed Gary's. What about me? What draws these freaks, these sociopaths, to me? Is there more wrong with me than just seeing these ghosts? Hearing these voices? Am I a bad person?"

"I see darkness in you."

"Darkness?" Haylee's mouth dropped. She expected something depressing like loneliness or sadness. But darkness?

"You said, in the woods, you don't remember what happened?" Lydia asked.

"I don't remember," Haylee answered. "I blacked out. I woke up in the hospital. Spent a week at a psych ward after."

"You do remember. I know you do. Because I saw what happened in Aaron's apartment, I see it inside you, now. You did so well, opening up earlier. But you haven't been honest with yourself."

"I'm not lying, I swear to you."

"You think you don't because your reality has bent to your will," Lydia sighed, her mind raced how to explain the situation. "It's not lying when you believe it. That's the power of the human mind. We can shape our world; we can alter it physically even. I'm sure you've heard of the paradox, what came first the chicken or the egg?"

Haylee shook her head, confused. "Yeah, of course."

"What came first, humankind, or earth?"

"Is that a trick question?" asked Haylee.

"Maybe."

"Earth, we live on earth, it had to exist before we did," she needed another strong sip of her drink for these questions.

"What if I told you we created Earth? It only exists because we willed it to fruition?"

"I would say that makes no sense."

"Enlightenment," Lydia smiled. "Something we would have discussed in length if we could have kept our meetings when you were younger. There is so much to this universe we get wrong every single day. It's always been mind over matter, even though the monetary matter is what we are led to believe is what truly matters."

"So, you are saying humans created Earth, so we had a place to live?"

"Sort of," Lydia frowned. "I don't want to get too philosophical with you. But technically, the collective human-mind came first. Even before any human was ever born, before any planets shaped, before this universe even existed. Our higher-being form, a collection of us, existed as a single entity. We made everything, every atom, molecule, star, black hole.

"That just makes my head hurt even more," Haylee finished off her drink, three long gulps down.

"Okay, forget the universe. Here, right now, our society. Strip away religion, and everything you know about where and how we came to live on earth. Because that's about how much we as a race, know about our existence: nothing, Haylee. We know nothing. A bunch of people are trying to explain our existence with our six senses. What we don't realize is that the blueprint was written to be understood with the seventh sense, and maybe even eighth and ninth sense too. We just can't grasp it. It's not our goal; by our own design, we are not meant to comprehend."

"What does this have to do with me? With all this? The murderer, my life? Robbie, the Simmons?"

"Enlightenment, Haylee. We are enlightened; we see beyond the design. Everyone around us tries to make sense of their lives through their physical experience, with their brains, their hands, emotions. But, they can't, not really. Don't even get me started on religion. We created that answer from the lack of the higher senses. The things we can't explain, our seemingly meaningless existence, our relationship with the universe, all the big questions about existence? We can't answer, and so we replaced that inability to understand with a single concept, faith. And we personified that concept. Its name is God, Allah, Yahweh."

"I need more alcohol..." Haylee frowned. "This is heavy stuff you're talking about."

"It's wrong, all wrong," Lydia continued, trying to keep Haylee's attention. "Everything we see here, in this world? Think of it as a single word on a page. Next, think of these words that sum up one page of a novel. Now, think of those words on those pages that form chapters, that add up to create a novel which in turn builds into a series. A series of novels that we call 'Life.' All of this: me, you, the sofa, Trayer, the pain from the loss of your mother, the way a hug feels from a loved one after a bad day. The food we eat, the sweet taste of sugar, the melody of a songbird outside, the smell of fresh-brewed coffee. It's all a part of us. It only exists because we, the collective higher-conscious, will it. We made 'us", we make 'us,' we create 'us,' we kill 'us,' we are, together as a collection, the lifeblood of reality."

"I just, I can't, it doesn't make sense." Haylee's head hurt. The tension was building in the back of her skull.

"We have it, Haylee. Listen to me. We are the few, the ones born with the higher senses," Lydia's words were fiery, passionate. "We have the ability to read it, to tap into the source. We see outside the lines. We can translate the human collective; we have access to the blueprint of life."

Look here, Lydia ripped out a sheet of paper from one of her notebooks. She took a pen from her bag. She drew a large circle.

"Inside this circle is reality. Everything we know. The universe, God, your friend Aaron, Trayer, your old high school. Everything you know to be true or real. It exists in this circle. Following so far?"

"I guess, yeah," Haylee replied.

"Inside that circle is where everyone lives, their conscious, their memories, their wants, needs. They use their senses to explain the world they see. We live in that circle, as well. Except we can also move our mind outside."

Lydia drew two stick figures inside the circle, then she drew two lines extending outside of the circle and wrote the words You and Me.

"We can traverse, out here. This is the darkness, not necessarily a bad term, its only dark because everyone else can't see into it. Their senses aren't capable of comprehending what's outside. We can because we can traverse outside into the dark area. They look within and outwards only. They live in the light, they can see in the circle, but will never be able to look into the abyss. We can move into the abyss; we can sit in the dark and adjust are senses in the blackness, and we can see. It's like when you sit in a dark room for a long time, and your eyes adjust. This is us. We are out there. We can see, tap into the higher senses and into the parts the grander design we were never supposed to see."

Haylee's head fell into her hands. She rubbed her eyes. "Look, this is interesting, but I failed miserably at spirituality and theory in college. My head hurts, I'm emotionally wrecked right now. I think I should call my dad, I just...I don't know what to do about my life, and I can't grasp this..."

"You see shadows, you hear voices," Lydia stood up, walked over to Haylee, put both her hands onto hers. She looked deep into her eyes. "Yet, what I am telling you, you push away, because it's scary. But you can't make sense of the voices either, can you? It's because you have no understanding of the higher senses. It's foreign to you. You see things you can't explain daily. I am telling you truth."

"My entire life has been a shit storm.," Haylee pulled her hands away. She broke her gaze. "I don't care what happens to me when I die. Why I am here, or what's outside that circle. Because, anything, even nothing, is better than what's in that damn circle. Anyway, what does this have to do with the woods?"

"Well," Lydia frowned. "It's going to get worse."

"What?"

"The woods," she explained.

"Okay?" Haylee questioned, growing slightly irritable now.

"In the woods, Haylee, I saw it. When I was attacked with the sickness, in Aaron's apartment, it came to me. I saw you in the woods, clear as day. The creature, it was communicating with me. Your life, all this sadness, confusion, death, then the pregnancy. The miracle with the married man, Dennis. Cheating on the one person you loved. How much did that hurt? You were angry with Robbie's cheating, angry at your own infidelity. You broke, your mind snapped Haylee. You can't blame yourself with everything you have gone through. You were a victim your entire life. This is how the creature was able to get in, how it was able to get through the veil. It came from outside the circle, in the abyss. It knew you because you knew it because you were the connection between the two worlds. It used your mind as a vessel. Out there in the circle, that's where our madness forms. Your darkness, the pain, and suffering of your life, first you manifested it out there. Then, unknowingly you gave it life here in the circle. You birthed it here in our world. It came from you, Haylee." Lydia's warm hand fell onto Haylee's chest right above her heart.

"What...what are you saying?" Haylee stammered. Her heart pounded uncontrollably.

"Mind over matter. That's something that we can do, and it's a real thing. The few us who share the gift, our curse, whatever you want to call it. We can tap into. Others can too, but it takes a large group of people with the same message. Have you heard of the group of Monks in New York city praying for weeks to decrease crime? It's a real thing, and it worked. But even I have never seen or heard of a case like this. One person manifesting their ugliness, anger, hate, all for lack of better words, into our world." Lydia sighed, the look on Haylee's face, the sheer disgust within her eyes.

"Don't you see?" Lydia continued. "All that pain, suffering, those secrets you shared with us? The death of your mother? The baby you always wanted, but with a man who you cheated with, already married twice your age? You physically altered your child within you, because of your connection to the veil, because of your ability to communicate with the higher sense. The alternate dimension. It was not a miscarriage. The doctors didn't know better, how could they? That child, early in its development was transformed and altered into the thing that has been haunting you. It grew in your womb, twisted, vile, something unnatural. You ran into the woods, lost in your fear. The pain overbearing. You were alone in your home when it happened. You panicked, and you fled, bleeding between your legs. You ran into the woods. You gave birth to the monster, the creature, and you tried to bury it in the woods. You clawed and clawed, buried it into the half-frozen earth. Then you turned on yourself. You lashed at your wrists. That's when the dreams started, right? When Robbie went crazy?"

"Robbie?" Haylee frowned. She held her tears back; anger coursed through her body.

"He was the first to stumble upon the creature. While you were away, in the ward, he went back to the spot they found you. I saw it there too, the creature, whether or not it wanted me to know, I don't know. I saw its memories. It was weak then. Small, dying. Robbie heard it yelping. This creature, alien-looking, half-dead, left to rot. It had already grown slightly. It feasts off your misery, drinking from your agony, your mental breakdown, your depression, it kept the creature clinging to life, barley. See, you share a thread with the creature. Your souls connected, and when you are in pain, it grows, strengthens itself. But it also has to feed. Your misery keeps it alive, but when it feeds, it strengthens."

"I feel sick..." Haylee walked away, entering the kitchen. Her face went pale.

"I saw Robbie lost in its gaze..." Lydia explained.

"Stop!" Haylee yelled. Her stomach lurched.

"This is the truth. It is what we are dealing with. We need you to stay strong. To stop running from it. It's a manifestation of your pain, grown outside the circle where the minds of man manifest their emotions. These creatures are only a small part of that world. But it is a part of it. And we are vessels. It knew you because it is you. It was able to use you as a vessel, manifest in this world with your unborn child in your womb."

"This is crazy," Haylee fell to her knees at the sink. Lydia gave her hand, helping her back to her feet.

"There is more, if you're able to hear it," Lydia helped her over to the kitchen table.

"I don't know if I can take more of this," Haylee answered.

"If you don't, more could be hurt. Killed."

"I don't want that," Haylee replied. "Tell me what you know about it, the creature."

"The creature is both male and female. It's androgynous. It uses its eyes, its gaze, to hypnotize its victims. I saw that too. I saw what it did to that man Gary. After it hypnotizes them with its gaze, it fornicates with them, plants its poisonous seed. Or rather, a parasite? Either analogy works. Either way, the poison quickly takes over its brain. The person becomes like a puppet, a husk of sorts. When I walked into Aaron's apartment, the creature's conscious was still there, lingering just enough for me to make a connection with. At least, some part of it. It immediately attached itself to me. I became a part of its hive mind. I had to purge it out of my body."

"Jesus!" wanted to sob, to cry. She wanted to give up. Crawl into a corner and numb her brain until the day the light on her candle finally burned out.

"Anger, sadness, fear it all empowers the creature," Lydia explained.

"Why me? Why us?" Haylee's face burned with anger.

"Because we are special. We see the truth, and because we are not alone in this universe. We are but a mere fraction of what lies out in the abyss. We are portals, gates to these other beings."

"What the fuck," Haylee stood up from the table. She went for her pills, slamming the cupboards. She opened the baggy but struggled with the bottle due to her shaky hands.

"No!" for the first time, Lydia struck Haylee's arm. The pills spilled to the floor. "The pills, the alcohol, they mask your pain. It strengthens that thing. It's killing these people. Don't you see?"

"I need them!" Haylee fell to her knees. She picked up the oval white pills, collecting them in her palm.

"Haylee," Lydia spoke softly.

Haylee ignored her.

"Haylee!" she yelled. "Robbie, and that man, Gary. They didn't kill anyone. They were poisoned by the creature. They acted out because of your pain, you. You are the one. You killed them."

"No!" Haylee stood up, her knees unsteady. "I didn't kill my sister! I didn't kill Dennis or his wife!"

"You did, indirectly. You are a victim, but so were they. We need to figure out how to kill that thing. It's time to stop hiding. You want to be a survivor, to take control of your life? Let me help you. We end it. Before someone else is killed."

"...How?" Haylee fell against her sink counter. She looked at the white pills in her hand. She wanted more than anything to swallow them down, the whole handful. Instead, she dropped the pills into the sink. She turned on the faucet. She watched as they disappeared down the drain.

"We need to confront it..." Lydia said.

FORTY-SIX

Aaron was told to stay on the phone, but his conversation was cut short. With all the commotion over the last twenty-four hours, he'd never gotten the chance to charge it completely.

Fucking idiot, he cursed himself.

Aaron was antsy; he paced back and forth near Vanessa's vehicle. It was getting late into the afternoon. He was sweating profusely now, even in the freezing Michigan Winter.

"Fuck..." it dawned on him. Jeanie could still be in the home. Should he enter, grab her? Get her into safety? Who knows how long it would take the cops to get there? The country road was out in god-forsaken bum-fucking-nowhere, Michigan.

He had to go in. Make sure everything was okay. Maybe her phone was charged, although he wasn't sure, she wasn't answering the calls previously.

He took a big sigh, it was decided. "Time to nut-up," he spoke to himself, feigning something that was a mixture of bravery or complete ideocracy, he wasn't quite sure.

Aaron grabbed his walking cane from the passenger seat. He made his way cautiously up to the porch. Vanessa hadn't had a chance to enter the home. He heard her knocking, yelling for her, to no avail.

Fuck it, he thought.

He was going in. The door was unlocked; he slowly entered the home. The living room was large and spacious, completely empty. He took his time, scoped the place out. His eyes panned to the opening into the kitchen where he saw what looked like a puddle. He moved closer, and before he could even get through the door frame, he saw the horrid sight.

Blood.

So much blood.

It was everywhere, splattered on the wall, pooling on the floor.

Aaron almost buckled. Such violence, his stomach turned, but he held it together.

It was clear the attack happened in the kitchen. There was a trail of death leading towards the stairs. Aaron guessed the body had been dragged into the basement. It didn't take a blood splatter specialist to figure that out. Aaron understood nothing good was going to be found down there. He swallowed hard. So much blood, there was no way she was alive. Or could she be? Down there, bleeding to death, barely hanging on to her life?

He had to look, stay on guard, ready himself for the worse. He saw the man fleeing from the home; he was reasonably sure he was alone. He had to look. He could never forgive himself if she were alone down there, scared, dying.

"Fuck me, fuck me," he whispered to himself, careful not to touch anything. He used his cane to swing the partial basement door open. The blood trail led down, staining the carpeted steps with more red. He slowly made his way, the path turned left, exactly where Haylee had found the body of her dead sister. That's where he found the corpse of Jeanie, mutilated. Her head missing.

Aaron lost it.

His stomach retched. He ran out of the basement, puking up on his jacket.

He couldn't get out of that house fast enough.

FORTY-SEVEN

The call came over from dispatch to Clent, who was out making rounds calling for backup at 1918 Orr Road. He had just finished with a routine speeding ticket in town near the strip mall when the call came over the radio.

"What the hell is she thinking?" Clent was quick to acknowledge the call. He was about ten minutes out from Orr road.

God-damned Orr road. Nothing ever good comes out of that god-forsaken road.

He tried Vanessa on her cell; she didn't answer.

Fuck. This was bad. Call it intuition. Client learned early on in his career, always trust your gut. His gut was telling him: *get to the fucking scene, pronto!*

He needed Pike. He was probably working late at the office, going over notes from the attack on Aaron Hauser and struggling to make sense of what it had to do with Haylee and the Simmons. This just escalated. He found Pike's name in his contacts and hit call.

The phone rang three times before he answered.

"Hello, Clent? What's going on?" Pike's voice was gruff. Exhausted.

"Did you hear?" Clent had his sirens going, speeding to the Orr house.

"Hear what? I just pulled into Haylee's driveway. Something happened there. Vanessa asked me to meet her there. I'm knocking on the door right now."

"She's not gonna be there anytime soon. She was headed over to the Orr Road house for some stupid reason, off the clock. I guess she spotted a man running into the woods, and she took off for him. Thinks its Gary."

"What?" asked Pike. His voice stern. Suddenly the exhaustion was gone.

"I know, I am on my way there now," Clent added. "She isn't answering her phone either.

"How far out are you?" asked Pike.

"I will be there under ten," answered Clent. He heard Pike talking to someone in the background.

"Give me twenty," Pike hung up.

"I hope she gets that son of a bitch..." Clent ran through a red light, hurrying to the residence. Every minute was critical. "God damn it, Vanessa!"

FORTY-EIGHT

"Detective Pike?" Haylee answered the door, her face puffy, eyes red, mascara ran down her face. She looked rough. Her breath smelled of booze. An older woman, mid-fifties, was with her. Pretty, sharply dressed, tattoos on both arms and chest, she remained calm and collective.

"Haylee," Pike put his hand over the phone, Clent would have to wait for a second. "Sorry to bother you. Give me one moment, please. I just got an important call as soon as I knocked."

"Sure, come in," She opened the door for him. Pike obliged, giving his attention back to his cellphone.

"How far out are you?" asked Pike. He waited for a response. "Give me twenty," Pike hung up the phone.

"Is everything okay?" asked Haylee. Her voice wavered.

"I should ask you the same," Pike replied.

"We've had a rough afternoon," Lydia chimed in. "My name is Lydia, a mentor of Haylee. We were discussing some...things."

"I see," Pike pulled out some trident chewing gum. He popped one out of the plastic packaging into his mouth. He offered some to the ladies; they both declined. "I was called by Vanessa. She wanted me to come here and meet with her? But I hear she won't be showing."

"Excuse me? Why not?" Lydia asked, masking the twitch of a frown. "She is supposed to bring my partner back with her."

"I'm told she went to your old home?" Pike looked towards Haylee for clarification.

"Yes, her and Aaron both. They went to pick up Lydia's friend, Jeanie," she answered.

"Hmm," Pike stroked the itchy stubble on his chin, vigorously chewing his gum. He needed a cigarette. This gum shit wasn't working.

"What? What's wrong?" asked Lydia. "is she okay?

"It's nothing. I need to get going. I'm sorry to have disturbed you. Bad timing is all." Pike tipped his hat to the ladies. "Pleasure meeting you, Lydia."

"Where are you going? To Orr road?" asked Haylee.

"I'll be honest with you," Pike nodded. "Vanessa spotted a man entering the forest from the backyard of your old home. She went to follow him."

"What about Aaron and Jeanie?" asked Lydia.

"I will make sure they contact you. I'm headed there now. Stay home, stay safe. Leave this to my team." Pike was blunt, emotionless with his words. He gave them a friendly half-smile before stepping back out into the cold. He entered his vehicle, flipped his siren on, and floored it down their residential road.

"Something happened," Haylee paced in the living room. "What are we gonna do?"

"We're going," Lydia grabbed her bag.

"We are?" asked Haylee.

"It's time we take control. Jeanie and Aaron are there. They could be in danger. The police have no idea what they are up against."

"Shit, okay, one minute," Haylee left. She was quick in her bedroom, calling Trayer in behind her so he wouldn't be out roaming. She went under her bed, pulled out a small silver gun case. She took the firearm out, loaded it, placed it back in her purse. She met again up with Lydia in the living room.

"Let's go," Haylee swallowed hard.

"Can you drive? My nerves are shot," she trembled at the thought of going back to that place. Images of Robbie's head opening up from her gunshot. The sickening noise of his body tumbling down the stairs. The image of her sisters' dead body. Her stomach sunk, nauseousness followed.

"Hand me the keys, and give me directions," Lydia nodded. Both women made their exit out of the home and into Haylee's small compact car.

FORTY-NINE

Clent pulled up next to the other two cars, exiting quickly from his cruiser. He saw Aaron immediately, sitting on the porch, hunched over on his hands and knees. A discernable amount of vomit puddled before him. He was gasping for air, holding his stomach continuing to upheave. Clent exited the vehicle.

"Sir, are you okay? What's going on?" Clent approached.

"My God," Aaron fell to his side. He pushed himself away from his stomach's contents. The image of Jeanie's headless body burned into his brain. "She...she's dead..."

"Who? Where?" asked Clent.

Aaron pointed into the home, "...the basement."

Clent drew his weapon, and he entered the home firearm raised. He cleared the first room. He made his way carefully into the kitchen. There he saw the scene of the murder. The blood was everywhere, a trail of it leading into the basement. Eerily, it was very similar to the first time he was called to the residence two years prior when he and Pike found the bodies of Camille and Robbie in the basement. Haylee weeping in the corner. He shook the thought; he needed to stay clear-headed, in the moment.

"Jesus," he whispered to himself. He needed to move. He made his way down the stairs, softly on each step. He remained calm. Clent hit the basement floor, spun the corner, weapon drawn. There Jeanie's lifeless body lay. Her head missing. Her body mangled. "...Fuck." The word slipped from his lips.

Aaron sat outside. He crawled away from his vomit, knowing he was too dizzy to stand. He sat himself up on the porch steps, his body still shuddering. His knees were weak as if they were replaced with jelly. What had he seen? His brain couldn't comprehend the image of Jeanie's body, the bloody stump where her head once was.

He cried—warm tears streaming down his reddened cheeks.

He took a deep breath; the cold crisp air filled his lungs. Breathing life back into his stupor. He realized he soaked through his shirt with sweat. Despite the bitter winter weather, he peeled off his vomit-covered jacket to cool off. Steam came off his skin. About five minutes passed before Clent came back out.

"I'm sorry you saw that. What's your name," asked Clent?

"Aaron, sir," he stammered.

"How do you know Vanessa? The victim in the home?"

"Haylee called Vanessa after some shit went down at her place," he explained. "The woman in the house, her name is Jeanie."

"Okay, wait, what shit went down? Is everyone okay?" he asked.

"Obviously not, Jeanie," Aaron replied.

"Back at Haylee's home, they OK?" Clent corrected himself.

"I think. We didn't know who to call. Lydia got sick, started freaking out, talking like she was possessed or something. Vomiting everywhere, way worse than me. Fuckin' freakin' out, screaming, lashing around, like a scene out of the Exorcist. She said we couldn't call an ambulance, she…" Aaron was barely breathing, spewing forth all this information incoherently.

"Calm down, just tell me where Officer Velasquez went. We can hash out the details later." Clent pulled out his cell, attempting to ring Vanessa one more time.

"Behind the house, into the woods. She followed the man I saw."

"Why isn't she answering her phone?" Clent hung up, pocketed his phone.

"She left it in the car," Aaron explained.

"God-damnit, son-of-a-bitch. What is she thinking?" Clent grabbed his radio, "631 I have a code one. I need responding units to set up a perimeter. Central, get me a dog and see if MSP can scramble the Bird for an overhead. Give me a five-mile radius around 1981 Orr Road, suspect Gary Thom is on foot. Off-duty Officer Vanessa Velasquez is in pursuit. She entered a heavily wooded area south behind the home, chasing the suspect." Clent looked at Aaron. "Was he armed; the man headed into the woods?"

"He had something in his hands. A bag, and something else, like a crowbar or a hammer," Aaron explained.

"OK, stay here. I want you to go in the vehicle, lock the doors until back up arrives," Clent ordered. "Do you understand? Detective Pike should be here soon. I'm going to go check out back."

"Yes, sir," Aaron got to his feet.

Clent made his way around the back of the residence. Two sets of footprints made their way into the forest behind the home. A small trail of blood, thick droplets followed with the prints. Perhaps the perp was injured, or worse, Vanessa. But, no, that couldn't be. Vanessa was on the chase. She hadn't struggled with the man. If he was injured, they might just get the son of a bitch.

He wouldn't get far, and he wouldn't outrun Vanessa. Oh shit, maybe the sick freak had the head of the woman from the basement? Clent pushed aside the thoughts. He had to wait, despite wanting to give chase. He needed to secure the area, wait for backup, set up a point. He checked his watch. Pike should be here soon, any fucking minute. Once he showed up, he would be ready.

"Fuck, hurry up," he began to pace.

• • •

Vanessa was on foot, close behind the suspect. She could hear him running through the foliage. She was able to catch a glimpse of him through the trees, his head bobbing up and down as he traversed the snowy landscape. He was running with two items in his hands, a sack with its bottom wet. This was the cause of the blood droplets on the snow. In the other, his right hand, he had a blunt object, a claw hammer.

Velasquez's chest was heavy, her lungs burned, but she did not stop her pursuit. The manhunt ended tonight. Justice would be served. He was fast, not seeming to tire, and yet, her legs burned. Thankfully the blood trail made him easy to track. She followed it to a small clearing. A derelict building came into view—some sort of run-down hunting lodge or cabin.

Gary was nowhere to be seen, gone. He was possibly hiding within the deserted hunting lodge. She spotted the blood-stained burlap sack sitting out in the open a few yards in front of the building. It was the one he was carrying. Vanessa held her firearm steady, kept her eyes on her surroundings. She approached the sack, kneeled, pulled it open, pouring the contents out into the snowy earth. It contained two severed heads, both female, one younger, she guessed in her thirties. The other an older woman, grey-haired, wrinkled skin. Her stomach heaved; she held it down, composed herself. She wouldn't allow herself to get sick this time.

Velasquez heard a noise within the building, approached it slowly. Her gun drawn.

"Hello? Gary? Exit the building. I'm armed!" she yelled.

She saw something move from within the darkness. A large oblong-shaped head curiously poked out from the shadows, behind the opening of the building.

"Exit the damn building!" she yelled again.

Two bright red eyes peered from the darkness, and they were spellbinding. Velasquez stared into them, losing her thoughts in the beauty of them. A fuzziness crawled up her body like ghostly fingers. Her mind befuddled, her surroundings began to blur together.

What was she looking at?

What was this thing?

Fear swelled up in her throat; she knew it wasn't right; this thing, the red eyes, stealing her breath from her. Her arms went heavy. Her gun fell between her feet. Vanessa was frozen, knees locked in place. Was it from fear? A trance? She tried to make sense of it, any of it, but she couldn't. Why was she unable to move? What was she looking at?

What the **fuck** was happening to her?

From the side of the building came Gary Thom, a bloody hammer in his right hand. He looked at her with a sick twisted smile across his face. He approached, carefree, the hammer swinging at his side, covered in blood from head to toe.

"Hello," Gary spoke, his voice calm, relaxed. "Don't worry. You can't fight it. Mother likes you. I wanted to stick the hammer into your brain, but when she saw you walk up. She fell for you. Pretty, pretty. She will have you as she had me. Maybe you will call her Daddy instead of Mother. She is both, you know? She is all everything. You will be a part of her, just like me. A family, brother, sister, mother, father."

Vanessa tried to bend down, reach for her gut. But no matter how hard she tried, she couldn't break the gaze of the glowing eyes. Her brain was telling her one thing, but her body was not listening.

"It's better this way, Mother will love you," Gary walked up in front of her. He grabbed one of the heads. It was Jeanie's. He tossed it closer to the building. The glowing eyes moved forward, away from the shadows, closer to the daylight.

"She is so beautiful," Gary's mouth stretched from ear to ear.

A tall, lanky creature broke into the natural sunlight. Horrorstruck, Vanessa couldn't scream, her throat seized, her body shook. Frozen, unable to move, she watched in a trance as the creature made itself known.

The thing, its grey skin rotted, dangling loosely from its ghastly frame. Exposed bones were protruding through the most rotten parts of its body— the smell of it, decay, rotten flesh. The odor settled in Vanessa's throat; she could taste the death. The creature's oblong head cocked quizzically at her; its huge antlers spiked into the sky.

A grotesque freak of nature.

It crawled towards her, its belly nearly touching the earth, its massive saggy tits dragging into the snow. It sniffed the decapitated head. Snarled with satisfaction. Its tongue hung from its sharp jaded teeth; thick hot drool dripped onto the snow. The creature took the head into its palm; its long boney fingers plucked one of the eyes out of the head. It swallowed it down. It did the same for the second eye. Next came the tongue, plucked from the mouth with ease.

"The best bits," said Gary, watching while his Mother enjoyed the fruits of his labor. He was rubbing himself between his legs, moaning sexually. "Next comes the brains," his mouth salivated. Despite his stomach full of the older woman's flesh, he hungered for the brains.

The creature cracked the skull with ease. It devoured the brains, slurping it up with its long-wet tongue. The creature looked over to Gary. It purred loudly, lovingly.

"I'm glad you enjoyed," he said, his voice soft.

The creature took the second head; this one belonged to Jeanie. It tossed the head to the feet of Gary.

"For me?" Gary's eyes lit up. "But you must eat." He lifted the head up, staring into Jeanie's lifeless eyes. "Thank you, mother." Gary dug his thumb into one of the eye sockets. He plucked out the left eye. Plopped it into his mouth, bit into its tenderness. He moaned, the sweet taste overcoming his body. He fell crossed-legged into the snow. He chewed slowly, savoring every ounce of it before swallowing and going for the second eye.

The creature now turned its attention back to Vanessa. Still, she was transfixed there, watching in agony. The creature moved forth, its head, resembling that of a half decomposed deer, hovered an inch from her nose. The creature sniffed her long, taking in her scent, smelling the fear. Its hot wet tongue drug across her cheek. Wet, rough on her skin. The stench was god-awful, putrid.

The creature purred loudly once again. It turned back towards the hunting lodge, Vanessa found herself following it. Her legs were moving on their own accord. Her instinct was to flee, to run, but her brain was not working. Her body ignored her instinct to flee. She entered the building.

She moved towards the creature who took a seat in the darkest corner. She moved closer, her hands now undoing her belt, she pulled down her jeans. Vanessa wanted to cry, to scream, but she did neither of those things. Instead, Vanessa gave her body over to the creature. She allowed it inside of her.

The last thing she remembered was its deathly breath on the back of her neck and a sudden flash of pain in her midsection.

Then blackness.

FIFTY

"Thank god you're here," Clent shouted from the back yard, running towards Detective Pike.

"Clent, what's going on?" Pike exited his vehicle. He took note, two civilian cars, one he recognized as Vanessa's. Clent's cruiser parked adjacent to them both, still running. Inside of Vanessa's car, sat the kid, Aaron, a friend of Haylee. His face white, sickly. He did not open the car door. Instead, he rolled down the window.

"Detective," Clent's voice was rushed. He filled in Pike with the details. The request for a K-9, a helicopter, and the five-mile radius. Suspect Gary Thom was on foot in the woods. Backup called and on its way.

"Your girl has some balls," said Pike. He spat out the chewing gum from before. Popping in a fresh piece. "Fuck, I need a smoke."

"Don't stop me," Clent warned. "I'm not waiting for back up."

"Don't be dumb, we need the dogs," replied Pike. "We have a protocol to follow."

"They are on their way," Clent pulled out his Maglite and his service pistol. "You're here now. Vanessa went in solo with a mad man. There is a clear trail of blood. I can follow it. I'm not asking. Fine me, fire me, whatever." Clent turned his back.

Pike sighed, but he did not stop Clent. Backup was ten minutes out. He looked at the kid.

"We need to talk."

• • •

Clent didn't wait for Pike to object. He needed to get to Vanessa. He broke into the thicket of the forest following the two sets of fresh footprints and a blood trail. It shouldn't be hard to track. Time was of the essence. If he waited another ten minutes for the backup, it could easily be too late. Pike was there. He ran the show. This god-damn piece of shit Gary was a lunatic, and he had been living in the woods for over a week. Vanessa, even if she had her firearm, was out of her element.

He moved as fast, careful not to lose the tracks, following the blood. Was Gary injured? If so, he would be moving slow. Perhaps Vanessa would catch up to him. He half expected to meet up with Vanessa, gun drawn on Gary, working their way back to the home. Vanessa was a tough S.O.B., and she could hang with the men on the force, take some of them out even.

She would be fine.

Clent had been in the woods for what seemed like eternity. He'd lost track of time. He came to a clearing. A large, broke down cabin came into view. He stopped, caught his breath, steadied his hand. He turned off the Maglite, raised his firearm, and closed in. He sat at the edge of the clearing, scoping out the scene. A man sat with his back to him, sitting cross-legged in the snow, hunched over. Vanessa nowhere to be seen.

It was him. It had to be.

"Freeze!" Clent broke through the clearing. He lined up his shot, center mass. "Arms up!"

The man stood up. Turned to him. It was Gary. Both his arms above his head. Clent circled him. His firearm centered on his chest. Gary's face came into view. Between his feet was the head of a young woman. Her eyes tore from her head, and it looked as if Gary had been gnawing on the victim's tongue. He had been eating it when Clent interrupted.

"Jesus, fuck," Clent cursed. "On your stomach, face down!" Clent demanded, his weapon not wavering.

Gary looked at him, dead square in the eyes. No fear, no worry. He smiled through the crimson mask of his victims' blood. Gary lunged; the hammer wielded high in the air. He took two steps before Clent got off three rounds square into the man's chest.

Gary fell over, his body crumbled into the snow.

"Stay down!" Clent ordered. He approached Gary, kicking the hammer behind him. Gary laid on his back with three holes in his chest. He coughed up blood, spraying it into the snow. His breathing labored, his eyes glossing over. He was dying fast. He tried muttering something, but it only came out in gurgles of blood. He took his last breath staring at Clent, looking for the first time like a human and not a bloodthirsty monster.

Clent never heard the soft approach from behind him. His adrenaline was pumping. The sight of Gary dying in front of him, taking in his last breath, making sure the danger was over, kept him distracted. He let his guard down. A fatal assumption that Gary was the only threat.

He was wrong.

Vanessa had come from the hunting lodge. She approached silently while Clent was checking for the pulse of Gary Thom. Vanessa had watched the scene go down. Watched Client kick the hammer behind him, out of Gary's reach. Vanessa approached it, picked it up. She heard her partner mutter to himself something about Gary being gone. She heard him sigh. She was closer to him now, standing only a few feet behind, she could hear him breathing heavy, the smell of his cologne lingered towards her.

"Nice shot," Vanessa spoke plainly.

"Jesus," Clent jumped. He spun halfway around before the contact of the hammer struck his right temple. A bright red flash exploded in his head. A sick cracking noise thundered from his skull as the first blow dropped him to the snow-covered earth. He fell backward. His vision blurred; his body too heavy to move. Vanessa stood above him, hammer in her hand.

He tried to call out her name. He tried to lift his hands to protect himself. He could do neither. His life was about to be snuffed out in the snow-covered Michigan woods. His partner smiled before delivering one more swift blow to the top of his head. His skull cracked, and chunks of his brain spilled onto the snow.

The urge for human flesh consumed her. Clent, her onetime partner, now dead, meant nothing to her than a meal. His blood covered the snowy clearing. Her mouth salivated at the sight of his spilled grey matter.

Loud barks came from the woodland. Vanessa, emotionless, popped her head up before getting to taste the sweet flesh. She sensed the danger; felt it in her blood. She would not get to taste her hunt. She had to flee, flee with Mother. Deeper into the woods, deeper into the dark. They would hide, hide in the shadows. Retreat into the depths of the wild. She would be patient; she would feast when the time was right.

Vanessa fled. The Hunting Lodge was no longer safe.

FIFTY-ONE

"Aaron!" Haylee jumped out of the passenger seat. She ran, wrapping her arms around his massive frame. It was good to hold him in her arms, safe, secure. He returned the hug, his strong arms gripping her tight. He was trembling. Haylee wanted to wash away his pain. It was evident by the look on his face, something horrendous happened. His skin was pale, eyes sunken in their sockets. He smelled of sweat and vomit.

"You OK?" she asked.

"I will be," he did not let her go.

Haylee's former home was surrounded by police cruisers. Their lights flashing brightly, lightening up the dreary grey-washed sky. Officers and paramedics were everywhere. An ambulance was further down the driveway, its back end open.

"Where is Jeanie?" Lydia exited the vehicle.

"People, this is a crime scene," An officer approached, waving his hands to get back. "We're still setting up the area. I need you all to get back into your vehicle and leave the premise."

"Where is she?" Lydia ignored the officer. "Aaron, where is Jeanie?"

"I got this," Pike walked up from behind a group of police cars. He patted his officer on the shoulder. "Let's get that yellow tape up, block this entire yard off as well."

"Yes, sir," The officer nodded. He went on his way.

"Detective?" Lydia frowned. "What's going on?"

"I asked you to stay put," he said.

"Well, we didn't," Lydia frowned.

"What's going on?" Haylee interjected.

"There's been another murder," Pike answered stone-faced. "I'm afraid it was your friend. We found her purse with identification. She had a tape recorder, other belongings, including her wallet."

"Oh god," Haylee gasped.

"Jeanie," Lydia's face was void of emotion. She stepped away from the group. She looked at the grey sky. She took a deep breath, held it for as long as she could.

Jeanie was dead.

So young, so much potential. Now she was dead.

There was nothing more that could be said or done. It was her fault; she hadn't understood the severity of the situation. How could she be so reckless?

No, how could she have known? She'd never experienced a case like Haylee. It didn't matter, no excuses. Jeanie was dead because of her. She would carry this burden until the day she joined her.

"I'm so sorry," Lydia let the words escape her pursed lips. She swallowed the lump in her throat. "Haylee," Lydia called her over. "We need to leave. Now."

"Yes," Pike answered. "We got a mess on our hands. The three of you go home. We will be in touch. Aaron, I will need to get your statement later. For now, let us do our job. Take care of yourselves and Lydia..." Pike frowned, his words soft. "Sorry for your friend. We will get the bastard who did this."

"Please do," she replied. "Aaron, Haylee, come on." She opened the driver's door, entered the vehicle.

Haylee and Aaron said nothing. They followed—Haylee in the passenger seat, Aaron in the back. Haylee wouldn't argue. She wanted nothing to do with her old home.

"I'm so sorry, Lydia," said Haylee.

"Don't be," Lydia replied. "It's not your fault."

"Are you OK?" asked Aaron.

"I will be," Lydia backed out onto Orr Road. She shifted the car into drive.

"Where are we going?" Aaron asked. "Please tell me home. I need a shower; I'm mentally fucked right now. Too much, too fucking much."

"No, this ends tonight," Lydia looked back at Aaron. "Either you come with us, or you get out and walk. We can't afford to lose any time. It's close. Very close."

"Jesus," frustration spilled over Aaron's face. "What's the plan? What exactly are we finishing?"

"We confront the thing," Lydia turned to Haylee. "You are the only one who can do this."

"Do what?" Haylee asked. "What do I have to do?

"Let's hope we figure that out when we get there," Lydia sped down the road.

"Five-mile radius," she explained. "You heard them, right? That means they will have the roads blocked off. We drive far enough down, pull over. We're going for an evening hike."

"A hike?" asked Aaron. "I'm not built for hikes. I just want to crash in my bed. I can't deal with what I have seen. Guys, seriously? This is not a good idea. We're all exhausted, mentally, and physically, right?"

"We know it's in the woods," Lydia ignored Aaron. "We know its home is close to here. Even if they get Gary, the deaths won't end. There will be another Gary, another puppet, and the cycle will just continue. You feel it, don't you, Haylee? Because I do. I can still sense its energy from the woods. It killed Jeanie. It killer her, not you, not I. *It* did. We confront it. We end it."

"That sounds stupid," Aaron protested. "Good way to get us killed, lady. I mean it, Haylee. This sounds like a god-damned fucked up terrible idea."

"Aaron, this thing kills for food. It also kills to keep Haylee depressed, miserable. It hunts people she loves; she cares about. It feeds off her misery, her depression. Its why it took over Robbie, its why it killed her sister, its why it killed Dennis, and Nora. Its why it tried to kill you. You will never be safe. It will hunt you forever. Or worse, it will take you over, as it did with Robbie and Gary. You'll do the killing for it. You will be a monster, craving human flesh, that's why the bodies were cannibalized. Look at the big picture."

"Fuck," Aaron shook his head. He was trying everything in his power not to freak out. "I don't even understand what the **fuck** is happening."

"The creature from my dreams, it's connected to me. It's a part of me. It won't stop," Haylee's words were strong, confident. "No more, it ends tonight. I'm with Lydia."

"Damn it," Aaron frowned. "Okay, let's do this."

So, they drove down the road. Haylee stayed silent. Her mind stuck, muddled with the thought of that night in the woods. The blackout. After Lydia explained to her what had happened, it was like waking from a bad dream. She remembered it. Crawling into the woods, the pain, the blood. Suddenly this strange creature was crawling out from between her legs. The horror, it had struck her mad. She dug and dug, buried it in the earth the best she could. She then turned on herself, slashing her wrists with her already bleeding fingernails, digging her own grave. She couldn't finish burying herself before she passed out from the loss of blood.

The creature must have crawled out of its grave, fled into the woods. Then she was found. Half buried in the earth, bleeding from between her legs and her wrists.

"Here," Lydia pulled the vehicle to the side of the road. "Small clearing. We can enter there," she pointed to a break in the forest.

"And go where?" asked Aaron.

"Into the Woods," Haylee answered.

"It's going to be dark in like an hour, should we wait till morning?" he asked.

"No," Lydia opened the driver seat. "We do it now."

"Fuck," Aaron exited. He grabbed his cane; his head was still pounding from the head injury from his assault. His winter jacket was stained and stunk of his stomach bile.

"How do we know where to go?" he followed.

"It knows Haylee. The connection will bring them together," Lydia explained. "It's connected to her conscious. Its why she gets the visions. We need to follow that connection. I think it knows she wants to kill it. It kept its distance for a reason. It worked better from the shadows. So, I am not sure how it's going to react, knowing she knows what it is. Maybe it runs from us, but I feel like it will be drawn to her. It wants your love, your affection. You are its mother."

"Yes," Haylee replied. A lump formed in her throat. This thing, no matter what it was, it was her child. The darkness of the woods, her child. She wondered what it thought of her, burying it in the earth. Maybe that's why it wanted to destroy her, keep her miserable. She had turned her back on her child.

Haylee sighed. Shrugged the thoughts aside. She made her way through the forest, leading the others now. She was drawn to it. She could hear its heartbeat in her head. It grew louder as they went deeper into the darkness.

"The connection is there," Lydia followed.

"Fuck me," Aaron frowned. "We're really doing this?"

Again, they ignored him.

The group walked for what seemed like miles, through the thicket, dense foliage. The sun was setting now, the air growing ever more chilled as it hid behind the trees in the distance. A soft orange hue stretched across the Michigan sky. The snow was still deep from the multiple severe winter storms over the past week. It made the trip difficult. The snow still fresh, untouched. White and pure, knee-deep in some parts where the wind caused snowdrifts.

Aaron's body ached; his cane hardly helped to navigate through the thick forest. His lousy leg throbbed. His chest heavy, lungs burned.

"We're lost," said Aaron. "How are we getting back?"

"We're getting closer," Lydia said.

"How do you know that?" he asked.

"We are," Haylee answered. "I can sense it. It's mad, like...I can feel its anger. It's making me dizzy."

"Yes," said Lydia. "It's close to us now. I feel it too. Be careful, Haylee. It may overpower you."

"What do we do? How do we fight this thing?" asked Aaron.

"I don't know," said Lydia.

"We have no plan? Like, literally zero ideas?" Aaron was beside himself.

"I have an idea," Haylee said. "But I don't know if it will work."

"What is it?" asked Lydia.

They heard a noise before she could explain—a loud rustling from a grove of pine trees. Aaron jumped, the startle caused him to lose his footing. He fell to his knees in the snow. A shadowed figure emerged with its arms raised forward, pointing something towards the group. A gunshot rang out. It echoed through the forest.

Aaron screamed in pain as the bullet tore through his shoulder. It was a clean shot, exiting out his back. Blood sprayed out his body into the snow. His body swung backward from the force. He fell unto his back, buried in the snow.

His blood sprayed onto Haylee's face. She screamed. She grabbed the top of her head, covering herself in fear of another shot.

"Shit!" Aaron screamed. His voice frantic, shaky. "I'm shot! I'm shot! Fuck, I'm gonna die!"

Haylee crawled to Aaron's side. Lydia ducked behind a tree, taking further cover.

"Quiet," Haylee reached to him, grabbing his hand.

"Hello," Vanessa's voice broke through the silence of the forest. Her firearm still raised. "Move so that I can taste him. I want to taste him alive. I earned my feast. The last one was taken from me."

"Vanessa?" Haylee frowned. She walked out from the shadows and into their view.

"I'm not allowed to hurt you," Vanessa's voice was calm. "We are one and the same. Please move." She spoke to Haylee.

"Haylee, stay calm, don't give in to emotion," Lydia whispered from behind the tree.

"Mother is here too," said Vanessa. "She is back there. Behind me, we heard you calling. She wanted to see you. You left her, your own child, to die. Out here in the woods. Why? You made her sad. She wept here in the woods for a long time. Weak, dying. Until she met that man, Robbie."

"Shut up!" Haylee yelled. She shielded Aaron with her body, holding both her hands firmly against his wound.

"Vanessa shot me?" Aaron winced in pain, holding his shoulder. "Why did she shoot me?"

"It's not her," Haylee answered.

"Mother!" Vanessa yelled into the forest. "She is here."

From the darkness of the wood, the creature's eyes broke. They glowed red, just like in her dreams. Haylee stood up, lost in them.

"Haylee, be careful! Don't look at its eyes," Lydia whispered.

"Go, see her," Vanessa pointed back to the woods.

Haylee said nothing. There was no fear in her body, no anger. There in the woods, the glowing red eyes called to her. The monster, the wicked thing that has ruined her life. It came from her; she carried it in her womb, gave birth to it in the woods. Her child. Somewhere, despite everything, there was only love for it. She left the side of Aaron, releasing the pressure on his wounds. She moved towards the eyes, to her grotesque child.

"What are you doing? Don't leave me!" Aaron begged.

Haylee ignored him. Motherhood, she felt the warmth of it for the first time. The unconditional love for a child, the yearning be with it, was all empowering. She thought of her own mother. She thought of her father, as well. His stubbornness, his unrelenting love despite everything that had happened to their family. She wanted to see her child. To hold it, to cradle it in her arm.

Vanessa said nothing. As soon as Haylee moved off Aaron, she darted towards him. She met with Haylee halfway through the clearing. She did not stop her pursuit of Aaron.

"Haylee, please!" Lydia watched in horror. "Don't let it take you!"

"Haylee, come back, please!" Aaron begged.

Vanessa's crazed eyes centered on him. She was a few yards away. Her mouth already salivating at the thought of her first taste of human flesh.

Aaron closed his eyes; the warmth of urine soak his pants. He'd pissed himself. Awaiting death, he began to pray.

FIFTY-TWO

Time slowed.

Haylee couldn't break the gaze of the creature.

There was a connection with it immediately, beyond what any words could fathom. Haylee had known love before, with Robbie, before he cheated on her back in Ohio, perhaps even after, although it was different. This, the connection with the creature, her child, it was a different kind of love. Not physical, but spiritual. The vision of her mother's brilliant smile came to her mind, her vibrant laugh. Was this what Haylee's mother experienced the first time she set eyes on her? This mixture of unfiltered joy, pride, an overwhelming and unwavering unconditional love?

Haylee stopped a yard or so before the thicket of the woods. She knew it was there, her child hidden behind the sizeable thick pine trees. She could hear Aaron screams for help, begging her not to leave him. She listened to his feint prayers. She ignored it all.

Vanessa hadn't made it to him yet. She would be there soon, ripping into his flesh, eating him alive. Lydia wouldn't stand a chance to save him. Haylee understood this, yet did nothing.

The creature made the first move. It stepped out into the clearing. In all its repugnant glory, it stood before her to see. Its dreadful, putrid body, decayed, deathly. There was no fear. She was not disgusted by its appearance. Nor was she off put by the putrid smell of death that settled in her nose. She only felt love. A single lone tear rolled down her cheeks.

"I'm so sorry," she whispered.

Haylee heard the struggle behind her, Vanessa made contact with Aaron. She'd gone on the attack. Haylee pulled her firearm from her purse, held it in her hand. The gift from her dad. The same gun she used to end the life of her fiancé, Robbie. Sweet Robbie, a puppet of her own evil. Camille, Dennis, Nora, and now Vanessa, maybe even Aaron. Victims of her, victims of her child born from her disease, her unfiltered emotions. She raised her hand. Her lips wrapped around the cold barrel. She realized what she had to do.

Kill the source. Kill the creator.

The creature knew it as well. Its eyes gave it away. Haylee peered deep into them, and for a fleeting moment, she saw the first real emotion the creature would ever know.

Fear.

Haylee pulled the trigger.

A flash exploded in her head. A loud bang thundered in her ears.

Her head snapped back, the bullet exited out the posterior of her lower head. She fell, tumbled over.

The creature mimicked Haylee's body. Its head exploded out the back of its skull. A murky liquid, thick like tar, sprayed across the towering pine trees. It stammered for a second, it's knee's weakened, it fell backward, limp. A massive pool of maggots spewed from the creature gaping hole in its head. They quickly overtook the creature's body, devouring its flesh, growing fat on its death—a feeding frenzy. The insects were making quick work on the monster, stripping it bare and fast.

Vanessa's body immediately went limp. The minute the trigger was pulled and the bullet ripped through Haylee's head, causing the creature's head to be blown half off as well, the bond between the beast and Vanessa was broken.

"Fuck me," Aaron cried. Lydia ran to his aid. Vanessa was dead weight atop of him.

"Did she get you?" she asked. She helped pull her body off of him.

"A little," Aaron's forearm bled where Vanessa bit down during the attack. "I managed to fend her, off mostly."

"Thank god," Lydia helped him sit up. He swore, grasping at the gunshot wound.

"Is she dead?" asked Aaron staring at the motionless Vanessa. "What happened who shot the gun? Where's Haylee?"

"Haylee shot the gun," Lydia said, pointing to her lifeless body.

"My God, what happened?" His voice trembled.

"Save your strength, you were shot," Lydia stood up, "We're miles away from anyone out here. You need to just sit and relax. Vanessa shouldn't be a threat anymore."

"Haylee? Is she?..."

Lydia did not answer. She made her way over to Haylee's body. Blood collected around her head, the snow melting from the warmth of it. She looked at the long skinny body of the creature, or rather the little of what was left of it. The maggots made quick work of its body, feasting on its carcass faster than anything she'd ever seen. Like piranha's in the wild, shredding their prey. The maggot-like insects already consumed half its body, straight down to the bones, and even those were getting devoured. She'd never seen anything like it.

She looked down again to Haylee.

She wasn't moving.

"What happened?" Vanessa lifted her head from the snow. Her body weak, like she hadn't eaten anything for days. Shaky, light-headed, she couldn't catch her bearings. Her vision blurred; her head pounded loudly with every racing beat of her heart. She thought it would burst from her chest at any moment.

"Don't eat me, you fuckin' freak," Aaron tried to kick at her head.

"What?" Vanessa rolled to her back. She sucked in the cold air, long and hard. "What happened?" her voice was shallow, soft.

"Are you, you?" Arron winced, scuttling away from her. He held his open wound with his good hand. He was losing blood, feeling faint himself.

"I think she is dead," Lydia returned. She kneeled, applying pressure to Aaron's wounds once again. "You are bleeding bad."

"Haylee?" Aaron's voice shook. "Dead?"

"I think so, yes. Or close to it."

"I can't remember...anything," said Vanessa.

"Save your strength," said Lydia.

"We're going to die out here," said Aaron. "No one knows where we are. Haylee's dead. Jesus, c'mon, she's really dead?"

Vanessa sat up. Her entire body ached; both her legs cramped up. Muscles stiff, sore, like she was running a high fever. Dizzy, disoriented, she couldn't make sense of much only that she was in the middle of the woods. She remembered chasing the suspect, then the red eyes. Her body heaved at the thought of the eyes. She spit out some blood. Finding her words were hard, she stammered, "Where are we? How did I get here?"

"She shot herself?" Aaron couldn't take his eyes off Haylee's body.

"Don't look at her. Focus on me. I don't want anyone else dying today," Lydia pulled his face towards her. "Look into my eyes. Stay with me. I got you."

"...Do you believe in god?" asked Aaron.

"Do you?" Lydia diverted the question.

"I used too..." he said.

"Well, we could use a miracle. You'd better start believing, and fast..."

FIFTY-THREE

"Glad to see you're awake," Pike pulled out a packet of Trident gum from his jacket. Popped one of the white squares into his mouth. "You were out for a while, kid."

"I heard," Aaron sat upright, pain shooting through his side. He winced. He muted the small white television that swung on the hospital bed's large white arm. He hated hospitals. They always seemed to follow disastrous life-altering events. This time made no difference.

"Cartoons?" Pike motioned at the small television.

"After what I have been through?" replied Aaron. "I can't stomach much else."

"You got lucky, you know that?" asked Pike.

"Yeah? How's that?" Aaron chuckled. "I don't feel lucky, dude."

"Clean shot, exited out the back shoulder," Pike nodded, motioning towards the wound. "Lucky to be alive. You're a survivor kid. Or maybe just stupid lucky, I dunno which."

"Probably the latter," Aaron half-smiled. It was not genuine.

"They told me you woke up early this morning," he dropped a greasy brown bag over the top of Aaron's lunch tray. "Bad Luck Lager House, the best burger in Emmett county, and fries. I know the food sucks in here. Eat up. You're not on restrictions for a diet."

"Fuck, yes," Aaron ripped the bag open. A handful of fries were already in his mouth. "I ate fuckin' oatmeal for breakfast and a shitty turkey sandwich for lunch. I'm starved for some real food." He spoke with a mouthful of greasy fries.

"Glad I could make your stay here a little more homely," Pike pulled up a chair and sat.

"They said I was out for a week, little longer," Aaron washed the fries down with a large gulp of ice water.

"Yes, that sounds right."

"You're the first visitor, minus my parents. Of course. They just left about an hour ago. Nurses told me they had been here since I arrived, never left. Took turns sleeping on that shitty couch." He pointed to the small faux leather hospital couch. I told them to go home and rest. They looked worse than me. I gotta stop almost getting myself almost killed before it kills them."

"I spoke to them a few times," Pike smiled at the jest. "Worried sick, you were touch and go for a bit. Lots of blood out there in the woods, a lot of it was yours."

"Yeah?" Aaron bit into the juicy burger.

"That's why I'm here," he pulled out his yellow legal pad. "A lot happened out there. A lot of stuff I can't make out head or tails. Strange stuff. Stuff..." Pike chose his words carefully, "stuff that just doesn't add up."

"Yeah?" Aaron replied again.

"A good man lost his life out there in those woods. His funeral was a few days back. I had to tell his wife and two kids their daddy was dead. He died in the line of duty, a hero; he was a good man. We didn't always see eye to eye. But, shit, I respected him."

"Jesus," Aaron frowned. "I didn't know that I'm sorry."

"Two other victims, too. The woman you found in the basement, Jeanie Cunnings. When we set up the five-mile radius, another officer found a dead dog slaughtered in a back yard of a nearby home. One house east of where Dennis and Nora lived to be exact. Found a cannibalized corpse of an older woman, head missing as well. It's all over the internet and news. Bastards are having a field day right now."

"I don't know what to say," Aaron pushed away the burger.

"Sorry, didn't mean to ruin your appetite," Pike frowned. He sighed heavily, ran his fingers through his thinning grey hair. His beard was thicker now; he hadn't shaved since the Simmons' murder. His eyes still sunken, sleep still evaded him.

"It's fine," Aaron frowned. "I didn't know about your friend or the woman. I am sorry for both."

"We don't know what happened to Officer Clent Moore. All we know Is he died from blunt force trauma to the head. No defense wounds. Baffles me how a decorated cop gets dropped like that without a fight."

"I don't think I can help you with that. I wasn't there."

"I know you weren't. The only people at the scene of the murder were Officer Moore and Gary Thom. He was found dead at the scene near Clent's body. Logistics found Clent's bullets in his chest. Vanessa had given chase. We *suspect* she was there, but she has no recollection of the events that transpired. She's a mess right now; something's wrong with her head. She is getting help. She can barely remember what year it is, let alone what happened to Clent. She also wasn't there at the scene. She was there with you folks when the dogs found you."

"What do you need from me?" asked Aaron.

"Lydia won't talk, lawyered up. Claims she saw nothing, knows even less."

"She's probably telling the truth."

"We found Vanessa's bullet in your shoulder. It matched her gun. She shot you."

"She did?" Aaron attempted to sit up. He winced in pain again. It hurt him to move.

"We got photos of the wound on your forearm too. A perfect fit for her dental records, she bit you? You two scuffled in the woods? But why?"

"I don't recall that, sir," Aaron frowned. "I was shot, bleeding out. I don't know who shot me. You're telling me it was Vanessa. But I don't know."

Pike sighed heavily. Frustration setting in. "I'm not the bad guy here. I want to know what the hell happened out there. When the K-9 unit sniffed you guys out, it had been almost an hour. You were near death. Thank God Clent called in the copter, he saved your life. We airlifted you out of there. It's a miracle you're alive talking to me right now. Do you understand that? I need to know what the fuck happened."

"Dude," Aaron shook his head. "I'm telling you; I don't know. If Vanessa shot me, it was an accident. The last thing I remember was Vanessa pushing Lydia away and trying to stop the bleeding. I passed out after that. I don't remember, man."

"We found black tar, or something, smeared all over the pine trees, on the snow, it was everywhere like blood splatter, but not blood. We're running tests on it now, but we have no clue what it was. There were fragments of fresh bones, a pile of dead maggots, mounds of them in the snow near the bloody tar. No maggot I have ever seen before. When we tried transporting them for tests, the fuckers disintegrated into the same black tar. They ate through most of the bones. Just fragments left behind. We're running tests on those too, but I'm guessing results will be inconclusive. What am I dealing with here? I need to know."

"I'm sorry, detective. I don't have answers for you. I wish I knew," replied Aaron.

"Okay," Pike wallowed in the bitterness of failure that flooded over him. "I lost a friend out there. Maybe two, because Vanessa..." he struggled with the phrasing. "I don't think she'll ever get her mind back. You say she helped apply pressure to your wound. But when we found you, folks, she was in a mental breakdown. She could barely form a complete thought, let alone save your life."

"Instinct, maybe? Look, detective. We all lost a lot out in those woods," Aaron shook the detective's hand. "I will pray for us to heal."

"You do that," Pike nodded. "Enjoy the burger." He turned from Aaron, defeated, angered. He walked toward the door. He paused, turned to look at him one more time. "If you change your mind and want to be honest with me. I left my card on the table."

"Thanks," Aaron frowned. He didn't want to lie to the detective. He saw the pain in his eyes. But he made a pact in the woods.

He would honor it.

"After they let you out of here, make sure to visit your friend," Pike opened the heavy wooden door.

"Who?" asked Aaron.

"Haylee is down the hall," He closed the door behind him.

FIFTY-FOUR

Gerald awoke. His body stiff, sore. He missed his bed back in Ohio. He had spent every night over the past two weeks sleeping next to his daughter, crammed on the small couch in her hospital room. He would not leave her side. He didn't know much about what happened. Only what the doctors were able to share, which wasn't a lot. Haylee had taken her firearm, stuck it into her mouth, and pulled the trigger.

What was a father to do?

He lost one daughter from a madman. Now, his second daughter laid in a comatose state in a hospital bed from a self-inflicted gunshot wound. He was a failure, a failure at everything in his life. His career, his marriage, both his daughters. He failed them all. He struggled, every night he wept, cried, wailed in the darkness of the sterile hospital room.

Haylee had few visitors. The bitch physic lady came in once. He wanted to curse her out, blame her for what happened. He fought back the urge to wrap his large hands over her throat and choke the life out of her. Instead, he said nothing. He left the room with a simple nod, waited for her to leave before reentering. She left behind some flowers and a strange stone. He decided not to touch them.

That was three days ago.

Today there was another knock on the door. Gerald opened it. Aaron stood before him with flowers.

"Hey," Aaron shook Gerald's hand with his good arm.

"Aaron," Gerald returned the handshake.

"She still hasn't shown any signs?"

"Nope," Gerald frowned. "Still in a coma."

"I brought her these," Aaron handed the flowers to Gerald. "There, from the little store on the main level. I haven't had a chance to get home yet. I just got discharged."

"Tulips, her favorite," Gerald took them, placed them near her bed. "I'll see if I can find a vase. Get them water."

"...You think?"

"—She will wake up? Gerald finished the question for him. "She has to. If she doesn't, then what's the point of going on?"

"Yeah," Aaron couldn't' take his eyes off her. Her pale skin, her head wrapped in gauze, the machines that were monitoring her.

"The bullet went through the back of her skull. She has a long process to go if she ever wakes up. Reconstructive surgery to repair the physical damage. As for the mental damage? Time will tell. Doctors have hope. But the part of the brain that was damaged, there will be a lot of relearning how to live her life, verbal, motor skills. *If* she ever even wakes up." Gerald sounded forced. His words shallow.

"Gerald," Aaron hugged the towering man. "Please, call me if you need anything."

"What's in your hand?"

Aaron hadn't noticed he'd been fiddling with the flash drive in his hand. He wasn't sure he wanted to leave it with him. But he hadn't much a choice in the matter.

"When she wakes up," Aaron set the flash drive on the small table littered with Gerald's things. "She wanted to read it. I finished it while I was recovering. I had my parents bring me my laptop."

"I see," Gerald frowned.

"I should get going," Aaron shook his hand one more time. "Let me take you out in a few days? Grab some food? It looks like we're both do for a good meal."

"Yeah," Gerald found a smile. "I'd like that. She'd like that."

Both men looked over to Haylee. No words were spoken.

Sorrow filled the air.

FIFTY-FIVE

Pike had one last stop. He'd buried his friend; he's seen another lose her mind. The only two people in the world that knew the truth hid it from him. Pike was tired. He didn't understand the world anymore. What he thought he understood; all came crashing down in the woods behind Haylee's old home. He felt like he lived in a house of cards, and he let a tornado into his life.

Life. He thought long and hard over that word for the last week.

Had he even lived? Did he do it, right? Was he happy with where the road led?

He wasn't sure. But he chose where the road led him on this eerily warm winter morning.

A cozy-looking farmhouse. Blue window panes, white sidings. Two garden gnomes greeted him at the porch steps leading to the front door.

He knocked on the door.

His heart was pounding in his chest. His mouth went dry, and his nerves tore his guts up into submission. Pike was a hard man. He'd seen blood, guts, death. He'd handcuffed bad men, who had done bad things. Shot his gun with the intent to kill, been shot at with the same intentions. He hadn't known pure gut-wrenching fear for a long time.

Today, that very moment, He'd never experienced more fear in his life. He'd also never felt more alive.

He thought of Haylee waiting for the door to open. She had done it wrong, in the heat of the moment, she put the barrel in her mouth then pulled the trigger. The bullet missed most of the brain, leaving her mostly dead. Pike knew the correct way, barrel to the temple, brains blown out the side. Grey matter blew sky high.

What waits behind the large red residential door, will cement his fate.

He heard rummaging behind the door. A faint voice broke the silence.

The door opened, and a man in his mid-thirties opened the door. He was well dressed, clean-shaven, soft sandy brown hair, a strong chin like his father. He looked shocked to see the disheveled and worn-down Detective standing on his porch.

"Son," Pike choked on the word, it came out more of a squeak than a voice. Warm tears streamed down his cheeks.

"Dad?" the man replied.

"Who's at the door?" A second man came to the threshold, his arm around his son's waist lovingly.

"Can I come in? Pike asked.

"It's been over ten years," his son said flatly. "I don't even know you."

"This is your father?" the second man asked. "The Detective?"

"Maybe a drink? The three of us?" Pike rubbed the tears away, sniffling.

"I don't think so. Please, never knock on this door again," the man frowned, his eyes redden with tears himself. He closed the door.

Pike heard the lock click.

Pike's head fell low. He tightened his jacket, turned, and walked back to his car, parked in front of the suburban home. He sat in the driver seat, swallowed the lump in his throat, tried to keep the tears from spilling, which he failed at, miserably. He grabbed his gun from the glove box. Felt the weight of it in his hand. He stared at it. He thought of Haylee, out in the woods. What caused her to do it? To swallow the bullet? Why had Vanessa shot Aaron? Why did Clent drop his guard? Nothing made sense.

No, he waved the thoughts away. The real question, the only one that mattered. What brought him to this end? Sitting out in front of his son's suburban home, hated by the only family he had left, with a firearm in his hand.

Why was he the way he was? Why did he disown his son? Why was he a shit person?

Questions he would never get to answer.

He was no longer fit for this world; he hadn't smiled in years. He'd lost his chance with his son. He knew what came next.

He was tired. So tired.

He lifted the gun, barrel to his temple.

"If only life had a reset button," he mumbled. "I'm sorry I was a miserable fuck."

He wrapped his finger tightly against the trigger. "Maybe I will see you wherever this takes me, Clent. I owe you an apology or two."

It was time, time for a new beginning, or a simple end into an eternity of blackness. Both sounded better to Pike than waking up another day in this mad, mad world.

ABOUT THE AUTHOR

J.L. Hickey is an author from Mid-Michigan who graduated from Saginaw Valley State University with a bachelor's in creative writing. He loves horror and the supernatural. When he isn't writing about creepy monsters, he is enjoying his life as a father of three crazy boys and time spent with his babe of a wife.

NOTE FROM THE AUTHOR

Word-of-mouth is crucial for any author to succeed. If you enjoyed *It Was Born in the Darkness of the Wood*, please leave a review online—anywhere you are able. Even if it's just a sentence or two. It would make all the difference and would be very much appreciated.

Thanks!
J.L. Hickey

Thank you so much for reading one of our **Horror** novels.

If you enjoyed our book, please check out our recommendation for your next great read!

Doll House by John Hunt

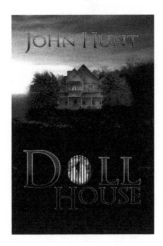

"This book is not for the faint of heart. It's deliciously dark and gruesome."
– Where the Reader Grows

View other Black Rose Writing titles at
www.blackrosewriting.com/books and use promo code
PRINT to receive a **20% discount** when purchasing.

CPSIA information can be obtained
at www.ICGtesting.com
Printed in the USA
BVHW071213060421
604325BV00002B/41

9 781684 336654